Mission Prodigy
Gvonni Avner

ARCANA VOX SCRIPTORIUM

Arcana Vox Scriptorium

ARCANA VOX SCRIPTORUM

To the adventurers out there who constantly strive to make the world a better place.

1

I am soaring high over a dense forest. Trees line up one after the other, none right in front of the last, each spaced out and non-symmetrical. Down below, the lighting is surely dim, but from where I am, the sun shines at its brightest. Up ahead, I can see the scenery change from lush green to plain desert, painted with only three shades of a sandy dirt brown. My Sonars is too big to squeeze through most of the forest, so I have to fly over it. But I notice just ahead there is an area where the trees aren't so closely grown together, and I can have fun for a minute or two below.

I dive down towards the ground, pushing the silence button on my dash to quiet the warning alarm. At the last second, I pull up, narrowly missing a brutal crash into the talvor. The forest thins out but hasn't yet opened to the dry desert. Trees fly past me as I curve upwards here and there. I swing around, weaving between thick trunks and overly large roots. I open the sunroof window to feel the breeze rush through the top of my head. I glance in the rearview mirror and smile.

I am *most definitely* having the time of my life here.

The trees space out even more. My excitement dies a little because the difficulty level drops with all the extra room, but I still have fun with what I have. I zip through two closely grown trees, tilting the Sonars sideways to make it through.

I didn't see it before. Staring right at me with an imminent crash is the hard rockface of a moderate plateau. I brake hard, turn my vehicle upwards slightly, level myself, and reverse quickly. A blast of fiery fuel blinds me momentarily as it pushes out enough force to prevent me from smashing right into the cliff. Sonars don't usually use any type of fuel, but most have some in reserve just in case an extra and sudden force of energy is required. I never thought I would have to use it in this sort of emergency. The heat makes me sweat, though that may have started right before I almost collided into the wall. I close the sunroof and silence the blaring alarm. Once my Sonars is still, I rise upward and make it over the plateau. I turn my head back to look over the plateau and the forested valley below.

"Huh," I say out loud to myself. And then I laugh for a moment, with the passing of the possibility of a blazing death. Though I've taken this route several times, I never noticed the plateau. It isn't tall by any means, and its top spans far out of sight, which means that without paying close attention, I would have never really known that there was a difference in elevation, only a drastic change in terrain from forest to bare desert.

Usually, I fly high over the forest, mainly because most of the time I'm running late on a delivery. This time is different. I'm almost half a day ahead of schedule. I shift the Sonars back into gear and head towards my destination. Behind me, inside my vehicle, is a bed almost large enough for two. A small backpack sits on the floor at the foot of it. The contents of the backpack are mostly useless stuff, such as pens, random paper notes crumpled halfheartedly, or empty packets of gum and wrappers. In other words, things no one would care to steal.

But there is a secret pocket, right in the center and almost in plain sight. That's where I hide the valuables that I am delivering, if they are small enough. Usually, it contains pieces of jewelry. But even with the jewelry shipments, I don't use the "super-secret pocket" often, mainly because the deliveries are too delicate to put inside. I also sometimes worry I'd forget it was there.

For the past four years, I have worked as a private delivery service. I take on clients who are willing to spend more for a quicker, less invasive postal service. Everything that goes through the UWS — United World Shippers — is inspected before being mailed out. Even with our bullet trains and super jets, it usually takes five to seven days, or more, to get something delivered. Though people can get next day deliveries done, the prices for that kind of service are so high that even the wealthiest of people opt out of it. Plus, cross-continent shipments usually require stricter laws that delay packages. Our governments keep a close eye of most everything. But I don't have to follow those laws since I don't work for or operate as a company. Personal travel between countries is easy, as it is mostly without restrictions. Business travel or shipments do come with them, and those restrictions delay delivery times. It is odd, because in school we were taught that mailing packages used to be much faster back in the day.

Bottom line, UWS cross-country shipping can take about a week. But if you hire me, I'll average one to three days. And I don't give a carcass's shit what you want me to deliver, so long as it isn't overtly immoral. Here's the best part: what I do is totally legal. Of course, some deliveries can take up to five days or more, depending on how far across the world I need to travel.

About thirty minutes out, I begin to feel hungry. Looming over the hazy horizon, I can see the tall mounds of rock that make up the buildings in Velro. I had eaten my last meal bar a few hours ago. Looking back at the floor, where the wrapper lay alone, I wish I hadn't. I wasn't even hungry when I ate it. I was just bored.

The open road reaches a point with a clear path. I lower the Sonars to hover just above the road and follow the white lines into the city. They call this grounding, even though we don't actually drive on the ground. It is required by law when entering most cities. Standing at a height of seven stories, most of the buildings are made of hard rock and are reinforced with steel beams. There are more vehicles here inside the city, but most are smaller than mine. The traffic lights have always been a downer. They aren't used much except in a few cities. Because it's midafternoon, there isn't a rush of traffic, and soon enough, I pull into a garage and park in a guest spot.

Once I step out of the vehicle with my backpack, a high-pitched beep sounds from a short pole. I tap the screen with the identification card on my phone, and my car is lowered beneath the ground and out of sight. I walk over to the lift. My client gave me a three-digit code. Punching in the numbers, the platform descends to my level, and the doors open. I step onto it. A light blinks yellow for a moment, verifying my code and waiting in case I plan to go to a different floor than the one I pressed. When I do nothing, the doors close, and I quickly go up through a dark shaft before slowing to a fast stop.

The platform rotates slightly, facing me in the direction needed before opening the doors and welcoming me to a large living room overlooking the city.

"You must be Arch," I hear a voice say. A man about my height walks in. He has graying hair and is wearing oval lensed glasses. He puts down a few pieces of mail and steps closer to me. "Like Arch Caldor, I suppose."

I crack a smile.

The man does the same. "You probably get that a lot," he says. He walks up to me, holding out a transparent card that glows green around its edges.

"I do," I say with a straight face, reaching around to take my back-pack off my back. I open it and pull out a letter-sized envelope. In my head, I laugh. I do get "like Arch Caldor" a lot. That's because I am him. Made slightly famous because of my father, Aldon Caldor. Five years ago, there was a serious scandal involving the CEO of PlatTech, a company that makes Platforms. The silent hero, Aldon, became the new CEO. Most people don't know that he was the one who discovered what the previous CEO was doing, but the company's founder did, and that's how he got the position. I don't know all the details because they were kept quiet to save face for the company. But my father's life changed after that, and so did mine. He gave me more than enough money to start my business, and then he went off to run his. I haven't seen him in four years. He actually gave me so much money that I probably never need to work again.

But my face has rarely been shown to the public, so almost no one ever recognizes me. It's just the name that's famous. Something I am extremely grateful for.

I hand over the envelope. The man takes it and holds out his card more prominently than before. I take my phone, press a button on its side to make it glow blue. He taps my phone with his card, and I've been paid. Uber rich people have these cards to carrying money around, rather than it all being digital. I never saw the point in it, but I suppose it help ensure your money isn't all in one place.

"I left you an extra tip so you can get yourself a Sonars charge and a nice room for the night. I know my delivery was quite far, with my son living halfway across the world."

Halfway is a bit of a stretch. If you were to travel all of Talvor at its circumference, you would journey about fifty-five thousand kilometers. I just traveled eight thousand. Sure, I crossed an ocean, but it was just a short journey as the two continents are quite close to each other. Those ocean journeys are what keep me in business.

Even with personal vehicles that can travel that distance on a single charge, most people don't want to risk it.

Still, I smile and say, "Thank you. I appreciate it." It isn't a lie, but I don't need the tip.

The man nods awkwardly, which I take as my cue to leave. I head back down, call my Sonars and drive back out into the sunlight. In the little time I spent on my delivery, the traffic picked up, and I am left waiting at red light after red light, just to get to a charging station.

My stomach growls. Yeah, I'm still hungry too.

It only feels like an eternity, waiting behind a Sonars that doesn't even notice when the light turns green. I hate cities that still use these traffic signals. They are just so *archaic*. I turn left and pull into a charging station and go up to the second floor to park, hovering over a Platform as the ones below were all taken. Platforms recharge vehicles by recalibrating their electromagnetic properties that make them run, the same kind that they use to hover over the ground. I tap the payment pole, authorizing it to charge up fully before heading inside to grab a snack.

Four escalators lead down, with another four bringing people up. I head to one of the "to go" screens and punch in my order of a fish cake with potato sticks. Seconds later, my order arrives on a tray, wrapped in a green bag. I take it and head back to my Sonars.

It can take up to an hour to fully charge if a Sonars is fully depleted and is an older model. Mine wasn't quite on empty, but I still wait over twenty minutes before I can leave. I also think that the Platforms here are ancient compared to the newer models in the large cities, and thus slower.

"Hey CHAD, find me the nearest and cheapest hotel," I call out to my car's virtual assistant system. "Hold up, get me a monarch suite. I'll indulge a bit." I remember my last client implied he tipped me well enough to pay for a nice hotel. Again, not that I needed the tip, but I might as well use it.

"Would you like me to set a course for your destination?" CHAD asks me.

"No, just show me where," I say. "I'll get there on my own."

CHAD turns on my screen with a map and pinpoints my destination. It's only three blocks away. I head towards the hotel, cutting in front of vehicles that I consider are going too slow. The sun begins to creep beneath the buildings.

When I get to the hotel, I notice that it is taller than most other structures, though still not nearly as high as they are in the larger cities. I pull into their garage, and a lift takes me up five floors. I park in the nearest open slot. I turn my body back to grab a few items and stuff them in my backpack before exiting my Sonars and locking up. When I leave, the Sonars is moved below into wherever they are stored, ready for me to call for it when I need to.

I step onto a mat that immediately moves forward, speeding up my long walk to the hotel lobby. The glass doors slide open, and the previously dark hall lights up. I turn a corner and am welcomed by the front desk.

"Welcome to the Canabana Hotel, Velro District."

I look up and return the warm smile from the pretty girl standing at the front desk. I am surprised too, as there are usually automated screens that check you in, so I was not expecting anyone to be here. The lady senses my puzzlement.

"You haven't stayed with us before, have you?" she asks. "Canabana Industries favors human contact over machines. While cleaning and restocking of suites is done by our exclusive line of droids, decoration, food prep, and transactions are handled by people." She shrugs and winks at me, "Most of the time."

I smile and nod. "I didn't know that." I never cared to stay at high-end hotels or resorts so I've never even been inside one of the Canabana hotels.

"Hmm." She doesn't open her mouth, but gives a brief smile. "Now you do."

Only now I notice her name tag.

MAYLENE

"There you go," Maylene says after punching several things into her computer screen that I can't see. She hands out a small card. I grab my phone and hold it near it. There is a small *ding*, and I now have access to my room 023.

"Our luxury suites start one level beneath the ground floor. Instead of views of the terribly dry and bare desert, you will be welcomed to a vast variety of biomes. And we'll have live music in our elite club." She looks at me mischievously and leans forward to whisper, "But I suggest you shower first." She's hinting that I should make an appearance. "And you ate those fish cakes at the charging station, didn't you?" She gives a slight grimace.

Yikes. I not-so-subtly check my breath.

"It's not that bad," she says, laughing at me. "But get cleaned up before walking into the club."

Duly noted, not that I really intend to go. I nod my head and smile awkwardly before walking away. The elevator requires me to scan my phone before it takes me down seven floors. When the doors open, I am welcomed to a vibrant hall with plants growing out of the walls. The temperature feels cooler here. Only when I pass through one of the stray leaves do I remember that I am inside and notice that the plants are not real, just holographic images at their finest.

There are small lights in the shape of numbers above the suite doors, which is how I find my room. There is a small fob where the handle should be. I tap my phone to it and the door unlocks. I push it open.

Luxury has been something that I could afford for many years now, but I never cared to use to my advantage.

I've been missing out.

There is a bed so large that it must sleep at least ten people. The curtains are drawn back but open upon my arrival to reveal a starry atmosphere that seems unreal. Its images pop out and immerse the room in dark shades of clouds and bright stars. Two end tables hold up large lamps that give the room most of its light.

But there is only one thing I have really been looking forward to all day. A shower. The bathroom is large, has two sinks, and a small separate room for the toilet. There is a large resort-style bath and a separate shower with black tiles.

Water sprays at me from all directions. I take my time in the shower. When I'm done, I look in the mirror before drying my brown, dark-orange-tinted hair. My brown eyes almost have bags under them, but that may just be my imagination from the utter tiredness I feel. There are a few options of complimentary cologne, but I pass on them. I may have money, but there's no need to smell pretentious about it.

I lay on the bed and close my eyes. I'm physically exhausted, but that may be more from sitting in a vehicle for several days. Naturally, I don't feel like going anywhere or doing anything.

There is a knock on my door. I groan but don't get up. The knocking happens again. With a sigh, I heave myself off the bed and answer the door. A gracious but expressionless man awaits just over the threshold.

"I have come to politely remind you that you have been invited to attend our elite club tonight," he says in a monotone. His head is raised slightly, and he speaks almost as if he were looking down on me. "It would be unwise to refuse such an offer, especially by such a beautiful woman."

I tiredly raise an eyebrow and say, "Okay, I'll be there in ten minutes."

The butler-looking man nods. "I will be here."

"No need," I say before gently slamming the door on him.

I put on some decent clothes, though nothing fancy, and make my way towards the door. I am gratefully surprised to find that the man is not waiting for me right outside. I head towards the elevator and go down one floor.

Inside the elite club, the tile floors are lit with small and round lights. There's a stage centered against a wall with a live band, and opposite to it is a large bar with two people attending it, though there are several kiosks available for ordering, which are most likely there for when it gets very busy.

There are about twenty people inside, including those that work here. The lack of people makes the place feel empty considering how large it is. While I look around, Maylene catches my eye. She smiles flirtatiously and looks away. I put on my best pretend smile, while also trying to act confident, and head towards her.

When I get to her table, she giggles. I don't know why. Several inaudible thoughts swarm my head. I sit down nervously, any attempt of a smile long gone.

"You don't do this a lot, do you?" she asks.

"Do what?"

She smiles, catches my eye for a moment, then leans in to whisper. "Talk to girls."

I blush. Due to my pale complexion, I know my flushed cheeks show. "I talk to whoever I need for my line of work. There's been plenty of women in my jobs." I curse myself silently, knowing I sound profoundly lame.

"Hmm," she says quietly. "I see. So, you're saying you're experienced in working with women."

Puzzled, I stutter. "I, uh, ahem."

Maylene raises her hand lazily and twirls a finger. I look over and see a bartender nod and start preparing a drink.

She turns back to look at me and laughs. "Sorry. I can't help myself. I enjoy making people feel uncomfortable."

"Why?"

Maylene smiles again. Damn, those teeth are white.

"Maybe it makes me feel more secure about myself," she says. Maylene lets out a soft breath. "And now you've made me feel bad about it."

"Oh, I'm sorry," I say awkwardly, not really meaning it.

Maylene laughs again. "I'm just shitting with you!"

Oh.

Haha.

Luckily the bartender comes by and places two drinks on the table before walking off. Usually I'm more reserved, but I quickly grab one of the drinks and take a few gulps.

"Who are you?" I ask after a minute of silence.

"That, you are about to find out," she answers cryptically. "But until then, enjoy the drinks and try not to lose your cool when I mess with you."

Joke's on her, I lost my cool the second I walked into the club.

We talk for a little while. I learn that she has traveled a lot, just like me, but has taken various jobs, all of them wildly different from the last. Occasionally she'll brush back her lightly curled and dark hair. I get the feeling that there is something she isn't telling me.

Before I work up the courage to ask her, an older man with bright blue eyes draws up a chair and sits down at our table. Immediately, my stomach growls.

I had forgotten how hungry I am.

"Ah, I see," the white-haired man says, staring at me with eyes like they know the very core of my soul.

I sit there awkwardly for a moment, but then a large platter of finger foods arrives, as well as trays of chicken wings and sushi.

"It's a good thing I ordered all this food," the man says.

I stare at him, and I'm pretty sure my mouth is gaping.

"I-I, uh, I don't have enough money to pay for all of this," I lie. I do, I just don't want this much food. I try to tell myself that I am not hungry, so that I don't eat any of this food from the stranger. But my stomach won't let me forget.

The man smirks at me. "I know that isn't true, but no matter. It is on me. You see, I own this place."

I raise an eyebrow out of astonishment.

"Yes," he chuckles. "I am Edward Canabana, and I own, and still run, all of Canabana Industries," he tells me. "So, enjoy yourself. We have something very important to discuss."

I nod once and gulp nervously while noticing Maylene eying me with an odd look of interest. I feast on the wings and slices of cheese before doubling down on the fruits. I am beyond starving. Water is supplied to me regularly throughout my dinner.

When I look like I'm finished, Edward promptly ends the call he was quietly on, puts his hands together, leans forward, and smiles.

"I have a job for you," he says.

"Oh," I say, relieved. I'm not sure what I was expecting, but I was a bit nervous for whatever reason. "What is it?"

He pulls out a screen from his bag and turns it on. You can barely tell that it's a physical object and not just a projection. I see blueprints for a large building. I recognize it as the government building in the largest country in the Pacan continent, the place where I'm from. Of course, all the continents have their single governing body that presides over the countries, and the countries inside have local governments, such as where the Tall Building is. I heard that on Earth, each country used to have its own government, but the whole world has been united, and just one elected official presides over the world along with his governing body.

"Do you know what this is?" he asks.

"Yes," I say. "It's the Tall Building."

Edward nods his head. "Quite right. Though I'm sure you've heard rumors that the president isn't actually running the country? That he's just a puppet?"

I don't want to get into a political talk. Or conspiracy theories.

"I've heard both sides," I say dryly.

Edward smiles. Maylene does as well.

"I see that you aren't much interested in the politics of the world," Edward states wisely.

"I mostly keep to myself," I say with a false smile. The thought of calling it a night crosses my mind.

Not that we have gotten very far technologically, but we are, to use a pun-phrase, light-years ahead of Earth. It's been decades since we had our first communication with Earth, and we still have no way for people to travel outside of our planet. Though, as far as I can tell, neither does Earth. What I do know about Earth and Talvor is that Talvor is larger than Earth, has a similar day-to-night cycle, and that we both speak what we call English, though they used to speak many languages according to what we're taught in school.

"A travel time of six years to the only discovered habited planet other than our own, and most of what we learn is that they are years behind us. They even speak our language, for the most part," Edward states with slight disdain, stating things I already know. "But I do enjoy some of their music and their food."

He looks at me as if I would appreciate his small talk. I can tell that he knows I don't.

"Never mind that," he says, putting away the screen. "The chip I just showed you contains a program that can override any other on our planet. It was sent to us eighteen years ago from Earth, and I have been keeping it a great secret since. By override, I mean take total control of anything that contains even the slightest bit of technology."

My ears feel as if they point towards Edward. Admittedly, he has me curious. I make eye contact with him, to show my interest. He cracks the smallest smile.

"Recently, I have heard of...rumors to use this as a weapon for planetary control. What I mean is changing people's medical information, altering their bank accounts, and even so far as erasing identities in minutes. They would be able to turn off pacemakers, neuro-implants, or assisted eyesight."

"What do you mean?"

"I mean, one minute you could walk into a bar, and the next your records show you're a wanted fugitive, and the next thirty years of your life are spent in prison, at best. Or someone's grandfather could drop dead because their life-saving implant was shut off."

I look at him confused. "How could someone do that?"

"By using that program chip I just showed you," Edward answers. "In the Tall Building rests the exact equipment needed to run such a program. Of course, there are other structures that can use the chip too, but the Tall Building is the most promising, at least from what I have gathered." His voice becomes more intense and urgent. "In the wrong hands, a single person could conquer all the continents in the world without starting a single war. Not one that anyone could see, at least."

"And what could it do in the right hands?" I ask.

Edward leans back and sighs. "I had been hoping to find out, but the threat is so imminent that I cannot take the chance to wait any longer."

"So, what do you want me to do about it?" I ask, not fully believing his story.

"Take it to NEAST, the National Exploration Agency of Space Techno—"

"I know what NEAST is."

A silence follows my rude interruption. I don't like it when people think they can fool me, especially when they think they can get away with it because I'm younger, or naive, or whatever they think the reason is that makes me a supposed easy target.

"Then please take it there," he almost begs. "I have a contact who will see that it is sent back to Earth."

I breathe out through my nose. Maybe it's because I'm tired, but my patience with this old man is thin. There have been deliveries I made and didn't get paid for, or I only got half. I've even had people tell me a sob story as to why I should do it for free. While I am prone to be trusting of most people, if there is even the slightest hint that I might get scammed, I become very wary.

"Think about it," he says, slowly getting up. "But while you do, share a dance with my lovely assistant. She traveled all the way here just so she could get you to me. Maylene even gave that guy you delivered a package to today the money to tip you. I just hope all her hard work pays off."

With that, he leaves with one last smile.

Shocked wouldn't begin to describe how I feel. I am disappointed that the man from earlier didn't actually tip me. Irked that I was basically forced to come down here and confused as to whether Edward Canabana is telling me the truth or not.

The music that I had been blocking out reaches my ears. A slow song begins to play. I look over at the band and notice only an empty stage. They must have left sometime after I ate. Before I can work up the energy to get up and leave, Maylene stands up and holds out her hand, offering me a dance.

Too tired to refuse, I take her hand and let her lead me to the dance floor. We dance to the song, with me less than uninterested about it. Maylene leads the dance for the most part, except when she pulls back, probably hoping I would take the lead.

I start to feel bad for treating her this way, even if she was some ploy to get me here.

"Look, I'm just not in the mood right now."

She stares at me with a look that tells me she thinks I'm a jerk.

"Not in the mood to what? Dance? Or avert the enslavement of everyone who lives on Talvor?"

A chuckle escapes my mouth. She pulls me a bit closer, and I look down at her, inches from her face. Our eyes meet for a moment with a seriousness I don't usually like being a part of. I look away.

All of a sudden, my hands get sweaty, in perfectly bad timing, as I am currently holding both of hers in mine.

"He doesn't mean what he says," I say.

"Oh." Maylene lets out a smirk. "He definitely means what he says."

I shake my head, pulling away from her and dropping one of her hands.

"I'm sure he does," I reply. "What I meant was that he isn't telling me the truth."

"Hmm," she says before leaving me feeling awkward in the middle of a short silence. "That's why he transferred half a million *Uwan* to your bank account. Because he isn't telling you the truth." Sarcastic wouldn't begin to describe her tone.

I drop her other hand and stumble backwards a couple steps. I look at her skeptically.

She nods her head. "Yup, that's right. You are half a million Uwan richer. And that's not all. Upon successful delivery, you will get an additional two point five million."

Though I feel frozen with doubt, my body lazily dances to the next slow song.

"Now I don't believe you," I say.

Maylene moves closer to me and wraps her arms around my neck. She leads us into a slow sway back and forth. "The threat is real," she says. "I've been doing my research and spent the last month reviewing every company and everyone that does any type of delivery. And I hand-picked you."

"So?" I laugh. "I have tons of customers for a reason, but so do a lot of others."

"You have the best record, flawless, even," she tells me. "Edward couldn't take a chance that someone would fail. And even then, he is worried."

"Why is he so worried?" I ask. "He's way later in years, probably only has a few left. Why isn't he just enjoying them?"

Maylene raises an eyebrow. "As much as you like to play the careless, and *lazy*, I might add, young man, I know that you would do the right thing every time."

The song ends and a new, more upbeat one, plays. There are a few cheers from the crowd, which has gotten larger since I stepped onto the dance floor, and I am surrounded by several people looking to have a good time, and I just want to get out of here.

Maylene gently grabs the back of my head and pulls it down so she can whisper in my ear. "Besides, I'm only dancing with you because we need to convince you to make this delivery."

I smile but don't move my head. "And here I thought you were just into me."

She releases her hand from my head and drops it. "You're cute," she says. "But you're not my type."

I twitch my head an inch with the feeling that she's about to tell me what her type is. She smiles wide and jerks her head towards the bar. I look and see another woman cleaning up some empty drink glasses. She catches our attention and winks. I'm sure that wink wasn't for me.

"Oh," I say. "Well, now I take it even more as a compliment that you think I'm cute," I blurt out.

Maylene laughs. "Hey, I find beauty in everyone," she says softly. "That's why I work for Edward. Even with all the money anyone could want, he still strives to be the best person he can be. And if that means sacrificing his last few years to ensure that the younger generation like us have a future we can freely live in, then he will do that. He is doing that."

I lower my head. I gotta say, she is getting to me. I even feel a bit bad now. I take her hand and lead her back to the table. Edward still isn't there.

The woman from the bar comes over.

"Can I get you two anything?" she asks with a genuine smile.

"I'm good, thank you," I say.

"I would like your number," Maylene says with such confidence that I almost feel like giving her mine. But maybe part of me already wants to.

The bartender smiles and walks away without a word.

I look at Maylene with an awestruck expression. "How?"

She shrugs. "I know what I want, and lately I want something to help relieve the stress."

I lean back and nod, impressed.

"Okay," I breathe out. "I'll do it."

"Excellent." I feel a warm hand on my back. He came out of nowhere.

Edward takes a seat next to me with a funny-looking smile. The bartender comes back with a napkin and places it in Maylene's hand.

Edward laughs. "Well, I see two of us got something we wanted tonight." He looks at me, a small twinkle of youthfulness in his eye. "Why don't you enjoy tonight yourself? I'm sure there's someone here who would catch your fancy."

I smile politely. "I'm good. What I want is a long night's sleep. It has been a long day. Plus, I really need to use the bathroom."

Edward puts his hand on my shoulder. "Then let me take just a few more moments of your time, and you can be off to bed."

I agree wholeheartedly with heading off to bed.

"The chip is with my dear friend in Yesfborne."

Yesfborne is less than a day's drive from here.

"Take your time though, Gary won't be ready until the evening, sometime around nineteen o'clock. But then, you must deliver the chip as fast as you can to NEAST. Gary or Maylene will give you further directions. So, enjoy your sleep tonight. You can check out whenever. The room is on me."

I just remember that I never actually gave any payment. Maylene just handed me my room card when I checked in. I catch a twinkle in her eye.

"And if you change your mind, I'm sure the crowd down here will still be quite large." There he goes again, with that smile that feels almost naughty. It would usually put me off, but by this time all I can think about is sleep.

"Have a good night, Arch," Maylene says pleasantly.

I give a tired smile and return a "you too" before heading back upstairs to my room.

2

Despite the convoluted dreams I had last night, I wake up feeling completely refreshed and ready to begin the day on a high note. I then realize the day has long since started, in that it is half past noon. I get up quickly, stressed that I am running late. But then I slowly start to remember last night. It feels like it was all a dream. What I remember most from yesterday was the long drive I made and delivering the package. Everything that happened since I got to the hotel feels like an entirely different day. It feels like it was so long ago.

I check my watch just to be sure. Yup, it is still tomorrow. At least, today is what I thought tomorrow would have been yesterday.

My thoughts make sense to me. Most of the time, at least.

Thinking confusing thoughts immediately after waking is not the best way to start a day. To clear my mind, I clean up in the bathroom, pack the minimal items I brought, and head out to grab a quick lunch from one of the several restaurants in the hotel. As I walk down the hall, I notice a small box-shaped robot unlock one of the hotel rooms and start cleaning it. A robotic broom hops in behind it and shuts the door.

My choice of restaurant is on the third floor. Maylene was right, these hallways look normal compared to where I stayed the night; sleek in design, two colors of deep red and yellow, and nothing like the holographic plants my hallway looked like, or the desert wasteland with a looming moon that it displayed this morning. I push the door open to the restaurant and take a seat. A waitress comes over immediately to take my order. It doesn't take much time before my food is served. Eagerly, I chow down on my meal.

I am happily surprised that my lunch is comped. Good thing too, because even though I only ordered a half-wire burger with fries (one of the best things Earth taught us), the meal would have been quite expensive. Our potato sticks just aren't quite the same as Earth's fries. I'm not one to be flashy, but I have to say, Edward definitely has style.

When I'm all done, I leave the restaurant and go up the elevator to the fifth floor so I can talk to Maylene before I head out on my trip. The doors welcome me to the floor, and, of course, Maylene isn't there. It's some blonde girl who looks like she will grow up to be a librarian. Or already has. Not that there's anything wrong with librarians.

"Uh, hi, excuse me," I say, walking awkwardly up to the counter. "Is Maylene around?"

The girl smiles and shakes her head. Her glasses almost fall off. I then notice that her name tag is upside down. I point to it, not wanting to be rude.

She looks down curiously, then looks up at me. Then it hits her, and she lets out a burst of laughter that causes me to jump slightly.

"My bad," she says, adjusting her tag. "I thought that there was something off about my aura." Her words are unnecessarily drawn out. She smiles a cheesy smile at me and flutters her hand lazily in the air. "Thanks for that."

Her name is Clarissa.

I nod, smiling back, still waiting for an answer. We look at each other sheepishly for a few seconds. Something lights up in her eye.

"Oh! Sorry, no, Maylene isn't around," she tells me. "She doesn't even work here anymore."

"What?"

Clarissa gives me a generic customer service smile. "Maylene is the pretty brunette girl, right? Has this kinda action movie star vibe to her?" Clarissa raises both hands like she is carrying a large weapon and then wiggles her body oddly after dropping her arms.

Here I thought I was weird.

"Sure. Yeah. Her." I regret asking her anything.

"She's an unusual chick," Clarissa says. I chuckle inside. *Yeah, Maylene is the weird one. And you, Clarissa, are completely normal.* "She started yesterday, asked to take two shifts, and then quit first thing this morning," Clarissa explains to me. Then she leans over the counter and whispers. "I think either she got with one of the guests or someone scared her off. Probably the first option though. She looks the type."

"Right," I say. "Well, thank you."

"Yes, of course," she says. "And Mr. Canabana wishes you a pleasant rest of your week."

I shoot a look at her. Is she also working closely with Edward?

"He gave you a message for me?" I blurt out, not really thinking about what I'm saying.

Clarissa eyes me with a worried expression. She probably now thinks I'm the cooky one. "He wishes everyone a good week when they check out," she says slowly to me. "Because he owns the hotel."

Understanding dawns on my face, but not fast enough as Clarissa adds, "It's part of our script when checking out guests." She puts on the best fake smile I've ever seen.

I close my mouth and nod my head slightly. "Of course," I say as I walk out the door.

With how fast I want to get out of here, it seems everything stands in my way. Two elderly women drop one of their suitcases, and naturally, it opens, and personal belongings fly everywhere. My good-neighbor senses kick in, and I help them get their luggage back in order.

I hurry towards the call stand to get my Sonars. Of course there's a line of about five people. I look around for another, but they are all the same, with multiple guests checking out.

The line goes by very quickly as the system is efficient. But I can't shake off this feeling that Clarissa is watching me, but no matter how many times I take a peek back, there's no one there except some passersby going about their day.

After what feels like forever, despite it being not much more than five minutes, I am driving away. I exit the garage and turn sharply onto the road, cutting off another driver, and speed away.

The roads turn around building after building, and I start to get impatient with being grounded. The people here move about as if they have nowhere to be. As much as I would love to disengage from the road and fly off, I'd likely get caught, and it wouldn't be good for me. Violation of grounding laws is a serious offense.

In the middle of the afternoon, the city feels desolate. More accurately, the land feels desolate. This is despite the numerous people moving about. I am nearing the borders of the city. There is a large screen playing from atop one of the condominium buildings. A commercial for PlatTech plays on it. Then another, this one for a new chain of hotels. Finally, there's an ad for a new medicinal pill for some obscure disease that apparently several people over ten years ago suffered from.

The traffic signal lets me pass, and I drive out of Velro boundaries and lift my vehicle into the air before setting off at a much higher speed. The view up here is beautiful. A couple of Sonars zoom past me, but most are fading out of sight in my rearview mirror. It takes hours to get past the barren landscape, and I am soon welcomed by small mountains far in the distance and a winding river below me. I avoid going over the heavily forested area and keep by the grasslands. I peek down every now and then and see large animals slowly gather towards their drinking spot.

Yesfborne lies near the foot of the mountains but I am still half an hour away.

That was one of the many things we have learned about Earth. We use hours, minutes, and even years to tell time. Though our days are slightly longer at just over twenty-five hours, and we have fifteen months in our three-hundred and fifty-nine-day year. I don't care enough to understand the scientific math behind both planets and why it is that way. They also use kilometers as we do, but we also use Milkateet, which approximates the old Earth use of feet. And our "wire" is like the "pounds" they used for weight back in the day on Earth in select countries. Our schools teach us several facts about Earth, and you can even go to higher education solely to study Earth. Our language is even the same as theirs, and though this isn't usually taught in our schools, though Edward knew it, they used to have several languages years ago, before they were united.

The sun begins to deepen its color, and soon enough starts its descent. Glowing lights are blurry in the distance but come into focus soon enough.

I have been to Yesfborne before. The smallest building must be about ten stories tall. Even the charging stations are a whopping fifteen floors and still get backed up every now and then. One part of the town holds houses perched on top of translucent ground that seems to float in mid-air. I would never be able to live in one of those, for fear the ground would give in, or disappear, and you would go crashing down nearly four-hundred Milkateet, or just about an eighth of a kilometer.

Yesfborne is also a major metropolis, and when grounded, it can take over an hour to drive through it. As such, those glowing lights stay blurry in the distance, but I can see well enough. I can even see the many Sonars that are traveling through, changing their road, or slowing down before turning out of sight.

As I enter the city, I look at my screen to see my destination. I ground my Sonars on the road and take a ramp up to the third elevation. I pass by many traffic lights before the road narrows and the lights turn into traffic signs.

Of course, these aren't actual roads. They are just fluorescent beams of an easy yellow that mark the way with a grid of thin, pale green lines between the beams, acting as the ground. I am much too young to have experienced the effort and disastrous mistakes when this was implemented, but the sheer amount of people made it necessary in heavily populated areas. I've heard that Earth uses a similar system. Though it disappoints me that there are traffic lights, the ones here are much more efficient, and far less hindering, than the ones in Velro.

Potted trees with wide leaves stand over twelve Milkateet tall on the concrete sidewalks, the ones that float magically in the air without issue.

Cities like this give me anxiety, though they operate on the same idea and properties as my Sonars does, and I have no fear of my Sonars dropping to the ground from way up in the air.

The residential area isn't as crowded as the main part of the city. I turn down many roads and make my way further. By this time the sun has set, and the bright light of the moon over the dark vibe of the land sets a quiet tone for the evening.

A call comes in through CHAD.

"Answer," I call out.

There's a fuzzy noise in the background before a jolting, croaky voice overcomes it.

"Are you here yet?"

Startled, I take a moment to answer.

"I'm sorry, who are you?" I ask.

I assume it's the man I'm headed towards, but there was no indication of identification on the call, and he didn't introduce himself when I answered.

"Bah! You know who I am," he shouts out. "Hurry, we're running out of time."

He hangs up.

I look at my clock. It is twenty on the dot. I'm not sure what the old man is going off about, but I suppose if being ready around nineteen means be there at exactly nineteen, then I suppose I am late. Being late for a delivery would be a first for me. Luckily, I'm doing a pickup, so my flawless record stands.

I speed up but stay careful to avoid crashing into anything. I'm not used to driving in such restricted environments, and I always fear that I'd crash while having an important delivery on board.

I turn into a driveway that sits in front of a sleek house covered with dark gray walls. The lights are on inside, though the place feels empty. There is no Sonars here. I park and step onto the concrete, taking careful steps as if it were going to collapse soon.

I look up and see several Sonars hovering in the air. They are more than a couple of elevations above me. Then I hear a quick zipping noise, and my Sonars disappears out of sight, having been parked beneath the house like the other Sonars are. This is one of the few cities in the world that does this.

There is a stone path lined with shrubs and budding flowers that I take to the front door. Before I can knock, it opens, and a tall, bony, and elderly man greets me.

"You must be Arch," he croaks out. "I suppose you look like him enough." Saliva spits out with every other word he speaks. "Well, come inside already!" he shouts at me before I can greet him back.

I lean forward and step inside.

The front door leads to a large living room with floor-to-ceiling windows on the back side looking out over the rest of the city. The view is one equal to views like on the higher floors of buildings, but this house is only one story tall.

The living room is sunken in, with two steps on all sides. There's another set of windows, these ones arched, that face the mountain. A tatami mat is spread across the floor, with a screen standing at the edge behind a large plant hanging from the ceiling. The furniture is all made of wood. I can't help but walk around a bit, though I am considerate of his property.

"Do you know why you are here?" The way his voice sounds I can only describe as a *grump*.

"I am here to pick up something from you," I answer impatiently.

"Yes, but do you know what?" He shakes his finger at me. Gary stumbles down the steps, nearly falling over, and walks right up to me. "What are you picking up from me?" he whispers intensely.

"A computer chip."

"Yes!" he exclaims, raising a finger into the air and turning around. He walks to the kitchen area. "But this isn't just any ordinary computer chip."

"So I've heard," I reply.

"No," he shakes his head angrily. "No, I don't think you fully understand how devastating this can be. In the wrong hands, this will destroy our world as we know it. Millions would die, and those that do," he says, his right eye twitching while both of them widen. He lowers his voice to a whisper. "They will be the lucky ones."

I wonder if he spent the day practicing for this very moment.

"Why don't we just destroy it ourselves?" I ask. "If it is so dangerous?"

"There's a protocol programmed into it that would spread its data to multiple sources even if they are out of range. That would be even worse. Phillip there, over there," he says, pausing for a moment while pointing in some direction that I assume is towards where this Phillip guy is. "Phillip is skilled enough to disengage the program before sending the chip back to Earth, which is where it came from." He pauses and looks down, confused. "Is it Phillip?" he asks himself.

There's one question that bothers me.

"If Edward thinks that this chip is so dangerous, why hasn't the effort to destroy it sooner been taken?"

Gary laughs with old man mirth, forgetting his pondering. Part of me wonders if it's an act. "When NEAST acquired the chip, several people sought to use it for their own desires. Fallon, there.... He managed to pull it away from the others without being caught, but certain people were suspicious of him, which is why he gave it to Edward. Even to this day, they don't trust him, but Michael has kept a low profile, and nobody there has any proof of what he did."

Fallon? Phillip? Michael? I'm not sure what to say, but I understand the answer and accept it. But clearly, Gary doesn't know who he is talking about.

Luckily, when Gary gets on a roll, he keeps at it, so I don't have to say anything.

"Not only is this able to alter or even delete anyone's identification at will, but it can also be used to send blank signals out across the planet. These signals can consist of nanoparticles that carry viruses. Supercharged electron-like particles. One could wipe out an entire city by using such a device as a bioweapon. Theoretically, one could wipe out an entire city by electrocution with this chip." Gary's left eye is quite big as he stares at me.

"Is that even possible?" I ask.

"Yes," he wheezes heavily. "On the surface, our world may seem united, but there are deeply repressed grudges amongst world leaders. Not to mention those who seek only to have total control and authority over everything and everyone. Give someone like that this chip, and they will have people begging him to stop, promising to do whatever he asks. Plus, some think we're way overpopulated and that we shouldn't have to build structures as tall as they are."

Last night, I thought Edward Canabana had some wild ideas, but this guy is on a whole other level. But despite the absurdity of what he says, I believe him. It is safe to say that he believes it too.

"I understand," I tell him. "I have my assignment, and I will complete the delivery. I will head out first thing tomorrow. It shouldn't take more than three days. Two if I really book it."

"No!" Gary shouts. "You can't leave tomorrow. You must go tonight. Get out of this city." Without explanation, he scrambles away down a hall and out of sight. Shocked, I stay right where I am.

Gary is back within a minute, carrying a small velvet pouch. Then he hands it to me, and I take it.

"Guard this with more than your life," he tells me. "We cannot afford for you to fail."

The gravity of the situation is dire. I knew that from last night. But Gary has taken that necessity and raised its seriousness. Of course, the thought that I am being conned crosses my mind, and I would be very upset if such a thing were happening. I'd be a fool.

But that thought lies deep down. My gut tells me that Gary and Edward are telling the truth.

"They will know that I had the chip, and they will come looking," Gary explains. He gently ushers me to the front door. "You must be far from here when they arrive. Don't stop until you are at least three cities away."

"Who is coming?" I ask.

"I don't know," Gary answers. "They have been quiet about their plans, but they are getting impatient. This is why you must trust no one. If you were found, they would kill you without a second thought."

"What will they do to you when they find you? And if they think you had the chip? Or when they find out you gave it to me?" I ask.

Gary chuckles a bit, his painfully aggressive attitude subsided. "I am not long for this world. There is nothing they can do to me. And they will never know that I gave the chip to you."

I nod, and he returns it. I almost feel as if I have made a strong bond with the grumpy man.

"Now go!" he shouts, pointing at the door.

Stepping outside, I turn my head back just in time to see the door close. I stand there for a moment. Gary's paranoia is contagious, and I feel as if I am being watched.

There is a loud rapping of something that makes me jump at the sudden noise. I look to see where it came from. Gary is staring at me angrily through his window, pointing to where I need to retrieve my Sonars.

My senses were right. I was being watched. But only by wheezy old Gary.

I walked over to the concrete pole and place my hand on it. I hear the familiar zipping noise, and my Sonars appears. I walk up to it and take one last look around. The night is still. The bustling lights out in the city remain lit, causing a pleasant glow to emit from the faux valley made of buildings. I hop inside and get going.

Passing through the small streets, unable to fly over the city and out, I look around. There are other vehicles passing by, probably coming back home from grocery shopping. Unfortunately, being this close to the main city limits, the stars are hard to see.

It takes close to twenty minutes to drive down into the main part of the city. I pass by two Sonars that drove off the designated roads but were caught by three law enforcement vehicles. I understand why they take it so seriously. With so many Sonars and other vehicles of transportation crowded into just one city, it would be mayhem to let them drive of their own accord.

I take a quick stop at a charging station just to grab some snacks and water. I don't charge, as I'm set for the next few cities. But if I am going to be driving all night, it isn't caffeine that's going to keep me going. It's food. I love food.

Something in the corner of my eye catches my attention. On one of the screens hanging from the ceiling, there is a news report about a known wealthy family that has gone missing. There is little to no sound, but the news caption tells me enough.

"They've been more frequent."

I stare at the screen for a moment. Then I hear someone clear their throat behind me. I turn back to see a shorter man with a belly and an unkempt face walk closer to me.

"The missing people," he says. "It's happening more and more. Makes you wonder if they knew something they shouldn't have."

"Yeah, I guess so," I say, though I haven't really given it much thought.

"They say that the world is going to be more united than ever before," he grunts out while nearly choking on a cheese chip. "But before that happens, I suppose some people have to go."

"You think these people were kidnapped?" I ask him, having thought that they went on a trip and never came back.

Someone turns up the volume, and I can hear the reporter speak.

"—just days after Mr. Fiski was reported missing by his secretary, she herself has now been absent from work for two days. Could there be a devastatingly raunchy scandal going on here?"

A man answers her.

"I don't think so, Polly, but it is possible that in a week we hear of a divorce between Mr. Fiski and his wife. She believes he's out enjoying a vacation somewhere, but highly doubts his secretary is with him. But she might be surprised when she finds out what we're going to reveal next."

The screen shuts off. I feel odd that the man stated words exactly as they were in my head.

I hear the crunching of chips. "There's no scandal there," the man says, still stuffing his mouth. "Jill Formore was loyal to Mr. Fiski, but she was already in love with someone else." He pauses for a moment. "You think they're lost somewhere hiking in the woods?"

I shrug, wondering why the screen went dark.

"I say they're dead, and anyone getting too close to the real story is going to end up the same way."

"Do you believe every conspiracy theory you hear? Or do you make them up?"

"Eh," he says. "You look too pretty and rich to care. Don't even know why I said anything." He walks away and disappears into a crowd of people.

I shake off the guilty feeling he leaves me with. He doesn't know what I'm currently up to. If Edward and Gary are right, then missing people are not of my concern, even if they are tragic.

I've also never been called "pretty" before, let alone by another man.

With my hands carrying bags of sweets and other "snacks" that I probably shouldn't eat in one night, I head off. From the lowest road elevation, the enormous buildings look daunting, towering over everything else and seemingly impossible to scale. But the brilliant lights and their colors make them seem less threatening.

Looking up, I can barely see the houses that sit atop the tallest buildings, just one more elevation higher. At least there, if the system were to fail, you wouldn't fall as far as most other houses. But I can tell you that the person and company that developed the technology to solidify the electromagnetic properties of Talvor with the use of light are the richest in the world, second only to the largest banking corporation - Hunt Banking.

A Glider passes by overhead, though it seems to only be a few elevations above me. I crane my head to follow it, but it goes out of sight. I put it out of my mind for the moment. The traffic down here is heavier than it should be at this time of night. I then realize that the traffic flow has been interrupted because one of the ramps that take you to a different elevation has been shut down. Most people who were planning to go that way move around slowly, not knowing where they should go instead.

I would understand if someone like me was in that position, not knowing the roads or where another route could be, but most of these people live here. I guess they just aren't used to their routine being changed.

Soon, I notice that some of the drivers are actually trying to get a look at what's happening, effectively making the traffic worse. I take another peek up, but I still can't see anything. It takes me a little while, but I get around the Sonars and make my way down a larger road to get out of the city.

My plan doesn't quite work as a stampede of emergency vehicles rush by. I turn my head to see where they are going. They also go up a few elevations. I then notice they go to the third. My heart stops for a bit. They wouldn't be heading to Gary, would they? I'm quite a distance from where he lives, and surely if something was wrong, there would be a closer unit to respond.

I keep driving. But in the back of my mind, worry sinks even deeper into my thoughts.

Making an illegal turn that pisses off a random person, I head back towards where Gary lives. I take the closest ramp up to the third elevation.

Up ahead I can see the mayhem caused by several first responders and drivers getting caught in the middle. I sharply turn down many streets, trying to get around the blocked roads and traffic, but I don't manage to move around quickly as so many others are doing the same. I turn on my radio to hear any news reports. The screen turns on, and a woman is speaking. I promptly turn the screen off but leave the sound on.

The woman goes on about a robbery that had taken place downtown, states the suspect, and then says they will be back with a breaking news story. Cursing, I tell CHAD to change the stations and find information about what is currently happening. CHAD shuts the radio off and reads out a report to me.

"Three homes in Yesfborne have caught fire just under an hour ago. Evacuations are still taking place while one family remains trapped underneath the wreckage inside their home. As of now, the other structures are still intact, but the Department of Fire Emergencies tells us that they do not know how long they can withstand it. Traffic in this area is heavy and is expected to remain so well into the morning. The elevation that has been affected is the third, near the heart of the city."

"Thanks, CHAD," I say, prompting him to turn off. I feel at ease now knowing that Gary lives further away and that his house did not catch fire. I look at the time. There's still about a couple hours until the new day, and I have backtracked far enough that I figure I might as well check around Gary's residence just in case. I don't even know why I'm so concerned for the guy. I just met him, and while he seemed well-intentioned, he wasn't the most pleasant to be around.

I suppose I feel it's my responsibility what happens to him, as he risked a lot giving me the program. But then again, I'm risking a lot, apparently, by taking the program chip to deliver it.

Once the traffic clears up, it doesn't take long for me to reach Gary's house. The streets here remain quiet, but by this time most of the house lights are out. This applies to Gary's house as well. I let out a sigh. I am relieved that he is fine, and presumably asleep, and grateful that he isn't keeping such a close eye on me.

I pass his house and turn down another street to head back out of the city.

CHAD turns on suddenly and announces a call. Before I get the chance to accept, or decline, I hear her voice.

"How's it going?" Maylene asks. Her darker skin isn't quite as intense as those who came from the high desert continents, but it has more color than my skin, which is very pale in comparison.

"Fine, I got the chip—"

"What are you doing there!" she shouts out, not really asking the question, though I am sure she will want an explanation. "Leave now! It's dangerous!"

I shake my head, confused. "I was just here, and everything seemed fine."

"Get out of there!" she yells at me.

I mumble "fine" to myself, but as we're still connected, she sees me and rolls her eyes. I look into one of the mirrors. I see a Glider fly by, and a beam of light is directed at Gary's house. I stop the Sonars and turn it to go back.

"Keep moving, don't go back," Maylene says. I ignore her.

My mistake. Within seconds, I lose control of the Sonars and I cruise down some of the streets without doing anything. I look back to see his house. I can see a trail of smoke rise, and shortly after, there's a small spark that I can barely see through one of the windows.

"What are you doing?" I lash out at her. "I have to make sure he's okay!" "Gary is fine," she says. "He told you that you couldn't stay in the city for the night because it would be too dangerous. Do you really think he planned to stay the night himself? He's probably ways ahead of you, and you're still in Yesfborne, worried about some old man you just met."

My Sonars still travels on without me driving it.

"I wonder if I made a mistake choosing you."

"Oh, now you're mad that I started giving a shit?" I ask, annoyed. "His house is probably burning down now!" I look back, hoping to get a view, but I am too far away now. I can see hazy smoke in the distance, but I could be just imagining that. It certainly looks like it is close enough, though. I quickly turn my head to look at where the other burning houses are. I can't see those either. "There were already three other houses that caught fire earlier tonight."

"And they were probably done by the same people who are going after Gary," she snaps at me, as if it were obvious. "Their tactic is to get enough of the city's resources handling a diversion while they go after their real target. Collateral damage has a fluid definition with them, and it is the first word in their vocabulary."

I don't respond. I didn't think about that, but it would make sense. If they caused something big enough to happen that grabbed the attention of most of the population, then they could do something else on the side completely unnoticed. In this case a fire that threatens three homes while one family is still in danger, makes for a much more exciting story than some old man goes missing for a few days.

She stares at me, waiting for me to say something. When I don't, she sighs and looks down for a second.

"I'm just mad that you're not following our instructions," she says with a much kinder voice. I can tell that her frustration was with the idea that I could be in danger. "It is my job to watch you, and everything else, to make sure that you have the smoothest and safest trip possible. I can't promise that it'll be perfect, but I can assure you that myself, and those who are on our side, want to make sure you deliver the chip safely."

My Sonars stops moving. For a moment I don't know what's happening, but then I realize I probably have control of my vehicle now. I test it and find that it drives on my command once more.

"How do you do that?" I ask after I get going.

"I work for Edward Canabana. I have access to technology most of this world hasn't seen yet."

"But hacking into a Sonars is technology that already exists," I respond. "I even have software to ensure that it doesn't happen to mine, and I paid a lot of money for it. It has always worked, until now at least."

Maylene smiles shrewdly. "Don't blame the software. I'm sure it's one of the best. But, like I said, I have access to advanced technology."

"And that's also how you bypassed my communication protocols."
She nods proudly.

"I am going to let you go now," she says as she yawns. "I'm getting tired, and I have already looked at your path, and all seems fine. I installed extra security protocols into your Sonars system that will alert me if anything seems threatening, but you should have an uninterrupted ride tonight."

"Gary said I should stop at least three cities away," I tell her.

Maylene nods. "He is right. I sent you the directions for Halav. You're going to be traveling for most of the day tomorrow, mainly because you are headed on a detour. It isn't too far out of the way. The purpose is to make sure you aren't being followed."

"I thought we wanted me to deliver the chip as soon as possible."

"Yes, but your survival and success are far more important than the speed of delivery. If they figured Gary had the chip, they would follow a route that's fastest to anywhere it could be threatened. And there is only one place."

I nod.

"No one can do anything with it as long as it is in your possession. And we can't destroy it if you never make it." Maylene pauses for a moment. "Now, take the route I'm directing you on. It will get you out of the city much quicker than if you travel down at the first elevation. You might be moving slower up here, but there will be less stopping."

Before I can thank her, she clicks off and her image disappears. There is another click, and CHAD's communications system turns off. I let out a sigh and keep going, following the directions on my screen.

Maylene was right. I travel through the residential area fairly quickly, and soon enough, I reach the city limits. The lights still shine brightly in the downtown district. There are plenty of Sonars moving around too, though few of them are actually leaving the city. If anything, there are quite a few coming in. Most of the shops and restaurants here remain open. Yesfborne is one of those cities that is always awake. I hear Earth has a few of those too.

I zoom down to the first elevation. The traffic here is immediately worse than above. But I am at the edge of the city, and I start to exit it.

It's just me and two other Sonars, and once we cross the border, we all soar into the air and go off in separate directions, but we move much faster now that we are no longer grounded.

It isn't long until the brilliant lights are way behind me. With the pure darkness ahead of me, I think to myself, "It is going to be a long night."

3

What feels like hours is barely just one. The constant black of night followed by a different shade of dark makes the drive overly mundane. This is even with the glowing stars, which I have seen hundreds of times. But looking into the heavens makes my mind work, and I soon lose myself in trails of thought that are comprised of wishful thinking and hopes for the future. Unfortunately, after a while, even the beauty of the heavens can seem to lose its appeal if that is all you ever see.

With how much I travel, I don't really have a place I call home. Home is just back at one of the houses my dad owns, and I stop by every now and then if I am a day or less from the house and want to take a break. Usually it is empty, though sometimes one of the maids will show up. I don't talk to most of them, though Elisa seems to genuinely like me, and we have chatted for hours at a time. It is odd, though, because her daughter and I dated briefly, but she broke it off because she was moving across the country. I knew that she knew it wouldn't really matter how far apart we were, but we had been drifting away from each other emotionally already. It was a good excuse for the breakup. Elisa and I still hang out like we've been friends for years, which by this time we have been.

My plan for my future is to make enough money on my own that I can comfortably own my own home and still have enough to try different business opportunities without losing everything else in the process, and feel like I did it on my own. The thing is, there isn't anything specific that I want to make a living out of. I've had it pretty easy for most of my life. While I am grateful for it, I sometimes wish that I had to struggle a bit. My father made my life so easy, but I feel like there is no purpose to it.

Of course, it would be nice to have a family as well, but with all my travel, I don't have much opportunity to make lasting relationships. Or I just haven't found the right girl yet.

First thing's first, and that is to make lots of money, and forget all about the money my dad gave me. That's why my current job is handy. The only downside is that during drives like this, I feel even more lonely than usual.

I pass by a few Sonars that are coasting along, clearly not in any hurry. There are even a few who pass me, swerving along and dive-bombing as if they were cutting through traffic or heavily forested trees, though neither applies. They're probably just having fun or are impatient.

Eventually I catch up to them, but only because they grounded themselves because they were caught by an Impositioner, or Impo. Sometimes those who really don't like them resort to calling them "Imps". It is not normal to be pulled over for breaking the law while driving between cities, as there are so few laws to break. But some of those laws include driving at too high an altitude or, in their case, unnecessarily moving about in a chaotic fashion, posing a threat to other drivers.

I shake my head as I pass. I understand the desire to have fun while driving, especially during long or nighttime drives, but there is a point of common sense that everyone should have and follow.

More time passes by at an unimaginably slow pace. I shoot down some caffeine and eat a small snack. When I'm done, my small snack becomes a large snack as I proceed to finish the bag of small cookies

I bought because they just taste so good that I can't help but finish them all.

As I crumble the last of it, with morsels of cookie falling out of my mouth, my screen turns on, and I see a very entertained Maylene smiling at me.

"Oh, if only I felt bad telling you that I had your camera on for about a minute before calling you," she tells me, doing a bad job of holding in her laugh.

I choke and spit, losing control of the Sonars for a short moment.

"You can turn the camera on in here without me knowing?" I ask, already knowing the answer. I shake my head for longer than I mean to. She nods her head, smiling. "Remember," she says slowly, but I cut her off.

"Yeah, yeah. You have access to technology this world hasn't seen yet," I say, throwing my hands up slightly and mocking her. I pause for a moment and then add, "And apparently the perverted tech too."

She lets out a short and offended laugh. "I would never!"

"What if I was doing something? Or if I wasn't clothed?" I ask her in a light-hearted tone, but I am also quite serious.

While she lets out bursts of laughter, I take a closer look at her surroundings. She's inside a darker room with two lamps at her desk. She sits in a rather ragged chair and is wearing an oversized maroon sweater. I can tell she has multiple screens on her desk. The room has an eerie underground vibe to it, but I am certain she's sitting in an office on an upper floor of a skyscraper.

"Wh-what would you be doing in your Sonars! I guess you sleep sometimes, but there would never be a time where you weren't dressed," she says. "Oh! Of course, unless there's a girl involved!" She drops her amused tone and sets her face straight. "What's her name? Do you even remember her name?" Maylene scoffs. "Ugh, this is why I don't usually deal with men. They can be so *self-centered,*" she spits out without giving me a chance to defend myself.

"Whoa," I say. "There hasn't been any girl. Not since we met, at least. And I am not self-centered. And I don't just hook up with random girls just because I can. I'm not one of those guys."

She scoffs. "Oh, yeah, and I bet you can just pick up so many girls whenever you want!"

I chuckle under my breath and say with a much more cocky attitude than I could ever have with people I don't know, "If I wanted, I could have gotten you."

"Mmm, funny," she says as she rolls her eyes and makes a face. "But I was just doing my job, checking in on you. And remember, I was *paid* to flirt with you."

"Ouch," I say, but a huge grin passes over my face.

Maylene and I stare at each other for a second. Luckily I'm in open air because it would be so dangerous to not look at the road for so long.

Maylene smiles. "I'm kidding, obviously." I know she is. "No, of course not though, I wouldn't spy on you like that. I haven't before."

I nod, both thanking her and showing her that I believe her.

Then she adds, "You know, I could see your browsing history too, if I ever wanted. Even if you tried to hide it."

I make a mental note to never look at anything on my phone ever again. Not that I do it often, which is something I tell her.

Maylene nods slightly, and a smile cracks on her lips. "That's because you're a cut above other men."

I don't get a chance to enjoy the compliment. Someone walks into the room Maylene is in. As he walks, he asks, "Who is a cut above other men? I know my favorite hater wouldn't be talking about me." All I see is a large silhouette.

Maylene rolls her eyes and rests her chin on her hand.

A tall guy comes into view. He is much more built than I am, has bleach blonde hair, and stunning green eyes. Yeah, I just called this guy's eyes stunning. The closer he gets the more I realize how tall he is. Taller than me for sure, at over six Milkateet. I stand at an average height. This guy meets the standards of some girls who "only want tall men".

"Oh, hey bud," he says to me. "How's the famous Arch Caldor doing this late night?" He smiles a cocky smile.

He's earned it.

"Not bad. But, uh, I don't know you, so I'd prefer if I could keep talking to Maylene," I say as politely as I can.

"Of course," he says with a respectful smile. "I understand. Sorry to bother you," he puts a small piece of paper on Maylene's desk. I hear him say to her, "Edward wanted you to get this." He looks at me again, waves a friendly goodbye, and walks out of the room.

I would feel bad for my attitude towards him, but I hate the guy for being so damn perfect-looking.

Maylene takes a moment to read her message.

"Is everything all right?" I ask her.

"Yeah, Edward just wants to make sure I check in on Halav. You know, make sure that there isn't anything unusual going on, and more importantly, that no one is tracking you. I already did, though, but I plan to verify all is well at least three times before you make it there. Your hotel for the night is also all booked and paid for." For some reason I don't think a paper note told her all that. The note is something else.

I nod, telling myself that Edward is just paranoid so that I don't get so paranoid myself. "And how about with the other guy? Who is he, anyway?" I ask.

"Oh, that was just Matt." Maylene shrugs. Even with her attraction to other women, I can tell she still finds Matt appealing. "He also works for Edward. He's decent at his work, but quite unpleasant to be around most times," she informs me with a half-hearted grunt of disgust. "Don't worry about him. As long as we don't run into any trouble, you may never see him again."

"What does he do?" I ask.

Maylene lets out a sigh. "A lot. He deals with intelligence and logistics, but mostly for preventing disastrous events, which range from a large drop in revenue for Canabana Industries to things like rescue missions. Like me, he works directly for Edward."

Whoa. I'm taken aback, but thinking about it, I suppose Mr. Canabana would be well prepared for anything and would have a personal team to assist him with his business activities. He probably has hired security that follow him everywhere, likely always hidden in plain sight.

"The 'rescue missions' part doesn't really happen often," Maylene says. I was going to ask about that, but good to know. "Matt usually deals with press and charming people to take Edward's side in deals and whatnot."

I let out a small chuckle. "I can see why."

Rolling her eyes again, Maylene says, "Not you too. Oh well, I suppose you're right. Even I admire him a bit." She then gives me a death stare. I can tell she didn't mean to say it out loud. "Don't tell anyone, especially Matt, that I ever said that. Seriously, or I'll drive your Sonars into a mountain."

I laugh. "No worries. After all, you are his favorite hater." Maylene rolls her eyes. A moment passes, and I ask, "How was your night with the bartender chick?"

"Which one?" She smiles mischievously.

I look surprised for a moment, but Maylene adds, "I'm just kidding. I don't get around that often. But it was nice. Something I definitely needed for the night. It had been a stressful day."

"Why was it stressful?"

Maylene chuckles. "Because I had to make sure you made it to your final destination for the day, and warm you up so that Edward could convince you to take his delivery." She looks proud with her wide grin. "It took a lot of careful planning and practice." She leans in closer to the camera. "But the hardest part was waiting for you to show up to the hotel. I was so bored!"

I laugh. "I bet. How long were you there for?"

"Just a couple of hours, but still," she trails off.

Not knowing what to say, I set the Sonars on autopilot, cross my arms, and nod.

Yawning, Maylene announces that she should get to bed. It is about two in the morning, and I understand. I am pretty tired too. With a last goodnight, Maylene clicks off.

And I get back to the banal drive, turning off autopilot, thinking that it would have been smarter to engage it when Maylene first called me.

Once again, I am passing over green field after green field. Not that I can see much of it because it is still in the middle of the night. And honestly, if I had to choose between an endless view of black or green, I'd choose black. Most times. It keeps me on my toes, figuratively speaking. Green fields can make me feel sleepy.

Before I know it, the early morning sunlight creeps over the horizon. The light reveals long farmlands of various animals and crops. I move higher in the air so that the other Sonars attending the farms can do so without my interference.

There is a city ahead. This one has low buildings, indicating a smaller population than other cities. It is likely, though, that the structures go beneath the ground. It would also mean that most homes are apartments or condos. Instead of windows with expansive views, they are given screens as walls and can change the look to whatever they feel like.

As directed, I don't stop in the city. If it weren't so wide, I would go around it, but it would be quicker to ground the Sonars and pass through it. Plus, I've heard of people getting pulled over because they went around a city and, as such, looked suspicious.

I won't be that person. Especially with what I am currently delivering.

It doesn't take long for me to pass through the city. There aren't many vehicles around. Most people here prefer to walk or scoot around with muscle-powered transportation. The buildings are mostly wide and flat, giving the city a look as if it were a huge network of warehouses. I've never been here before. I make a mental note to come back one day so I can truly visit it. There are plenty of cities already on that list, and I continuously add more.

After just under twenty minutes, I leave the limits of the city, and I am soaring high in the air once again. A large aircraft passes over me. I look back to see where it is going. I can see it starting its descent and I see a port for it at the edge of the city. Even with the power to travel continents, most vehicles can't last long with such extensive trips, and there are faster ways to travel, so few ever do it themselves.

I pass over smaller mountain tops but travel through the valley when the peaks get too high. I can tell it is cold outside because of the light snow sprinkled across the land, even though it is still summer in this hemisphere.

The bareness and emptiness of the mountain is calming. The peacefulness of being alone here makes me wonder if this is what I want for myself. Deep down, I know that I'd start to feel it—the loneliness. And it would eventually get to me. Just as it does on long drives.

It takes a few hours to get through the mountain pass. When I'm out, I glide down for a bit before leveling off at the base and drive over a quiet forest.

The route Maylene has sent me on takes me off the beaten path. If I had gone my normal route, I would have easily passed through another two cities. And it would have been much quicker.

I end up passing through what I would call a small town. Though the normal laws of the land are generally more lax in an area like this, they still hold strong to the grounding laws. There aren't many of these left in the world. Most cities have become so populated that it takes a couple thousand city workers to handle day-to-day stuff. Here there are old structures still made of wood. While they are bigger than I am sure they used to be, there are no large business buildings. The city hall here consists of a two-story church-esque building with a bell hanging up top in the center.

There's a narrow building that is advertised as the only hotel in the area. It would be nice to take the rest of the day off and stay the night, but the town of Maldmar isn't my goal for the day.

I have to stop for a little while to recharge my Sonars, even though Maylene would have preferred I didn't. Inconvenient as it is, I learn that the town has only one Platform, and I have to wait about an hour before I can charge up. I go into the dinky convenience store. The first thing I notice is that it lacks self-serving kiosks. There is one man behind the counter and no one else inside. I hold out my phone to pay for my drinks and lunch. He grunts what I take to be a thanks before walking off towards the back.

I wait another thirty minutes, and my Sonars is ready to leave.

I'm out of the town in just under another ten minutes. I didn't pass by one single Sonars. The ones that were charging must have been traveling, just like me.

Maldmar is more of a mountain town than I thought because when I leave, I still stay quite close to the ground, going down yet another hill.

Roadways have been carved out of the mountain, but I still must drive slower because of the narrow space between the jutting rocks.

Hours pass by, and the ground levels out once more. I peek behind me. The full height of the mountain is hard to see, and I wouldn't have known it was so tall if I had not just passed through it. The sight is pretty, though. Way up, it is snow-capped, but otherwise, the mountain is littered with evergreen trees of varying shades. I am sure many creatures live there, but I unfortunately did not see any.

Though the scenery remains mostly the same, I don't mind it at all. There's a sense of calm that this wilderness brings to me. One day, if I'm not too busy, I'll also take some time off and maybe go bare-camping for a few days. No tent, limited technology. If my delivery mission didn't hold the importance that it does, I would stop and spend an hour or so relaxing outside.

This is one of the rare times when I enjoy driving in the day rather than at night. The skies aren't cluttered with other vehicles here, and the scenery is just simply beautiful.

A few more hours pass by before I see the city of Halav. With towering buildings and three floating stadiums, this is the largest city I have been in since I started this delivery.

The sun is beginning to set, but by no means is it nighttime. As I approach the city, I lower my Sonars and merge with the other traffic. There are so many vehicles, countless billboards, and several homes that look cheaply built. There are cracks in the structures, and trash piling on the ground. Not all of the lights are lit.

It is rare to see anything like this.

For about five minutes, I drive on the main road, but soon the road brings me up to the fifth elevation. I look down. There are houses on top of houses, or condominium buildings where houses would be. In this city, like so many others, it appears the wealthier you are, the higher up you live.

I crane my head to look up. It is hard to see, but there are other houses alongside and above the skyscrapers.

Traffic here moves seamlessly but at a slower pace.

I come to a point where new buildings rest on higher ground. For a moment the road leads me down. There are structures built into the steep rockface.

Eventually I come to a stop. There is a quick-changing light that lets one to two Sonars through at a time. This might be the only traffic light in the whole city. When it is my turn, I follow the road up more elevations than I can count. The ascent is steep, and it takes a minute before it flattens out. When it does, I am welcomed to the amazing world of the city proper. Using both the electromagnetic technology and the natural landscape, varied-sized structures seem to levitate next to each other, while others are floating at another elevation above. But then there are also areas where the ground is easily ten elevations higher than the city limits. Not all the plateaus are drilled into, though. There are also some houses that jut out of the cliffs.

Skybridges connect buildings to buildings, and the roadways are cleanly and carefully set between them. Glass panel walkways line the roads. These are solar-powered and most likely supply enough energy for the entire city and beyond. The mechanism that holds everything in the air can be seen, just barely, if you pay attention. I think the city was purposefully designed that way. It's almost like fuzzy circles beneath all the structures, vibrating at such high speeds that it gives it the appearance of glitching out. Truth is, you want it to stay that way. If they seem still and unmoving, you could be in trouble pretty soon.

It takes me almost an hour to reach the hotel district. Sitting atop yet another plateau, hotels line each other, each at least twenty stories high. The road is lined with placed palm trees, and the ground is a reddish color, making it the only place in the entire city that has a natural looking ground. Old models of Sonars line parking areas facing the hotels, though I know most vehicles are parked in the normal garages.

I turn into my destination. The driveway takes me below the hotel building, and I wait in line before I am able to park. When it is my turn, I get out, grab my stuff and scan my phone so that my Sonars disappears out of sight, parked somewhere hidden from view.

From what I can tell, the hotel boasts all its floors as indoor living spaces, none of them corporate offices. The parking garage is dug deep into the plateau, impossible to tell from the outside.

One of the first things I notice when I walk into the lobby is that this is not a Canabana hotel. It is still quite elegant by all means, but a row of kiosks awaits me rather than someone to welcome me. I scan my phone. My room pops up, and a key is distributed to me. The screen tells me that my room is paid in full for one night. All thanks to Maylene. Or Edward, I should say.

Normally I would head straight to my room, shower, and pass out, but I am so hungry that I find the closest restaurant to me. It is located on the same floor, just around the corner. With the restaurant being the same as the main lobby, I am greeted only by a mobile kiosk that takes my order, gives me my food, and takes my payment. It rolls away quicker after I pay than when it was serving me.

I now see why Edward Canabana likes hiring people. The lack of human interaction can feel lonely and rude, something I would not have noticed if I hadn't spent the other night in one of his hotels. In about five years, I believe it will be the new trend.

It would be great to see that happen.

Several screens hang from the ceiling. Most show a news channel, but a few air the last game of the Spherewars Championship. Simple enough of a game, but it is quite exciting to watch three teams of Sonars defend their tower while trying to, essentially, capture the flag from the other towers. Each team has fourteen Sonars, though these are larger than common ones and each are manned by three people. The flags are hidden inside a fortress, each uniquely designed to destroy anything that attempts to enter it. It sounds quite dramatic, which it is, but despite the crashes, the fatality rate is quite low. Each team has about fifty people. Any of the games can last up to a week, and they only stop at night when all teams agree to a ceasefire for a specified time. Breaking the ceasefire is grounds for immediate disqualification.

The teams in the championship match were the *Fireflies*, the *Woke Dragons*, and the *Iron Hooks*. The Fireflies won this year.

But something on the news catches my attention. I press a button on the end of the table by the divider, and a small speaker turns on, just loud enough for me to hear it. A man speaks into the camera.

"Just a friendly reminder, tonight is the first of three nights that Halav will be under lockdown. No curfew has been issued, but no one is allowed to leave the city boundaries between the hours of twenty-three, and four."

I don't care to ask someone why the city is on lockdown. But because it is set for three days, it is likely because there is a military base near and their next operations, whatever they might be, will be ongoing during the night.

It also doesn't affect me because I intend to sleep way past four in the morning.

Once I'm all finished, I head to my room, number 306. There is a revolving elevator ahead. When it slows down, I step on it. If someone were to not be properly footed on it, or if they weren't fully on or off, the sensors would halt all motion so that no one would get crushed. I refuse to embarrass myself like that, and my ride up to the third floor is smooth.

When I get into my room, a message from Maylene pops up on my phone.

"Glad you made it in alright. I'll let you have your good night's sleep. Don't be late in the morning. Please be out and on the road by ten."

I drop my phone on my bed and take a shower. Once done, I plop myself down and fall asleep instantly.

4

There is a rapid clicking noise. I am flying high in the air. Sirens go off behind me. I hear the clicking again, only this time it sounds more like loud knocks. I turn my head back. Instead of the sky, all I see is darkness.

I open my eyes.

The rapid clicking noise stops for a moment. Even with the curtains shut, I can tell it is very late at night. I don't want to wake myself up any more than I already am, so I don't turn on the lights. I close my eyes to go back to sleep.

The clicking noise returns, this time sounding more like a heavy tapping, as if someone were running. This time, the sound doesn't stop. It gets louder. Now it sounds like several people are running. There's a brief moment of silence before the tapping is replaced with a cranking sound. I think I hear a few doors shut. I turn the light on and get out of bed. I'm wearing minimal clothing, so I decide to put on a pair of pants.

The cranking stops. There's a high-pitched whistling as if a firework were going into the air. Where there should be a pop, a loud blast shakes the whole floor. After a few seconds, there's another, following the same whistling sound.

Then another, this one even closer than the last. With the ground shaking violently, my heart begins to race. I hastily put on my shoes.

Another blast happens, rattling everything on the walls around me.

Then another, but this time the frames fall to the floor. I could tell that the blast happened in the room right next to mine.

Without thinking, I open my door and jump out of my room. The first thing I see is a man carrying an air launcher, a firearm with rocket power, though all it does is send a destructive blast of air out, one that can tear you to shreds if you were caught in it.

The man points it at me.

I jump back into my hotel room. I hear the high whooshing of the projectile before it blows open a wall in the hallway. I hear footsteps approaching. In hindsight, it probably wasn't one of my smarter ideas to run back into my room, because now I have nowhere to go.

The footsteps sound closer, and soon a man appears in the doorway. He is wearing all black, with a mask of the same color covering his face. There are no eye sockets, but I know the guy can see very well, probably with enhanced night and ultrasonic vision capabilities. He points the blaster at me.

At least at this point, I know I'm the target, if I didn't figure as much before.

Frozen with fear, I think of nothing better to do other than imagine what my death will feel like. Millions of thoughts race through my mind. It just feels like such an anti-climactic end to what would have been such a great journey.

And then I hear it. The faint click, a pop, glass breaking, and the whistle of air that will surely feel like five Glider blades tearing through me. The man standing in front of me is blasted off his feet. In my blurred vision, I can see his body split apart, his blood leaping into the air in thin slices before it loudly splatters on the hallway wall. There is barely a body left to see.

I turn my head back, wanting to see where it came from and who had just saved me. I see no one, but there is shattered glass littering the floor. The blast had been so loud that I didn't even hear the glass break, somehow I just knew that it did. The curtain has been blown to bits. Cold air sweeps into the room. I'm not sure how late it is, but all I see outside are city lights and buildings; not many vehicles are in the air.

Instinctively, I feel the back of my head and neck. Some shards managed to nick me, but I'll be fine. Small cuts aren't my biggest problem at the moment.

I have seconds before my imminent danger is very real. I know there must be more out to get me. Dashing out of the room, I trip over the remains of the douchebag who was trying to kill me. My mind is racing, and I can barely see, though I know nothing is in either one of my eyes.

My fists bang against the wall as I push off of it to race down the hall. The first corners I turn, I clumsily smash my body against the wall and bounce off it. My hand slams against another door to a room. I stop for a moment, with everything being quiet for the time being. I worry that the person inside the room will angrily open the door. No one does.

I hear another blast and instantly go on the run again. I curse the hotel for being so big. I then curse at myself for thinking that I had a moment to stop. There must be an emergency exit somewhere nearby.

The hallways are long, and I can barely see the end of them when I first turn down another one. I hear another rush of air. My reflexes make me step to the left. Just in time, the wind blast misses me, though scratch marks tear into the back of my right shoulder. Luckily, the longer the distance, the less lethal the air blasters are.

I turn another corner again, this time without bouncing off of the wall. I'm still running as fast as I can. Finally I find a staircase. I barge through the door, hurting my elbow as I do so, and nearly topple down the stairs. I go down two flights before crashing into the hallway on the first floor. The emergency lights are on here because the normal lamps hanging in the hallways have shut off.

I race down another hallway, looking for the exit to the hotel. Nobody is around here. I'm running through halls of hotel rooms, wondering why I can't find the open spaces, such as where I entered the building and where I had dinner.

When I begin to feel like I am in some sort of post-apocalyptic era, I barge through double doors into a kitchen area. I can tell that this is not the same restaurant I ate at before. Blasts echo through the room, and I feel a gust of wind behind me. I don't even look back, but book it straight ahead, turning around a corner as soon as I can.

Luck is not on my side. The corridor I run down leads to a staircase that only goes up. I know it would be too risky to turn back, so without slowing down, I head back upstairs. I try the second-floor door, but it is locked. I run up to the third. It is also locked.

Cussing loudly, I go up to the fourth floor. Also locked.

It isn't until I get to the seventh floor that I find a door that is open. I'm panting heavily and beyond out of breath, but fear keeps me going. I swing the door open and run down another hall of hotel rooms. It is also empty up here.

I turn another corner. To my left are doors that look like they lead into large suites. The right is just a sleek wall. Ahead, there's a large double door that swings open both ways. I push through and run into a long hall. This time, to my left, there is just a plain wall, but the right side is lined with one large window, floor to ceiling and as wide as the hall.

The stunning view of the city distracts me for a moment. In that moment, a blast knocks me off my feet and into the wall. I crumple to the floor, dizzy, and try to get up.

Instead of ringing in my ears, I hear a strong, yet dull, whooshing sound. My brain replays the noise of shattering glass over and over. I know I'm still alive because of the pain I feel. Honestly, I can't believe I'm not dead.

There's stinging in my arms and side, probably due to the glass that cut through my skin. A shard stuck itself in my triceps. Instinctively, I yank it out and simultaneously let out a squeal of pain.

The thought of getting up on my feet occurs to me. Slowly and with great difficulty, I stand, leaning on what's left of the wall for support. The cold air from the night blows in. My body shivers. For a moment, I wish I had put on a shirt when I was back in my room. I can hear sirens in the distance. Flashing emergency lights obscure my vision. Blood spills out of the cut and runs down my arm, pooling into my slightly cupped hand before leaking onto the floor.

The sound of wind and glass shattering fade, and is replaced by thumping. I squint my eyes and look around, trying to see clearly. An alarming thought crosses my mind. What if there's another blast or explosion? With the entirety of the window shattered, there's nothing to dampen the blast, which would mean I'm pretty much already dead.

A rough hand clasps my shoulder and pulls me back. Flinching from the surprise and pain shooting down my body, I turn back to see who grabbed me, but manage only to nearly tumble back to the floor.

The guy who grabbed my back catches me, and my face falls into his chest for a split second before I am lifted back to my feet. For a moment, my face is a little too close to his for my comfort.

It's Matt.

"We have to get out of here, now," he says. Matt pulls something out of his pocket. Next, I am stabbed with a small needle near the tip of my spine. A warm trickle flows down my back and arms. I get dizzy for a second.

All of a sudden, I feel like a new man. I no longer feel any pain, and I am able to hold myself up. My eyes are wide as if I overdosed on caffeine. Additionally, the lack of body movement causes my body to shake.

Matt then slaps something on my arm where the cut is. It stings horribly for a bit, and I let out a gasp of pain. The pain quickly subsides, and the cut feels like it has healed over. Of course, it isn't my real skin, but a bandage like material covers the cut and stops the bleeding.

"There you go," he breathes proudly. "Follow me."

He leads me back down the halls with the hotel rooms. He stops in front of one of the doors, looks up and down, contemplates, and then kicks the door handle.

The door doesn't budge.

"Ah, worth a shot," he mumbles. He grabs something else from his pockets. It's a blank card chip. He scans the keylock, and the door clicks open. Matt shoves the door hard, causing it to bang against the wall.

The suites on this floor are huge, and they have floor-to-ceiling windows that line the edges, which are very tall as they go up two stories. The main area inside has a wide floor plan and is flanked with bedrooms on the second floor of the suite. The flooring is made of a smooth, glossy rock that shines just like marble. On the left, the entire wall is covered by a screen, switching between short videos of forest lands, metropolitan views, and even various neon shapes.

"We need to keep moving," he breathes out, grabs my arm, and walks over to the window, taking me with him.

"Damn it," he cusses. "They should have been here by now."

I don't have a moment to ask who he is talking about. The door to the hotel is smashed open, and another blast zooms in, knocking over several pieces of furniture.

Before I can process anything, Matt takes something out of one of the many pockets in his pants. He uses the metal object to crack the window. It isn't a large crack, but he must have used a great deal of strength to create it. He then pulls me to the floor, and I fall on top of him. Once more, my face is so close to his that I can feel his warm breath.

It's only a second later that I realize why he did it. Another air blast comes through, this time hitting the window right where we were just a moment ago. The window shatters. I cover my head and Matt's as the glass falls on us. Without looking, Matt twists his legs around mine and rolls me off him before rolling on top of me. Our eyes meet for a second. Eerily, it feels like he's apologizing for something.

Like everything else, there is no time for me to process what's happening. Matt rolls again, this time wrapping his arms around my torso.

And we fall out of the window.

The freefall almost feels relieving, like the end is near and bliss awaits.

Matt holds me tightly with one arm, his legs still wrapped around mine. His chest is pressed against my back. He uses his other arm to reach into another pocket of his. I feel the pull of a parachute jerk us to a slow descent. Matt hastily pulls a small orb from one of his two straps crossed against his chest. He chucks it at the building we just jumped from. When it hits one of the windows, the glass shatters so quickly that it almost looks like it dissolves. With a grunt, Matt lowers his head over my shoulder. A strong gust of wind pulls the parachute down and away from the hotel. Matt shoots out a grappling hook towards the opening he made in the building. With a zip, we are pulled towards the hotel, but we are pretty far away, and it is clear that we won't make it.

As we swing down towards a hard and smushing collision with the building, Matt tosses another orb. Just in time, the window we're about to hit dissolves, and we fall into the building on the second floor, into a conference room occupied by small robots doing their nightly cleaning. We slide to the end of the room until we hit the wall.

Our entrance does not disturb the robots.

"Let's go," Matt says, quickly jumping to his feet. I follow suit. Under normal circumstances, I would be aching all over, but the serum Matt injected me with is still working. Though I expect heavy bruising tomorrow. If I make it that far.

We push open the large conference room doors. The hallways are largely unlit, though the dim backup lights are on in some areas. As we jog down the hallways, taking care to stay away from windows, we pass a few flashing emergency lights. I can hear sirens outside, but the hotel remains hauntingly empty, meaning we aren't the emergency, or that they haven't found it yet.

Matt stops for a moment. We are in an elevator foyer that is normally hidden from the guest's view, meaning there are no windows here.

"Something isn't right," Matt says to himself. I am curious to know what his thoughts are, but don't ask. He takes my hand and leads me away from the elevators, continuing down another hall. I slip my hand out of his grasp but continue to follow him.

These hallways are not nearly as elegant as the ones that are parallel with the large windows. There is no carpet, and the walls are painted a dull teal. It feels too long that we silently pass through hall after hall. Most doors are locked, but when we find ones that aren't, they don't lead anywhere.

"Where are they?" Matt asks himself angrily. But it isn't just anger; it's fear. He had a plan, but someone hasn't done their part yet. This means that Matt is most likely starting to panic, but he's keeping a cool front for my sake. Or his. Or both.

All of a sudden, Matt stops and presses his finger to his ear. I didn't realize he had an earpiece, but then again, they are so small that you can't really see them. And the wealthier citizens generally have one literally inside their ear. I realize this might be the case for Matt, as he works for one of the richest men in the world.

"I've been trying to reach you!" he shouts out into the wind. "Where have you been? Where are you?"

His voice is raised, but I can't hear anything that is being said to him. After a moment, Matt says "Fine" before looking at me and jerking his head in the direction we need to go.

I follow him for a bit before he leads me to another staircase. I tell him that the doors might be locked on the upper floors.

"I'll find a way to open them," he says. He is no longer angry or scared. There is determination in his voice. He sounds like he's fed up with the situation.

We jog up the stairs, Matt skipping a step each time. I do the same but fall back because I am not nearly as fast as he is. He looks back at me and waits on the eighth-floor landing.

"Buck up; we have a long way to go, and we don't want them to find us in here," he says.

"Where are we going?" I pant out, despite the adrenaline injection I had.

"To the very top," he says, and without waiting for a response, he leaps up more stairs. I grit my teeth and do the same.

I focus on the stairs right in front of me, seeing only the top of each floor in my peripherals. I avert my eyes slightly for a moment and almost miss the next step. I have to reach out of the guard rails to keep myself from falling onto my face. I recover quickly and keep going. Matt is much farther away than I am.

Too long. It seems like too long, but I keep going. I stopped looking at the floor numbers after fourteen. I don't know how many floors there are, but I know if I force myself to keep going, I will eventually make it.

Eventually I do. Matt is waiting on the top floor, the door to the grand hallway open. There is a ladder that leads up to the roof.

Thinking he is holding the door open as a gesture for me to go first, I make my way towards it. Matt puts his hand out and places it on my chest. He looks away for a moment as if he is listening intently.

Just then, I hear a window shatter. The sound is deafening, but only for a moment. Matt pulls me back and slams the door. Before it closes, I hear a faint plop.

"The roof!" he shouts out, panicked. He grabs my shoulder and shoves me into the ladder, then pats my back quickly until I climb up. As I go, I can hear another faint plop.

I shove the escape door open and pull myself onto the roof. Matt follows right behind, grabs my wrist, and takes off at a sprint towards the end. There is a large, bus-sized vehicle hovering just over the edge. I see it carefully move closer to the building.

As we're running toward it, I hear another plop, this time a bit louder. And now I understand the urgency and horror in Matt's voice. The small, circularly shaped bomb slowly blinks red. The light reflects off of its metallic casing.

Matt tosses me into the Sonars. There is a three-foot gap between the roof and the floor of the vehicle. Matt jumps in, crashing into me, and we start sliding towards the other side of the vehicle until we hit the wall. The door is closed as the Sonars tilts and pulls away from the building.

I look up just in time. From out of a window of the Sonars, almost as if in slow motion, I see one last blink from the round object, and the building collapses. There is no large explosion; no visible fire. Just one moment the building is standing strong despite all the damage it sustained, and in the next it is falling to the ground, taking only seconds before collapsing into rubble.

5

My mind is numb. Irresponsive. Lost.

Hours have passed, but I am still in such shock that during those hours I was mostly unaware of anything that happened. All I remember is lying on the cold metal floor of the vehicle, slightly curled up and shaking due to its temperature. I barely saw Matt during that time, but I could hear his voice. I never saw who was driving us or anyone else who may have been on board. I knew I could hear the words that were said, but nothing registered in my mind.

By the time I was able to center my thoughts around the collapse of the hotel and the inevitable perishing of those who were staying or working there, we had landed wherever it was that we were going. I was steered inside by Matt, but soon someone else helped guide me while we followed him.

All those innocent people in the hotel. At best, it would have been in the hundreds. But that hotel could easily accommodate thousands of guests. *Could have*, considering it no longer exists.

Soon my senses slowly come back to me. I am still being guided by someone. I recognize Matt as he leads us through a long hall with easy lighting that lines the floor. He is talking to someone I don't recognize.

"I need Mr. Canabana to meet me in Maylene's office now," he tells the man. "I already tried contacting him, but he hasn't answered." Matt's voice is even. Direct. I can tell he is doing his best not to spread panic or alarm. But I doubt that many people wouldn't know what happened.

The other man nods and hurriedly runs down the hall. Matt looks back at me briefly. Our eyes meet. He takes that as a sign that I'm no longer in total shock. He nods to the person who has their hands on me, gently making sure that I am following Matt. I now just realize that there is a blanket wrapped around me.

"I'll take him from here, thanks," Matt says to the man.

The guy takes his hands off me and goes through one of the several doors that line the hall. I didn't notice them before.

"How are you feeling?" he asks me.

I don't respond.

He lets out a quick sigh and puts his hand on my shoulder, though I feel it is more to quicken my pace than to comfort me.

"Look, I am sorry for how things went down," he says. "It was my job to ensure nothing like that happened. I had been watching you, just like Maylene, and I missed something." There's something about the way he speaks and the words he uses that makes me think that maybe this guy is just like everyone else, and not some overly cocky man who pretends to live the best life ever.

I can hear him. I understand what he is saying. But I don't understand everything. I'm the one who is missing something. Something that doesn't add up. I just don't know what to say or ask.

We go through wide doors and enter a welcome foyer. It is early in the morning. The sun hasn't quite risen yet. The lights are dim, and the large circular reception desk in the center of the room is empty. There are glass waterfalls on both sides. Live plants line the room, packed in their beds that are made of brick. Matt scans his phone, and an elevator comes down and its doors open. Once we're inside,

Matt scans his phone again and presses a button near the top of the panel.

"Look, I know you might be mad at me, and you have every right to be. But the second I found out that every reservation for that hotel was cancelled and the guests were being moved out, I knew something was off, and I came as fast as I could."

The elevator zips us up to the hundred and fourteenth floor in just under half a minute. The reservations were cancelled? I don't understand what that would mean.

As we exit, I am surprised to see a room that looks so familiar to me, though I know for a fact that I have never been in here.

Swiveling around in her chair to greet us is Maylene. She jumps out and gives me a long hug of relief. She even gives one to Matt.

"I'm so sorry," she breathes out. "This is all my fault. If I had checked the hotel's guest list more often, I would have known something was wrong."

Matt shakes his head. "This isn't on you, Maylene. When Arch checked in, there were still hundreds of guests in the hotel."

There is a short span of silence, but I can't take not knowing anymore.

"How many?" I ask.

Matt and Maylene stare at me.

"How many died?" I almost shout.

They look at each other before Matt answers.

"No one," he says.

I blink at him and take a step back.

"What do you mean?"

"He means no one died," Maylene answers. "At least in the hotel collapse, if that is what you're asking. The entire building was evacuated before the attack. The entire building except you, that is."

I walk around the room. The closing of doors I heard before the attack makes sense now, if that were the last of the guests leaving. But still, they must have left hours before that. Whoever was responsible took calculated steps and even went so far as to minimize collateral damage. In that respect, I'm impressed. Otherwise, screw them for trying to kill me. I'm just relieved that no one died. Of course, other than the man that was torn to shreds in front of me. The memory of the building collapsing still terrifies me.

"My Sonars!" I cry out, suddenly remembering that I had parked in the garage, which is now completely wasted underneath more weight than I can comprehend. Then I remember something far worse. I didn't think to grab my bag from my room when I was fleeing from whoever was attacking me. That's understandable. But the chip was inside that bag.

"I failed," I say quietly before slumping into a chair near the large window. "The computer chip was inside my bag. If it got destroyed, that program is probably in the hands of a lot of people right now."

Matt gives a look to Maylene before walking over to me. He kneels and waits for me to look at him.

"I picked up your bag when I first got to the hotel. It took a while for me to find you after that, and I suppose that when I finally did, so much was happening that you didn't notice that I had it on me."

I think back to those late hours. I remember the multiple pockets that still adorn Matt's clothing, though his clothing has been torn and looks seared in several places now. I can remember a strap across his chest, but I didn't think much of it. Between almost dying, the shot Matt injected me with, and the death-defying stunts he put me through, it would make sense that I didn't see my bag.

"Where is it now?" I ask.

"I had our pilot bring it in. It should be with Edward by now, and you'll have it back soon."

I sigh.

"What does this mean for the mission?"

Maylene comes over to join us. She kneels as well, the two of them looking at me like parents comforting their crying child.

"Edward will make the call on that," she tells me. "It is clear now that despite our efforts to keep this quiet and keep you safe, the word is out there. People know what we're trying to do. And they know what we have."

"The severity of that is still unknown," Matt tells me. "I don't think everyone who has an interest in the device knows that you have it, but I am sure that they all know Edward Canabana has it. There is nothing that ties you to him — on record at least. So, unless someone from inside his company betrayed us, you should be safe."

"Except that I wasn't. I'm not safe," I say. I'm not angry. I'm not disappointed. But a new understanding of how much the chip is worth and how dangerous it is dawns on me. "I'm not blaming either of you, but if people are willing to destroy an entire building or kill me to get their hands on the chip, then I need to get it back and keep going. I will drive for days with no stops if I must. If no one died in the collapse, then at least we were lucky this time. But I can't take the chance that something else might happen."

I feel like an entirely different person than I was just a day ago.

The elevator doors open. There is no mistaking his brilliant eyes. Mr. Canabana walks in. Matt and Maylene stand straight very quickly and professionally greet Edward.

"We're moving past formalities here," Edward says gracefully, but with a hint of authority and resolution. "Tell me everything you did after Arch was given the chip in Yesfborne. I want detailed reports and verification. You first, Maylene." He sits down on a lounging chair nearby.

Edward Canabana doesn't sound angry, but he is clearly not happy with how things went down. I don't blame him. With things not going according to plan, this mission is going to be a lot harder now. And a lot more dangerous.

Maylene follows her instructions and tells Edward everything, including the times she called me and messed with me. Though my attention to her story comes and goes, I learn a great deal about what her job consists of and how much work she puts into it. I learn that there have been at least three attempts to track me and two to scan my Sonars. Scanning is illegal and can only be done by the government if warranted and legally granted. What it does is detail every part of something, inside and out. If anyone had done that to my Sonars, they would have found my chip. And if I was in it when they did, I would have been subjected to high amounts of what they call suppressed radiation, which means I would have no signs of poisoning until I was about to die. Hence the illegality of it.

Maylene shows Edward a computer pad that recorded everything that she said and was said to her in full video. I also learn why I was taken on such a long detour. One of the cities I would have passed through had Impositioner Checkpoints that would have scanned my Sonars and there would have been no hiding anything in my possession. Maylene didn't want to take the chance that they were corrupt.

When Matt tells of his work and the progress he made, I can tell, by the sound of it, that he is technically Maylene's boss, but he gives her space to work and only rarely asks for reports from her. Matt had been doing something similar to Maylene, tracking me and my route, how long it was taking me to get to various locations, and seeing if there were any hostiles near me. Apparently, some of the people after the chip have invaded, tortured, kidnapped, or outright killed anyone they suspected to have the chip, or even if they *might* know any information about it.

Like Maylene, Matt didn't notice anything odd about the hotel that I checked into. The whole street is almost purely hotels, so a guest list in the low hundreds wasn't out of the ordinary, especially during a slow season. Luckily, Matt kept tabs on the hotel, and when he noticed the large number of guests checking out, he told Maylene that he was going there to check. On his way to the hotel, the list reached zero, even wiping me off the record, and that's when he called Maylene and told her to send backup and to prepare for a rescue. Maylene tells her part of this story, something she had previously left out because Matt was ultimately responsible for the rescue and the reason why it was successful.

"If you hadn't prepped the team together so quickly, Arch and I both would probably be dead," he tells her.

At this point, Edward stands up and paces around the room slowly. The three of us sit in silence, waiting for his response. No one wants to rush him, and while Matt and Maylene feel they did the right things, I'm sure there is an uneasiness inside them that fears Edward isn't as satisfied.

In these minutes, my deep appreciation for how much Matt and Maylene have done for me to make sure that I stay alive fills me. The threats to the mission are unknown, but that number is growing. It would be impossible to predict everything that anyone might do. This is something Edward seems to understand.

"Well done, you two," he says, breaking the silence. "And to you too, Arch, for staying alive. The danger to your life was far greater than I had hoped that it would be, and if you wish to discontinue your work with us, I will understand and will still pay out what I promised."

I stare at him in disbelief. I know he doesn't know me well, but there should be no doubt about my dedication at this point. "It was never about the money," I tell him. "Sure, that helped at first to sway my decision, but when Gary told me his fears of the danger the world would be in, I started to believe everything. And the longer I was on the road, the more I realized how serious this was."

Matt and Maylene smile at each other. They know me and know that I will not back out. It's as if we've known each other for a long time.

"With all due respect, I am finishing this job," I firmly tell him, locking my eyes with his. "I've been through too much to not see the end of it."

Edward cracks a smile. "I am pleased with your choice to stay, but please be patient. There are a few kinks that we need to iron out before you go back out on the road again. And for that reason, I am going to ask that you do not step outside this building until further instructions." He starts to leave the room. "Matt and Maylene will assign you quarters and new clothing, and ensure that you are comfortable during your stay here. I do not expect that it will take more than a few days."

I nod. He smiles one last time and leaves down the elevator. I turn my head back to look outside the window. I tighten the blanket around me so that it isn't as loose. I can see the sun rising from here, creeping above the tall skyscrapers. The easy yellow and green lights that make up the roads of the many elevations deepen in color to make it easier to see in the harsh sunlight. Some of the early-goers are out and about. The city is large, like Yesfborne, but it doesn't have many houses; most homes are probably condominiums inside the skyscrapers that cover the city.

"It would probably be a good idea to assign you a room for your stay here," Matt says, echoing Edward's order. He looks towards Maylene, who nods and takes a few steps towards me. "When you're ready, Maylene or myself can show you around, where to get food, and where to occupy your time if you feel bored."

I don't say anything. I take another look out towards the city before facing my two friends. At this point, that is what I would call them, even if we haven't really known each other for that long. But there aren't many people I keep in touch with currently, and I have a feeling that when this is all over, I'll still stay in contact with them. Maybe I'll even get a different job with Edward, and I can finally settle down somewhere and really start putting together a life that I want.

I'd miss the traveling for sure, but there isn't a reason why I couldn't do that whenever I wanted.

"I'm ready," I say, standing up. "You can show me my room, but I would like a quick tour so that I know where things are. I'll probably spend the rest of the day sleeping."

"Sounds fair," Matt says. "I'll probably do the same." He pats me on the shoulder and leads us out of the large office. Maylene follows behind me. I know she is tired, but I'm sure she wants to hang around as much as possible.

There is an employee kitchen and dining room on the tenth floor, with the kitchen area probably taking up most of half of the floor. The rest of it is sitting areas, with some tables packed together like a military mess hall, while others are more spread out, facing windows or otherwise secluded.

"For Edward's employees in this building, most of us don't have any assigned mealtimes, but there is always food to grab and chefs available to cook a specific dish. And you have your choice of seating, first come, first served. For stressful days where you feel like being alone, the corners do just fine," Maylene says. "Or you can be social and sit at the round tables near the center." She pauses for a second and walks closer to the windows that line the mess hall. "Or enjoy the view of the city."

"Do you want to see the game room?" Matt asks excitedly, not giving me time to respond with anything else but a nod. I almost say no because at this point all I want to do is shower and sleep, but even with the no sleep we have all had, his eyes light up.

"Sure, quickly, though," I tell him. "I need to shower, get a change of clothes, and get some sleep."

"Good old shut-eye," Maylene says, another slang term we've read about from Earth.

The game room is just one floor above, and it takes up the entire floor. The building layout confuses me. I barely understand what the building is for. But I stop thinking about that when the lift doors open. Instead of a brightly lit room, I am welcomed to an impressively dim, inviting, and short hallway. There's a closed double-door just steps ahead. Matt scans his phone into the reader, and the doors unlock.

The next room is even darker, but there are enough lights, warm and neon, from the floors, ceilings, and arcade games to give more than enough light to see easily. At first glance, the room appears to be just one large room with a maze of games running through it. As we walk along the machines, including many games from a distant past, I see several walls or partitions that divide the game room (or lounge, I should say) into many different parts. There is even a bar against one wall, and despite it being early in the morning, there is a bartender.

"People usually spend their free time in this room," Matt says. "There's an array of activities to keep you occupied, and since most employees in this building live far away and are here for weeks at a time for work, they don't have much else to do."

"Where do you live?" I ask him.

"I live in this building," he answers. "Maylene and I are part of the few employees who do make this place our permanent residence."

"But as you probably know," Maylene says. "We are easily accommodated if we travel out of town for work. Edward has hotels all around the world, and if a city doesn't have one, there is a building just like this, or he just pays for another hotel for us."

Something bothers me for a moment. Maylene had been communicating with me from that room upstairs ever since she left Velro. I have covered quite a distance since then, even if I was taken on a long detour. So, where are we?

I ask her the burning question.

She holds in a sigh and answers, "Candalance."

My eyes widen.

"Candalance? That—that doesn't make any sense!" I cry out. "Why would—?" I stutter in disbelief. "How come we're here? How are we here?"

My detours may have taken me on an odd path, but at least I was still headed in the general direction of my destination. I would eventually cross the continent and make my way towards the heart of the next large piece of land. I crossed a continent, alright, just in the opposite direction.

A delivery from here would take me about four days. No detours, just my normal stops and breaks.

This continent is connected to the one I was just on only by a sliver. The connecting land is smack in the middle of the equator. Because of its narrowness and naturally low elevation, it is usually sunken under water and is largely a swamp. Few people cross it on their own due to its unpredictable weather, swamp gas, and tales of monstrous creatures.

"This was the safest place to take you at a moment's notice. The drive wasn't more than a few hours," Maylene says. "We flew above Passing Altitude at speeds faster than commercial jets."

I'm stunned. Passing Altitude is higher than I can legally fly; only commercial or military ships can do that. Legally, at least. My Sonars probably has a built-in feature that prevents it from reaching that altitude. I never had a reason to fly that high, so I didn't care to disable it.

And, like I said, only military ships can legally fly above that level, and almost always do.

My head gets foggy, and I stifle a yawn, which causes my eyes to water. It still doesn't make sense to me, but I know I won't be able to figure it out now.

"I think it's time to get some sleep," Matt says matter-of-factly.

He took the words right out of my mouth. I turn around, assuming we will go back the way we came. The doors in front of me open inward, and Gary walks through them. Surprised and exhausted, I fail to hide my groan.

"I see you still aren't too fond of me," Gary says sarcastically. "I simply came to check that you were okay," he says, walking up to me and placing a gentle hand on the side of my shoulder.

"No, it's just—"

"Have a good rest," he says sharply, not missing a beat. "I'll still be around. And truthfully, I came down here to enjoy myself. Running into you was a complete accident."

Gary smiles and walks away.

"Alright, let's get you to your room," Matt says, clasping my shoulder in a friendly manner and steering me into the elevator.

"I'll see you guys later," Maylene calls out to us, waving goodbye before slickly walking back into the gaming hall.

The hundredth floor welcomes us as an angled lobby, shaped like a half-moon with the curves on either side of the elevator. Matt leads me to the right. The hallway is ornate, with a plush carpet of a warm color and a neat, basic design of spirals, almost in the shape of musical notes. There are no windows, but there is plenty of lighting. Doors line the left side of the hall, though they are noticeably spaced far apart. While the other floors I've been on had a more modern, business-like vibe, this floor feels more homier, almost like a hotel, but instead of splendor and attempts-to-awe galore, this floor clearly wants you to feel at home. It feels safe.

We turn another right, and Matt stops at the second door. He whips out his phone and tilts it towards me. It takes me a second to catch on, but I grab my phone and lightly tap his. There is a small ding.

"There you go," he says.

I nod and scan the phone over the key reader. With a faint click, the door unlocks. Matt gracefully opens the door. Even with how tired I am, I find his demeanor unusual. That is, until I see the unit.

For whatever reason, when I was told they would show me to my quarters, I imagined a small room with a single bathroom and maybe even two beds or a bunkbed. This is something entirely different.

The edge of the condo is lined with glass windows that oversee the entire city, just like the executive suite just floors above. At one end of the windows, a projection plays of an under-the-sea experience. As we walk into the condo, lights turn on in the living room. There is a large kitchen connected, and stairs lead up to two additional floors.

I have money, but not this kind. Apparently, Edward Canabana does.

"It's not as large or nice as our permanent housing," Matt shrugs, dismissing certain pieces of furniture as he casually walks around. "But I hope it'll do." He stares at me, waiting for my reaction. I don't give him one.

Matt chuckles, walks back to me, and pats me on the arm. "I know you're tired, but lighten up! You're being treated like royalty here. Seriously, only a few people have housing like this. The floors under us don't have condos this large. Most of this floor is actually unoccupied."

A random thought crosses my head.

"Where does the elevator go to on the next two floors above, if the condos are three stories tall?"

Matt raises an eyebrow. "You can be an odd one sometimes," he says, almost sighing. "That's okay, though; I still like you. But if you're so curious about that, well, there are hallways above us, just like outside, but they only lead to maintenance rooms."

I don't blame him for calling me odd. It was an odd question.

With a sigh, Matt says, "Well, I didn't get much sleep either, so I will see you later. Feel free to call me if you need anything, but you should find plenty in here. I'm on the same floor, just on the other side of the building, and Maylene is just down the hall."

Matt leaves the condo, and the door closes. I walk over to the first couch I see and collapse onto it.

It's so sudden. The jolting. The panic. The feeling that I have missed something very important.

I look around. It takes me a while to adjust my eyes. I fell asleep with the same blanket I had wrapped around me earlier. The sunlight from the window glares brightly through the thinnest fragment of a window that isn't fully blocking the light with projected images of a dark curtain. I look at the time. I check the date just to be sure. I did not sleep for long. I don't feel well rested. But I'm no longer exhausted.

There are several bathrooms throughout the condo, but I choose one on the second floor, across from the first bedroom that I come across. I shower and find a nice change of clothes that fit me well. I suppose someone must have prepared the room for my arrival, most likely before I even got to the building.

I look down at the pile of worn clothes. These are done for, especially my old shirt, which can no longer be considered one. I kick them off to the side, wondering if there is a hotel-type service that will clean these up later.

After several detours to different floors, most of which I chose incorrectly, I make it to the mess hall. A decent number of employees occupy it. As Maylene mentioned previously, the employees are scattered around, some more social than others. The kitchen portion of the floor is mostly blocked off. It is about dinner time, after all. I look around, not knowing where to go to get food.

I jump slightly when someone puts their hand on my back.

"Didn't mean to scare you there," Gary says, almost wheezing. I can't tell if it's because he's old or if he is laughing at me. "Come with me; let's get something to eat."

Gary gestures to the room and looks at me. I get the idea he doesn't mind where we sit, though I thought he was going to lead me to a table. When he doesn't, I walk over to one of the smaller tables by the windows.

A small, circular bot rushes over. It's just a ball levitating at about chest height. Two antennae-like arms stick out, and holographic menus appear. There are three generic choices for the main dinners of the day, but there is an option to choose a different plate.

Being too hungry and not feeling picky, I choose a meat-packed sandwich and salad. I'm asked several customization questions, but Gary points his finger, and I swipe away the screen, bypassing the customization options and completing my order.

The small robot thing whizzes away. I thought Edward preferred human interaction to machines, but I'm too tired to ask about it right now.

Gary stares at me, making me slightly uncomfortable. He grumbles a lot but doesn't say anything. When I try to speak, he quickly shushes me. I do not understand this old guy.

When we get our food, he proceeds to eat very quickly. There isn't much on his plate, and since I am in no rush, I take five minutes longer than he does to finish.

"Are you feeling better now?" he asks me, pushing his plate away.

"Yeah," I tell him. "But I don't want to stay here long. I want to finish what I was paid to do."

There is a brief pause in the conversation.

"That eagerness is both a gift and a curse," he says in a warning tone. "Use it to your advantage, but remember that sometimes you need to think before you act. There are times when the best path to take is a step back, so that you may see a bigger picture."

Maybe I'm still tired, because I don't understand what the guy is getting at.

"With everything that you went through, you're still determined to finish this mission," he goes on, making statements in such a way that it sounds as if he is talking to himself. "You know that the attack on you in Halav was calculated, and as it was unsuccessful, people will get desperate. Maybe not everyone knows that you carry such a powerful weapon, but soon enough they all will." Gary trails off into almost a whisper. He mumbles to himself for a bit. "You know, there used to be many of them out there."

I have no clue what Gary is talking about. Getting drowsy again, I struggle to keep my eyes fully open.

I am immediately jolted fully awake when someone brushes their hand against the back of my head. I turn to see a tall man with spiked hair dyed pink-blonde wink at me and say, "It's nice to see you've got some proper clothing on now."

Before I can ask what he means exactly, he walks away. Things are getting a bit weird for me.

"He just means your shirt was in pieces last night," Gary says with a strong voice, reading my thoughts. I turn to look at him but don't say anything.

"I won't be around much longer," he tells me. "But do know that I will always be looking out for you."

My mouth opens as I struggle to understand what he is saying. At this point, I almost feel that Gary is senile. Or getting there, at the very least.

"What do you mean?" I ask him. "Are you going back home?"

"This is my home," he replies. "I left that old one just a couple days ago."

"So where are you going?"

He sighs. "I'm old. Did you not notice? All I care about is getting that chip destroyed. If you can do that before I pass, well, let's just say it is my dying wish."

I look away for a moment. I have always known that Gary was old, but plenty of people have lived longer than he is. There is the possibility that Gary is much older than he looks, but even then, I would expect him to have some years left. It sounds to me like Gary doesn't care much for this life now, but he has just one last order of business to get to.

While I don't think it is fair for Gary to say such a thing to me, with all the pressure that this mission already carries, I force a small, sincere-appearing smile.

"I will finish this mission with haste," I say, sounding more proper than I mean.

"That is very good!" I hear an energetic voice from the side. Edward Canabana pulls up a chair and joins us at the small table. He waves away the round bot that comes by, not caring to order food.

"Here," says Edward as he proceeds to place my bag on the table. The plates underneath make a loud noise under the sudden force. "I thought you might be missing this."

I grab my bag and instinctively look through its contents. I don't have anything in mind I'm worried about, but it makes me feel better to see that everything is still there. Not that there was much at all before. It doesn't have the chip, though, but I half expected that.

"The chip is still in my hands," Edward says, leaning in closer so he can speak more quietly. "I expect that I will be able to let you leave in two days' time."

"Why two days?" I ask him.

"There are searches happening for you. I want those out of this area and out of your path before you continue on your journey," Edward explains. "The risk right now is too high. All around the world, the government is shaping the news as they see fit, slowly creeping into their next phase of planetary control. Getting their hands on that chip may very well be part of their plans."

"What do you mean their next phase?"

"For decades, centuries even, people have always wanted the power to rule an entire planet. Now, most people would object to such a ruling. But these enslavers, if you will, are cunning. By teaching the 'right' things in school and telling a news story in just the right way so it sounds completely true, the government has slowly taken control over the population. There was a time when the separate countries had their own laws and government. It isn't the same now, even if the world is divided into sub-sections. They even attempt, and with some success, to delude the citizens into thinking that each other is the enemy."

I shake my head. "I don't know if I am well enough rested to talk about this."

Edward nods. "Forgive me. I tend to get carried away with my stories, and I know you don't care much for them. But know that I mean well, and while the chip I have is just one step in a long road to helping the people of this world, it is currently the most important. Rest assured, I still believe you are the best man for this job."

Mr. Canabana gets up from his chair. "Matt and Maylene are around if you need them. Your stay here should be quite comfortable, and you will be on the road soon enough. I bid you a safe journey."

Without a word, Gary leaves as well. I look around the cafeteria. Most people either didn't notice Edward's presence or didn't care. It is possible that they also leave him be when they see him. I've never worked a corporate job, so I don't know the etiquette regarding interactions with the CEO. I get up and head back to my quarters. The elevator ride is lonely and short. I'm not in the mood to talk much, so I don't look for Matt or Maylene.

I stumble back into the suite. I feel almost drunk, but I've had no alcohol recently. I'm coming to realize that my nap earlier was even shorter than I thought, and I probably only woke up because my stomach wanted me to get something to eat. Heading upstairs, tripping as I do so, I look around at the condo, admiring the view of the city outside. I force myself to go up another flight of stairs, and I soon find myself lying on the bed in my master suite.

6

I wake up in the late afternoon with the sun still blazing down over the city. The long night's sleep has given me back my normal state of mental capacity. I no longer feel a burning urge to complete my delivery. Of course, I still want to, but yesterday it felt more like a passion; some form of manic revenge. Today, I feel like finishing it so that there is no longer this threat to the world.

I take my time to dress and clean myself up before heading to Maylene's office. When I get into the elevator, I realize that I can't access her floor without an unlock code in my phone. After cussing silently to myself, I head down to the cafeteria, a place I've now visited more than any other in this building.

With nothing else to do, I grab a small snack. It isn't a mealtime currently, so the kitchen is open and there is only one small bot floating around, ready to take an order. I order some nachos loaded with chicken, cheese, and other stuff that doesn't belong in a properly balanced meal.

Some people mill around, grabbing a late lunch or early dinner, but I don't talk to anyone. I know I've been here for only a day, but I don't recognize anybody that passes through. It makes me wonder how many people work in this building.

After slowly eating my snack, I make my way to the gaming floor. When I push the button, nothing happens. I groan. The floor is probably locked as well. I scan my phone just for the sake of it, and

I am genuinely surprised when it works. I scan my phone and press the 114th floor button, but nothing happens.

The elevator reaches the gaming floor, and I stroll through the hall. There are a few people inside, more than there were when I first came here.

After wandering aimlessly for a bit, I settle on a classic game where I shoot three balls into the arena, and I have to make sure they don't fall through the holes at the bottom by manipulating levers that I move along the bottom of the arena and pushing buttons to make them bounce the balls away from the holes. Apparently there is a similar game back on Earth, though their every attempt to send one of their game machines has failed.

"I've got some good news."

I jump at the sudden sound, having been so engrossed in the game. Immediately, the three balls find their way into the slots at the bottom, and it is game over. I turn my head back and see Matt standing there with a small smirk on his face.

"Then tell me your news if it is so great," I reply, referencing a line from a book I read years ago. There is a slight chill in my tone because I am annoyed that he interrupted my best game.

He gently pushes me aside and starts playing the game. Matt gives me a quick glance, a half-smile on his face, and the look in his eye as if he is annoyed at me. If he didn't have his looks, I would have walked away by now, but part of me wants to keep eye contact.

As he plays the game, he tells me, "We will be leaving tomorrow morning. Edward made a slight change to our plans that lets us leave here sooner, but unfortunately will make this delivery of yours take longer."

"How much longer can the delivery take?"

Matt doesn't answer right away, concentrating on moving the single slider carrying the two levers back and forth to catch all the balls before they fall through.

"There are some places that manage to just be, let's say, more isolated than others. It should only take an additional three days than it would to just leave from here."

"Why don't I just leave from here and make my way towards NEAST?" I think about the odd routes Maylene would probably take me on, so it'll be about a seven-day trip.

Matt shakes his head, though I'm not entirely sure if that's because he just lost the game or if he doesn't like something that I said.

"Due to logistics and environmental disadvantages, I would say that three days would be added to our journey. That is, once we get there. We'll be riding for a day. Edward has directed many of us to this remote location for our safety in case we've been compromised. A ship that large won't do well traveling at our normal speeds." He stands up straight. We look at each other for a second. He nods, gives me his usual slap on the shoulder, and says, "Be ready by seven in the morning, in the basement. Your phone has access."

Matt walks out, though I see him slide into another part of the gaming floor. I sigh, look around as if I'm expecting someone, and then head back to my room. I have a momentary thought about packing my stuff, but I remember that I don't have anything now. A sadness instills itself inside me, thinking about my Sonars and how it was completely crushed, its parts unforgivingly unsalvageable.

The rest of the day passes by unbearably slow. I don't see Maylene or Matt at all, despite visiting the eating area several times and making a few trips back to the gaming floor, playing a random game so that it would not look like I am wandering aimlessly. Two hours after dinner, I head back to my room and turn on the TV. The screen-windows play shows with short episodes, and I mindlessly watch while pacing around.

Closer to ten, I turn off the screens. The windows are clear, letting me see the city in full view, bright with the shine of the moon, the traveling vehicles across the subtle neon elevations, and the warmth of the street lamps lighting up the world.

My shoes press against the metal floor with each step I take, a small clinking sound accompanying each footstep. I move forward through the belly of the airship, but I don't yet know where I am going. Many people move around me, preparing for takeoff. Slowly, I keep walking deeper into the belly. I know there must be more welcoming and comfortable spaces above.

I climb a metal ladder. This part of the ship serves as a lounge, with large, curve-shaped couches decorated with red cushions, a holographic fireplace, and a small restaurant bar in the back. A command station at the bridge lies at the bow, raised half a story higher than the main part of the lounge. Two staircases on both sides lead up to it.

Without knowing where to go, I take a seat on one of the couches. I feel out of place and useless, sitting here doing nothing while everyone else is doing their jobs.

Not wanting to catch anyone's eye, I lean forward and look at the ground, contemplating what happens next.

I don't know what I was expecting today to be like, but for some reason it wasn't being on a large craft that is about to haul what probably adds up to thousands of people to some remote, safe house. But this does makes sense.

This morning I had gotten up around six, eaten a quick breakfast, and packed some new clothes in a backpack, both of which were right inside the condo I was staying in. When I went to the basement and the elevator doors opened, I was worried that I had gotten stuck, as it looked as if there were only a wall right in front of me. But that soon opened, and I was invited into the airship by someone who recognized who I was, but he quickly left without so much as an introduction. I was in the airship with ten minutes to spare.

The world around me hastens its pace. Clearly, the time to leave is approaching. There are so many people here — way more than I thought there would be. I have been given very little information as to where exactly we are going and when we were leaving. I look at a clock behind the bar. It's half past seven. I don't know why Matt made me come here so early, but then I think to myself, maybe we are just running late.

Some more time passes. I end up scrolling through my phone to avoid anyone's gaze, though they are all too busy to notice me.

"Working hard or hardly working, am I right?"

The deep yet delicate voice is accompanied by a slender man around my age with spiked hair dyed a dark purple with blue tips. He smells strongly of soap. He perches himself atop the arm of the couch, close to where I am sitting.

"I've been doing my part," I reply dully. "You?"

The man sticks his nose up and makes a motion with his head as if he were flipping his hair, though it is nowhere near long enough. It's also glued in place, so I'm not sure what it is he thought he was doing.

"I've already finished all my assignments and helped my cowork-ers with theirs. I've earned my free time."

I don't reply but nod so subtly that I doubt he sees it.

"When are we supposed to be leaving?" I ask him.

"Precisely at eight. So, in just three minutes, in case you were wondering," he answers politely, despite my disinterested tone. After some awkward silence, during which he stares at me as if trying to read me, he says, "I heard that you had quite the close encounter a few days ago!"

"Yeah, Matt really saved my life there."

The man sits down next to me, closer than my comfort level allows, especially since there is an entire lounging couch available and a whole other one nearby.

"Matt is so hot," he says. "But you're not bad yourself."

"I'm sorry," I say, talking as politely as I can. "I'm not into guys like that."

The man lets out a laugh so loud I'd call it mirth.

"Oh, heavens no, I do apologize!" he says, and puts his hand on my shoulder momentarily. "I have a fiancé, and we are happily committed to each other. I am into guys like that, but I didn't mean to come on to you."

"Oh, uh, congratulations," I say, feeling embarrassed, even though it absolutely felt as if he were coming on to me.

"Yes, yes," he says quickly, jumping into an explanation of himself. "I do get that a lot, though, where people think I'm hitting on them. Even the women! Which is funny because I purposefully make it plainly clear that I have no interest in them in that regard."

As he talks, I nod. It isn't that I mind the company; I was just expecting someone else. My mind wanders for a while. I think of exotic places that could only exist in fictional worlds as the destination of where we are heading.

"—but there was this one time where the waitress insisted on giving me my number, even after Daden had proposed in that same restaurant minutes ago! He wanted to wait until our evening walk, but she was determined to get in my pants!"

I snap back to Talvor, fantastical thoughts gone from my head. Most of the motion around me has ceased. I notice that fewer people are coming up and down the ladder, and the command station is fully manned.

"Looks like it's about time for takeoff," he says. "My name is Andre, just by the way. I work in public relations for Canabana Industries. I mainly charm the big dogs of other companies into deals for Edward. But Matt deals with the difficult ones." He pauses for a moment. "Maylene asked me to keep you company while everyone else prepared for our departure."

I make a mental note to talk to Marlene about the kind of people she sends to "keep me company."

Andre stands up and respectfully holds out his hand. I take it briefly, giving him a quick shake, and nod.

"I hope to see you around after you're done with your mission," he says genuinely. "You seem like someone who would be fun to hang out with."

With that, he walks away to the back rooms and out of sight. The airship rises off the ground. There is a tunnel ahead that we drive through for a bit before slowing down to a stop. I can see light coming in as the gate above us opens. We rise through it and are above ground.

The tunnel took us out of the city limits and into the dry grasslands that surround the city. Candalance was once a high desert, but due to population growth and self-sustaining efforts, water now flows through it in a man-made river, and the desert is slowly becoming a light marshland.

Once the aperture beneath us closes, we take off, slowly ascending and gaining speed. Once we hit what I believe to be our top speed, we are passing most Sonars below us, though our elevation isn't much higher than theirs. I now understand why it is taking us a full day to get to where we're going. While this ship surely could travel more than double its current speed, flying above Passing

Altitude with a ship this large would attract unwanted attention, and traveling too fast at this elevation would do the same.

Even still, this "secret location" must be far away, maybe even towards the other side of the world, if this speed is considered slow and it'll take us all day to get there.

Someone taps my shoulder. I jerk my head back and see Maylene with a pleasant expression on her face.

"Come back here with me," she says. "Matt and Edward are waiting."

Maylene leads me around the back, behind the bar, and up what feels like two flights of stairs. I feel the ship ascend as I follow her. There are no windows where we are, but the lights are dimmer and give a quiet and cozy feel to the ship.

We walk into an oval cabin. The cabin is lined with a plush sectional with red seat cushions tasseled with gold. There are no windows in the room. Lights hang tactfully and are directed so that no shadows are cast. A large circular table sits in the middle, and on the left, just past the entry, there is a mini cooler and a small stand with glass cups. As Maylene said, Matt and Edward are here. As is Gary.

While every other part of the ship I've seen has a metal floor, this one is wood. Sleek, elegant — all in the same style and class that Edward loves. Gary nods to me, moves slightly as if he is about to stand, but then crosses his legs.

"Ah, Arch," Edward says pleasantly. He looks much happier now than he did a couple nights ago when he was getting Maylene's and Matt's stories on what happened that night. "Come on in; help yourself to any drink if you like." He points to the cooler.

"Thank you," I say, walking in but not getting a drink. Maylene follows behind me. With a gentle, though forceful, push, she seats me down next to Matt, and she then sits next to me.

"So, how is everything?" Edward asks.

"Uh, all good," I say.

Matt chuckles. "Man, you've got to stop being so awkward," he tells me. "It isn't like you aren't used to expensive things. You have money. Your father owns one of the largest companies on the planet."

Telling me not to be so awkward makes me feel more nervous, but I don't show it. Instead, I stand up and walk over to the cooler. When I open it, all I see is a black screen. I tap it to turn it on. Several drink choices appear. I swipe until I get to the hard liquor. I almost select a shot of Ancanine, one of the more potent alcohols, but decide on a soda/alcohol mix so that I don't appear so desperate.

When I sit back down, Matt eyes me and my drink and chuckles but says nothing. I take a sip. No one says anything. So I drink again. Gary has resorted to looking at a hologram tablet on his knees. Matt keeps his attention mostly focused on me, hiding it poorly. I ignore him.

Edward closes his eyes.

I drink again.

Before I know it, my glass is empty. I get up to get another.

The room remains mostly silent. Maylene is now moving her head to the music she started playing on the speakers in the room. Edward and Gary whisper quick words to each other as they share a screen. Matt continues looking around, though there is a hint of amusement on his face.

Once again, I have finished my drink. I go to get another one.

Halfway through my third, I can't take it anymore.

"What eez it that we need *totalkabout*?" I blurt out.

Maylene barks out a laugh. Matt leans his head back and laughs at the ceiling. Edward and Gary look up, a look of concern in their eyes. Gary moves, though he becomes a bit blurry in my vision. I stand up to make myself more visible, even if that makes little sense. But once I stand, that is when I realize I've made a mistake.

By this point, the room is amused by me. The ceilings dance, and the light dims. Gary and Edward are laughing. Maylene gets up and grabs another drink from the cooler. She tosses a can to Matt.

Laughing, Matt catches it and pops it open. Gary gets himself and Edward a glass too, though they drink a light wine. I sit back down. My senses numb, and the room slowly becomes still once more.

"Arch," Edward says jovially. "We're here to relax. There isn't much to do at this very moment, especially for you. Once we make it to Verdrayson, Maylene will set your destinations, and you can continue your mission."

Verdrayson is the coldest landmass on our planet. Void of almost any life, only a few people own any structures there. It is largely unpopulated and therefore has little value for political, governmental, or personal purposes, unless you wish to be entirely secluded from the population. The temperature gets so low that to be outside, you must wear a full suit to keep your body temperature warm enough. A couple minutes of exposure to its climate can have catastrophic effects on the body. There have been instances of people going out with a compromised suit, such as a hole in the glove, and auto-amputation of a finger would occur. Generally, the medical attention required would have had the whole hand removed to prevent the spreading of such a severe frostbite that would begin to spread as a disease.

It has been a long while since such an incident occurred.

"How long will we be in Verdrayson?" I ask, talking much slower now. My head spins for a moment.

"At this rate, longer than I intended," Edward says with a laugh. He gets up, places his half-empty glass on the table, and motions for Gary to follow him. "But I am pleased to see that you are more at ease. I was beginning to wonder if I had somehow forced you to work for me." Edward smiles brightly and walks out of the cabin with Gary. Gary takes his unfinished glass with him.

"Who is ready for another drink?" Maylene calls out louder than necessary, though that might be inaccurate. I might just be a bit drunk.

Haha.

I just might be.

I stand up. As loud as I can, I shout, "Another!"

Matt jumps up next to me and shouts the same. I respond, and soon the three of us are shouting "another!" while Maylene pours shots from a bottle.

The cabin door slides open. Andre walks in. "What is this?" he calls out, looking offended, though he has a playful smile on his face. He walks up to us and snatches the bottle from Maylene, which at this point is three-quarters empty. Andre chugs the rest of it in what looks like one gulp. He proudly slams the bottle on the table. It makes such a loud bang that I almost think it shatters. It doesn't.

Andre then shouts, "Another!" and we all cheer with him.

Maylene rushes to the cooler to get another bottle. I honestly don't know how the tiny cooler carries so many bottles, but truly, what do I care for? I don't. I really don't. I blurt out a laugh and snort. Matt looks at me.

"Bah haha!" Matt puts his arm around me and pulls me closer. "See, this is the side of Arch Caldor that I want to see more of!" he exclaims. "I always knew he was in there."

He leans closer to me. Drunk me thinks of how devilishly handsome the man is, though I know I would think the same sober. He makes a point to lock eyes. Matt is so close that I can feel his warm breath and smell the alcohol that adorns it. I'm sure I smell the same way.

"You'll miss out on opportunities if you remain so reserved all the time," he whispers to me. "You have so much potential," he says as he jabs me in the chest, spilling some of the liquid in his shot glass onto my shirt. He lets go of me. Andre comes in between us and wraps his arms around us. "This isn't supposed to be the serious room; this is the fun room!" he shouts as he jumps up and down.

The lot of us are somewhere in our twenties, with Andre maybe being the youngest, though that appearance might be due to his slim figure and wild hair. It is amazing that I can stand here, knowing that I am intoxicated, something that hasn't happened in many years, and feel such a connection and friendship in this room. That includes Andre, a dude I met just this morning and wasn't particularly fond of.

Just then, Andre's phone rings. It plays a pop song, and he excitedly answers it with the hologram projection. All phones can do it, but not many people use the function for every call they make.

A man with dark, slicked-back hair answers. He has a strong jawline and tan, smooth skin. With full lips and teeth that are treated often to shine white, I see what type of guys Andre is into. He has a slight accent that comes from one of the countries further south that used to speak a different language.

"Oh Daden!" Andre happily shouts out and blows a kiss to the hologram.

"I am very sorry. Am I interrupting?" Daden asks politely.

With this, I can tell that Daden is most likely about ten years older than Andre.

"Not at all!" Andre answers. "We're just on our way to Verdrayson now. Tomorrow we'll probably set Arch here on his way to Borough. It is still to be determined how long I will be in Verdrayson, you know. Mr. Canabana evacuated all of the staff stationed in Candalance as a safety precaution after the incident in Halav."

"Of course," Daden says with a smile. "How are you, Arch?"

I burp accidentally before answering. "I'm dandgood." I cough. "I-I'm good." I almost said dandy, but I also almost said Daden.

Daden smiles politely again. "Glad to hear it," he says. "I also work for Mr. Canabana. I manage his Chlorofyx hotel."

I raise my hand as a response, choking on my inability to decide what words to speak.

Daden waves his hand. "I will leave you guys be. Love you," he says, looks at me and winks, then clicks off. I'm confused for a moment, but then I realize he was speaking to Andre. He probably winked at him too, but I don't know.

"Andre is in love!" Matt claims. "That was so adorable!" I know Matt is teasing Andre, but he isn't serious about it. "I wish I had someone like that in my life."

Maylene comes over with another bottle. "Well, you might if you weren't such a conceited ass," she sneers. "Hell, if you weren't so vain, I'd be into you."

Maylene just let something slip that I know she will regret.

Matt laughs. "Hold up. I'm not vain." He gestures to himself. "But I do look for certain qualities in a woman. And no way you'd be into me. I'm not your type!"

Maylene nods in agreement. "You're right; if I were to be with a guy, it would be someone more like Arch." She comes up next to me and gently pinches my cheek. "He's almost just as hot but is way more charming than you are."

I take being almost just as hot as Matt as a major compliment.

"Ah, okay," Matt says, defeated. "My point, though, is that you're not into guys like me."

"Yes, that is exactly my point," Maylene says. Matt looks to the ground. Maylene must have felt bad because she walks up to him and gives him a kiss on the cheek.

"Aw, does Matty need some affection?" Andre says, and he too gives Matt a kiss on the cheek.

Maylene and Andre look at me.

"What, do you not like Matt?" they ask in unison. "Come over here!"

I oblige. Matt looks at me.

"My day will be much better if I got a kiss from you, too," Matt says, looking at me with a pouty face and puppy eyes. I kiss him on the cheek.

"There we go!" Maylene says, and takes a swig from the bottle she holds. "We all love you, Matt! You know we do!"

Andre and I shout out, "We love you, Matt!"

I swear Matt blushes at this. We take another round of shots and stand in a circle, arms around each other. We dance around, led by Andre, until we fall over on the sectional.

"All right, it's time for a round of water!" Matt says, getting up. He brings over four bottles of water. "No more drinking until you drink your water!"

"But drinking water is drinking!" Andre says childishly. Matt smiles and shoves the bottle into Andre's chest.

I down my water very quickly and find that I want more.

Maylene claims she wants more alcohol after drinking that "disgusting water" and grabs another bottle. But the rest of us can't bring ourselves to drink anymore.

"Pathetic," Maylene says, and chugs the bottle. She doesn't make it more than a few gulps before she runs out of the cabin, presumably to puke.

When she returns, I am lying on the couch. Matt sits nearby, arms outstretched and head leaning back, and Andre is curled up on the floor, his choice.

"I'm done for," she says gloomily. "I'm the epitome of wasted and pathetic." She groans and lays on the couch, though she lays partially on top of me, despite there being so much more room on the sectional.

"Nighty night," she says quietly.

I look up at Matt. He closes his eyes tiredly, plays with my hair for a moment, and passes out.

I don't know if I am the kind of tired that needs sleep. But it is very comfy here, even with the weight of half of Maylene's body on my legs. I think my legs go numb. My foot surely does. But with everyone passing out, I just stare up at the ceiling, wondering how they could be so tired that they are already snoring. And considering they pretty much started it all with the drinking, it makes even less sense. I didn't even want to drink. But I sure am glad I did.

7

Mindless. I had passed out suddenly. I wake to being aware of dreaming. The dream slips away quickly, vanishing into forgetfulness. I feel very hot. I can feel my damp shirt stick to my skin. My jeans feel tight and uncomfortable. My eyes snap open. I look down. Maylene is drooling on the floor, her head resting on my leg, somehow balanced so that it doesn't fall over.

I had fallen asleep on my chest. Matt is no longer here. Neither is Andre. I shake my leg delicately, not wanting to rudely wake Maylene, but enough so that she does wake.

"Oh shit," she says, getting up quickly. She wipes the drool from her mouth and shoots me a look, telling me to never discuss it. As she sits up, she groans and puts her hand to her head. "Water," she croaks out, and she stumbles to the cooler. I sit up and grab one of the many that were placed on the table. A waking present Matt left us, though clearly Maylene didn't see them.

I sip on the water. My throat feels dry, and my stomach churns. Once I finally drink enough water to not feel sick, I start to feel hungry. Standing up, I walk over to Maylene. Her head is hanging low.

"Let's go," I say, gently guiding her to the exit. I don't really know where I am going, but I know that we have made it to Verdrayson. Only a few people move about; the stragglers, or those with duties to tend to on the airship.

Maylene holds on to me as we go down the stairs, but when we reach the ladder, I am at a loss as to how to help her down it.

"There's a lift this way," she says, pointing to the command room window. I look out. We are inside a gray structure, some sort of parking bay for the ship. Three engineers are working on the exterior of the ship. Maylene then leads me in the opposite direction of where she pointed. She still clings to me as if I am her life support.

Blended in with the wall, there is a lift near the lounge bar, adjacent to the ladder, only a few strides apart, about twenty-six Milkateet. The lift only goes to the main floor of the ship and its belly. We walk out of the ship and down the parking bay. A red door connects the bay to the rest of the building, something I have not seen.

I can tell the hallway is one of many that are intertwined. Doors lead to various rooms, though I can't see what's behind them. May-lene, still hanging on to my arm, leads the way slowly. She turns a few times, and I have no clue how she knows where she is going. Everything looks the same — grayscale, dull, but with bright lights. Several vents blow warm air into the halls.

We reach double doors with a sign overhead that reads *West Wing*. Maylene doesn't take us through them. Instead, we go into a lift and go up one floor.

The building is narrow but long. We must have been underground before, where the structure was much more expansive. I had fig-ured we were underground, as there were no windows. Above the ground, the whole building is lined with windows, from the ground to the roof, making it look as if the building were made entirely of glass. In the far corner, there is a food-court restaurant-like stand with a few people lined up in front of it. Maylene haggardly walks towards it, her pace brisk. She ends up letting go of me and promptly falls over. *How much did she have to drink?* I help her get up. I don't laugh. I feel bad for her. And I know she must be very embarrassed. We make it to the stand. When it is our turn, we order from a person stationed behind the counter. Maylene gets a large drink loaded with vitamin shots to hopefully make herself feel better.

I order two chicken and egg sandwiches.

It doesn't take long for our orders to arrive. Though it does seem odd that here we have someone to take our order, in the true style of Mr. Canabana, but it was not the same back in Candalance, with the small bots and their order screens.

"With the size of the building and number of staff, it was more efficient to have those small bobbly droids take orders back at the main headquarters," Maylene says, reading my mind. It is quite impressive that, in her current state, she can still guess what my thoughts are. We sit down at a round, raised table in the eating area. "Real people still cook the food, though," she says. "But especially during normal mealtimes, there are just too many to serve; it's much less frantic to have those guys zip around. Here — well, here usually there aren't so many people."

I eat quickly. Maylene is quicker, though. She sits there, blankly staring at my food, until I am finished. I pick up my tray, but Maylene presses my hand down and takes my fingers off of it. She pushes a button, and the table opens up, swallowing the contents of it into some chute. The table then sprays itself with a disinfectant that dries immediately.

The concept is so simple, but it has been so long since I ate in a public cafeteria, which is what this place resembles, that I had forgotten that most of them have automatic cleaning tables.

By this point, Maylene can walk by herself, though she still goes at a slower pace and stumbles every now and then. We go to another lift and go up just one more floor.

Immediately, I can tell we have entered an infirmary. There is a clean welcome desk with two people behind the counter.

"One vital shot, please," Maylene coughs out at the counter. I guess the vitamin drink she had just now didn't help her as much as she hoped it would. The brunette girl wrinkles her nose, but smiles politely, and goes to the back to retrieve the requested item. Maylene turns to me. "How do you feel?"

I shrug. "I'm okay," I tell her. I mostly feel fine; my head just feels a bit heavy mentally.

"No nausea, no headaches?"

I shake my head.

Maylene groans and puts her head down on the counter.

"Here you go, Miss Mayfield," the nice lady says, handing Maylene a small vial of green liquid.

Maylene mumbles a thanks, pops the cap off, and shoots the contents like a shot. It clinks lightly when she puts it back on the counter. Seconds pass, but then the change in Maylene seems immediate. Her eyes open fully, her normal color fills her face, and the bags beneath her eyes disappear.

"Much better," Maylene says peppily. "Thanks Krissy."

The girl named Krissy nods and takes the vial back to the back. Maylene takes my hand and leads me back to the elevator. This time Maylene pushes button 106, and we go to the top floor.

The floor is nothing more than one large lounge. Adjacent to the elevator are a few bathroom doors. There is a kitchen area to the left at the end of the building and a screening room on the other side. The marble floor is gray with amber veins, with the occasional white striation. All sorts of seating are scattered throughout, all with varying-sized and shaped rugs of ocean blue or black. Beyond the windows is a marvelous view of snowy wind and ice dust that slightly smothers the view of a frozen land. But beyond the pure white, glacier-blue water gleams in the sunlight. The sky swirls with gloomy hues of blue, gray, and white.

Even though the landscape is hard to see, there is something very magical about the view.

There is no one else up here at the moment. Maylene swipes and types into her watch's hologram, though I can't see what exactly she is doing.

She walks over to the kitchenette.

"Wanna drink?" she asks me with a laugh. She pulls out a glass jug of water from the fridge and pours herself a glass. She takes a sip. "Mmm." Maylene closes her eyes. "Want any?" she asks me, eyes still closed.

"Sure," I say, thirst coming to me as I walk over.

Maylene pours me a glass.

"Matt will be up here in a few," she says. "He messaged me saying that even though we are taking the day off, we need to get you out of here tomorrow morning, and that he and I have some work to do."

I nod, drinking the water. I look back out the windows. The place has a lonely, calming, and peacefulness to it that I am almost sad I am leaving so soon.

As I'm gazing out the windows, the elevator doors slide open and Matt walks in. He looks perfectly normal, showered, and without any adverse effects of excessive drinking.

"Had fun yesterday?" Matt asks me. That confirms my suspicion of having slept through the night.

"Ten-ten would do it again," Maylene says, holding up the jug of water.

I don't answer. I sit in an armchair facing the window.

"That much, huh?" Matt says sarcastically. He joins me on the other pair of armchairs. Maylene refills the jug with water and comes over with it and her glass. She sits on the couch and places the drinks on the table in front of her.

"Nah, I did," I say. "I had fun. It's been a while since I drank like that. Last time I did it, I was still in school hanging out with friends I don't even speak to anymore."

"I know what that's like," Matt says. "Five years ago, I had friends that I now no longer keep in touch with. I tried though, but they kept hanging out without inviting me anywhere."

Maylene frowns. "That sounds so sad."

Matt shrugs. "It's like they say, if your absence doesn't affect them, your presence won't either. And it's all cool. Better to see the truth in things than hide from the facts."

"Still sounds so sad," Maylene says after a short pause. "But I hear you."

"It would be sad if I kept pretending that I had those friends," Matt says. I'm surprised at how deep and vulnerable he's letting himself be. "I'm happy with how things turned out. Now I've got you two, and I wouldn't have it any other way."

"Same," I mumble loud enough for the others to hear. When I think about it, the last few years have been quite lonely for me. I didn't really have any friends. I don't have much of a family. The only thing that kept me busy was my deliveries. Looking back at it, that solitude is probably why I feel so awkward around people.

"Let's talk about tomorrow," Maylene says, changing the subject. For a moment, I reflect on yesterday. I smile, knowing that the friendship we share goes beyond intoxication and that there is something very real here. I believe that Andre would feel the same if he were also present.

"We've got a surprise for you," Matt says excitedly. He stands up. Maylene does the same, and the two look at each other. "Shall we?" Matt has a wide smile on his face.

"We shall," replies Maylene.

The two grab me and bring me to the elevator.

"You're gonna love this," Matt says. We go all the way back down to the first floor. We then go to the lift that only accesses this floor and the basement.

Instead of walking back through the long corridors, Maylene and Matt lead me through the double doors into the West Wing.

A similarly designed layout presents itself. Long halls, crisscrossing each other. Though these are a sleek black with small lights that turn on with our presence. The walk is long, but we get to the loading docks quick enough. We go through the door with a red number "4" above it.

Just like the parking bay for the large ship, this one looks the same, though instead of just the single ship docked, several Sonars are lined next to each other, each with their own set of stairs.

The one in front of me is dark in design, like the hallways. The other Sonars that are parked are of the same model, but some have slight color variations. This model is an upgrade from what I had. It is the latest high-end one. There is no exhaust. Most Sonars have one, but they are subtle, and only when a quick and powerful maneuver is made, do they release any sort of jet propulsion. This one will never do that. Even at its top speed, it'll come to a full stop in mere seconds.

"Gosh, this thing is sexy," Maylene says. Matt looks over at me, his face full of excitement.

"You'll be able to travel much faster in this thing, and you can fly at a higher elevation than most road vehicles, but still be sure to stay within legal range," Matt tells me. "There is also a cloaking mode, but that's illegal except on military crafts, so don't use it unless you absolutely have to."

I'm stunned. I can't speak. My sorrow for losing my old Sonars drowns in my thrill to have this new one.

"And as you've probably guessed, this is yours," Maylene says. "So even after you finish the mission, you get to keep it."

"It's beautiful," I say, walking down the metal stairs. I do a circle around the Sonars, eyeing its smooth finish and fine details. I stop in front of it. Maylene and Matt join me.

I feel Maylene grab my hand, but instead of holding it, she places a small chip in it. I hold it up to my eyes. It's a programming chip that I can download into my phone, and my phone will act as the key to the ignition. Because I am using a physical piece of technology to gain access to the Sonars, that means that it has never been driven. I'll be the first.

"This is going to be a fun ride," I say.

"I've already mapped out your destinations," Maylene tells me. "Bring food and drinks with you. It will take you all day tomorrow to reach the closest city, and there is nowhere to stop for a break until then. Once you cross the frozen desert, you have a long way to go across the ocean. The shortest distance, unfortunately, is not quite in the direction you need to go, but it is the safest, so you'll stay the night in that city. Only a large ship would be able to safely travel across the distance that heads directly to NEAST from here."

"How long will it take me to get to NEAST?" I ask.

"With my new calculations, about four days. This is accounting for three stops a day plus nights," she tells me. That's a lot better than I was expecting. So many days have been added to this job since I started it. At this point, I am more than eager to wrap it up. Though it has been less than a week, that night in Halav seems like a lifetime ago.

Matt places his hand on my shoulder, indicating we should leave. I follow him back up the stairs and into the corridors.

"There is a Canabana hotel in Borough," Maylene tells me as we make our way back to the lift. "I've booked you a room for the night.

Nothing too fancy like the suite you stayed at in Candalance. But it should feel like that first room you stayed at back in Velro."

"I appreciate that," I tell her.

We make our way back to the cafeteria for some food. Andre finds us, and we take a long lunch together. Despite his seemingly frivolous disposition, I find Andre quite pragmatic. He talks with varying tones of airiness and changes in pitch when excited, but when it comes to deep, serious talks, he speaks with an appropriately expressed tone of voice. I have no doubt that he believes in Edward's humanitarian endeavors.

There isn't much to do. We finish lunch. Andre goes back to his work because he did not get the day off. Maylene and Matt show me around the building, but there isn't much to see. Most floors are just offices. There are sleeping quarters here, just like every other Canabana building, but none are as massive as the ones in Candalance.

"This place is not used very often. In fact, usually the cafeteria isn't open. There are kitchens on the fifth floor that the workers stationed here usually eat in," Maylene explains. "But with the influx of personnel staying here for a few days, some were given a new job for the time being."

"Did everyone in Candalance just hop on the ship and come out here?"

"Oh gosh no!" Maylene says. She lets out a laugh that sounds almost embarrassed. "We were all told of this being a possibility the morning after you arrived, and everyone was given the option to go home for a bit or come out here. Some people who came even brought their families. But it was their choice to come out here. For some, it's probably like a vacation, but with work."

"Well, not everyone was given the choice," Matt says sarcastically. "But if I had to choose, I'd still come."

"Yeah, well, we're all still on a job. It doesn't matter much where we are," Maylene says.

Just before sunset, Matt bundles me up in clothes that make me feel extremely hot. I think I start sweating, but that could be made up in my mind because of all the layers I wear. He gives me a mask to put over my face. The goggles are very clean, and when I put them on, I can barely tell I am wearing them.

We meet Maylene at a loading dock beneath the first floor. This, like my new Sonars, is in the West Wing, but some ways away from where my cherished vehicle rests. She is waiting on top of an ancient vehicle. A Snowgadget. It rests on the ground, gliding across frozen lands. Some of the "newer" models would rise above the ground, but not very much. It wasn't long before these became outdated, with only a few people caring to have any collection of them.

I'm excited. It's been a long time since I rode one.

Matt and I mount our Snowgadgets and chase Maylene down the tunnel. Up ahead, a door slowly opens forward, and we slide off of it onto the snowy terrain. Small shards of ice fly around. I can hear faint clinks as they bounce off my face guard. Maylene leads the way at first, but Matt overtakes her.

We climb up some hills and race down them again. Through the small valleys, underneath the ice tunnels, and all the way to the mountain side. We all skid to a stop, throwing snow up as we do so.

It was impossible to tell earlier, but Verdrayson is actually a mountaintop that overlooks the icy ocean. By the edge of the cliff, the colors of the sunset clash with the snow-white of the atmosphere and the colorful streams and waves that glisten in the coming night sky.

This is something Maylene really wanted to see. I don't blame her.

We don't say anything. We just sit there, hands on the handles, and look at the view. Only when the sun is close to disappearing beneath the horizon do we head back. This time, we move at a quick but calm pace. With the sun going down, there is even less to see on the way back.

After a quick dinner, Matt shows me where our room is. It is a two-bedroom suite with one bathroom. He tells me that there are a limited number of sleeping quarters and that most people are paired up. Some of the families are quite cozy, but they get the bigger suites.

"I usually have my own suite," he says playfully. "And I've actually only been here twice before. And both times it was just a small crew."

I nod.

"Mind if I shower first?" he asks me.

I wave a hand, telling him to go ahead. I walk into my bedroom. It is noticeably smaller than the other bedrooms I've stayed in, with only one small dresser and a normal-sized bed. There is a little closet inside, but it is completely empty.

There is a large bag on my bed. I open it and find several pairs of clothes. I suppose Edward wanted to make sure I got anything that I lost replaced. I appreciate the gesture, especially since I won't have to go days wearing the same clothes the entire time. I lay on the bed for a little bit, but I get bored of doing so quickly. Now I feel like showering. I grab the bag and stand up.

Yawning, I make my way back to the common area. It too is small, with just a tiny nook in the corner with a radiation oven and a small freezer. I drop the bag on the floor and lean against the counter, staring out the window.

Matt walks out of the bathroom, which is closer to his bedroom than it is to mine. He wears nothing but a towel around his waist. Chiseled abs, corded arms, and a strong chest. His arms are so toned, I see muscles I didn't know existed. His toned waist shapes down into a "V" and honestly, I have no clue why this guy isn't a model. Nothing about him looks unnatural, either. There are body-builders who literally inject protein and use non-invasive surgery to shape muscles on their body. None of them look normal or natural. Matt isn't like that.

This man must stop being so attractive. It does not help my self-esteem.

"All yours, bud," he says before disappearing into his room, closing the door behind him.

I look out the window again, firmly deciding to start working out when I'm done with my delivery. I have more than enough money to take off for a while and really start focusing on myself, improving my overall health, and stabilizing my life rather than always living on the road.

My shower isn't long. When I get out, I find Matt sitting on the couch, facing the window. There is a screen, but it is turned off. Matt has a notebook in front of him. He looks at me as I pass by. He jerks his head, telling me to hang out. I nod, put my bag down in my room, and join him on the couch.

"The main thing I hate about this place is that it doesn't have a gym," he says. "So I resort to doing pushups, but they aren't the same."

"What's that for?" I ask, pointing at his notebook. I can see scribbles inside it, but his writing is unique, and I can't easily make out any of the words.

Matt chuckles. "I just keep thoughts I have in here," he says, closing the notebook. "It isn't really a diary or journal, just a place for me to write something down in case I want to remember it later."

"Oh," I say.

He laughs again. "I know it sounds odd, but I promise you I don't write how my day went. What I do write, though, are any achievements I feel I made in the gym, at work, or in life. It's good to look back at them if I ever feel down on myself."

My instant thought is that I can't imagine why Matt would feel down on himself, but I do understand that everyone has their own things that they are dealing with. In the last week, I've learned that people find me more attractive than I thought I was. Or maybe I just never saw myself as anything like Matt. And I'm not. But the point is, I might think Matt has it all, but he doesn't feel that way about himself.

"How long have you been working out?"

"Five years," he tells me. "Though it really is seven, but I wasn't consistent for the first few years. I was also impatient and didn't care much for the gym. At the time, it felt more like a social appearance thing. Now it's therapeutic."

I've heard that a lot, though many have also told me it's pure torture.

"I want to start working out when this is all done," I tell him. "It's time I find who I want to be and become that."

Matt gives me a huge smile. "That's what I like to hear," he says. "When you're done taking that chip to NEAST, head back to Candalance, and I'll be your personal trainer in the gym."

I smile too. "Sounds like a plan."

He looks out the window, a smile still on his face. The night here is darker than I'm used to, as there are no city lights to shine across the atmosphere. But the stars look so much more majestic than I've ever seen before. Powerful. Elegant.

"Any ideas of who you want to be?"

I think about that for a moment. I've always considered myself to be a good guy and humble. But now I am not so sure. I've taken things for granted. What I considered to be polite conduct has probably come across as rude and condescending to others. A good person will always find a way to help others. I've never really done that. I haven't spent all my waking hours doing something that I know will benefit the world at large. After meeting Edward and his employees, I've come to realize that I have done nothing meaningful with my life.

While that is a sad understanding, it's an understanding that will change the very essence of how I view myself.

"I'm not too sure yet," I tell him. "But I know I want to make it worthwhile. I want to be someone who will spend their whole life making our world a better place."

Matt smiles again.

"Sounds like you want to be like Edward," he says. "But really, that sounds like you are already just like all of us. And that, my friend, is why I like you so much. Maylene was right about you. You're real. Genuine. And you actually give a damn."

I look down at my feet for a moment. I hear the words Matt says, and I plan to live up to those words.

8

The morning comes too soon. The sun, even though it has only risen above the horizon for a few hours, shines brightly over the frozen wasteland. The bright white view of constant snow is beautiful, but I'm sure it quickly loses that attractiveness to those who spend all their time here. We hadn't discussed a time for departure. I don't know if I am running late or not.

I open my eyes groggily. I'm not super tired, but some extra hours of sleep wouldn't hurt.

Matt and I ended up talking late into the night. He asked about my home life and told me of his. He has a family that he stays well connected with, whereas I am almost the total opposite. I didn't feel jealous, but it made me want to get back in touch with my father. Though, as he said before, and like me, he doesn't much have anyone else who he is really close with, whether that be a friendship or romantic partner. When I asked him about Maylene, his answer was that I knew she isn't into guys like him.

As I work through my morning thoughts and fight for the will to get out of bed, I hear panicked banging on my door. Matt charges into my room.

"Oh, good, you're awake," he says.

From underneath the covers, I groan at him. "Do I have to be?" I ask.

"Yeah, ideally you would have left an hour ago," he answers. "The journey to the next city is long enough already, and we don't want you to get there so late."

"Okay, fine," I say, throwing the sheets off me. Matt leaves and lets me get ready. I take a quick rinse to wake up, pack some clothes from the dresser into my new bag, and head out.

Matt is waiting in the living room and leads me downstairs. We don't talk on the way down. Something feels different now. This is the first time in about a week that things have gone back to normal. Normal, as in me being on the road all alone, except for when Maylene calls me. I don't tell him this, but I hope Matt does the same. Not that it would matter. This journey is one that will keep the three of us connected for a lifetime.

The loading bay is silent except for the humming of the heating system that circulates warm air throughout the entire building. Maylene waits, leaning against the hood of my new Sonars.

"Ready, baby girl?" she asks.

"Uh, yeah, I suppose," I answer uncomfortably.

Maylene scoffs. "I wasn't talking to you," she says, but then smiles. "I was talking to her." She nods emphatically to the Sonars.

"Oh," I say with a short laugh. "That makes more sense."

Matt chuckles.

We stand there in silence for a minute.

"So, this is goodbye," Maylene says.

Before I can answer, Matt does. "Only for now. But in a week, we'll be partying together again. The only question is, how does the future look?"

"I think it looks bright," I say with a large smile.

"And after your return and after our amazing party time, we'll go back to what we do best," Maylene says.

"And what is that?" Matt and I both ask in unison.

"Saving the world, of course," Maylene declares. She then tilts her head slightly. "And, uh, other, extreme sports."

I give her a puzzled look. "Is that a reference to something?"

Maylene shrugs.

"I feel like that should be a reference to something," Matt says. "Sounds like something I've heard before."

"You aren't leaving without giving me a chance to say goodbye, are you?"

Andre dances into the bay. He jumps down the few steps and runs over to me to wrap his arms around me in a tight embrace. "I'll see you soon, good friend," he says and kisses me on the cheek, a little closer to my mouth than I'm comfortable with, but I appreciate the gesture all the same.

With that, the four of us share a silent glance at each other. I hop into the Sonars and start its engine with the driver's side still open. I give them a nod and pull the door down to close it. I hear the latch lock, and I start up the navigation system.

My destination is already programmed in.

The others walk back up the stairs, a safe distance from the Sonars. I raise the Sonars off the ground, wave to my friends, and head down the bay. Up ahead, the large gate lowers. Soon enough, I'm soaring across the wasteland. I turn my head back. The building is barely discernible in the blowing frost.

And just like that, I am on the road again. Borough is quite far. Per my navigation system, I won't make it there until well into the night.

Traveling across Verdrayson is not as enjoyable as riding across it on a Snowgadget. Up here, everything looks the same, and as such, it doesn't look like much at all. The view is almost like staring at a blank, water-stained canvas. The snow storms around much more violently up here than on the surface of the land, and I have to heat the windshield to stop the snow from building up on it.

Luckily, the travel time through the wasteland is short, and soon I launch off the cliffs and glide over the icy ocean. At this point, I set my Sonars to autopilot and set it so that it warns me when we are nearing land. I would prefer to steer the Sonars myself once I'm in the city.

From glaring white to glistening blue, the colors of the scenery blend into one, and I don't much care to look out the windows.

The Sonars I have now is larger than mine was. It has a bigger cab and plenty of space to sleep. I lay on the bed on my back and stare up at the ceiling. There is a screen on a full-motion mount. I don't turn it on yet. I let my mind wander and drift off. There is plenty of time to watch movies or series during my travels.

It is hard not to appreciate the top-of-the-line luxury class of this Sonars. Like everything else, Edward Canabana has impeccable taste. Which reminds me, I didn't actually see him in Verdrayson. Thinking back to it, I wouldn't expect to. He is a busy man and already has two employees of his taking care of me.

I nap for a few hours. When I wake, I decide to sit in the driver's seat, but I keep the autopilot on. Three Gliders pass above me. They move over to the side and drop down a net. Fishermen. The Gliders rise higher, lifting the net carrying a bunch of flopping fish. They move in closer together. Dangerously near each other's spinning blades, a small board shoots out of one. Two people are on it. One of them steers while the other weaves a rope and hook through the net, tying it together at the top. The three Gliders still carry the net, as the net, now filled with fish, would be too heavy for just one Glider to carry.

The two men on the hoverboard return to the Glider they came from. And the three Gliders fly out of sight.

I raise the screen in the back, revealing a large window. I can't see anything but water all around me. The front screen turns on. Maylene comes into view.

"Hey baby girl," she says mockingly to me.

"What's up?" I ask, chuckling.

"Do you want to see something cool?"

I shrug. "Sure."

Maylene smiles and holds up a finger. My Sonars drifts down towards the sea.

"Hey," I say, starting to panic.

"Just wait, relax," she says. "Don't you trust me?"

I nod.

"You might want to buckle in, though."

I quickly strap on the belt. I do it just in time as the Sonars hits the water. It goes smoother than I anticipated, but there is still a jolt from the impact.

The Sonars continues to descend, deeper into the sea. I can't see anything out of the window. Bubbles fly everywhere, and I think chunks of seaweed smash against the windshield.

"One second," Maylene says.

The brights of the Sonars flick on. It takes a few more seconds for the bubbles to clear up, but soon I am immersed in a gorgeous sight of beneath-the-sea life. Colored plants sway around. Small fish swim through the marine garden. Oceanic mounds spit out bubbles. The Sonars doesn't fly too deep, as the varying elevation is too erratic for the auto-pilot function to navigate safely and I don't think Maylene wants to drive the vehicle the entire time.

"How is it?" she asks.

"It looks pretty freaking awesome," I say as a school of fish swim over my Sonars.

As I go further, I see more aquatic animals, all of them small and non-threatening, though I know most everything is carnivorous except for the fish. I even see a few plants that are nothing more than traps, waiting for the smaller marine life to get tangled before devouring them.

"Yeah, that sure is breathtaking," Maylene says slowly, looking at her screen, which shows the view from my Sonars' front camera.

"Oh, I just remembered," I say, slightly frantically, but I'm sure everything is just fine. "Where is the program chip?

"Didn't you get a new bag?" Maylene asks.

"Yeah, uh," I start to say, but she interrupts me.

"It's inside. There is a small pouch in the main pocket."

I nod. "I figured," I say, playing off my panic.

Maylene and I enjoy the aquatic scenery for a while.

About an hour or two in, I lose track of the time, and Maylene tells me that she has to get going. She asks if I want to stay underwater or go back up. I tell her I'd rather go above the water as I want to rest for a bit. My Sonars starts to ascend. It beeps for a moment as it nears breaking the surface of the ocean, indicating a vehicle is passing above, and it stops itself from hitting it. When the vehicle passes, it continues its ascent until I am well above the sea.

"I'll talk to you later," she says, and clicks off.

I spend the next few hours lying back in the chair, my eyes drifting off to sleep for small spurts.

The sun moves across the sky, high and higher, and then lower and lower. It drops beneath the horizon before I reach land. I expected it to. Borough is on the coast, and I won't make it there for yet another four to five hours.

The moonlight glistens on the ocean's surface. Glowing plankton burn bright green and pink in waves as they move through the choppy waters.

Another set of three Gliders passes by, already carrying their prized net of seafood. There have been few journeys that have felt this lonely. Something about traveling across the sea for hours. If I were in an industrial jet, the time would have been cut in less than half. But those are quite large, and all of them are regulated. Even if I wanted to drive one of those for this mission, it would be unwise to do so.

The twenty-second hour approaches. I am less than an hour away from Borough, but in the dark night, I can't see anything ahead of me. I rest a bit more in the bed.

Vaguely, a distant memory with my father comes to mind. I was much younger back then, but I had already began to feel the loneliness that filled me while my dad was gone for work for so long. Even before he was CEO, he still worked too much. Too much, that is, to take care of his only child. But he spent a week with me. I remember being so happy then, but then feeling so abandoned once he left.

Bitter memories filled with joy and sadness remind me of how much I resent my father for barely being there. But I also feel the urge to reconnect. That's something I can do once I am done with this delivery. I will probably see my friends first, and then take some time for my dad.

I turn off the autopilot half an hour later, knowing that I am getting close to the city. Soon enough, I see tall buildings and wide bridges ahead of me. In the distance, the lights of Borough welcome me to a coastal city that feels calm with its glowing light radiating over the sea. Luxury liners are docked along the shore, old ships from decades ago made into a sort of novelty experience. When I'm done with this job, I may just spend a week on one of them. I'll just add that to the ever-growing list of things I'll do. It is amazing at how much more open the world seems, and how much more inviting life seems, once I've set goals to strive for.

The flat semi-submarines are anchored down, some sitting atop a heavy bed made for parking the *flatboats*, as many people call them. They are much bigger than what I would call a boat, though.

Borough has a unique grounding law where you fly across the coast and sandy areas and only ground your Sonars once you've reached the main roads. I wouldn't have known that if the navigation in my Sonars had not alerted me.

The Canabana hotel I'm being directed to lies on the outskirts of the coast, atop a small cliff overlooking the ocean. As the cliff juts out over the edge, thick metal beams support the cliff and building.

I steer my Sonars into the parking building across the street. The parking building is nearly as tall as the hotel, and three breezeways connect the two structures. Only two elevations are marked out in the city, but it is legal to fly above those so long as your destination is within the city. Most people don't care to fly that high either way, so only a few Sonars soar above me.

A message from Maylene is read out loud by CHAD.

"Park on the seventh floor; that's where your room will be."

I do as I am told.

I'm just a little bummed, having counted nine floors in the hotel, but I suppose there is no reason to waste a top-floor suite on me, especially since this is one of the most tourist-filled cities in the world.

It feels snobby to think it, but I am a bit more excited when I have to scan my phone for access to the seventh-floor garage. I've been too spoiled the last few days that I now want to live luxuriously.

Unlike the other parking garages, my Sonars stays put when I leave it. I suppose the floors below might have a complex parking system that hides your vehicle in some basement until you call for it, but up here, the guests must be paying for privileged parking. Of course, while the usual mechanics allow for five Sonars to be "parked" in the same spot, here that isn't an option. Again, like the old ships, this is an experience of days past.

I walk along the carpet and through the automatic doors that glide open. A waterfall, brilliantly lit and that falls down in front of the door, stops pouring water, and the decorative drain on the ground closes, leaving the floor completely dry.

When the doors close behind me, the water starts to fall again.

"Welcome! You must be Arch Caldor."

I look up to see a young man with slicked-back blonde hair and a clean face. He smiles genuinely at me and then inputs data into his computer.

I walk up to him. I knew that Maylene wouldn't be here, but it still feels a bit weird that she isn't.

"You're all set to go," he tells me with another wide grin. "You're in room 7010. Please enjoy your stay with us. We've sent a directory to your phone. If there is anything you need, please do not hesitate to call."

"Thank you," I say politely. I feel relieved as I walk down the hall, and with the greeter saying nothing else, that is, nothing that references my name.

I unlock my room and walk in. The curtains open automatically, revealing a wide window that overlooks the ocean. I toss my bag onto one of the beds and look out.

Even in the dark, I can make out the beach beneath, which is private for hotel guests. Lit torches line the sand. It even looks like there is an outdoor kitchen, and it appears to be open. With my stomach aching for a real meal, I immediately head downstairs. It only takes me a few wrong turns before I walk out of the hotel and down the ramp to the beach.

There is no line. I look around, noting how many people are about, and I walk up to one of the bartenders. I give him my order of Flite fingers. Like chicken fingers, but the Flite has more texture and meat on its body. The order comes with salty Starchips, made from vegetables and plants found in the ocean.

It isn't long before I'm sinking my teeth into my dinner. Someone comes up to order as well, but I don't pay them much attention. The person is a couple stools down.

The food is just too good. As there was nowhere to stop, all my food today consisted only of "meal replacement" sticks, bags of chips or cookies, and a small protein shake. I close my eyes and savor the moments of each bite. I can smell the smoke from the grill, the fresh vegetables, and the cooking meat.

When I'm done pigging out on my food, I grab the cloth napkin that was left for me and wipe my face. As I do so, I look up.

The person who ordered is still there, though now she eats her salad slowly, as if she were in deep thought. She has brown hair, a small nose, and smooth skin that is a light caramel color. She hiccups and then burps subtly before laughing at herself. Before I realize it, I chuckle. She looks over at me with a hand to her mouth. I quickly look away. She laughs again.

"It's okay; it was funny," I hear her say.

Unable to help myself, I grin, the wide smile almost turning into laughter. I look over at her.

"I mean, I just didn't expect it."

"Oh, that's coming from the guy who just devoured his dinner like a starving stray dog," she says, laughing at her own joke.

All of me wants to present reasons why I have to leave, why I can't stay, and get to know her for a bit. But all of me also wants to make a move, a feeling I haven't really had in a while, if ever. I just don't understand why I feel this way all of a sudden. But this feeling inside could be nothing.

I at least have to try to see if there is something there.

"Let me guess," she says, catching on. "You've got an early day tomorrow and can't stay."

I let out a short chuckle.

"Well, I do have an early morning," I tell her. "At least, I think I do. But it doesn't mean I can't stay."

She smiles and shrugs her shoulders. That tells me she might be as awkward as me. If only that were true. Could the odds really be in my favor?

"I'm Kaedy," she tells me, gently holding out her hand.

I take it. "I'm Arch."

"Mmm," she says. "Interesting name."

I shrug, not knowing what else to say. My empty plate is cleaned up, and the bartender wipes off the counter.

"So, tell me a story," she says, placing her chin between her hands, which now rest on the bar counter.

I give her a puzzled look. "What do you mean?"

She moves to the seat next to mine. "I don't know, just anything," she says. "You're out here in the middle of the night, all alone, at a place lonely people don't frequent. There are clubs for that, but those are down the road."

"Are you not here alone?" I ask her, my heart sinking just a bit.

She laughs. "Oh, I am. But I am here on business," she explains.

"Me too," I say.

She gives me a small smile and narrows her eyes. I feel myself turning red, and I can't hold my gaze on her, so I look away.

"You're not really 'dark' enough to be the mysterious type," she says. "Of course, one shouldn't judge a book by its cover."

I shoot her an offended look.

She gasps. "No, not that your cover is bad! I mean, I'd read you," she says, then scrunches her face awkwardly.

I wait for her to say something. I know she will. I know the feeling of realizing you just said or did something cringy.

She does.

"That was kinda weird, wasn't it?" She shakes her head.

I cock my head slightly. "Just a bit," I tell her. "I wouldn't call it smooth. But it was cute." Those last words escaped my mouth before I realized I even thought of them.

She shakes her head, but there's a large smile on her face. She laughs again.

I'm starting to get used to that sound. I don't know what it is. I just met her. And yet....

I look out towards the beach. The breeze filters through, occasionally picking up sand. The lights of the hotel and the shine of the moon sparkle in the dark oceanic waters. There are some people about. Like Kaedy said, most of them are couples. If any families are here, they are tucked away in their hotel rooms.

It's nearing two in the morning, but I don't want to leave. While I know I need to get on the road as soon as possible, Maylene wasn't pushing me to get up early. She hasn't mentioned when I should get going at all, and I expect that they're giving me time to sleep in, knowing that today's drive would be very long.

As I focus on the gentle crash of the waves, I start to zone out, almost as if I am in another world, one where only happiness exists.

Even if I never see Kaedy again, this still would be some of the best days of my life. Of course, seeing her again would make all this so much better.

It sounds childish, but I can't wait to tell Matt.

"I don't mean to leave after that *embarrassing* moment," she says as she gets up. "But *I* have to get up early tomorrow, so I will be going to bed."

She stands next to me and holds out her phone. It takes me a minute to realize what she's doing. I take my phone and tap hers, syncing our contact info.

"Well, Arch, I do hope to see you around," she says, and starts to walk away. I can feel a twinge of sadness build up. I'm worried I might never call her, or that she may never call me. I've been so used to being alone that it's almost like I forgot how to have normal relationships. "Don't be a stranger, seriously. I'll call you when I'm done with my business trip. I expect you to do the same." She holds a stern look for a short while, but then leaves with an easy smile. I watch her go for a moment. Part of me thinks that she knows I'm watching her leave, but she doesn't turn her head back.

The sounds of the waves splashing onto the sand and the water crackling as it buries itself give me a quiet, lonely feeling, but also a full feeling. I look down and can't help the wide grin that stretches across my face.

9

Realizing what the time is, I ask for my check. The bartender tells me that it's already been paid for by Mr. Canabana.

"Oh, okay," I say, appreciating Edward. I'm in a good mood. I'm probably still smiling. "Well, at least let me leave you a tip," I say.

"No need," the man says. "Mr. Canabana already did." He pats the bar and walks away, drying a glass.

Tips aren't expected much these days, but for higher-class resorts, they are generally expected as a nod to wealth. Most people who leave tips don't think down on those who don't; it is more of a societal gesture of the upper class. Generally, I wouldn't stay somewhere like here, but I have before and understand the customs.

It is kind of Edward to leave a tip for his staff, even when he pays a meal for someone that they serve.

As I head back to my room, I begin to replay my talk with Kaedy in my head. I never did tell her a story, as she asked. I will the next time I meet her. There are so many things I could tell her, but I am more interested in hearing her story.

The generic style of seashell-designed carpets line the first floor, but as you go up to the rooms, the halls become polished in design. I would suppose most beach resorts host a similar style throughout, such as bright colors and tropical pictures, but Edward keeps his signature touch of a simple, elegant look.

I walk into my room and take a long shower. I'm still smiling to myself. There are just a few more days of this job, and then I'll take that vacation Matt and Maylene talked about. Maybe I'll even invite Kaedy.

In good spirits, I lay my head on the pillow and sleep for the rest of the night.

After a quick breakfast, I am driving out of the parking garage. It's mid-morning, and most of the local traffic has dissipated. I make a quick call to my dad. He doesn't answer. I figured he wouldn't. He's been so caught up in his work, something that I understand.

Still, after talking to Matt the other night, I hope I could spend more time with my father.

I have just under an hour of driving before I get out of Borough. Most of the city sits upon jutting rocks, and the further inland I go, the higher the elevation gets. This is another place that I would like to come back to and visit. I've been here before, though I don't remember it much as I was very young. That was while my mother was still around.

Palm trees are planted along the streets with colorful bushes in between them. There is also an assortment of other trees, vividly green in appearance in a mountainous shade. Rather than immersing it in a tropical setting, the city itself uses its natural landscape and indigenous vegetation, though I believe the palm trees were brought in. The city is quite wide, with a gorgeous route that lines the beaches. As I head deeper into the city and away from the ocean, the land will turn into tall hills and canyon-like areas.

Sadly, I leave the city limits. I raise my Sonars above the ground and pass over small hills, gliding in between the canyon.

I get an incoming call from Matt. I answer it.

"Hey bud, how's the drive going?" he asks.

"Where's Maylene?"

He looks taken aback. I laugh. "I'm just messing with you," I say. "It's all good. I left just a bit ago."

"Oh, you left already?" he asks. "Your next stop is Chlorofyx, which, compared to the distance from Verdrayson to Borough, is less than half."

"I didn't even check to see my destination," I say, raising my eyebrows. "I just got going."

"Did you charge your Sonars?" he asks.

My heart stops. "No, I, uh..." I look to see how much charge I have left. It is well under a quarter, but not yet empty. "I can turn back."

"Let's see," Matt says, looking at another screen of his. I look to see where he's at. He looks like he is in a ship, probably traveling back to Candalance. "You have enough charge to make it to Laviere," he says. "It's a small city situated in a valley. Their grounding laws are strict, and the elevations don't make sense to me," he comments. "But it's quiet and you'll be able to get a full charge there."

"Sounds good," I say.

"Even with that, you'll still make it to Chlorofyx before dinner time. Your new Sonars can hold more charge than your old one, and it charges much quicker."

"Perfect," I say, wanting to talk about something else.

His brief silence gives me my chance.

"I met a girl," I blurt out.

Matt sits back in his chair. "What a player," he says. "You say it like we're getting back in touch. It's barely been a full day since I saw you last!"

I laugh. "Yeah, it, uh," I stutter, feeling embarrassed.

"When did you have the time?"

"I was starving for a proper meal last night, so I went down to the tiki bar at the hotel. That's where I met her."

He nods his head, looking at me expectantly.

"We just talked for a bit. She had to go, and it was better for me to get to bed," I tell him. "But I have her number, and I'll call her after this delivery."

Matt raises an eyebrow. He looks at one of his other screens briefly before asking, "You didn't tell her what you're doing, right?"

I shake my head. "No, of course not," I say. "She was pretty, but I'm not stupid. She told me that she was there on business, and I said I was too. We didn't go into any details."

"Good, good," he says. "What was her name? I don't want to shit on your good news, but I have to make sure she checks out."

"I understand," I reply, wondering why I wasn't suspicious of her earlier. That's not true. I know why. "Her name is Kaedy. I don't know her last name."

"That's okay," he says, entering info into his computer.

I start getting another call. It's Kaedy. What a coincidence.

"Uh, she's actually calling me now," I say.

Matt smiles but doesn't look up. "Maybe she really is into you," he says playfully. "Take it. I've got some work to do. And just so you know," he says, now looking at his camera, "Maylene is on a different ship. She's headed somewhere nearby Chlorofyx, but has other business to attend to, but if she can, she's going to see you before you take off again."

"Okay, sounds good," I say, getting anxious that I'll miss her call. I almost hang up, but I have one last question. "You don't need to listen in to the call, do you?"

Matt laughs, again now looking at his other screens. "No, I don't need to. Even if I did, I wouldn't before I got your permission." I nod appreciatively. "I can check the hotel records for yesterday. In fact, I've already found her. I'll let you know if I find anything concerning about her." He looks back at me and winks. "Make me proud."

The screen turns off, and the incoming call flashes at me. I take it.

"Damn, I thought you were ignoring me," I hear her say. There is no visual on the call.

"No, I was just on another call," I say.

"So, where are you headed?"

I don't answer immediately. I look at my screen, hoping for a message from Matt. Nothing comes in.

"Uh, I'll be heading to Laviere for a bit," I answer. "I just need to charge my Sonars, I forgot to before I left this morning."

"Oh!" she says happily. "I had a meeting here that just ended," she says. "But I'm in no rush to get back home, which is in Iccircus."

Iccircus is a city close to Velro. The thought crosses my mind that she has been following me. I push it out. It is merely a coincidence. Must be.

She is being a lot more open than I'm comfortable with. Especially since I can't return the favor.

"I can hang around if you want to meet up for a late lunch or something," she says. "I think a redo of last night is in order." I hear her laugh.

I laugh too.

"I wouldn't mind that," I tell her. "Hey, why isn't your camera on?"

"Well, I'm driving right now," she says. "I don't like being distracted while I drive. Why, do you talk with visual while you're driving?"

I cough. "Um, no?" I say, giving myself away.

She laughs. "Okay, well, fine. Maybe one day I'll give you the honor of video calling you while I'm driving."

"Sounds good," I say, relieved that she doesn't mind much. It might not be illegal per se, but the penalties are double, and you are always at fault if you're in any accident while on a video call when driving.

"Where are you driving to? I thought you said you just finished a meeting, and that you would stay in Laviere for a little while."

"Yeah, I am! But I'm heading to the library now. I figured I'd find a good story to read while I wait for you."

A message flashes across my screen. Because I am on a call, it is not read out to me.

"She checks out."

Relief floods me.

"Sounds good," I say, probably sounding slightly absent-minded. "I should be there around thirteen or fourteen."

"That gives me plenty of time!" she says excitedly. "I send you the address of a good lunch spot close to then."

"Okay, I can't wait," I tell her. I feel like she is smiling.

"See you soon!"

Kaedy hangs up.

The drive seems to go by quickly. The valleys and canyons are a pretty sight. Changing from lush green to rocky surfaces and back again, I take my Sonars along some weaving paths for fun.

When I fly high enough, I can still see the ocean behind me, but it's just a blur of blue that blends with the sky. I can make out some of the city, but most of it hides beneath the horizon.

Soon enough, I start to feel anxious, and the time seems to slow down. For a while, I drive alongside other Sonars, but then I move faster than them and leave them behind.

I begin to get hungry and start snacking, but I stop myself as I don't want to lose my appetite. I end up drinking water and regret it as my bladder fills up. It's astonishing that I was able to drive all day yesterday and not have an issue with needing to go to the bathroom, but on this short drive and with just a small amount of water, now it is a problem.

The drive begins to feel never-ending. Overwhelming. I do my best to ignore my restroom needs.

I can't.

I end up pulling over on an open prairie and do my best to shield myself with my Sonars as I do my business. Some other vehicles pass by overhead.

When I'm done, I hop back in and keep going. There was a message that Kaedy left for me with her location. I have CHAD navigate me there. Then I realize how close I am to Laviere and shake my head, as I probably could have made it without stopping for a piss.

Most of the canyons are gone by now, but there are still hints of mountainous land. Like Matt said, Laviere is located in a small valley. I pass by a large dam that moves water away from the valley. I ground my Sonars well before entering the city.

There are a few elevations, but most of them line both sides of the hills, leaving the center open. The only tall buildings are on the other side of the city, and they are also along the hills; none are in the center. The middle of the valley is covered in small houses, though they all have large yards that surround each one.

The elevations and roads are one-directional. There are many ramps to the higher elevations, but up there are fewer roads to turn around. I don't need to go up to them.

Tucked away in an inlet is a charging station. It only takes less than ten minutes to get a full charge. Afterwards, I let Kaedy know that I'm almost there and head her way.

Parking is located on the side of the streets, though most of the spots whisk your vehicle away beneath the ground.

The first elevation is mainly small shops and large retail stores. Interspersed are the family-owned cafes and restaurants, as well as the big names.

Parking is full right in front of the sandwich bar that Kaedy is at, as the available spots beneath the street only hold three Sonars per spot, so I have to park a little further down the road. I walk back up the street and enter the lunch spot.

The place is a lot larger than it appears to be. A lot of people are inside, and I can hear the staff bustling around. Kaedy is not far from the front door and looks up at me brightly when she sees me walk in. I sit myself down at her booth. She is holding a book, full-sized and made from paper. The only places you can find such things are libraries or museums. There are probably collectors, though, who cherish their prized treasure.

She closes the book gently and tucks it away in her purse, which sits just next to her.

"You hungry?" she asks me. "I already ate, so go ahead."

I nod and, because I am quite hungry, start punching in my order on the screen that pops up from the table. I look around at the interior. Most of the restaurant staff either bus away dishes or sanitize the tables because there isn't enough room to have an automated system for that. That's when I notice the booths and tables are packed quite tightly.

The food must be good if this place is always this busy.

As I wait for my food, Kaedy asks me how my trip was.

"Not bad," I say. "It was nice driving over greenery and hills rather than white snow and blue ocean for over half a day."

My throat tightens, and I feel a lump grow inside. I swallow it down, worried that I had just let on too much.

"Oh wow, where did you come from, Verdrayson?" she laughs.

I take a second too long to answer.

"Really? That's so far away! Did you drive yourself?" She seems genuinely curious.

I take a moment to answer.

"Yeah, I did it myself. It was exhausting, but mostly just boring," I tell her, coming up with a lie. "My friend's dad wanted some pictures, so he paid me to go all the way out there."

I feel bad for it. Lying. Kaedy has been nothing but sweet, and I am taking a liking to her that grows every time we speak. But still, even though Matt said she's good, I have my doubts. It feels almost like I don't want myself to be happy. Or I am giving myself reasons why I can't be.

I force myself through it. After I'm done with the delivery, I'll tell her the truth about everything. But for now, it's safer to lie.

A waiter drops my food off, asks me if I was able to order everything I wanted, and then leaves. The slight human interaction is probably one of the reasons why the place is so popular.

I take a bite out of the bacon and chicken sandwich. The food. It is also the food that makes this place so favorable. Kaedy smiles at me.

"What?" I say, mouth full of food.

"I knew you would like this place," she answers. Kaedy brings up the ordering screen and gets two milkshakes. "You're gonna love this."

Right as I'm done with my sandwich, the milkshakes arrive. Light brown in color, whipped cream filled inside, and topped with a fudge drizzle and *strawberries*. Strawberries are considered plain as a fruit and are more of a delicacy than something people consume often.

I take a sip of the milkshake. Yet once again, Kaedy was right. I do love this. She giggles as we both drink our shakes, almost as if we are racing each other.

"So what do you do?" I ask when we're done.

"Well, I am a collector," she tells me. "A hired collector, I should say."

I squint my eyes.

"What do you mean?" I ask. "Do people hire you to just buy stuff?"

"Exactly," she says happily. "But I buy it for them, not for me, obviously," Kaedy explains. "Like a client I just had is really into poisonous frogs, so I spent a week in the Ulessis getting five of the slimy things."

I nod.

"Sounds like fun," I say.

"Actually, it is!" she answers. "And for that last job, I had to catch one of the suckers myself because the store only had four available. There's something about the adventure that I really like."

"No, I totally get it. That's why I like driving around all the time," I say, then quickly realize my mistake. "So, when my friend's dad asked me to get some pictures for him, I was more than happy to."

I might be overthinking all of this.

"That does sound nice," she breathes out. "Any plans for when you get back home?"

"Yeah," I say, trying to act as smooth as possible. "Calling you up for our first date."

She opens her mouth in surprise.

"But isn't this our first date?" she asks. I forgot about that. She has a point.

"Well, yeah, but this is more of a lunch date," I say. "I mean, I want to take you somewhere."

"Where?"

"Uh, not sure yet," I say, tongue-tied.

She laughs, and then I do too.

"I'm just messing with you," she says. "I'm sure you will think of something both romantic and adventurous."

"That I will."

Kaedy gets up and places her phone on the table, paying for her meal. I do the same. She walks us out.

"I have a few more items to collect while I'm in town. And I was just offered another job, so I won't be heading home just yet," she says as we step out into the sunny atmosphere. "Where are you headed next?"

I pause. There isn't much harm in telling her.

"Chlorofyx," I say. "Have to make the most out of my trip."

"Oh, I'll be going there too! But I probably won't leave until late at night, or even tomorrow morning," she says sadly. "But I'll see if I can catch you there! Otherwise, I'll be looking forward to that first date."

I smile. "Me too," I tell her.

She looks at me briefly and then gives me a quick kiss. I wasn't ready for it, so I stand there, doing nothing and feeling like an idiot. I blink a lot, and she looks up at me.

"Until next time," she says slowly with a small smile, starting to walk away.

"Wait," I blurt out. I gently grab her wrist and pull her back to me to give her a kiss. This one lasts longer, and it's only when I feel like I am overdoing it that I pull away. We lock eyes for a moment. I can see a few strands of her hair stick to her face.

She's so freakin' beautiful.

"Until next time," she says, but this time with a much larger and more genuine smile. She walks away but turns back and gives me another wide grin. I smile back at her and watch her turn around a corner.

I stand there for a moment, staring at where she had been. I've been in relationships before, but never have I felt something like this about anyone — I never understood how anyone could just after meeting someone, but now I do.

Sometimes everything just seems right.

I head back to my Sonars. I pay the parking fee, and my Sonars is returned. I hop in, set the engines, and head out. I travel through the rest of the city. I stay on the first elevation; it being the direct route in and out of the city.

Once I pass over the elevation markings, I lift my Sonars up, getting a bit above the normal height for traveling.

The hillsides and canyons remain the same. There is farmland out here. The wide-open spaces and unincorporated land make it easy for meat and produce to be exported, as there are no grounding laws.

Chlorofyx is less than half a working day's drive. When I get bored of the scenery, I let the autopilot navigate while I rest in the back. And when I get bored of doing nothing and am uninterested in music or entertainment for the time being, I turn on the news while I space out to my thoughts.

Not much is said. A reporter lightly discusses the building collapsing in Halav and mentions that there were no casualties. Two of the major energy companies are at odds with each other, with several lawsuits in the works. That is new, but only because it is unusual for energy companies to compete with each other as most of them have monopolies on the services they provide. There is nothing new about major corporations taking each other to court.

I patiently wait for a phone call, but none come in. I feel like I am getting too comfortable with this new life I'm making for myself. After failing to reach my father again, I hop back in the driver's seat and numbly make my way.

The sun is nearly set when I arrive in Chlorofyx, one of the largest metropolises in the world. There are about ten elevations in the city. Some buildings are built from the ground and reach all the way into the sky, just above the highest elevation. There are other buildings that only go up halfway, but right above them are other structures resting on their mostly invisible platforms. In this city, the roofs of all structures hold magnetic properties with both similar and opposite polarities. I never understood the mechanics of it, but this is how heavy constructions are supported, even when supported by an elevation.

As such, between the fifth and sixth elevations, it is absolutely and disastrously fatal to travel between the elevations except in the marked areas, as the electric and magnetic forces are too powerful for the body to handle. Best case scenario, your heart stops. Worst case, well, there's been news coverage about criminals fleeing from Impositioners meeting their exotic ends by improperly traveling between the two. Each elevation accounts for about ten stories of structure.

The only other area that supports new structures is at the very top, where most of the upper class look down on the world from their high-rise-style homes.

Atop the tallest of the buildings are large rings that generally consist of penthouses, though some are still business-related.

The Canabana Hotel is in the heart of the city, and it is one of the few buildings that stands higher from the lowest elevation. Because of it, there is a circling elevation road that surrounds the entire hotel, making traveling between all the elevations easy.

The roads are marked with a faint baby blue and faded pink, each with its own direction of travel. With the sheer number of vehicles on the road that are always on the move and the clashing colors of the elevations, the city can appear quite daunting to pass through. Because of the rush hour time of my arrival, it takes me almost an hour to reach the hotel. Maylene had already set my final destination for the seventh elevation, all of which is parking for the hotel. As usual, my Sonars is taken away after I park it. I enter the main lobby of the hotel and take a quick peek at the directory. Most floors below the sixth elevation are office spaces that have been rented out. Two elevations are for parking, and then the hotel starts on the seventieth floor and goes almost all the way to the top, where there are offices that I am sure Edward uses when he is in town. The ring above the hotel are penthouse suites for hotel guests.

A small woman smiles as I enter. She has wide eyes and a pink headband that attempts to tame her wild hair. She looks quite young, almost as if this is her first job. "Hi! Welcome to the Canabana Hotel, Chlorofyx district," she says brightly. "Do you have a reservation?"

"Yes," I tell her. "Caldor."

She nods excitedly and punches data into her computer.

"Right, here you are!"

I hold out my phone to her. She takes it for a moment before handing it back to me.

"You're all set!" she says. "Your room is on the eighty-eighth floor, number 8808. I'm sure you know this, but you also have meal credits, so feel free to dine whenever you please!"

I smile at her.

"Not that you couldn't dine when you wanted, obviously," she hurriedly blurts out with a nervous laugh. I chuckle inside, feeling for her. "But I mean—"

"I know what you meant," I say gently.

She closes her mouth and smiles gratefully.

"Have a nice stay," she tells me.

I thank her and start to walk down the hall towards the elevators. One of the lift doors open. I see a well-kept face and slick black hair that I recognize.

Daden smiles and says, "Well, well, well." He steps out of the elevator and walks up to me. He holds out his hand. "Is this real? I finally get to meet, face-to-face, the one and only, Arch Caldor."

10

"Nice to meet you," I say as I give Daden a firm handshake. He squints his face, almost as if in disgust, but he smiles genuinely. He releases my hand but casually caresses my fingers as he does so.

I ignore it. He holds his smile. I understand why he and Andre are together. They both have a flirtatious nature, but Daden is far more reserved, his flirting apparently subtle to onlookers.

"Come, let me give you a tour of our finer establishments," he says, gesturing for me to follow him down the hall. I sigh quietly to myself, swing the strap of my bag over my shoulder, and nod my head.

We go through a set of double doors. I hear a small click as the doors shut behind us. Even the echoes of our footsteps are quiet in here. The hall is well lit. The carpet is a clean indigo, while the walls are mostly off-gray and striped.

Daden leads me down most of the hallway before saying anything. We turn a corner and walk along the edge of the building, with large windows to my left that overlook the marvelous city. It reminds me of the hotel where I was attacked. I push the image of the building collapsing out of my mind.

"You can tell by their plain design that these are our low-end rooms, but what they offer in size and exquisiteness is so grand that most other hotels can't even come close to comparing." There is a snobbish attitude in the way Daden speaks, but I wouldn't think it is meant to offend anyone. With what he is saying, he probably treats all guests with the same respect. It might just be that he's proud of the hotel he runs.

"Let's visit the Earthling," he says as he pushes the button to call the elevator.

"What's that?"

Daden smiles widely. Obviously, he was hoping I'd ask. The elevator arrives, and we step in.

"It's our most popular restaurant, with its design and food style based on our good friends back on Earth! It took a lot of research, having to collect the photographs they sent us and learning about the kind of food they serve," he explains. "It is quite sad that they seem so behind on their technology. I hear that their Sonars are on wheels and can only drive on the ground! What horror!" He looks aghast for a moment. "Alas, that is why I was born here, on Talvor, as I could never survive such a peasant-like, unsophisticated world. But we've sent them our vehicle designs and roads, so they should be upgrading their technology any time now."

I chuckle. "But weren't they the ones who sent us a computer program so powerful that it could change our world into something so slave-like?"

I try to speak like him, but it doesn't flow well.

"You mean such as the very one that you carry on you? Let's not speak of it now."

He doesn't say anything else. The doors open, and he walks down the center of the large atrium. We are on the ninety-seventh floor.

"You do have it on you, right?" he asks, his curiosity getting the best of him. There is something more inquisitive about his voice that I don't like.

I shrug. "Yeah, it's in one of my bags. I'm pretty sure it's in my other one, the one I left in my Sonars."

"Hmm," he says, smiling again. "That's probably very safe, and it isn't like *this* hotel is gonna collapse."

I don't appreciate his attempt at humor.

We reach a narrow part of the atrium, where the windows are foggy from this side. There is a large red door, decorated with gold trim, before us.

"Well, we have arrived," Daden says with a bad attempt at an even voice. He's too excited. I don't understand the man. He works here and probably sees this restaurant at least three times a day.

He lets me push open the door. I do.

Inside is what seems to be half of the entire floor. Steps lead down to the seating area. Live trees are planted all around, vines hang from the ceiling, and there is a river that runs right through. As this building is circular in design, the whole crescent side overlooks the city, while the wall behind me is a large holographic screen that shows a silent tour of what I take to be Earth. I wouldn't even know where we got those video recordings of Earth, but if anyone had them, it would be Edward Canabana.

Earth seems to be very similar to Talvor. Daden was right, though. They appear to be years behind us in technological advancement. Their cities are nowhere near as large, though some are bigger than the small towns we have. They have an abundance of natural landscapes that vary throughout the planet. Apparently, there are only a few places that speak the same language we do, but a few stand out as ancient languages that we used to speak, such as Latin, Chinese, and Greek.

There are some weird names for places with just as unusual a language, such as Mexico — and underneath it says the language they speak is Spanish.

"Mex-eye-co seems like such a beautiful place," Daden says. "And I wonder what that Spaynish language sounds like, but I imagine it to be very romantic."

I don't respond. I look back to the videos. From what I can tell, Earth has cities that are much closer together than ours are currently. We used to look like that, though, but soon we got so populated that many cities became one.

A butterfly passes in front of me. It is quite large, and it is brown in color.

"What's with the butterflies?" I ask, looking around and noticing a lot more.

"Apparently butterflies are considered a great part of nature on Earth," Daden answers.

"But we have butterflies here, and we even call them the same thing."

Daden nods. "I believe that is the point. Mr. Canabana envisions a great future where Talvor and Earth work together; where we could travel back and forth. While Earth has several differences from our world, we also have so much in common. I believe that is the theme Edward wanted to bring to this restaurant."

We walk down the stairs and along the path woven into the carpet. We pass over the small, arched bridge that crosses the river. He sits me down in a private booth by the window.

"There is a lot more of the hotel that I would like to show you," Daden says. He doesn't sit down but stands next to me. "Unfortunately, I don't have the time at the moment, but if you're not too tired later tonight, you can always call me."

He hands out his phone. I tap mine to his, regretting it immediately.

"If not, there is no pressure. I am sure when you're finished with the job, dear Andre will bring you out here. And hopefully at that time, you won't be so pressed for time."

Daden barely smiles before walking away.

I don't wait long until someone comes over and asks me if I am ready to order. I quickly look over the menu and ask for the "American Burger" meal.

"Good choice," the waiter says. "You're in for a surprise." He flashes his teeth at me with a smile before walking away. I am served a water shortly after that. I am then served a small salad with thin pieces of shredded cheese, though it isn't like any cheese that I've seen. It tastes good, though. When the burger comes, I am a little taken aback by its size. Grease drips from it.

"Don't worry, it won't kill you," the server says with a wink. My waiter comes back and tells me the same thing. For a moment, I think they are going to wait until I take a bite out of it, but they both walk away. I brave it.

With the first bite, it tastes almost just like any other burger I've had, though there are more juices in this one. With the second bite, it becomes something else.

There are strips of bacon; crunchy, tasty, and greasy all at the same time. An egg pops and leaks its yolk out, covering my hands and spilling over my mouth and down my chin. There is a red substance that leaks out, and I find that it is some kind of ketchup, but has other flavors involved.

I wipe my hands after the bite and keep eating. My hands get all messy again, and this time I don't care.

My waiter was right. This is delicious. I don't understand why we don't make all our burgers like this.

I am served a plate of "French fries" with seven different dipping sauces. I've had fries before as served on Earth, but these are even better. My burger plate is left there by the waiter. Getting the idea of what to do next, I scoop up some of the leftovers with my fries. After trying each sauce, I can't choose a favorite, so I keep using them all.

When I am done with those, all the plates and small bowls are taken away. They are replaced by a small plate with a chocolate round cake on it. I use my fork to cut off a piece. Warm, melted chocolate leaks out. It's all chocolate, and it all tastes so good. I don't even clean my hands.

I am then served more water to wash everything down.

By the time I finish this plate, I feel extremely full and ready for bed. My waiter thanks me for dining and gives me moist wipes to clean my hands. I use them, and then I get up to leave.

I find my way back to the elevator and go to the floor my room is in. The hallway is the same color as the one on the seventieth floor, but the rooms are more spaced apart, indicating that they are much larger. The doors also have gold trim around the room numbers.

8808

I unlock my room and enter it. This is almost just one wide room, with a decent-sized bathroom to my right. There is a bed in the center, looking out the window. The city looks busy as ever, Sonars flying through the air and buildings reaching higher than this one, while others are not quite making the cut. I walk up to the window and stare out. My phone rings. I answer it, connecting it to the window screen so I can see Maylene.

"I am taking it that you've made it, and all is well," she says. She looks like she is in a Sonars, though she doesn't appear to be driving.

"Yeah," I breathe out. "This hotel is something else. This city is amazing. I've passed through it before, but I never realized how brilliant it is."

Maylene smiles. "Yes, Chlorofyx is something else."

I turn to look at the camera so that she can see that I'm looking at her.

"So where are you?" I ask. "I heard you were near Chlorofyx."

"Yes, I am just about forty kilometers north of you," she tells me. "I just made a quick personal stop before heading back to Candalance. But Edward needed something, so it worked out."

"Candalance is pretty far, though, isn't it?" I ask.

"Yeah, but I don't mind the drive," she tells me. "But with the distance growing between us," she stops speaking for a moment. We look at each other and laugh briefly.

"It is likely that both Matt and I are going to relocate somewhere near NEAST, just so we can be nearby in case you need anything," she goes on, the serious tone returning.

I nod, smiling. I look out the window again.

"Hold on a minute," Maylene says. The screen goes black for a moment before turning back on. Maylene walked out of her Sonars. I can't see her too well, but I can tell she lies on the ground outside. From the images projected to me, I can tell she is somewhere away from a city, surrounded by trees. The camera looks up to the sky. I can clearly see the stars, and because of the lack of light pollution, I can see the swirling mists of colorful clouds way out in the deep vastness of space.

"It is beautiful out there," Maylene says. "I hope one day we actually get to travel the galaxy. Earth would be nice, I guess. But there must be so much more out there."

I keep standing there. I know Maylene isn't looking at me. I look out across the city and back to the stars from Maylene's phone.

"I'm sure we will," I tell her. "With everything that we've accomplished, I am sure we're just years away. For all we know, NEAST already has a way for us to travel the stars."

I feel like I can see Maylene smile.

"Would you find out for me?" she asks. "I'm sure Edward's contact there can spill a few secrets."

"You mean you don't know?" I ask, chuckling. "I thought you knew everything."

Maylene sighs. "When it comes to Edward's work, yes. I know everything. But NEAST itself is a whole different world. Even Edward doesn't know all that happens there."

I nod, agreeing. "But I'm sure he knows more than he lets on."

"Probably," Maylene says.

We let the silence speak for us for a little while. I still stand there, letting the fullness of the food and the calmness of the city view consume me. Of course, the silence doesn't last. Maylene speaks again, though I can't help but smile when she does.

"I heard you met a girl," she says.

"That loudmouth," I say loudly. "Matt mention something to you?"

"You can't blame him," she says. "He's excited for you! And so am I. Who would have thought that during this *dangerous* mission you would have time for romance."

I shrug. "I don't even know how it happened. But I am glad it did."

"What's her name?"

"Kaedy," I tell her.

"That's a nice name," Maylene says. "I should tell Andre, just so he can tell Daden about her. Knowing him, he's probably made some moves on you." She laughs. So do I.

"Just the one," I say. "But I ignored it."

"Just play with him," Maylene says, then laughs loudly. "Oh, that sounded so bad. I mean, he's in love with Andre and is devoted to him. He would never cheat, but he likes flirting, so just flirt back. He would appreciate that." I hear her, but I don't intend to flirt with Daden.

I look out at the city again.

"Maybe it just doesn't come naturally to me."

"Or you just don't like him as much."

I don't answer. Maylene grabs her phone and looks at it. I can see her, though it is still quite dark.

"You probably just need to spend an afternoon getting drunk with him," she laughs. "Then you'll like him more."

"Yeah, probably," I say. "He's fine; he's just a bit odd. I get why he and Andre are together, though."

"They are kinda cute," Maylene says.

I nod, though she can't see me as she's already turned her phone to face the stars again.

"I should get going to bed," I say.

"Did you try the Earthling restaurant?"

"Yup," I say, choking down a burp. "I think it's making me sleepy."

"Yeah, that'll do it for ya," Maylene says. "And then will come the shits. I suggest you don't leave until you've released it all. It will come suddenly, and it will be powerful." I laugh. Maylene gets up from lying on the forest ground and walks back into her Sonars. "I should be getting to bed soon too. And here's a tip for leaving tomorrow: wait until mid-morning. That way, you miss the morning rush traffic."

"Will do," I say. "Have a good night."

"You too," she says before clicking off.

I spend some more time staring out the window. I want to call Kaedy, but I hold myself back. I know she's busy, and while she would likely answer my call, I don't want to distract her.

There are two locations on Talvor where the skies show off the "space clouds," as I call them. Chlorofyx just misses that, but we are close enough that the night sky still has hues of pink and blue in it, even though it's hard to see with all the city lights.

I move away and take a long shower. Afterwards, I do some pushups, just to get a head start on working out with Matt. While

I am quite sleepy, I don't feel ready for bed, so I look out the window again.

I check my phone and look at my next destination. Maylene is sending me north, and I will spend tomorrow night in Papilene. My course of travel appears to be more direct now, probably due to the fact that I am late for the delivery. If I had it my way, I would just travel all night long and get it over with, though I know it is unhealthy to do so.

I send Kaedy a message, asking how her trip is going and, if she makes it to Chlorofyx soon, if she wants to get breakfast. As I figured, I don't get any response. I'm sure I will wake up to her reply.

Lying down on my back, I stare up at the ceiling. There is a mural of mountains and skies on it. I daze off, letting my mind wander before my eyes feel heavy. When I am ready to pass out, I slid underneath the covers. I set an alarm for early morning, wanting to have time for Kaedy if she responds. Either way, the end of this mission can't come any sooner. It almost feels as if I won't have much of a purpose when this is done. That thought doesn't scare me the way it would have. It excites me because I know I can find more meaning in my life and make something of it.

11

As I guessed she would, Kaedy responds sometime in the middle of the night. When I wake to relieve myself of what Maylene warned me, I see her text telling me that she would not be able to make it in time for breakfast. I reply now, telling her that it's okay and that I'll see her soon. With that said and done, I go back to sleep for a couple of hours.

After getting up slowly, with the mid-morning sun glaring through the window, I take a peaceful shower. I didn't notice it last night, but the tile in the shower is a mural of mermaids resting on a rock in the sun, much like turtles do.

I don't feel much like having an other-worldly experience for breakfast, so I check out the other restaurants in the hotel on my phone. There is one on the twenty-second floor. It technically isn't part of the hotel, but meal credits for guests are valid. Not that I would have cared either way, but it seems like the most relaxing option.

It takes over ten minutes to get there, but luckily, once I get out of the hotel, I notice that there are lifts that are able to take you to any floor below.

The café is quaint, with rounded and curved walls creating a cozy vibe that otherwise shouldn't exist in a place so large. There are many people inside, but with the layout, I still feel closed off from the world. It isn't too much to ask to spend a morning alone before

I head out on the last stretch of my assignment, so I appreciate the design. I call it the last stretch, even though I still have some more days to go, though I forget exactly how many are planned.

I order flat cakes with poached eggs on top. I suppose because the restaurant is inside a Canabana Hotel, they follow the same rules of having someone take your order, rather than it all being computerized.

My food gets served to me with a small side salad of only leafy greens. All kinds of syrup flavors are readily available to me. As I eat, I think about how Kaedy would have loved these flat cakes. Maylene also would, though she might not admit it immediately. I'm not sure that Matt would eat them, and I almost feel guilty thinking about it. But I have another week or so before I start my physical training with Matt. So, a cheat meal every once in a while — or every day until then — won't be an issue. Plus, I did pushups last night. *I'm good*, I lie to myself.

A petite woman takes my plate away and thanks me for choosing the restaurant.

I head back up to the hotel. I grab my stuff from my room and head out. A dark-skinned lady looks up as I walk out. She's gorgeous; with her dark hair and dark eyes, she almost looks pure. Not pure in some weird way, just pure.

"Mr. Canabana thanks you for your stay, and he hopes you enjoyed your time with us!" she calls out, smiling brilliantly and genuinely sounding happy. I give her a nod of thanks and awkwardly force a smile out, which she replies by holding her smile.

Even now, I manage to be so weird. I guess it's just who I am.

I'm not the only one heading out of the hotel. Most of these guests are probably here for multiple nights and are just leaving for the day, but I notice that there are a lot of ethnically diverse people about. It might just be the city; being so large and overwhelmed in population, people from all over the world must have come here to start a new life, follow opportunities or dreams, or take a vacation.

Chlorofyx is one of the most expensive places to live, though the city itself does pretty well for its citizens, and it boasts one of the lowest homeless rates of all Talvor. There are rumors, though, that claim the municipality relocates homeless people elsewhere, though not one person has claimed that they were relocated, and as such, that rumor may not be true.

I drive a bit more into the city while I head for a Platform Station. I go down to the lower elevations as all the stations I passed by were so packed that there were lines backing up the roadways. I'm still well packed with snacks and beverages, so I just stand outside my Sonars while it charges. There is a news story playing, interspersed with irrelevant and low-budget ads about life tips or discounts on cheap food from the snack bars. I watch the news portion absent-mindedly and tune out the entirety of the commercials. Something catches my ear.

"The CEO of Helioux Weapons was found guilty of allegations of misconduct, and despite his claims of innocence, the evidence is apparently *overwhelming*. Unfortunately, details of the allegations have not been disclosed, and Jay Mingun will be sentenced via private trial."

The news reporter seems out of breath and looks quite uncomfortable, but he continues to read his script, moving on to other news.

Helioux Weapons is one of the two most prominent and successful military-grade manufacturers in the world, and they have been working on a project with NEAST, though they have been largely confidential and details are kept tightly under wraps.

A faint bell sounds, alerting me that my Sonars is now fully charged. I take a step towards it, ready to leave.

The ground shudders for a moment and then kicks back with a jolt. For just a brief second, the glowing lights making up the roads and elevations flicker. Again, the ground shudders. Everything seems to go quiet, despite the several Sonars moving about; most people not noticing a thing.

I look around. There are only a few people doing the same. Even many of the people who are also charging their Sonars don't notice anything. I walk right up to my Sonars and open the door, ready to get in. I steal another glance, this time looking out into the city. Layers of elevations line the skyline, all packed and full of Sonars making their way through the city.

The Sonars beyond the Platform Station drop from the sky. Cascading down with no warning, Sonars and Ships alike plummet to the ground below. As in waves, the vehicles closer to me follow suit.

I frantically jump into my Sonars and get the engine going. I'm not fast enough. The door is still open and I free-fall down. Warning lights flash and sound. I cling to the small steering wheel, willing my Sonars to move forward.

By some miracle, the Sonars hover in the air again. Everything is still for a moment. So many vehicles lay on the ground, completely demolished from the impact. I don't understand how so many Sonars became defective.

This is just the beginning.

As we all sit still in the still traffic, recovering from the fear of plummeting to an instant death, the skyscrapers sitting on the fifth elevation wobble. I stare out into the distance, focusing on the top of one of the shorter buildings. It drops just a bit.

My heart begins to hammer against my chest. I know what's happening, and it's always been one of my greatest fears.

I punch the accelerator, not wanting to be anywhere near this disaster.

Disaster comes too quick.

A sight of horror. The tallest of the buildings come crashing down. The elevations they sit on falter. Some areas remain intact until the colossal weight of the structures break through them.

Most of the Sonars that remain are safe, though some are unlucky and are crushed beneath a falling building. There are some other people like me, racing as fast as possible to get out of the city.

My Sonars' warning alarm sounds constantly, alerting me of potential collision after potential collision. I quickly tell CHAD to turn off any automated braking mechanisms.

It is impossible to see how far I am from the city boundaries. Quickly looking in my rearview mirror, I can see the Canabana Hotel still standing tall, just like the other buildings that are built from the ground all the way up.

Unfortunately, there are buildings that stand on solid ground that are being crushed by the buildings that had been suspended above them.

I quickly drop to the first elevation to avoid being crushed. I weave between structures and other vehicles. There are some emergency responders coming out, but they aren't going anywhere but up. One of them is unable to avoid a chuck of metal and is pinned down.

I do the same thing; I start heading up, almost vertically. I spin around falling debris, narrowly missing a jagged slab of concrete. Looking down for a moment, I have no idea how I survived this long. The first elevation is almost entirely covered in debris, with demolition dust still rising into the air, making it harder to see.

The higher I go, the larger the remains of the building materials are. Some of the structures were only about thirty stories tall, so they rose just three elevations. In addition to those collapsing, many were also crushed beneath larger structures that stood above them.

A pulse penetrates my Sonars, and I can feel the change in the electromagnetism in the atmosphere. Once again, my Sonars fails, and I plummet from the fifth elevation.

Frantically, I press all the buttons I can and push the accelerator, steering the wheel in all directions. Nothing happens. I spin out of control. In the seconds I have to see upwards towards the sky, I notice a four-story house falling towards me. My Sonars won't move in any direction except down. Everything is off, and I can't get the systems back on again.

Reigniting suddenly, my Sonars returns to power. I had my foot on the initial accelerator, and I launch forward at a slight decline. I am pressed back by the momentum. I pull away from the accelerator and move a lever that flips my Sonars about forty-five degrees. I shoot up. Adjusting my direction, I steer the Sonars into another vertical ascent. By this time, most of the structures have already fallen.

I look down. The last remaining ones seem to fall in slow motion. They hit the ground or the wreckage and disintegrate into clouds of dust.

For a moment, I feel safe from the pandemonium. I don't understand how most of the Sonars remain in the air, when they were the first to fall. Maybe taking out Sonars wasn't the intention. That is one thing I know for sure. This is no accident.

Taking a breath, I look around. The city is gone, save for the buildings that survived the attack, and those are only the ones that stood tall enough from the ground that they were mostly unharmed, though some of them were hit by the other structures and, while still standing, are heavily damaged.

There are more Sonars zipping about than I figured there would be. In my desperate attempt to escape, I didn't notice how many others were trying to as well. Most of the Sonars are flying straight out of the city, not knowing what else to do. Some are hovering in the air, like me, wondering what just fucking happened.

The last EMP confirmed that this was an attack. Someone wants to destroy the city, and they found something strong enough to disengage the elevation barriers and electromagnetic systems that support the city. Knowing how strong the EMPs must have had to be to cause this much damage, especially knowing that these support systems and structures are heavily guarded against such attacks, I wonder if had I been close to the source of any, would it have physically affected me. There is absolutely no way that these blasts were solely electromagnetic.

The emergency response vehicles appear from above this elevation. They had gone to the only place they could be safe, but now they have more work than they can manage.

A laser blast bolts past me, flipping my Sonars around. It hits one of the Department of Fire Emergencies vehicles. The bus blasts apart. After stabilizing my Sonars, I look in the direction it came from. Another beam shoots towards me. I turn off my systems to plunge my Sonars towards the ground to avoid it. It narrowly misses, skirting just over my Sonars. I turn my vehicle back on, suspending it in the air again.

The blast shoots off, missing everything, and goes beyond the city where it eventually makes contact with something. Due to the slow rise of smoke, the beam must have hit the trees far beyond the city.

Knowing I don't have time to do this, I look again at where the blast came from. Three military-edged Sonars drop in, heading towards me. The vehicles are shaped like missiles, rounded and curved in design to keep their mass small, making them harder to hit when attacking them, but they have wings that can emerge from most sides, making any maneuver for aerial combat a quick feat.

Punching the initial accelerator, I shoot away from the Sonars, making my way out of the city. I am at a huge disadvantage. There is nothing to help me lose them, and their Sonars are so much faster than mine.

They are right on my tail, surely attempting to lock onto me so that their next attack doesn't miss.

Remembering that I now have a Sonars from Edward, I ask CHAD if I have any governmental-right power in my Sonars.

Annoying but extremely helpful, CHAD tells me that my Sonars is equipped with the latest military technology that most of the armed forces don't even employ yet, but that the systems are turned off and locked unless I am in an emergency. My heart drops for a moment. If the Sonars doesn't know that it's an emergency at the moment, would I be able to turn them on? I am about to see if I can call Maylene when CHAD asks me if I would like to activate them.

"Yes! YES!" I shout, spinning my Sonars around to avoid another laser.

"Activated," CHAD responds.

I punch the accelerator again. The increase in velocity is very noticeable, and I push it harder. I propel forward, increasing the distance between myself and the guys after me. Unfortunately, they do the same and quickly catch up, but now my Sonars is just as quick.

I move my Sonars sideways, trying to throw them off target. It works to the degree that all of the shots they fire miss me, but they are still on my tail and gaining on me. I shift the gears, throwing the throttle into full force, and blast out of the city.

The Sonars still follow me.

Most of the survivors have left the city and are well in the distance now. Only the responders remain, but I am out of their range. The Impositioners have another matter to deal with, and don't notice the vehicles chasing after me.

I pull the lever and rotate the vehicle. The sudden change at this speed creates so much G-Force that I feel like I'm unconscious for a moment. The other vehicles are unable to follow me, and I lose them for just a bit.

Chlorofyx seems so far away now, though the smoke from the debris begins to clear out that I can see the remains, looking as if a bomb had detonated just over the city. It has been years since there have been any wars. Before my father's lifetime, even. Uniting the governments made it easier to control each other. And since the different countries are run separately, it would seems like they are commanded by a single entity, though most people know this is not true.

Only in my history lessons in school have I seen anything like this destruction. Something big is happening now. And I am the one carrying the reason for it.

The Sonars rise into view behind me. They shoot towards me, accelerating faster than they had before. Still, I press forward, chasing away from them. The remains of Chlorofyx are parallel to my line of flight. An aircraft looms in the distance, but it speeds in my direction. I don't know if it is a friend or something else, so I move away from it.

My screen turns on. Maylene's frantic face comes into view.

"Arch, I—"

The screen turns off, and she cuts out. I try to call her back again, but it doesn't work.

A beam shoots towards me. I move out of the way, but it isn't a laser blast like the others. This one is a constant output of energy, and it moves, tailing me and destroying everything it hits. It dies out before it reaches me. I look over at the aircraft. Definitely not a friend. I do my best to fly out of there, but I am already going as fast as I can. Luckily, the large aircraft can't keep up, but its firing range can.

The three Sonars that tail me turn into five. Some dip out of sight. They're trying to circle me. I go down and turn, trying to prevent any from coming up underneath me. It works. For a moment, I can see the five of them behind me. The aircraft shoots another beam, but this misses me completely, and it quickly dies out. I have the advantage over that. It will take some time to recharge. I just need to get as far away as possible from it so that it doesn't have a chance to hit me. A laser grazes over my Sonars. The impact jolts me a bit, but I mostly stay on course. There are now seven Sonars coming after me.

An eighth one drops down in front of me. I duck beneath it. Its fire shoots towards one of the other Sonars, but another blast hits me, and I am knocked off course, spinning. My Sonars recovers quickly. Emergency lights go off and the warning sounds blare through the speakers.

"Imminent and unavoidable impact detected, activating defense measures."

The Sonars voice speaks out, this time a woman's voice. It has shut down CHAD.

"Override!" I shout, not wanting the Sonars to take control.

"Override denied, closing Sonars in five...."

I unbuckle, knowing that the Sonars is now on autopilot. I have to get to my stuff. I don't know much about the defense systems, but I do know that the vehicle will close itself off and create shields to absorb any impact from attacks.

Another blast hits the Sonars. The hit knocks the Sonars to the side, causing me to slam into the side window.

"...two, one."

I reach out instinctively, trying to grab my bag, the things that carries the chip. Doors that I didn't know existed shut. I am relieved that my reach was short, as my arm would have been chopped in half. The Sonars breaks off into three parts, all independent of each other.

For the moment, the attacks stop. Shields go up around the cabin. I can see the faint blue hue of them.

The vehicles chasing me go after the cabin that holds my bag, leaving me alone. They shoot it down and five of them chase after it.

"Deploying pads," my Sonars calls out.

Another blast hits me, and I bang against the ceiling. Then the pads activate, cushioning me from any other blast.

With a second beam, my Sonars plummets to the ground. I can't see out any of the windows. All I can see is the beige color of the cushion pads that will attempt to save me from any impact while the shields try to absorb the shock. My stomach rises as I fall. The cabin increases its speed of descent. My body is suspended for a moment. My cab hits the ground. The shields absorb what they can but then falter. The force of impact slams me into the ceiling cushion. There is so much force that I feel the solid wall behind the cushion. My eyes water, and my vision fades for a moment. I grunt before I slam back against the ground. With one last jolt of impact, I can't even let out a small groan before everything disappears.

12

There is a knocking on the metal. The cushioned bags that protected me from hard impact have deflated. My face is pressed against the skin of the airbag, and beneath that is the cold floor. Or ceiling. Wall, maybe. The cabin I lay in had been turned around, flipped, and thrown into the ground without regard for what was inside. Which was me. I can feel the coolness of the metal seep up through the fabric and into my face. I let out an involuntary shiver. The knocking continues, firmly done, but with how thick the outer shell of the Sonars is, it sounds like an annoying tapping.

For all I know, I am dreaming it. Nothing that I know is real. I feel like I am sleeping, and the thought of waking up isn't pleasant. In my half-dream-like state, I can feel the physical pain encroaching on my moment of bliss. I fully remember everything that happened. Part of me thinks I'm dead. The other part knows I'm not.

The tapping ceases. My eyes are still closed. With each second that passes, I become more awake. I reach the point of consciousness, but I keep my eyes shut. There is no need to return to reality at the moment.

That choice apparently isn't mine to make.

I hear the tearing of metal, crunching, and almost the sound of something I can only describe as *scranking*. Discordant. A disturbance to the peace, if you will.

Beyond my closed eyes, I can see the light overcome the dark view that I was enjoying so much.

Something is heaved off into the distance. I hear a soft thump as it hits what I imagine to be grass. The next thing I hear is silence, a silence that almost sounds disappointed. There are eyes on me. I don't know if it is a friend or foe, though I suppose if it were a foe, I'd be dead by now.

"Are you going to keep me waiting?"

It's Maylene. I can tell by her voice. I pretend to be asleep, not wanting to do anything right now.

"I know you're awake," she says with a sigh. "I can see you breathing; your back keeps rising and falling. If I didn't know any better, you recently regained consciousness."

Grudgingly, I open my eyes. Everything is blurry for a moment. I try to push myself up. It doesn't work. Good thing too, because I don't feel like getting up.

Maylene hops down into the cockpit. She turns me over. I quickly close my eyes again. Maylene lightly slaps my face.

"Hey, we have to get you out of here," she says. "Get up!"

I sit up and groan. My arms rest on my knees, hands in front of them hanging down. I keep my head low. I don't want to face Maylene. I failed. How could I ever see my friends again? They counted on me so much, and I couldn't keep my promise. I have to start a new life, which sucks, because I was really liking the one I have.

"If we don't get moving, we're going to be in a lot of danger."

"Fine."

I stand up. Using all of my willpower, I look over to her. My eyes are set, almost in anger. There is anger there. And sadness.

Maylene displays one of the most compassionate faces I've ever seen. She doesn't look disappointed. She doesn't look angry or even melancholic.

"Up we go," she says, hopping up over the hull. She balances on it, reaching her hand down, though I know she isn't meaning to pull me up.

I grab the top of it and pull myself up. Maylene jumps down onto the ground, and I follow her. My legs, still half asleep, do not support my falling weight, and I collapse onto the singed grass. I quickly stand up.

The world around me is a mess. Fields of nature, tall-growing grass, and thin trees are mostly destroyed. Small fires still burn, though they have trouble growing. Scraps of metal are littered along the floor. The cab I was in is just a small part of what used to be my Sonars. I look around. I can see one of the other pieces that broke off when the vehicle knew it was about to be destroyed. That one seems the most intact, even though it was the end piece.

"Do you have it?" she asks. There is nothing accusing in her tone. It was just a question.

I shake my head.

She looks around. Maylene is smart. She knows that it was in my bag and is likely inside the part of the cabin that shielded itself off from the cockpit. I follow her as she looks around. As much turmoil that lies scattered across the ground, the sections of the Sonars are quite easy to discern from the rest. The sections are so intact that I have trouble understanding where the other scraps of metal are from.

We pass by a tree that had been ripped in half. Its now-short trunk stands splintered, looking as if it had been beheaded. For all intents and purposes, it has been. Its top lies near it, with branches broken off and leaves so surplus that they still spin around in the weak wind.

I spot it.

"There," I say, pointing off to my right. Maylene rushes over to it. I don't follow her with the same speed. From here, I can see it quite clearly. Like what Maylene had done to the sections I was in, this one has been ripped open. I can see my bag tossed on the ground, mostly mangled.

Maylene looks inside the bag and then inside the cabin. She looks at me and shakes her head. She doesn't have to. I already knew it. Those who came after me got what they wanted. The chip is no longer in our possession. They knew it was there. But how?

There is something that I don't know yet, and the questions burn in my mind. I don't know why. There's nothing I can do about what's been done.

"What lies in the aftermath?" I ask her.

Maylene walks up to me. "Nothing you want to hear," she says.

"I know, but I still want to know," I tell her firmly.

Maylene sighs. "The current death toll sits at three million. There are only a few buildings that remain, but none are intact. Not even Edward's hotel. Rescue missions and evacuations continue in the city. There isn't a single vehicle left there that is operational. Anyone who couldn't make it out is trapped there."

Three million. And that number is likely climbing fast.

"We need to go," Maylene tells me. She gently grabs my hand and pulls me towards the Sonars she came in. Numbly, I follow her.

I step on a thin slice of debris. It cuts into my ankle, and I start bleeding. I can't even feel the pain. Somehow, I was left only badly bruised when my Sonars crashed. That is, until now. Adrenaline fuels all my movement, but I know it's wearing off.

Maylene notices. "You okay?" she asks.

The cut isn't deep. "I'm fine," I tell her. "Let's just keep going."

Maylene landed her Sonars away from the field of trees and debris. I'm amazed that she found me so quickly. The sun is beginning to set, but it must have only been a few hours since I was blacked out. Her Sonars is of a larger size, almost like a transport van. The front latch opens upward, and a ramp with a gentle slope rolls out. She runs in and comes back out as I step onto the ramp. She stops me, kneels down, and wraps a bandage around my ankle to stop the bleeding.

I had forgotten that I cut myself.

The cut is deeper than I thought. I start to feel lightheaded, but I hide that as best I can from Maylene. I can't tell if she notices. If she does, she says nothing of it. My stomach feels weird.

When I sit down on a small couch behind the front seats, Maylene starts the engines. The couch has dark cushions, all one seat, though there are stitches in the seams to present four seats in total. We rise into the air before Maylene accelerates, elevating us as we move forward.

"Strap in," she says. "This Sonars looks like a military operations ship, so we will be moving quite fast."

I buckle one of the straps over my chest.

"Where are we going?" I ask her.

"Candalance," she answers.

"Candalance?" I ask in disbelief, just as I did when I was there last. "It feels like I'm restarting this whole journey."

"Without the chip, we are."

I shut up. I swallow my disappointment in myself so that I may choke out a single word.

"Sorry."

Maylene turns around. She punches a button on her dashboard and walks over to me.

"This isn't your fault," she tells me.

"They got me, I lost the chip, and an entire city has been reduced to rubble."

Maylene sits next to me.

"That isn't your fault. Someone found out that you were carrying that weapon and discovered that you were in Chlorofyx. Those things are not your fault. If anything, they're mine."

I don't say anything.

"And you aren't responsible for the city; whoever attacked it is."

"We don't know who attacked?"

Maylene shakes her head sadly. "Matt is working on that right now."

"But still, three million people."

"Yes. This might sound harsh, but in a city of over fifteen million people, that is a really low number considering everything that happened."

"I didn't even know that it was possible to dismantle the roads and elevations like that."

Maylene sighs. "We didn't know it was possible either. Someone very powerful is behind this. Which makes the situation that much more dangerous."

I let out a breath. I knew I was holding it. My breathing is slow, my way of attempting to calm my nerves.

"So, what's the plan?" I ask.

"Well, we have to get the program chip back," she says. "I'm not sure how we're going to do it, but Edward told us that we must do everything we can to get it back. He's also working with his contacts to try to find it."

I sit there silently for a moment. Maylene stays with me. She won't need to return to the pilot's seat for a while.

"I think I need some rest," I say.

"You'll get it," Maylene assures me. "Do what you can with what we have to rest now, but back in Candalance you will have a proper bed."

Maylene goes back to the driver's seat and disengages the autopilot. She doesn't turn back or speak to me. I know she is hoping to give me some rest. Rest isn't something I can get at the moment, despite how much I feel I need it. The seat is comfortable enough, but the straps put pressure against my chest. Normally I don't mind, but with my mind racing in all directions, the smallest things bother me tenfold more than they normally would.

I can feel my brain space out, though the nightmarish daydream flashes before my eyes. It's a funny feeling, being unconscious while simultaneously being wide awake. The half-rest I get makes me feel even more tired. My body begins to ache. The cut on my ankle stings. My head is pounding and my eyes are heavy, but they refuse to close.

With a sudden spasm, I jolt forward. The straps against my chest tighten, pulling me back. It was so sudden and I notice that Maylene jumps at the noise. She jerks her head back to look at me.

"Kaedy," I blurt out. "She was supposed to be in Chlorofyx."

Silence.

I can tell Maylene knows how worried I am and that she wants to help. Internally, she's battling with how to respond. I don't wait for her to. I unbuckle the straps. In my haste, I fall to the ground. I pull my phone out and make my call. My phone does not work. Evidently, it didn't survive the chaotic assault.

I hear a ring. I look around, still on all fours. Maylene is calling someone.

There is no answer.

"Who are you calling?" I ask, wanting to know if she's even helping me.

"Kaedy," she says. She turns back again to look at me. There is a simple expression on her face.

"I can alert some guys back in Chlorofyx to see if they can get any info on Kaedy, seeing as she didn't answer me." Maylene looks back out towards the sky.

"How did you get her number?

Maylene turns her head back towards me again.

"Dude," is all she says.

I look down at the floor. "Right," I say under my breath. I stand back up and walk over to the front. I sit down in the passenger seat.

"You don't want to get any sleep?" she asks me.

"I can't right now," I tell her. "Too much going on in my head."

Maylene sighs, but the tone of it was more of an understanding, not annoyance or tiredness.

"I told you, it isn't your fault," she says. "You can't beat yourself up over this."

I nod. "Unfortunately, that isn't even why I can't sleep," I say. "It's really gonna suck when the reality of that truly hits me."

Maylene nods. "Then what is it?"

"I—" The words are hard to come out. I don't know how to say it. "I don't know," I answer. There is something in the back of my mind trying to tell me something. I can't hear it.

Maylene keeps quiet. I appreciate her for it. It feels like there are a million places I should be. I force my eyes shut. Sleep doesn't come, but more physical pain does. With the adrenaline now quickly wearing off, I can feel my body hurting more and more. Nothing feels broken. Not yet, at least.

"How much longer?" I croak out.

"About four hours."

Four hours. That means we've been traveling a lot longer than it feels like. Another funny thing, waiting while your mind is flying in all directions, overthinking everything, and imagining only the worst.

Time feels impossibly still, yet it also feels faster than the speed of light.

We keep traveling. Maylene silences the calls she gets. She tells me that the ones who need to speak with her know what she's doing and where she's at. I nod, not really getting it but also not caring. Each time her phone rings, my head hurts more. I know I'm not in the right state of mind, so I keep all of my annoyances to myself. Her impatient tapping on the dashboard, the notification sounds she gets, the vehicle's various alerts — all of it. These things are completely normal, and right now I can't stand them.

I shift uncomfortably in my seat, pretending that I am trying to get some rest.

It must be some hours later when a return to consciousness overcomes me. I must have fallen asleep for a bit. My head feels hot, and I can feel the sweat all over my body. Something churns in my stomach. Everything that I should have felt earlier, I feel now. With no further warning, I retch. I fall over in the seat, hitting the ground as I vomit. I collapse fully to the ground, my face pressed against where my barf is spread across, chunks of it making the ground feel uneven. It is only for a moment that I can smell its stench. It makes me feel like I want to retch again.

My body begins to shake. First, it starts to vibrate, but it soon evolves into spasms. I can't swallow anything, and so my saliva spills out of my mouth. I feel my eyes roll back into my head. My heart is pounding fast. I vomit again.

I can sense that Maylene is frantically moving about, but I can't hear anything. I can see her shoes move in front of me and out of sight. But then my vision fades. All I want is for it to stop. I can't even feel the pain that I am in. I try to move my arms, attempting to stand up, but nothing happens. I have no control over my body.

If the color of pitch-black could blur, that's what I see now. Sound reaches my ears, but only in small spurts. Maylene is practically shouting, though I don't know at who or what. I can feel some sort of cloth under my cheek. Maylene must have put something there. I didn't notice when she did.

There is no longer a beating in my heart. Not one that I can feel anyway. Pain shoots up from my leg. I think I cry out, but I can't hear any sounds I make. A new sting shoots through my arm, starting somewhere in my shoulder area. The pain moves to my chest and tears through it. I scream. I can hear this one, but can't hear anything else.

Then everything stops. All I can sense is a still white frame in my mind that spins slowly. I don't even know how I can see it spinning.

Nothing else happens. Except I know everything does. Dichotomies. All I can sense are dichotomies. We're moving fast, yet we're not moving at all. I see nothing except white, but my mind fades to black. I can hear everything that is happening, yet the world remains silent. The ground presses against my body; I can feel the soft pillow under my head, yet I am suspended in limbo, touching nothing.

My back lies against something. That's funny. I thought I fell flat on my face. My perception heightens. My mind feels like it's in overdrive, in superhuman mode. The small details of the last hours hit my memory. I can feel the ghosts of the sharp pains, the moments I couldn't breathe, and the terrified screaming from Maylene's voice. I can remember the warmth of her breath as she bent down close to see if my heart was beating. I can feel her face press against my chest. Her hand on my head feels gentle, though her body trembles.

At this point I'm not sure if these are memories playing back, or the reality of the present. But then there is nothing.

I feel is an aching, dull pain. My head hurts. My body feels as if it is sore all over. I almost feel like I have a hangover. My eyes open. I am staring up at a white ceiling. My attempt to get up is useless. Three straps tie me down to the bed I'm in. I look around. With the silver walls of metal, the wide lights above, and the steel, raised bars around my bed, I think I've been committed to a mental hospital.

Patiently, I lie there, knowing it isn't the case. I don't know how much time passes. I have to pee, and then I do so. There's been a tube attached that drains my piss away.

I don't feel hungry, though I feel as if I haven't eaten in days.

This sucks.

I let out a sigh. As I do, the doors to the room glide open. Maylene walks in, followed by Matt and a young woman in lavender scrubs.

"How are you feeling?" the nurse lady asks me.

"Sore, and like I want to get out of here," I say, looking down at my body as best as I can.

"Sorry," Maylene says, and moves over to unstrap the restraints. Matt helps her.

When they are done, the nurse says, "These were used to make sure you did not seize again and fall over."

"What happened to me?" I ask.

Maylene shrugs. "Our best guess is that you got infected through that cut in your ankle."

"Due to the nature of the crash and its circumstances, it is highly likely you contracted the virus sometime between the initial major impact and when you boarded the ship Maylene rescued you on," the nurse says with a very definitive and scientific tone.

"The Kelcon Virus has killed people within one hour," says Maylene. "Most even faster than that."

"In other words, you are very lucky, Mr. Caldor," the nurse says. "Maylene's adrenaline injection followed by the anesthetic injection is most likely what bought you time to arrive here, and ultimately saved your life."

Maylene's lips curve into a small smile.

"I can't take the credit for that idea, though," she says. "Matt suggested it."

"In any case," the nurse says, changing her tone to slightly disapproving. "It was an unorthodox method, and I suggest not doing it again."

"I'd rather not get infected again," I say before sitting up.

"That would be best," the nurse says before turning around to walk out.

"What was your name?" I call out to her.

She turns her head back, gives me a short look, and says, "Caitlyn." She then walks out. The automatic door slides shut after her.

"You sure that you're okay?" Matt asks me. I look up at him. I swing my legs over the edge of the bed.

"Yeah, I'm fine," I tell him, feeling much better than I did, though I know I'm far from a hundred percent. I step down onto the ground. Matt makes a small movement as if he is about to catch me. I don't fall, and he doesn't touch me.

I'm about to ask them something, but Maylene answers, knowing what my question is.

"Two days," she says. "You've been here two days. Fed and hydrated through an IV. Once you stabilized, we had to make sure we fully cleared your system of the virus, so the only option was to have you put into a short, medically induced coma. Unfortunately, cleaning out your system meant that you, uh, essentially used the bathroom several times during your sleep."

An uncomfortable feeling comes over me.

"Here, I'll walk you to your room, and you can clean up," Matt says.

I gulp.

"Thank you," I tell them. "You guys have saved my life more than once."

"Come," Matt says after a short silence. We walk out of the patient room. The infirmary is located in the basement of the building. It feels like a long walk to the elevators, but I know we move at a slow pace. When we reach the elevators, Maylene gives me a gentle hug goodbye before walking off.

The doors open, and we step inside. Matt pushes the button for the ninetieth floor. "This elevator goes all the way to the hundredth floor, but only on the other side, so this way will be faster," he tells me.

I nod. We walk around some halls on the ninetieth floor before stepping into another lift.

"I'm sure you don't want to sleep at the moment, but take it easy," Matt tells me as he walks me to my suite. "You might feel fine now, but your body still needs rest to recover. I'll be nearby. Call if you need anything."

"Did we find the chip?" I ask.

Matt shakes his head. "No, but Edward believes it is being transported to the Tall Building, so we are working on a plan to retrieve it."

"Let me know when we have one," I tell him. "I want to go."

Matt laughs. "That's not necessary. It isn't your job," he tells me.

I shake my head. "It is now," I say. "I'm going to get that chip back."

Matt raises an eyebrow, but I can see a crack of a smile.

"Get some rest, Arch," he says. "I'll call you when I know something more." Matt closes the door behind him. I shift uncomfortably where I stand. There's an itch somewhere back there in my body. I move to scratch it. It doesn't take long for me to realize it's higher up in there than I thought it was.

Then I remember. But what? The thought is once again fleeting, and I feel that itch return.

I remove my clothes and take a long shower. I take a short bath afterwards and then clean up again with a quick rinse.

When I'm all done and dry, I lay on the same bed I used last time. Sleep doesn't come. It probably has to do with the fact that I slept for around forty-eight hours. Back in school, during what I considered to be one of the more useless classes, at least for me, I learned that people respond differently to being in a coma of any kind. I also learned that it was way worse decades ago, but medical advancements increased the chance of survival and quickened the recovery.

When sleep evades me after another attempt, I pace the room, looking out at the window. It had been late afternoon when I woke, and now the night view of the city dazzles with lights. All here seems quite normal. It is almost as if news of Chlorofyx hasn't yet reached Candalance. But that can't be. It was days ago, and an entire city collapsing isn't something that would not be broadcast to the rest of the world.

It hits me again.

Kaedy.

I hastily reach for my phone. It isn't on me. Right. I don't have one anymore. I haven't even dressed yet since washing myself. I scramble out into the main room. A phone sits on a pony wall near the entrance to the suite. Maylene must have left me a new one.

Before I can grab it, I get a call. It looks like Maylene was able to transfer all my data.

"Kaedy!" I shout into the microphone. "Are you okay?"

I am out of breath already.

"I was going to ask you!" she cries out. "I must have called you over fifty times! I'm back in Iccircus now."

Instinctively, I lower my phone and check the screen. Twenty-seven. Kaedy called me twenty-seven times.

"I-I'm sorry," I tell her.

She lets out an uneasy laugh. "Don't be. I'm just happy you're okay. I suppose you made it out of Chlorofyx. I never even made it in, and I'm grateful for that."

There's a short pause between us.

"Where are you now?"

"Candalance," I answer without thinking. My heart stops a beat. A horrible thought crosses my mind. It can't be. There's no way. But I can't be sure.

"Hey, I'm sorry to do this," I tell her. "I have to go. I'll call you soon, though."

I move the phone away from my ear. I can still hear her, though.

"Wait! Arch! How long are you going to be in Candalance for? Why didn't you answer my calls?"

I hang up.

The pain I feel inside is enough to kill me, more so than any Kelcon Virus can. My phone almost slips through my fingers. The world around me spins. My whole body begins to shake. This time, it isn't a seizure. I stare out blankly ahead. Conflicting thoughts barrage my mind, drowning out any silence or peace. The emotions that batter me — hate, anger, grief, hopelessness, foolishness, anguish — soar at supersonic speeds. I feel hot, burning with rage. I don't even know if it's true. There is no way Kaedy is behind any of this. But no matter how much I tell myself that, it does nothing to quell the feelings inside. She is the only other person that knew where I was headed.

I barge out of my room and down the hall.

13

Frantically, I look for Matt's suite, but there are no names on the doors. I swear loudly into the hall, my shout echoing into the emptiness. I pull out my phone to call him.

Matt shows up from his suite. I stare at him and then look back. I don't know how far I walked, but I can't see the door to my quarters.

"What's wrong?" he asks. There's a hint of worry in his eyes.

"Kaedy! She must have been behind this all along!" My words strain as I fight to raise my voice through the involuntary closing of my throat. "There's no other way it could have happened."

Matt stares at me incredulously and walks closer. I hear footsteps from behind.

"Is everything alright?" Maylene asks.

Matt talks over my shoulder. "He thinks Kaedy is behind Chloro-fyx."

Maylene places her hand gently on my shoulder. I fight the urge to throw her hand off me.

"How else?" I ask, but when they don't answer, I raise my voice again. "How else! How else did they know to go after me? How did they know I was there?"

Matt shrugs. "I-I don't know. But I did all my usual checks on her," he says. "And more. I didn't find any alarming ties."

"Well, maybe you missed something," I tell him coldly. He doesn't respond to the bait.

"Arch, we have no proof that she had anything to do with it," Maylene says, trying to reason with me.

"Here," Matt says, gesturing to walk back towards my room. I swat his arm away. There is a flash in his eyes of a momentary anger, but it disappears. "You need to get some rest," he tells me sternly.

I don't say anything.

"Arch, listen to him."

I look down at the ground and try to calm myself. Me. I blame me. As the anger flushes my face, I yell out and punch the wall. The wall is harder than steel, and I can hear my knuckles snap. The pain overwhelms me, and I can feel the tears form in my eyes. There isn't a dent in the wall, not even a meager scratch, but my wrist feel like it snapped.

"Hey," Matt says, this time grabbing me. He is gentle but has a firm grip. I am reminded of that night when I first met him and he saved me from that hotel. He and Maylene walk me back to my suite.

When we go inside, I hear Maylene tell Matt, "Go easy on him; he needs to rest." I can almost feel Matt nod.

He lets go of me as we walk into the bedroom on the first floor. Numbly, I walk over to the bed and fall face-first into it. I notice that Maylene doesn't follow us. Matt is silent for a little while.

"I know it seems bad," he says. The thoughts have been going around in my head on repeat. The tears in my eyes are no longer from the physical pain of hitting the wall. I don't move a muscle. I don't even let myself sniffle. He probably already knows it, but I can't let Matt see me cry.

"Tomorrow I will do some investigation and more background checks on Kaedy," he tells me. "But I don't think it was her. But I will find out who is responsible."

Still, I say nothing.

"I know you're still awake," he says with a quiet sigh. "I wish I could give you something to help you fall asleep, but I can't. It would be too dangerous after your time in the infirmary."

Again, I say nothing. I can feel my body wanting to sob, but I force it to be as still as possible. The tears still run down my cheeks. I listen carefully. Matt never leaves the room. I do my best to silence my thoughts, but to no avail.

After some hours, I feel tired enough that my mind runs through random memories. Some I don't even know if they are real. Kaedy pops into my mind again. I can sense the sadness in me, but I am too exhausted to truly feel anything.

Daring to move slightly, I turn my head just a bit to see if Matt is still there. His eye catches mine. He gives me a small, compassionate nod but otherwise holds his gaze. I turn away and shut my eyes. This time, I can feel the sleep arrive. Kinda.

Indeed, sleep eventually overcomes me, but it feels meaningless. I am haunted by dreams. My body does not feel rested. It is evident to me that I was not without adverse reactions from any medical procedures performed. My head feels like it was tossed off a third-elevation balcony and then stomped on, just for good measure. My nose is stuffy. My eyes ache, even if they are still closed. I can feel crusty, dried tears beneath my eyelids that give me the sensation that they have been glued shut.

If I think too much about it, the list of everything that's wrong would go on and on.

With great effort and serious willpower, I decide to get up.

It takes me another five minutes to actually do so.

Matt is fast asleep, slumped in an armchair. He never left the room. I'm not sure when he passed out, but I'm certain it was after I fell asleep. I do my best not to wake him as I walk around him. I am about to leave the room when I hear him move.

I turn my head back. Matt is staring at me with his piercing emerald eyes, wide open as if he had never been asleep.

"How did you sleep?" he asks.

I give him a slow nod, but I'm even slower to answer. "I knocked out," I tell him. "But I don't feel like I got any good sleep."

He takes a deep breath as he stretches in the chair and sits upright. His light hair shimmers in the rays of the sun that seep through beyond the curtain. He's tired, but his eyes hold a strong gaze on me.

"Yup," he says lazily. "That's how you're going to feel for a couple days. It will pass over, though."

I look around at the room. For some reason I'm feeling self-conscious again being around Matt.

"I'm going to get some breakfast," I tell him.

"Good idea," he says, getting up with a heavy sigh.

"Maybe consider brunch."

I jump slightly at the sudden voice. I look to my right and see Maylene standing in the doorway.

"It's a little close to noon," Maylene drawls.

"How long have you been there?" I ask.

"I got right here just now. But I slept on one of the couches out here last night," she tells me, indicating with her head to a couch that has a thin blanket laying over it.

I shrug, not understanding why she didn't use one of the other bedrooms.

"Whatever. If you're joining me, let's go," I say, knowing that they will because none of them want to leave my side right now. I'm both annoyed and grateful for it. I head out of the suite with Maylene right behind me and Matt stumbling out to catch up.

The lift is a little busy, and it takes a bit of time to get to us, but it brings us down in one go. When we get to the cafeteria, my head starts to hurt from the noise and buzzing around. There are so many people coming in and out, small bots whizzing by delivering food, and chefs going back and forth from the kitchens.

Maylene leads us through the mayhem towards a table by the window, but I ask her to sit somewhere without so much added light, so she leads us to the inner part of the mess hall.

As we sit down, a bot comes by and wipes the table clean. Another one follows right after it and displays our holographic menus using three of its small antennae-like arms. I look through, not really seeing anything as my mind is elsewhere. Where exactly it is, I don't know.

Someone sits down at our table. I give him a quick look and realize that it's Andre. He looks clean as ever. The bot displaying our menus immediately sticks out a fourth arm that presents Andre with a menu.

Andre takes no time to swipe through and order what he wants.

With a wide smile and long exhale, Andre says, "So, how are things?"

I shrug. Matt looks away, but I can see a small grin of amusement on his face. Maylene is kind enough to respond.

"Just taking it easy," she says.

Andre nods. "I bet. I would be too," he says. I can tell he wants to say more, but he holds himself back. I appreciate it. I don't feel like talking much at the moment.

As I flip through the menu, my stomach begins to make low growls. Nothing seems appetizing, so I am the last to order. Finally, I decide on some toast with a fruit-and-seed butter along with two eggs.

All the clanking of utensils, the rushed footsteps, the banging of the swinging doors off in the corner, and the wind that blows by with all the bots that zoom around, become nothing more than just static background noise. I can hear my friends talk to each other, but I can't always hear what they are saying. They don't talk too much, though, and I think Matt and Maylene are giving Andre polite but short answers.

I look at Matt and Maylene, both of whom sit across me. They too are looking around the mess hall. I think they are mainly keeping themselves entertained but also keeping a close eye on me. Or maybe I'm just paranoid.

Our food comes, but I am no longer hungry. I take some sips of water and force down small bites when I feel I am able to. Andre waits around for about fifteen minutes after he is done before he leaves for work. Matt and Maylene patiently wait for me to finish, or to tell them that I won't be eating any more, but I have an inkling that Matt will force the food down my throat if I say I won't finish my plate, so I say nothing, and swallow the small bits of food that I can.

The cafeteria clears out, though some employees taking a late lunch hurriedly walk in and order their food. My struggle to chow down on my meal continues. Matt and Maylene rarely speak to each other. All they do is wait. I have never seen such serene and persistent patience before. I almost feel agitated just looking at them.

After what feels like an entire day, I finish my last piece of toast. I ask a bot for more water, and it comes back in under a minute with a new glass. I chug that down, exhale a satisfied breath, and look up at my friends. This time, I feel ready enough to talk. I feel a lot better, too.

"All done," I say.

They smile but say nothing.

"Where to next?" I ask them.

Matt shrugs. "Wherever you want."

I nod slowly, thinking. "Is it too early to go out into the city?"

"We figured you might want to do that," Maylene answers. "We can use our prototype glasses on you, which would protect you from any camera feeds."

"Like what, it scrambles the footage?"

"Not quite," Matt jumps in. "If it did that, someone would think something was up. It just rearranges your face to make you look like someone else, so any software that might be programmed to catch you won't recognize you."

Maylene smiles. "It's not perfect yet, mainly because it has to find a similar face to yours that's also in the global database, but without activating a duplicate alert."

I shake my head. "That sounds impossible."

I can tell Maylene is very proud. "It should be, but Edward is a very intelligent man."

"Problem right now is that we still need to wait until we are sure the worst of the effects of your coma have subsided," Matt says. "So today would not be a good day to go outside."

I expected that. Actually, I expected worse. Truthfully, I was hoping they would say no. Waiting a day or two to go out into the city won't be a problem. My only issue with that is that every second I'm here, the program chip is most likely on its way to being in operation.

"Any news?" I ask.

"On what?" Maylene asks.

I know what she means. The chip or Kaedy.

"Both," I say.

She shakes her head. "From what I can tell, Kaedy had nothing to do with it, but we are looking for undeniable proof to put your mind at ease. No new intel on the chip's whereabouts."

There is a depressed silence that's fueled by my disappointment.

"I'm going to go back to our offices and check on things," Maylene says. "If anything changes, I'll let you both know immediately."

Matt gives her a strong nod. Maylene gently places her hand on my shoulder as she walks away.

"So, where to?" Matt asks.

I sigh. "Let's play some games."

The game room appears empty, but it's so large with its sections that you can never truly tell if it's occupied or not.

Matt and I play some air disk, a ball-basket game, and a flight simulator. We spend some hours going back and forth between games or playing "just one more" again and again against each other. After a while, the games succeed in taking my mind off of things, and I can feel myself relax. The dim lights make it easy to lose track of time. There is a main area to order food and drinks, to which I return on multiple occasions to drink more water.

At one point, Matt and I team up against some of his acquaintances in a maze simulation. The simulation is in a room tucked into a corner, and we jog in place on a floor pad while navigating the maze around us, projected onto all walls so that it feels as if we are in the maze. I try to see what would happen if I tried going through a wall, but all it does is nothing.

None of us make it to the end. The other guys say they have to get back to work, so we have to stop the game. I ask Matt if he and I could try to find our way out of it.

"We can try," he says. "But that was one of the more difficult ones, and I think the record is about four hours. And even that guy couldn't do it again. He already tried. Many times."

"We have the time," I tell him.

"True. But it's already half past eighteen," he points out. "We could be here until twenty-two, or even twenty-five. Even longer."

I think about it for a moment.

"Let's try," I say. "If it comes to it, we can just end the game."

Matt's lips curve into a small smile. "Yeah, as long as we don't get addicted to it."

We jump back in. There is something frustratingly calm about the game. We spend a couple hours making our way through. The maze starts off with hedges that seem to go up ten stories. But then the hedges are replaced with solid barriers, and one area of the game even has waterfalls as its walls.

Matt places his hand on me and shows me the time. Its twenty-one. I look up at him and nod, telling him I'm good with leaving.

We make our way to grab some dinner. I didn't realize how hungry I was, but I figure that it's a good thing my appetite is coming back. Maylene doesn't meet us for dinner, but I figure she already ate. I don't see Andre either.

Thinking about it, the fact of not finding the end of the maze is going to drive me nuts. It's a stupid thought considering it is just a game, and there are more important things to get to.

I ask Matt if he's heard anything from Maylene. He shakes his head but leads me up to their office. Maylene isn't here. The memory of when I was first here plays through my mind. It wasn't even that long ago, but I feel like a completely different person. I walk towards the windows and stare out, though I don't really see the city. My mind flashes with visions of that hotel collapsing back in Halav. That memory is followed by the city of Chlorofyx literally falling apart.

My blood begins to boil. That feeling is quickly replaced with sadness. I think Matt can sense what's happening because he comes by and stands next to me. He doesn't say anything. But his presence calms me. It isn't long that we stand there, but in those minutes, my love and respect for the man increases. A brotherly love, that is.

I can feel my normal self coming back to me. Weeks ago, Matt's mere presence would have made me feel insecure, the same way it did this morning. But now I can not only admire his good looks, well-defined body, and alluring aura, but I can also admire the great qualities that I have. That's something I never really was able to do before.

"You ready for bed?" he asks after some time. He turns his head away from the window to look at me.

I return the gaze and nod. He leads the way out of the office and to my suite. The elegant sleeping quarters feel unreal and empty. My head begins to feel heavy. Matt raises his arm a bit as if to catch me.

"You good?" he asks.

I nod. "Just tired."

He walks me to the room I slept in last night.

"Alright, Maylene and I are also going to stay here. She'll be in shortly. But don't worry, I won't be sleeping in this room like I did yesterday."

I chuckle. "Thank you," I tell him before climbing onto the bed.

Matt gives me a small smile, nods, and leaves. I can hear him go upstairs. I start to let my mind drift off to sleep. I can hear Maylene stealthily enter. She pokes her head into my room. Matt never shut the door. I don't look up but I can hear her relaxed breathing.

Tears don't come tonight. If anything, I'm too tired even for that. But I also don't feel as emotional now as I did yesterday. I'm sure some pain medication was used during the short coma, and those came with all kinds of aftereffects. I'm starting to think clearer now. I don't think Kaedy was responsible for anything. I owe her a call. And an apology. But still, I can't be too sure yet.

In the morning, I ask Maylene if she has any news. As I see her walking around slowly and cleaning up the kitchen nook, with her hair newly showered and brushed down, I become very self-conscious about how I smell.

"Almost," she says. "We are certain that the chip has made it to the Tall Building by now. Of course, immediately using it and changing everything worldwide would result in revolutions."

I stare at her blankly. Maylene shrugs. "Nothing solid on Kaedy's innocence, but I'm more than certain of it."

"Okay, thanks," I tell her. "I'm gonna take a shower, but I'll be ready for breakfast after."

"Sounds good," she says. "Oh, and we gave you access to our office." She walks out of the nook and into full view. I can tell she's very comfortable here. Maylene is wearing a loose, oversized shirt and shorts that barely cover everything.

I take a quick but thorough shower. When I get out, I see Matt waiting on one of the couches, with Maylene sitting on another.

"Shall we eat?" Maylene asks politely and with more grace than I am used to from her. She's also dressed more.

"I'm starving," Matt says, getting up.

I lead my friends downstairs. Breakfast seems like a busy affair, but even though people are moving about quickly, I feel much more at ease today. Ordering food doesn't take me as long, and soon enough I have a plate full of easy meats and eggs, along with a salad full of fruit. My usual appetite is returning.

"What did you mean by resulting in revolutions?" I ask Maylene. Matt looks up at the questions and lets out a single laugh with a wide, one-sided smile.

"Oh, yeah, so imagine this," she says excitedly. Maylene wipes her mouth with a cloth napkin and takes a sip of her juice. "You're minding your own business one day, and then all of a sudden you can't buy your lunch during your work break. Not only that, but you are soon arrested and charged with things that you have never done."

I'm skeptical. Even if that would work, I don't think people would believe all of it, especially those who know you.

"Trouble is, being far worse for you, is that all the people that would vouch for you and be your alibi, well, they too have been arrested. Or worse. Let's say one of them was being treated in a hospital for something, but their medical records were scrambled and they were given the wrong blood type, or that they were given some drug that they were allergic to. The possibilities could be endless."

I stare at Maylene. I have a feeling that she isn't done yet.

"Also, let's say that one day, PlatTech goes bankrupt all of a sudden. Now there are competing companies, but none of them ever really stood a chance. That's why you never hear about them. But now one of them just got very lucky," Maylene goes on. "You see where this is going?"

She doesn't give me a chance to answer.

"Chlorofyx could happen all over again," she says. "If they were able to hack into and override the right programs and security protocols, the ones that are literally impossible to break, then cities could be demolished in minutes. With half the population of Talvor dead, it would be easy to obtain global power. Whoever uses that chip's program," she says, letting out a short breath as she pauses between her words, "that person would not need to even pretend like they're the good guy. They could just threaten anyone's life. The rest of the world would have no choice but to bow down."

After a minute, I say, "Sounds pretty bad."

"It would be much worse than it sounds," Matt says.

I feel even worse now.

"No one is blaming you," Maylene says. I know she's told me before. She'll probably tell me over and over again. "My whole point is that no one can immediately start doing anything close to that. We have time. And we will get the chip back."

"Me too," I say. "I will be there."

"Yes, you too," Matt says. "Your dedication to see this through is more than enough to convince me."

"But we have no news yet," I say, stating what otherwise is a question.

"Intel is being gathered on the Tall Building while Edward is working on finding the exact location of the chip," Maylene says. "That could be that someone has it in their possession or it is being stored somewhere."

"I'm guessing there really isn't a way to track its exact location."

Maylene and Matt both shake their heads.

"The tracker that we had in it has been deactivated," Matt explains. "It was turned off within minutes of it being picked up from the crash site. The only lead we had then was the direction it started in. Funny thing is, the Tall Building was the other way."

"So how are we sure it's there?" I ask.

"Edward has many connections," Maylene says. "Come now, you should know better than to doubt us. But still, we do need to verify where it is before we can plan how to go about retrieving it."

I nod, agreeing with her. While my patience is lacking, I understand the steps that we are taking to ensure that we succeed. It would be a dangerous waste if we just went after it, especially if it ended up not being where we thought it was.

"We're almost there," Matt says reassuringly. "Another day or two, and we all will know exactly where it is."

The crowd of people inside the cafeteria neither increases nor decreases. People leave just as fast as they come in. Some more hurriedly than others. I stare out the window, admiring the city. The sun seems to sit just over the horizon. It gleams down into the city, permeating it with its warmth. The skies look pale, as if winter is nearing. I imagine the smell of fresh snow falling on top of autumnal leaves. Of course, not every part of the world gets to enjoy that. But everyone has the chance to, if they want.

"If you're up to it, I think we can spend an hour or so outside," Matt says, eyeing me with a knowing expression. He understands that I want to get some fresh air.

"That would be nice," I say. "And I already feel much better today than I have since I woke up from that short coma."

"Then let's get you ready," Maylene says. She leads us back to the suite. The lift makes several stops on its way. From what I can tell, Matt and Maylene are highly respected by many of the employees in the building. I am told to dress for cooler weather. I look through the closet of clothes. None are mine, but they actually might be now. I'm never quite sure how it happens, but whenever I stay here or anywhere owned by Edward Canabana, I seem to have a personalized closet of clothes that fit me perfectly.

I choose a stiffer jacket, gray in color, over the usual sweater I would wear. Underneath it, I wear a simple black shirt.

Matt is dressed in a black jacket that suits him well. Maylene is snugged inside something that looks so comfortable that I would wear it, even if it is normally regarded as woman's clothing.

"Let's get you under disguise," Maylene says as she puts a soft knitted beanie on my head.

14

The eyeglasses are clear, flat-looking, and make me feel like the only thing I care about is studying or reading. At least, that's how I imagine myself to look. I've never had to wear glasses before. I step towards the window, trying to catch my reflection. It's hard to see with the near-afternoon sun beaming down, penetrating the glass.

When I manage to see myself, I realize that the glasses don't look bad at all. They even suit me. The glasses have a thin, black rim. The dark-brown beanie looks silly, though that might be more of a personal opinion, as I don't usually wear anything like it.

"Perfect," Maylene says with a voice that sounds almost dreamy. I wonder what's gotten into her. Not that it's bad, but she isn't quite the same Maylene I met all those weeks ago. Then again, I'm not the same Arch that she met. "Now let me just check our feed to make sure it's working."

Matt shifts slightly, looking back out the window towards the city. Their office is otherwise empty of people. It feels like a comfortable place to work. Even though I've been here a few times, I still seem to notice things now that I didn't before, most notably how large this room actually is. I guess that just happens a lot in this building. It also doesn't help that every time I've been brought here, it was from a near-death experience. If anything, this building is like my own personal hospital.

Maylene swipes away at a data pad that she holds in one hand. She looks up at me and then back down at the screen.

"Perfect," she whispers loudly.

Matt and I walk over to her to look at the camera feed. Indeed, it looks quite perfect. You can clearly see Matt and Maylene. You can even see me, though I don't look the same. My face is skinnier, paler, and has more freckles. My hair is now a much darker shade, thinner and flat, but only visible creeping out beneath the beanie. Of course, none of it is actually me; the glasses are just distorting any images to make me look like this. Honestly, I prefer the way I look compared to this guy.

I move around slightly. The video looks alright, but my head gets a bit blurry for a moment.

"Hmm, maybe without the beanie," Maylene says, taking it off my head. "It might be a bit nippy out there, but this is the safest way."

"I'll manage," I tell her, smiling. I'm excited about venturing out into the city. With everything else that's going on, I feel like this is a small moment where I can just enjoy myself and take a break from all that I've been dealing with. I feel like a kid in school about to go on a field trip.

"Let's have you move again," Matt requests. I do so, shifting slightly, moving my head around, and shuffling my feet.

"We're good to go," he says, clasping me on my shoulder.

Everything seems to take forever. The wait for the elevator and the ride down, even though we made no stops on the way. As we walk through the entrance courtyard, I remember the first time I saw this place. It was empty then. Now there are a few people moving about. There is a quiet feel to the area.

Instead of going through one of the doors to the sides, which is where I came through over a week ago after Matt saved me, Maylene leads us out the front.

The first step into the air feels brisk against my face. My body gives an involuntary shudder from the sudden drop in temperature. I breathe in deeply. No matter how clean a ventilation system is, nothing is better than fresh gulps of atmospheric air. If my eyes were closed, I wouldn't put it past me to guess that I am in the mountains.

It's been too long since I've breathed in air like this. Even if it was just a couple of days or so.

A headache I didn't know I had dissipates. That sounds corny. Deep down, I knew I had it. But it was so constant that it had become numb.

We walk around the block. I'm used to it by now, having experienced it all my life, but I still can't get over how small I feel surrounded by all the buildings. Sonars glide by and over us. I look to the sky. I can see the faint road markings above through the glare of the sun.

Because of the altitude of the buildings and how many businesses and stores have separate accesses depending on which elevation you enter through, there are conveyors that constantly rotate, ascending and descending, so that pedestrians can get about. There are some lifts that can be called and entered at a slower pace, usually reserved for elderly or handicapped people. There are even some for vehicles, though they go mostly unused.

Matt and Maylene stand in front of me as we ride up to the third elevation. They haven't told me where we're going. After we reach the second elevation, a forcefield screen creates a wall between the solid steps and the open air below. Most people are used to such high altitudes that there isn't much of a fear of heights, but it can be quite unsettling when you're higher up, fully exposed, and with the wind gaining strength.

I run my hand along the screen as we ascend. It is warm, and I can feel some sort of energy surging through it, but it doesn't cause me any harm.

"This way," Maylene says pleasantly. She looks back and smiles, though I can barely see her with Matt standing in front of me.

She leads us to a lift. We wait several minutes before it is our turn to go up. We step inside. The lift is fully enclosed in glass. Even the base itself is glass, though it is opaque, probably due to the fact that most people would not be comfortable looking down an elevator shaft while they were riding in it. The lift starts slowly but gains speed as it takes us up many floors. We pass through at least seven elevations. As we slow to a stop, perfect timing allows a flare of sunlight to crest over the structure, just like it would if it were just creeping over the horizon during the early hours.

The doors slide open, and we step out onto a terrace. It is much chillier up here. Pyramid-shaped heaters are placed around the terrace, with a small fire blazing inside each one. There are straw huts that wrap around the center, with elevators between each of them. A structural roof covers most of the terrace, but the outermost edges are uncovered. I realize that this is a restaurant, and a popular one at that. There are more floors above; some may be office or business suites, but more than likely they are penthouses.

I can hear some people talking about Chlorofyx. I ignore them, put on a small smile, and look around. There is no need to let others dictate my mood, and since I feel at peace in this moment, I'd rather keep it that way.

Matt wraps his arms around me and Maylene and walks us out to the edge. A guardrail that goes up to just beneath my chest lines the terrace, with a glass screen used as a window so younger and smaller people can still look out. A similar wall hangs down from above, though this is made entirely of glass, which is used to prevent the worst of the high winds rushing through. There is enough space between the two to look out with a clear, undiluted view.

Breathtaking.

About ten elevations high, the entire world belongs to me. I can see beyond the city. Small moving objects come in and out as people drive away and to the metropolis. Below are thousands of Sonars whizzing by, all gliding across the translucent roads. It amazes me that, even though I have seen most of the world, I haven't seen much at all. Even when I would spend a couple days in a new city, I never managed to find the best spots.

"Can you feel the rush?" Matt asks.

"The wind, or the feeling inside me?"

He takes a short moment to answer.

"All of it."

Maylene growls a low, contented sound. She folds her arms and leans against the fence.

"I'll be back," Matt says as he walks off.

I stay there with Maylene. We don't talk. We just enjoy the view, like other people around us. The gusts of wind are frequent. I believe that the sky deck was intentionally built that way. My ears go numb from the cold, so I lean them against my shoulders, alternating every minute or so.

Matt comes back carrying three chocolate lotuses, a decadent dessert where each petal contains melted fudge inside, all while the entire treat is heavily sprinkled with sugar purposely dressed to look like snow.

"Oh, these are so good!" Maylene cries out, chomping a bite into the delicacy rather than plucking off the individual leaves. Melted chocolate spills out of her mouth, and she must make excessive use of her tongue to try to catch it all. It doesn't work, even with all the experience she likely has; there is just too much of it smeared across her face.

Matt and I eat the confection in a civilized manner, though I am tempted to dive my whole face into it just like Maylene did. I close my eyes with the first bite. There is little time to savor the moment. All of our phones alert us at the same time. Maylene takes a second to check hers, still grappling with the leaking chocolate on her hands. Matt and I look immediately. Edward is telling us that they have an exact location for the computer chip and to meet him immediately in their office.

Maylene slurps up the rest of her dessert and books it towards the elevator. Matt and I rush behind her, but we are more careful as we are still eating. Maylene fights against the lift's doors so we can make it. The ride down is quick, and time seems to blur. Before I know it, my dessert is finished, and I'm in another elevator, this time headed up to the hundred and fourteenth floor of the Canabana Building. Edward is standing by the windows and turns around slowly when he hears us come in. Andre is here, as well as another man around Edward's age. I don't recognize him. As we walk up to Mr. Canabana, I notice Gary sitting on one of the armchairs.

"Very well," Edward begins. "Let's get right to it." He briskly walks to what I would call the center of the room. He stands in front of the desk Maylene usually sits at and addresses us.

"As we surmised, the chip is located in the Tall Building. We have also discovered its name, thanks to my contact and friend, Mr. James Cropough." The older man I did not recognize bows his head slightly. "The chip, or more accurately, the program contained inside, is called Prodigy. As we well know, Prodigy was created on Earth. We do not know if it was successfully used on their planet, but I don't understand why someone would send us such a powerful program if they still needed it."

"Do you think Earth succumbed to this Prodigy?" Maylene asks.

"I don't see any reason to believe otherwise, unless, of course, someone was sending it away, hoping that we didn't know what it was."

"Is it a bad idea to send it back?" Matt asks. "What if they were trying to protect themselves?"

"You have a valid point, Mr. Schwae," Edward replied. "But however the circumstances are, or were, if Prodigy was sent to us with the knowledge of what it is, I fully intend to send it back. I will have a message carried with it, one that warns those who receive it exactly what it is. Of course, there will be precautions to ensure it can't be used, but we don't know all the technology Earth has, so there is no guarantee." Edward takes a few steps back and forth. "As it is, Prodigy was created with some sort of technology that we don't fully understand, which is why we have been unable to destroy it."

"But there is something in the Tall Building that can read Prodigy and activate it?" I ask.

"Precisely," Andre pipes in. "Though they are still in the process of discreetly engaging with it, so progress is slow. That's good news for us."

Matt steps forward. "So what's the bad news?"

"The Tall Building has extensive security that makes it nearly impossible to infiltrate, especially during the day. During the night, most things are secured with measures that even the legendary Edward Canabana has been unable to crack," James says. There is something irksome about his voice.

Edward smiles. "Something I am working on."

James gives Edward a half-smile. "Fortunately, I will be able to grant you access to most rooms while you four retrieve Prodigy and safely return it here."

"Actually, I will be having the four of them head somewhere secure and unknown, and then Arch will take his leave with Prodigy and complete his delivery," Mr. Canabana says.

"Oh?" James looks at Edward, who does him the courtesy of returning the look but says nothing more.

"So, will we be leaving tonight?" Maylene asks.

"We'll be leaving in less than an hour," Andre replies.

"You will be making this a twelve-hour trip and will be traveling in one of our smaller air ships," Edward says. "By the time you are ready to enter the Tall Building, coordinates will be programmed into the airship for your immediate departure after you are in possession of Prodigy."

"How dangerous is this going to be?"

We all look over to Gary, who is still sitting in the armchair. His back faces us.

"Well," James says, stepping toward Gary. "It is my duty to make sure that they are as safe as possible. I do have high security access, so it is just a matter of making as little noise as possible." James turns to face us. "If you can accomplish that, then you won't have any issues."

"How many people are usually in the Tall Building during night-time hours?" Maylene asks.

"Normally about ten, depending on the exact time," James replies quickly. "But since they have their covert operations regarding Prodigy underway, the amount of people inside will be closer to fifty."

"Fifty isn't too bad," Matt says.

"When most of those fifty guards are in the same corridor, it can make things tricky," James retorts. His lower lip trembles. "But let me worry about that. You guys just get the damn thing out of there before they kill us all."

"With no better way to put it, this is a stealth mission," explains Edward. "I want minimal use, but prefer none, of the weapons you will be carrying." He walks around us slowly. "Andre has a decoy chip that will be used to replace the real one. A decoy will not last long. While they won't know how to operate either of the programs, real or fake, they will soon realize that what they have is unusable."

The room is quiet for a moment.

"Pack up anything you would like to bring with you. The airship is already loaded with a month's supply for each of you, including food and clothing. I expect you all to be back within a week, but at any rate, they are there just in case," Edward says. "There are light-weight armored suits sized for each one of you. Please wear them; they could save your life. Manuals for how to use them are also provided. As these are a new line of technology I have developed, I suggest you read through it so that you know its capabilities, and its limits." He pauses for a moment. "Get going."

The four of us head towards the elevator. I hear someone call my name from behind. I turn back. Gary is standing, now walking slowly towards me. I can tell he is in pain. There is something different in the way he moves.

"None of us blame you," he says. "We all still have full trust and confidence that you will finish this. It's time you do so." Gary smiles. I can tell he speaks honestly and from within his heart. Something tells me I won't be seeing him again. I walk up to him and give him a hug, saying nothing, before walking away.

The elevator doors close in front of me.

"The air ship is in the second basement bay," Andre tells us. "I'm set to go. See you guys in a few."

"I'll follow you," Maylene says. "I'm set as well. I've already got what I need."

Andre nods to her.

"Arch, come with me," Matt says. "We're going to pick something up real quick." He turns to Andre and Maylene. "We'll be there in fifteen." Matt gently presses one of the buttons.

"Second floor?" Maylene asks.

"Second floor," Matt replies.

A second later, we reach the second floor. Matt walks out, and I follow him. The hall is a dark gray, made of what looks like thin concrete, but there are metal beams between the walls, presumably used for support. Simply lit, the hall bears no distinctive or attractive qualities other than a minimalistic approach.

"What is the second floor used for?" I ask Matt.

"You'll see," he replies without looking back. I can hear the excitement in his voice. He says nothing else.

The hallway is longer than any other I remember in this building. As we get closer to the end of it, I can see an unremarkable door. Matt scans his phone when we approach it, enters a code into a keypad, and then places his hand over a scanner, touching one of his fingers to it. There is no beep or other sound of granted access other than the faint click of the lock unlocking. Matt pushes the door open.

Large lights hang down from the ceiling, illuminating the room so well that you can't see any shadows. Metal flooring lines the room. Cases of glass shelves are parked throughout the room. The cases contain the largest variety I have ever seen of weapons, ammunition, and armor. There are guns that are too big to be carried by one person. Melee weapons are towards the right, ranging from small knives to luxurious tridents embellished with carvings and gems. There is no sound of footsteps as we walk. Matt walks toward them. He opens a door and picks out some small knives.

"Here, keep these on you," he says as he holds them out for me to take. I do so. "I'm sure the suits waiting for us have places to properly hold them."

I carefully stuff the knives into my pockets. Matt leads me across the room. For a moment, I think we're heading out, going back the way we came, but I realize that he is walking past the exit, down the room, to an area I hadn't noticed before. The whole floor is one large room, though sections of it are partially divided. We walk parallel to the hall that led us into the room. The walls are lined with more cabinets. Most of these are armor or suits. Closer to the end, the displays hold firearms. He opens up another glass door and picks out a small handgun. It has a thin barrel, which makes up most of its design. There is a small trigger located beneath it and a small, teal-colored button that sits just above it.

"This little guy is quite treacherous," Matt tells me.

"Treacherous?"

He chuckles. "Yeah, I know. Odd choice of word," he says. "But let me explain. You point this at your target, hold down this button, and pull the trigger." He makes the motions with his hand, pointing it down the room, but he doesn't even push down the button. "What this will do is pull your target closer and then blast him back as if you just detonated a bomb right in front of him."

"That doesn't sound pleasant," I say.

Matt laughs again. "No, it probably isn't. It can be tricky to use, especially since your aim has to be pretty good and your target can't be too far away, lest you pull something else towards you. But even though death by it is likely to be extremely painful, it will be quick," he describes. "I don't like thinking about it too much, but it is effective. The other benefit to using it is that if your target shoots something towards you and you use this in time, it will also blast back the incoming projectile, thus saving your life."

I nod. Awkwardly, I wait there, wondering if he is going to hand it to me. I do want it, but I don't want to look like I do, in case he doesn't think I should carry it. He does hand it to me after a bit. He takes another one for himself.

"I think that should be good," he says. "The airship will have other weapons, ones that Edward likely would rather we use. We can't leave a trail of bodies in the Tall Building, because once they are found, they will know something happened, and our bought time with the decoy will be lost."

He gives me a quick look. I nod again, not really knowing what else to say. Carrying weapons isn't something that I am used to, but it is something I need to get comfortable with really fast.

"Let's go," he says. He walks back across the room, turns around, and goes through the door we came through. "There is another door that leads to a lift that goes straight down to the basements, but Edward prefers that those be used only as needed, and I don't want to alert anyone else that we're loading up with weapons."

"Makes sense," I say.

We use the same elevator we did to arrive to this floor and we take it down to the basement. Matt leads us to another one that takes us one more floor below. The doors open up. The airship bay is cold, dark in design, and lit only enough to see the ships themselves. Maylene and Andre are inside the ship, sitting on laced chairs and reading the manual Edward told us to.

Maylene looks up when she hears us.

"Nice," she says, nodding her approval when she sees the firearm I carry in my hand.

"Ready to go?" Andre says, gracefully shutting the manual and standing up.

"Yes, we are," Matt says. He walks up the metal stairs into the airship. It is large, with a small deck above that looks out the bow.

I am sure there is something below, but I don't see any immediate access to the hull.

"Let's get going," Andre says. He hops onto a ladder and goes up. Maylene walks past it and into the pilot seats at the front. When Matt and I are inside, Maylene retracts the stairs and closes the ship. I look out the front window. The engines roar to life and then quiet down to a low grumble. The vehicle lifts slightly, and Maylene steers it out of its bay and turns it to face down the runway. Lights turn on down both sides. There is a moment of red lights that flash three times in the loading bay. The red lights disappear, and a second passes before green ones light up the bays.

"We're ready for takeoff," I hear Andre call from the intercom.

Matt turns to look at me. There is a childish excitement in his facial expression.

"Strap in."

15

The airship sounds silent from within. We start gliding forward. Our speed picks up quickly. The lights in the loading dock go red again. A second later, we accelerate out of there. The force presses my body against the back of my seat. For much longer, we soar through the dark tunnel, guided only by small blue lights, with the red ones far behind us back in the bay.

We begin a gentle ascent. I know this only because of how often I've driven. I can't tell how fast we're going, but I know that we are still gradually picking up speed. I have a feeling that when we fly above ground, we'll take off even faster.

Just when I think the moment is going to happen, when I'll see the light of the sun, the glow of the elevations, and the size of the buildings, we stay beneath the city. Once again, it happens, and I think we're going to break the surface. We don't.

Then it actually happens. The cargo door opens so quick. One second it was only the easy illuminating light that I could see, and not even the next I'm blinded by the sudden exposure to sunlight. The front windshield dims itself, easing the light from outside. As I predicted, we accelerate so fast that I bang my head against the headrest. Luckily, it's well cushioned.

We shoot up into the air. I see the sky immediately. I look around, confused. There isn't a building in sight.

As if he were reading my mind, Matt pushes a button and reveals a window at the rear. I turn my head back to look out. Candalance is far behind us. The buildings don't even look that tall anymore.

"The second basement has a long tunnel that spreads out in six directions, far beyond Candalance," Maylene explains. "Speeds while inside the tunnel can feel quick, but that's only because of the tighter fit inside. When we break through the surface, that's when we really go."

"Cool," is all I manage to say. I keep looking back, noticing how the city not only gets farther away but also lower and lower while we keep up our lift.

I hear footsteps coming down from the ladder. I turn back to face forward.

"All good up there," Andre tells Maylene as he skips the last two rungs with a small jump. "I've relinquished the controls from above."

"Great," Maylene replies. "I'll take the first shift."

"Sounds good," Andre says. He turns his head toward me. "You can unbuckle now."

Matt looks back at me as well and grins. Andre takes a seat near me.

"What did you mean by relinquishing controls?" I ask him as I unstrap myself.

"The tunnels are narrow, at least for these ships. Normal Sonars, even like the large one we gave you before, fit great inside," Andre tells me. "The main steering unit is here," he points to Maylene and the controls. "But up there is where I make sure that we don't make contact with the walls."

I nod.

For the first hour or so, we don't talk all that much. This time is much different than the last time we travelled somewhere, beyond the fact that this round, we're driving. The three of them exchange little conversation, mainly of other work-related stuff that I have no idea about. From what I can tell, the three of them dropped everything to be a part of this mission — the whole mission.

Even though we are traveling quite far, the Tall Building is closer to NEAST than anywhere else I've been so far since I started this journey. That is, it is closer by travel time, not necessarily by direct distance.

We travel for some more time, but nearly everyone is silent. I can't even hear the roar of the ship's engines. After fading out into my daydreams, it crosses my mind that it is now dark out.

"We have another ten hours to go," Matt tells me, getting up from his seat in the front and coming back to join me and Andre. "Choose whenever to sleep, if you want to. We have adrenaline shots in case you don't. It'll be nighttime again in Longfurd by the time we get there, but the time difference may throw you off."

"I'm good for now," I tell him.

"So am I," I hear Maylene call out from the front. Andre immediately gets out of his seat and takes Matt's old one. He gives Maylene a nod and takes over driving.

"It sure feels like a prime time to take some shots," she says gleefully. I can't tell if she's joking.

"I don't think so," Matt says. "Though it could ease the nerves."

"Oh," Maylene says, sitting right up behind Matt. She mockingly rubs his shoulders. "Big bad boy Matt is scared to do a stealth mission? What, not enough air rifles and buildings to crash into?" Her eye catches mine for a second. I can't help but spit out a laugh.

"Something like that," Matt says, lowering his head into his hands. "Actually, I think I'll get some rest for a bit. Andre, wake me when it's my turn to go."

"Will do!" Andre calls back without taking his eyes off the sky.

He gets up and walks down the airship. He pulls down on a string from the ceiling. Another ladder reveals itself and he climbs up it.

Maylene pulls out a book from her bag and begins to read. She doesn't notice the look of surprise on my face. I lean back and close my eyes. I'm not tired, but I am quite bored. Kaedy crosses my mind. I am glad that Maylene hasn't brought her up again. I want to call her to apologize. I'll be doing that right after this mission. Hopefully, she understands and gives me another chance. The thought of her not doing so makes my heart feel small, heavy, and barbed.

Hours pass. Maylene falls asleep on the seat. Andre puts the aircraft into auto pilot and hurriedly goes back to wake Matt up. I see Matt come down the ladder, but I don't see Andre, meaning it is likely he stayed above, snagging a quick nap for himself. Matt eyes me as he passes.

"Wanna join me?" he asks, nodding towards the front. I give a mental shrug and get up.

The seats in front are wide, but they aren't like the seat I was on, which was more of a small couch. The pilot seats are comfortable, though, and they have both chest and lap straps.

"Couldn't sleep?" he asks.

"No, wasn't really tired," I tell him.

"Me neither," he says. "Tired, I mean, but I got a small nap just now. But no worries. Like I said, when we get there, we'll make sure you feel as though you've slept for a whole day."

"That would be perfect," I say.

Something drops into my lap. It is the manual I was supposed to read.

"I'm guessing you forgot," he says.

"You are correct," I reply, clicking my tongue. He doesn't say more, but he lets me read. It isn't very long, and there aren't many instructions. From what it says, the suit can detect incoming attacks and strengthen the area that is likely to be hit. That includes the face area, which is uncovered and exposed unless it is necessary to guard your face. There is a disclaimer at the end stating that this is a prototype and is not available anywhere else yet due to its imperfect design.

I shut the manual.

"Don't worry about that last part," Matt says. "It was true when it was written, but these suits are ready to hit the market. They'll do a good job."

"Why haven't they hit the market?" I ask him. "And what is the market, exactly?"

"I think that Mr. Canabana has had other things on his mind," Matt answers with a sarcastic tone. "But who am I to know?"

He looks at me and laughs.

"No, I'm just kidding," he says. "Sort of, at least. The market for the suit is mostly the military or security type, so I would guess that Mr. Canabana isn't interested in selling these at this time, what with not knowing who is after Prodigy."

"Has it been a while since Edward sold anything like it?"

"Probably about three years," Matt tells me. "Canabana Industries is quite large, with many, many products and services. Honestly, I probably don't even know them all. But I've seen a lot and worked with several things. There was even a stint where I was basically a pretty boy by Edward's side as he made deals to acquire buildings and such."

I chuckle.

"He apologized a lot during that time. He told me that he hates to use me like that, but unfortunately, so much of the world only responds to that physical attractive charm, and that in his old age, he didn't have as much as he did years ago," Matt explains. "It just makes people want to trust you," he says. "And I get that, so I played my part when he asked me of it."

"Have you ever considered being a model?" I ask him.

"Is that all you think I can do?" he retorts. I'm not quite sure how to answer.

"No, of course not," I say after a moment of thought. "After everything that's happened and with all the times you saved my life, absolutely not. But just because you're a model doesn't mean that that you can't do anything else."

He laughs again. "I know. I was just messing with you. I was actually a model for a couple years when I was younger. But I wanted to do something more meaningful with my time. Plus, the constant pressure of not being good enough eventually gets to you."

"I get it," I say, though I know I don't truly understand it all, having never been in that position.

"I was a lot younger then," Matt goes on. "And it sucked too because all the girls I met weren't ever into me, just my body. The last straw was when I slept with this one chick, and midway through she let out this long, heavy sigh and told me that it wasn't how she fantasized it."

I bite back any smart retorts I can think of. The pain that he must have felt in that moment. I can feel just a fraction of that. Always worried that you aren't good enough, being told various reasons why you didn't get a job, never knowing who is telling the truth. And he probably had people be too blunt with him.

"After that, I called it quits," he tells me. "I cancelled my upcoming job and took off. I traveled for a while and took time to get my head straight so that I could figure out what it was that I really wanted. Then Edward found me. And the rest is history."

"So not only did you find what you want, sounds like you got it, right?" I ask him.

Matt smiles. "Yeah, for the most part. But there is still something that I'm missing."

"Maylene."

I don't even know why I said it. I don't know how I even knew it. Matt looks at me, almost as stunned as I am.

"I-is it that obvious?" he asks.

I raise my eyebrows and let out a breath. "No, I mean, I don't think so," I say. "I guess just after all this time I've gotten to know you. You also may have hinted at it before."

"Hmm," he says. "Yeah, I may have. But please don't tell her," he requests. "But it's not like she doesn't already know. I asked her out a couple years ago, and probably a few more times since then, though never as directly."

I can't help but laugh.

"What's so funny? Are you laughing at me?"

I look over to him. He had a wide grin on his face.

"No, I just think that you have a shot," I tell him.

It's his turn to laugh. "Yeah, I'm not her type. She's told me that many times."

I shrug. "I don't think she lets herself see it, but I think you are her type," I tell him. "Just give it time."

He doesn't say anything, but I can tell he's thinking about it. I give him time to dwell on his thoughts. I end up drifting off to mine and then drifting off to sleep.

Matt pats me on my chest.

"We're here," he says. He is already wearing his suit. It is one piece made of dark, reflective material. It looks made to fit tight. I get out of the chair and walk towards Maylene, who is gesturing frantically for me to hurry over. She hands me my suit.

"Go change," she says, pointing to a restroom in the ship. "You can't wear anything underneath it."

Somehow I missed that part in the manual.

The restroom is quite large considering it is part of an airship. I strip down and pull the suit on. It is a tight fit, but it is very flexible, and no part of it feels constricting. I look in the mirror. The reflectiveness of the suit is distorted. Probably meant to disguise you slightly from cameras, but not anything more effective than making it harder to see who you are.

When I walk out, the three of them are waiting for me. Matt is whispering into his comm piece. I look out the windows but can't see anything because they have been shut.

"Let's go," Matt says to us. I hear a beep in my ear. The suit comes equipped with communication devices. "We're connected to each other, Edward, Gary, and James. Edward and Gary will monitor us, while James will give us directions. Listen to him. He has access to every feed in the Tall Building."

We nod.

Matt opens the door and we follow him out. We've parked in a thicket of trees in the middle of the largest park in Longfurd. Most of the streetlights are out, though there are a few scattered about that are still on.

The suits muffle our footsteps. Matt leads us at a slow jog. As we pass over the bridges and through the small plant gardens, I see some homeless people asleep on benches, under the bridges, and even on patches of grass. When we reach the end of the park, Matt holds out his arm to stop us.

"Hold," I hear James tell us in my earpiece. The traffic light tells us to wait. I hear some clicking, and then the walk sign shows. Matt jogs across the street. There are no vehicles around.

Longfurd comes into view as I step out from under the cover of trees and darkness. Massive structures shoot up from the ground. Many of them have slanted roofs. Lights shoot up into the sky and shine down on the streets and sidewalks. The elevations are marked out with bright lights that have a hint of pale blue.

"Shutting down city feeds," James says. A second later, red lines enter my vision. The suit has computerized eyewear. The red lines mark out the path that we should take. We follow Matt down the road. He quickly ushers us in between two buildings. He pushes us back further, covering us with shadows. Passersby walk in front of us, not noticing a thing. When he deems it safe, Matt leads us back out and down the walk.

We go for over twenty minutes. Massive screens are attached to buildings. Some display commercials or feeds of sports, while others have a more niche presentation, probably having to do with the product of the company that owns it.

At long last, I see the front doors. The Tall Building is intricately built. Straight up and vertical; at several intervals, the building has long structural parts that slant down from the roof and jut out of the original dimensions. This occurs on all sides, but never two sides on the same five floors. From what I can tell, the roof is shaped like a square, but from the pictures I've seen, it is open in the middle, leading down to the enclosed courtyard, accessible somewhere on its hundredth floor. The building's exterior is made of dark and tinted glass, unable to be seen through and non-reflective. Flood lights shoot straight up into the sky from the rooftop. There is so much light pollution in the city that you can barely tell there is even a night sky.

"When I tell you when," James says, and I jump slightly at the sudden voice in my ear. "Run through the front doors. I will be deactivating the sensors on the doors, but I can only hold that for a few seconds. I will then shut down the feeds in the foyer. Once again, I only have about a minute of complicated tasks to do this, lest the alarms trigger, in which case you're all dead. As fast as you can, make it to any other floor; just don't stay on the first."

"Not a problem," Maylene says.

"Don't be overconfident," James snaps. "The foyer is large, and most elevators will not be operational. I can't control these, so it's best you don't waste your time trying. And don't use the main stairs either; they only lead to the upper foyer."

"Sounds complicated," Maylene says.

"That's what I want to hear," James replies.

The gut in my body tells me not to trust James. But there's nothing to do about that now. We're already here. I barely have a moment to compose myself.

"Go!" James hisses a quick order.

Matt runs towards the front doors. Andre, Maylene and I follow. The doors glide open. Andre, behind us all, barely makes it through when they shut.

"Countdown forty-seven seconds," James says.

Matt books it across the foyer. Other than it being wide open, with plants sitting at the edges and a large garden with running water placed in the middle, I am unable to notice more, namely any of the fine details that I'm sure there are. My focus is keeping up with Matt. Maylene struggles a bit, and she's faster than me. Andre stays by my side, and I'm not sure if he's not leaving me behind or if this is his speed.

Barely ten seconds pass before James alerts us to having fifteen seconds left. Realizing that this is taking longer than I thought because of my speed, I push my legs harder to catch up. Andre picks up his pace too.

We barge through a small exit door at the other end of the foyer. Matt stands by the alarm-activating door just on the other side to make sure none of us accidentally go through it.

"Zero," James whispers into our earpiece. The door clicks closed behind me.

"Make your way to the fifth floor. There are no guards there, and you will be able to use those elevators. But don't go through the door until I tell you so. It is locked, and attempting to open it will alert security."

"Got it," Matt says. He starts making his way up the open-well staircase. We follow him. Still, even with our suits, our heavy footsteps are muffled. We reach the fifth floor. Matt stops in front of the door. I am beginning to breathe hard. I can't hear the others, but I can tell they are tiring out too.

"Take these," Matt says. I clearly hear him through my earpiece, and that's when I realize these suits contain all sound from ourselves. He pulls out small syringes and hands them to us. Maylene and Andre inject in into their shoulders. I do the same. Matt doesn't do his.

All of a sudden, my breathing slows. My heart rate becomes normal, and I feel like I have enough energy to run for an hour straight, but the lack of motion doesn't make me jittery. If I was lacking sleep, I can't feel it anymore.

"These were specifically designed to inject enough adrenaline into you to keep you moving quickly for long periods of time, but without the adverse effects that feel like they could kill you if you don't move enough," Matt explains. "But taking any more than the dose I gave you in the same twenty-five-hour period will likely kill you, so don't ask for more."

"Go," James tells us before we can answer Matt.

Matt pushes the door open. The hallways here are far less attractive than the foyer. Gilded numbers adorn the doors that are spaced apart, giving me the idea that these are office suites.

"By the center of the floor are the elevators. It doesn't matter which one you take," James tells us. "You can ride up to the forty-fifth floor. From there, you will have to discreetly make your way around. The goal is to get to the hundredth floor. You'll want to find the elevators that are meant to be used by civilians for that. Once there on the hundredth floor, you can access the freight lift down to floor ninety-nine, which holds Prodigy."

"Got it," Matt says. There is something different in his voice. His words are more direct and unemotional. He's done this type of thing before. I get the idea Maylene has too. I don't think Andre has, but I feel like he's been training for this day.

Once again, Matt takes the lead at a slow jog, and we make our way down the hallways. We pass by three elevators, but Matt doesn't so much as glance at them.

Another turn, and we step into a wide elevator lobby. Clearly, this is where James was talking about. Matt calls the lifts. One arrives in a few seconds. We go up, and the doors open on the forty-fifth floor as James instructed. As I suspected would inevitably happen, someone turns around and points his gun at us.

16

Matt is much quicker to respond, and he blasts the guy off his feet. I can hear his thud, and I cringe at the noisy thump as he hits the ground. Someone else hears it. Still, Matt is the quicker draw and shoots him too. When I get closer to the first guard, I can tell he is still alive but has been knocked out.

"Dammit," James hisses, his sudden voice a stinging pain of annoyance. "Put the two of them in the elevator; I'll lock it out of use so that no one finds them."

Matt immediately picks up the second guy he shot over his shoulder and gently lays him down on the carpeted floor of the lift. Andre and I drag the first one.

"These guys weren't on my feeds," James explains. "This could be more difficult than I thought. Stay vigilant."

I don't understand how James could have missed this. An honest mistake, I try to tell myself. But the feeling of distrust in the man grows. I don't voice any of my concerns to the others. Plus, James can hear everything that we say.

When the commotion is over, Matt carefully places the other man next to the first. He spits out air as he leaves the elevator, leaving Maylene to jump in, hit a button and run out. I hear the elevator rise and then stop suddenly after James shuts it down.

Matt punches another button, and a different elevator greets us shortly. We get in and ride it up to the forty-fifth floor. I look at the others. Matt's face is set, almost with an annoyed look. Maylene tries to keep her face hard, but I can tell there is fear behind her eyes. Andre looks bored, but his eyes quickly fix on the closed doors as the elevator comes to a halt. I hold my breath as the doors open.

The floor is empty. Grand in size, there isn't much else going on. The open space breaks off into two hallways, but I can tell they are connected. The rooms in the center seem to be small utility closets, while the ends have rooms used for meetings.

"The board rooms are all connected. Don't bother with the doors in the middle; they will likely just get you killed. I know the floor seems empty, but patrols will come through randomly, and there are likely to be people in the suites," James warns us. "Unfortunately, there aren't any cameras inside the rooms, so I can't help you much with checking if anyone is in them. I will play back earlier feeds to see if anyone has entered them and let you know if I find anything. For now, all you want to do is reach the pillar towards the center. That is the back door to the main elevator, which will run straight up to the heart of the Centennial Courtyard."

Great, another excuse in case we run into danger.

As usual, Matt leads the way. He didn't say anything in response to James, so I begin to wonder if he is feeling the same way I am. As we move forward, I can't help but feel that the utter emptiness of the place means we're being followed.

"Go through the door to your left," James says. When we don't immediately follow his order, he barks, "Now!"

Matt shoves open the door. Maylene is right behind him. Andre trails off for a second, but I see what James was trying to have us avoid.

Before the man can raise his arm to point at us, I shove Andre through the doorway and jump in, locking the door behind me.

Barging into the conference room did little to resolve the situation. The room is long and has an oval feel to it, though it is quite rectangularly symmetrical. Doors remain closed at all ends, with four leading out into the hallway, including the one we came through.

Three guards quickly rise from their chairs and shoot. A bullet hits me in the chest. I stumble back, the pain shooting through me quickly but briefly. There is a slight distortion of light in my vision. The suit. The suit just saved me. The bullet never made it into my body, let alone the suit.

Without thinking, I raise my weapon and fire. I don't hit anyone, but two of the guards go down. Once again, it was Matt doing his work. Andre gets the third guy. Maylene runs over and begins to drag them under the table. Better than nothing, at least they will be out of sight upon a quick glance.

The door at the other end opens. Instinctively, I raise my firearm and shoot. Without aiming, I shoot him square in the chest, and the guy flies backwards, landing unconscious in the conference room next door.

Matt pats me on my shoulder and makes his way into the next room. Luckily, there is no one else waiting for us. Not there at least. James tells us to get back into the hallways. We do so.

I believe all of us are suspicious of the man, but we know he can't do anything overly drastic. Not with Edward also watching.

A woman steps into the hallway from one of the smaller rooms to our right. I thought those were closets. She looks at us with an eye of distaste, but she carries no weapon. Instead, she carries a metal staff used to recharge machines used to clean.

"I mean you no harm, but I cannot help you, whoever you are," she says. She wears a white cloth over her head and part of her face.

I believe her. Wispy brown hair filters through it. She is shorter than Andre. "Please just let me be, and I will tell no one."

Matt shoots her.

"Unfortunately, we can't take that chance," he says. I'm not sure if he was telling her that, us, or himself. "Also, unfortunate for you," he says as he walks up to her lying on the ground. We follow him. With her eyes closes and her mouth curved slightly, she looks peaceful. I know she isn't dead, but it's still a sad sight. "This weapon isn't lethal, so my backoff on using it is none." Again, I think he's mostly talking to himself.

He steps over her and makes his way towards the center. As we get closer, the middle set of rooms comes to an end, and the two hallways are joined once again like they were back in the elevator lobby. There is a pillar here, but that is all it is.

"Let's keep moving that way," Matt says, pointing to the hallway.

"No, use the other hall," James says into our earpieces.

Matt stops in his tracks, shakes his head just ever so slightly, but crosses the open hall to the other side. We barely make it twenty Milkateet before James shouts at us to jump into the door to our left. Matt does so quickly, followed by the rest of us, having learned our lesson last time. Funny how fast we listen to a man we barely trust.

I was right. The rooms in the middle are mainly utility closets. It feels as if I can feel every part of everyone else. Random cleaning tools stand out in their compartments, jabbing into my back. I don't know why they bother with these since no one uses them. They've barely been in use even before I was born.

As uncomfortable as we all are, we stay silent. The minute turns into two, and I begin to wonder if James is just messing with us. Then I hear the footsteps. I can sense someone walks down the hall, closer and closer, yet they move slowly, as if they know someone is here that shouldn't be. Then the footsteps get louder. Then they double. There are two people. I can hear them talk quietly to themselves, as if they are bored with their job but still pay enough attention to do it in case they need to.

My foot begins to slip. I'm not sure how it is; the floor doesn't feel slick, and it isn't like there is anywhere for me to fall. I feel Andre shift behind me. I get the idea that he also feels like he is slipping. My arm feels awkward, grazing against Maylene's butt. The room is dark, the only light seeping in through the crack at the bottom of the door.

Out of the corner of my eye, I can see their shadows. They stop talking. They stop walking. Not even a minute passes by, and they just stand there. Listening.

The minute passes. They go for it. One of them opens the door. Matt, much larger than the rest of us, leans backwards, pressing us down on top of each other, and punches the man in the face once it's exposed, sending him back reeling and dazed. The other man raises his gun and shoots. I hear the quick whistle as the air rifle blasts through. I can feel the wind against my head, but Maylene takes the greatest blow.

Her suit flares up, and I can see her face as it gets pressed in, but her skin doesn't get sliced into pieces. The range is so close; the solidified air bounces back, and the man gets blown away, layers of his skin evaporating as it is cut into minuscule pieces. The result makes his face ooze blood, his eyes appear to be charred, and the man had a painful, quick death brought on by his own shot.

"Shove the body in the closet."

At first, I think James said it, but then I realize it was Matt. He takes the man that he knocked out and shoots him in the chest, just for good measure.

"There's too much blood on the floors," James says. "Leave him there; your chance of keeping quiet is gone."

"A dead body is much easier to see at a distance than some blood on the ground," Matt snaps back. He then turns to Andre. "Move it into the closet. They'll find it eventually, but not tonight."

Andre does as he is told. Matt drags the other guy into a different closet. He then turns back and gives Maylene a quick hug.

"You okay?" he asks her.

Maylene chokes down a sob, but her voice is quite strong. "Yeah." She pauses for a second, then looks down the hall and jerks her head. "Let's keep moving."

Matt gives her a small smile, and we make our way, this time at a jog.

At the next open area, I see the pillar with the back-door access to the lift. Matt presses the button, but nothing happens.

"You need a key," James says. "Hold on. I'll bring the elevator to you."

We wait just under ten seconds before the doors slide open. This elevator is quite elegant, with stone flooring and gold handrails. The wooden boards nicely add a touch of taste. This elevator was designed to make visitors feel like they were in a place of peace. A place that is safe. After what's happened so far, I know it's not, and I find it quite nefarious that they put up this front.

It's just something else I don't like, and it makes my feelings for James worse, as he was the one to instruct us to use this elevator. I would imagine that there are other ways to get to where we need to go.

A quick trip to the hundredth floor, and the doors open to paradise. The courtyard is covered in a lush growth of trees, ferns, and shrubs. Blossoming flowers provide a pleasant scent that rides the circulating air. There are paved paths that walk over bridges that spawn small creeks. In the distance, I can see a lone bird fluttering towards a tree. Four fountains are spaced evenly around the elevator that we're in, which took us right to the center of the courtyard. The ceiling is clear, making it easy to see up towards the sky.

Matt steps out after a second, taking in the view. He walks slowly at first but quickly goes at a determined pace. I follow right behind while Maylene nudges Andre to move faster.

As we go, I can hear the water trickling and the leaves blowing in the fake wind. There are several benches plopped about, while some pathways lead to an observation deck. The whole room is so large that you could easily spend a couple hours wandering it. It must take up most of the floor.

"That elevator usually brings people from the second floor, straight up, and vice versa. Visitors pay a small fee to visit the place and then spend hours lost in the magical land," James says into our ears. There is something off about his voice, something disdainful. "Pity, these people can go out of any city and see things like this, but people seem to forget that there is a whole world out there."

Finally. James says something that we both agree on.

"Keep heading where you're going," James says. I see Matt shake his head again. "Doors line the floor in case of emergencies, but I've disabled the alarms so you can use whichever one you want. The tricky part will be entering the floor below."

We keep going. Knowing what lies ahead, the awe of the courtyard quickly loses its appeal.

Before long, we reach the end of the paths. Matt jumps over the wooden fence and splashes into the shallow river that lines the edge of the room. People aren't meant to be going this way. I do the same. When I look behind me, I see Maylene and Andre open a small gate and hop over the river.

Andre gives me an amused look as he passes. I follow the three of them out of the courtyard.

The hall that lines this floor feels cold and damp. There is nothing but structural stonework in the hall. Even though our suits silence our footsteps, I can imagine how they would sound here.

An alarm starts blaring.

"Shit, they found something," James hisses at us. "You guys should have been more careful!"

"We followed your orders!" Matt shouts back, turning around and facing us, though he looks straight ahead. "But that's already done; where do we go from here?" Matt lowers his voice. Just a bit. He holds his composure well, but I can tell from the way he acts now that he never trusted James.

"Calm yourself, Matt," I hear the voice of Edward say. "They just know there is some sort of intruder; it'll take them much longer to find you than it will for you to find them." Mr. Canabana pauses for a second. "Find the stairs and head to the floor below you. In fact, this might be easier now since the guards below will be distracted."

"Only if they move quickly," James says. "They have sensed motion on the hundredth floor. I was unable to wipe the feeds before they looked at them. They are headed up to you now. Less than one minute."

The four of us sprint down the hall, on the lookout for a door that leads to a stairwell. We find one. Before we can barge through the door, red lines flash on. Matt collides with the door, unable to open it. It's been locked.

"They're initiating a lockdown," James says. The franticness in his voice sounds strained. I clench my jaw and imagine all the possibilities, most of them with the four of us dying here. "Let me see if I can override it."

I feel like we're doomed.

"Let me."

The sound of Gary's voice injects hope into my soul. I don't even know why. I barely know the man's capabilities, but I trust him completely.

Seconds later, we hear a click. Matt kicks the door open, and we jump down the stairs. The ninety-ninth floor greets us with no less than five guards, aiming at the door we just pushed through. We all take the hits, though the suits absorb them, leaving us unhurt. The four of us fire our weapons, and the guards are blasted back unconscious. I don't know if, in larger doses, our ammunition is lethal, and I hope not, as I don't know that these guards even know what they're protecting.

The floor we're on looks like a maze. There are even more halls, though there are almost no doors. We run wildly through, ready to shoot anything that moves. The alarms still blare, but that noise has moved to the background in my head and remains nearly silent. The red lights stay on, not flashing.

We put down another dozen guards as we make our way. It feels as if we go in circles. Our earpieces remain silent. There is a large part of the floor that I feel we haven't covered, but there is no way to access it.

Minutes go by. We never slow down. Finally, we find a few doors, but they are all locked. When we do find one that opens, it is just another stairwell, very likely the same one we came down.

"There!" James shouts, slightly busting my eardrum. "I've done it. You can access the facility."

It takes a moment for us to understand what he means. In the large area surrounded by walls, I had guessed right. There is a part we haven't covered. It looks like it leads from near the middle of the floor right out to one end of the building. Up ahead, a door opens, retracting upward into the ceiling. It blends so well with the wall that I never would have known there was a door there.

Guards barge out of the room, their weapons aimed but not yet firing.

As we get closer, they start pulling their triggers. Two lines of guards, each line made up of around eight, take turns firing their guns. After enough hits, I start to feel like I am getting bruised, but the pain is still nowhere near what a bullet through the chest would be. Or an air rifle to the face.

With what feels like telekinetic teamwork, the guards lay asleep on top of each other. We jump over them into the facility.

Most of everything in here is white; with strong blue lights shining down from the ceiling, while white lights light the room from various spots in the ground. There isn't anyone here. I would expect more guards, and even those who are scientifically and technologically inclined, but it is possible they have already left.

The door shuts behind us, leaving us trapped inside.

"They haven't all left the facility," James says. "Now no one can, but the Lead Specialist has the chip. He wears a gray coat. Find him."

The four of us split up. I make my way around various appliances and shorter walls. A guard jumps out in front of me. I fire my weapon in shock. I miss. The guard doesn't. Three shots: two to the chest and one to the face. While the suit protects me, I still fall back. As I lie on the floor and scramble to gather my weapon, the guard walks up to me. I snatch one of the knives near the boot-shaped part of the suit and chuck it at the guard. It grazes his leg, not doing much to him, but still gives me enough time to properly aim my weapon and fire.

When I hear his thud, I jump to my feet.

"Got him!" I hear Maylene call out. I turn back, trying to make my way to her. I finally do so. The gray-suited man looks asleep, while

Maylene holds him slightly elevated off the floor by keeping a tight grip on his suit. Matt comes up. Maylene hands him the chip.

"Do we even need to use the decoy?" Matt asks. "They already know we're here, and they may have removed the chip."

Silence.

"Do you read me?" Matt asks, slightly frustrated. The four of us now stand close to each other, nervous, as we all feel like sitting ducks.

"Get to the main machine," Edward orders. "I believe that the gray man was a distraction."

Matt charges into action. Maylene drops the Lead Specialist, and we follow Matt. He leads us to a slick, black device that stands as tall as the ceiling. It looks simple. There is nothing flashy about it. The dark, shiny color of it is majorly contrasted by the bright white of the rest of the room. We walk up to it. Sure enough, there is a small chip hovering inside a reader.

"Don't bother using the decoy," Edward tells us. "But be sure to take that one."

Matt reaches for it. His arm jerks away. His suit falters. Matt turns to the source, takes an old, regular-looking bullet to his torso, and falls back. I whip my head, and my eyes open wide when I see the shooter. Maylene's eyes do the same. But nothing is more heartbreaking than the look on Andre's face. The sudden realization that the one you planned to spend the rest of your life with is your enemy, probably always, just in disguise.

"Good evening, *fiancé*," Daden says in his usual style of class. His hair is slicked back, and he wears a dark tuxedo. He smiles with those flashy teeth. "Surprised to see me here? I heard you might come, but I had hoped that the rumors weren't true." He walks closer to us. "Well, no time to talk now. I need you to leave now. Leave the chip where it is. You do that; no one else has to get hurt." He walks even closer. Maylene and I tense. I steal a quick glance down at Matt. His eyes are narrowed, teeth baring in pain. There was something potent about that bullet.

Andre is as still as the night.

"Don't make me shoot you," Daden warns. "I don't care about the others." He fires a quick shot at Maylene. She falls back, but her suit remains intact. "These weapons were designed to counter your suits. Apparently, they still need some work."

Andre taps his cheek three times, deactivating the silencing mechanism on his suit. "Why?" Andre asks, skillfully hiding the pain in his voice.

Daden cracks a small smile. "Perhaps, on our honeymoon, we can catch up," Daden says.

There is little to no thought to it. No hesitation. Andre nimbly pulls a weapon from a rear pocket of his suit. I know where he held it. I hold one of my other weapons that Matt had me bring in that same spot. Lightweight, strapped well, but made for easy access. It almost doesn't feel like a pocket at all. Andre flicks down the safety mechanism on his weapon and pulls the trigger. There is a faint pop. Two things happen almost simultaneously. Daden jerks from the impact, and then the small bullet discharges a quick, powerful jolt to his body, and with another jerk immediately following the first, Daden drops dead.

Matt groans and gets up to his feet. He snatches the chip from the reader but almost falls when he does. When the chip is removed, the device seems to shut down. He turns to look at Andre. Andre doesn't return it. His face is set with a look of pure anger and hatred. I can't imagine what the man must be feeling. And with how quickly he acted, part of me thinks he's going to have a hard recovery.

There isn't time to dwell on it.

"Get down!" The shouts ring through my ears, but I do as I'm told. The others get down too and cover their head with their hands. I notice Matt inject something into his shoulder. Blood leaks out of his side.

A mechanistic blasting gun fires, and I hear glass shatter. Shards rain down on us, though we are safe from the worst part of it.

"There's your ride guys! Get in!" Gary wheezes into our earpieces.

I look up. Way at the end, beyond the open window frame, is the airship that we rode in. I get up and start to make my way, but I feel something tug at my leg. I look down. It's Matt.

Matt looks in bad shape. Maylene places her hand on my shoulder to get my attention. I look at her. She points to Andre, who has tears forming in his eyes. I nod to her, understanding. She's going to take Andre to the airship. It's my responsibility to get Matt there.

Strong gusts of wind howl through. I look Matt in the eye. He closes his mouth and nods. I bend down. With all my strength, and then some, I heave Matt up. He is able to stand on his legs but needs me for support. His hand covers his wound, which is getting worse with each passing second. The bullet may not have worked on Maylene's suit, but it tore through Matt's.

As I help him walk, Matt's eyes start to fade. He keeps at it, despite everything. I can feel his muscles working to make his body move, and he does his best to not drop all his weight on me. I see a pocket of his with some syringes and get a sudden idea. I move my hand to grab one, but Matt stops me with his hand. I can feel the sticky blood. Matt falls to one knee. He is bleeding too much. I wonder what exactly that bullet was made of.

Not knowing what else to do, I remove my suit and wrap it around his torso, trying to stop the bleeding. I tie it as hard as I can, hoping that whatever it is that can absorb impacts can also help seal up Matt's growing wound. My body shivers, now naked in the wind, ninety-nine stories high. Giving it all he has, Matt stands up again. I wrap his arm around my shoulders the way it was before, and we take small steps to the airship. Matt's eyes are half closed.

The walk seems to take forever. I am amazed that more guards haven't barged into us, firing their weapons to kill.

When we're close to the airship, it moves closer. I can see the silhouette of Maylene inside, and she is waving her hand, indicating for me to stay back. I don't know why, but I follow what she says.

A ramp extends out from the ship. Adeptly, the ship moves even closer, and the ramp is gently placed on the floor. Good thing, as I would never have made even a small jump with Matt on me.

Once we get in, Maylene helps tug us inside properly, and the ramp retracts. The airship's door closes, and I can feel it fly into the night. Our speed picks up quickly.

I shiver again and cough out. Spit and mucus splatter the cold floor. Andre gives me a small blanket, but it does little to warm me or cover me up. Maylene attends to Matt, who is now almost fully unconscious. I want to help him, but the very real realization of being there naked on my hands and knees hits me.

I hear someone say something in the distance, but I can't make out any words. Andre goes towards the cockpit. I close my eyes and take a deep breath. I know Maylene would help, but she has more pressing matters.

I force myself to look at Matt. His eyes are open now. Matt stares at Maylene, not even flinching as she works to close the wound. Maylene sprays an antiseptic every other second.

"You took two of them," she whispers to herself, half amused. "You shouldn't have." That's why Matt stopped me earlier. He knew I was going to shoot him up with another dose, but a third one probably would have killed him. With shaking hands, she injects something else into his shoulder. Again, Matt doesn't even flinch. He is so still. Just when I think he might be dead, Matt blinks.

The sound of approaching footsteps catches my attention. I gulp and shiver again. I hope that it's Andre with a bigger blanket or some clothes. The seconds that pass seem too long, like so many other things tonight.

It is hard to believe that we were successful, though that success is already tainted with Andre's tragedy, and it all might get worse, depending on Matt's condition.

The footsteps took their time to arrive, but they finally do.

My heart stops when I look up. I had feared for so long that I had ruined everything, and now I lie here, naked, on a cold floor, having been rescued by the only girl who has made me feel any sort of love in a long time. My embarrassment doesn't help my nude appearance, and I try to turn away from her.

"Let's get you some new clothes, shall we?" Kaedy says with a playful wink.

17

Kaedy wraps her arms around me and leads me towards the back of the ship. She sits me down on a step and walks away. I can't help but do my best to cover my exposed parts. I am now constantly shivering, and the vibrations of my body are making my teeth chatter. The noise around me sounds too loud, and the noises I expect Matt to be making are too quiet. I want to get up, but something keeps me pinned where I sit.

When I'm about to stand, Kaedy comes back. She tosses me a pair of soft pants and a sweater. I glance up at her. My eyes feel wide, as if I'm scared. She gives me a slightly disapproving look and then turns away. I stand up and put the clothes on. The sweater is slightly big, but the pants fit fine.

"Are you done?" she asks.

"Yeah."

Kaedy turns around. She marches straight up to me and gives me a hug. I hug her back, forgetting all the embarrassment I just felt. When she releases, she gives me a quick kiss and then a mild slap across my face.

"That's for thinking I was anything less than a decent person," she says. I look at her, horrified at what I had done. But her face eases into a smile, and she gives me another quick kiss.

"Let's check on Matt, and then depending on how things are, we can catch up," she suggests. I nod. She takes my hand and walks me back to the front. Matt is sitting on the couch. He is still awake. He smiles a foolish grin when he sees me walk in.

"My unclad savior!" he shouts out. He shifts to get up off the couch, but Maylene holds him down. "Come here, you scoundrel; I need to give you a proper thanks."

Kaedy playfully pushes me forward. When I'm close enough, Matt kicks my legs, lifts himself up slightly, and brings me down with him, holding me in a tight embrace.

A million words go unspoken, but I understand the immense appreciation he has for me for what I did. Even with his moderate high, no doubt brought on by whatever Maylene had to do to keep him alive, Matt is able to wordlessly communicate a sober truth: that he probably wouldn't be alive if it weren't for me.

For me, it was a no-brainer. I definitely wouldn't be alive if he hadn't saved me on more than one occasion. This way, I've started to pay back that debt.

He releases me from his firm grip. I stand back up and look at him. He smiles again.

"I'm all good," he tells me. "In a few days, I'll be back to normal. Now go talk to your girl. You've both been waiting for this."

Maylene shoots me a mischievous grin as I walk away. Kaedy doesn't lead us far, just back to the cockpit, where Andre sits.

"Is he okay?" Andre asks.

I nod. I hesitate for a moment, but I have to ask. He has to know I care.

"How about you?"

Andre doesn't look at me. I never expected him to. Moments pass, and I presume he isn't ready to answer.

I lean back in the chair. Kaedy stands there, staying silent but reassuring. On and on, the night passes by as we soar through it. By this time, we are way past Longfurd. Andre increases our elevation, and we fly high over another city, though the city is much smaller than most. This maneuver isn't legal, but with our airship's cloaking capabilities, it is unlikely that we will get caught.

"I was sent this." Andre's voice is deeper than usual, somber, and his words are curt. He holds out his phone and presses his thumb to its screen.

"Dear Andre." There is a short laugh after the two words are spoken mockingly. *"Oh my, if you are hearing this, it means that for whatever reason, I am dead. Whether by your hand or another's, I do not know. It isn't always easy to predict the future. But you must know this. I was paid a lot of money to infiltrate Canabana Industries. The fall of Chlorofyx was just initiated, and I fear that our conflicting interests will come between us. Not that there was ever really much of an us. But,"* Daden's voice pauses for a moment, *"over time, I grew to like you. Of course, my true love, the one I am devoted to, doesn't share those feelings for me. No matter, I got to play with yours and pretend like something was there."* Daden lets out a long sigh. *"But, again, if you hear this message, I am dead, and you survived. Good for you, because it was my every intention to have you killed the day before our wedding. As much as I had fun playing your love game, you were never the one for me. Alas, with me dead, I am happy that I no longer have to spend time with you."*

The recording stops abruptly. I don't know if Andre stopped it early, concealing from us anything else in the message, or if Daden cut it out himself for whatever reason he had. I stare at Andre, not knowing how to respond. What kind of person even records something like that? Daden was messed up in more ways than there are numbers. Kaedy says nothing. With a direct stare out the windshield, Andre keeps his composure. It doesn't take long before he breaks down into sobs. Kaedy walks over to him. She leans down and gently tries to get him to leave the seat. She shoots me a look and jerks her head towards the control panels. I move the chair up, disengage the main driver controls, and take over driving the airship.

I hear something behind me. I take a quick glance and see Maylene, with Matt behind her, leaning against the wall. Maylene looks horrified. Matt's expression still holds a hint of physical pain, but his eyes are gloomy, and he looks down at the floor.

The four of us remain where we are while we let Andre grieve. I keep most of my attention on the sky, but it's hard to concentrate much with everything that we went through. My eyes form tears, but my feelings alternate between extreme sadness and rage, a pendulum striking the strongest chords of my emotions. Andre never deserved it. A good guy who thought he had found the love of his life, left shattered with the broken truth that it was all a hoax. Left with the knowledge that he had been played, used, and tossed aside without care. A naturally welcoming man told straight up that he was nothing more than a means to an end and a cheap substitute for something else. Daden always meant to harm Andre, one way or another.

But also knowing that Daden in some way played a part in the destruction of Chlorofyx infuses a hatred and anger within me that makes me feel like doing some extreme, violent things. If Daden was still alive, I'd probably use all my resources to hunt him down. That won't happen. Andre already did the work. He did it before knowing that Daden never truly loved him. He did it thinking that he killed his fiancé for the sake of his new friends, people who he met only recently.

A good man. Pissed and shat on by the evils of immoral human beings.

The dark sky begins to blaze with the dawn of a new day. Andre has fallen asleep, leaning on Kaedy's shoulder, who holds her uncomfortable position for his sake. Matt walked back to the couch a couple hours ago and now sleeps in his recovery. Maylene sits between the two front seats, saying nothing but being there all the same.

A call comes into the ship. I silence it before looking at who it is. It's Edward Canabana. Maylene presses a button on the left side of the panels and tells me to answer it. When I do, the volume is low, and the sound only comes out on the side I sit at.

"My deepest apologies for not calling sooner," Edward says. He sounds tired. "I knew you were all safe from the footage in your suits, but still, that doesn't excuse my not checking in."

I can tell there is more news, none of it likely to be good. We don't say anything, so Edward goes on.

"James was confronted on his lack of performance while guiding you through the Tall Building. Of course, and I had increasingly begun to suspect it, James threw a fit and attempted to kill us." Edward zooms out of his face. He is in Maylene's office, sitting at one of the desks. Chairs are tossed sideways on the floor, and one of the desks is splintered into three pieces. Papers lay scattered across the room, none fully intact.

"Long story short, Gary put him down," Edward tells us. Gary pops into view. In his old age, he seems younger than ever. His clothes are ruffled, and his thin hair stands up higher than it should.

"Oh, I got that sucker good," Gary spits out. "He never knew what was coming."

Edward lets Gary croak out a laugh before continuing.

"We are still determining if James is working for the same person Daden was or if it was a collaboration of two entities who shared the same goal." Edward pauses for a moment. He lowers his voice and says, "Speaking of which, how is Andre?"

I sigh and look over. Andre is still asleep. Kaedy listens intently, but I can tell she struggles to hear everything.

"He's having a rough time," I tell Edward.

"As expected," Mr. Canabana replies. "I'll leave you be. Give Kaedy my thanks for being there for the four of you, and Maylene, well done on recruiting such a wonderful girl. She has out-proven herself, even if she agreed only to this one mission. I am sure you all can agree that she is a life saver."

I look over to Kaedy. She hears that and wears a blush with her smile.

"When you reach your destination, call me," he says, talking to Maylene. She nods, and he closes the connection.

Andre stays asleep. Maylene gets up. "I'm going to check on Matt. I know we passed over a few cities under the cover of night, but ground the ship next time we reach city perimeters. We won't get away without doing so, even while cloaked."

"Okay," I tell her. She leaves toward the back.

I look over at Kaedy, a wide grin on my face.

"So Maylene called you and asked you to help us?"

Kaedy shrugs. "Yeah."

"That's amazing," I say. "I am sorry I ever doubted you."

Kaedy shrugs again, this time with a small smile.

"I understand why you did," she says. "The coincidence was just too great. It was probably very logical thinking, given your state of mind after what happened." She sighs. "I was freaking out because I thought you were dead. But then, after we spoke, I realized what you were thinking. Later that night, Maylene called me and explained everything."

I slowly turn to look at her again.

"I know that you're taking that program chip to NEAST, and I know what that chip does. So, when Maylene told me that she was going to need my help soon, I told her that I would be there. She later said that I'd most likely be saving her life and yours too. I didn't know Matt or Andre, but still. If they were your friends, I was going to help them too."

The sense of love I feel for her grows in my chest. I take in a deep breath. I almost leave the seat to go over to her. She can tell that I want to. She wants to sit by me too, but she keeps being Andre's pillow, a comfort that he needs more than I do.

We come upon a large city. The buildings reflect a hue of blue in the afternoon sunlight. The main road is wide, and we aren't stopped much as we pass through. With bustling crowds and bullet trams that traverse from one side of the city to the other, I am a bit disheartened that I don't have the time to enjoy the city, as I have never been here before.

I try to get a good look at what the city has to offer, but being surrounded by buildings close to two hundred stories tall, I can't see much other than what is right in front of me. Neon lights of purple and pink dominate the city. There are fewer elevations here than there normally would be considering its size. Towards the end of the city, the buildings are smaller, and then even smaller until we pass by large homes, the grand scale of the city diminishing and replaced with a countryside feeling. It is likely these are the homes of the wealthiest. The inner city is likely riddled with crime at night, in the darkest and dirtiest of spots. It amazes me how they can get away with it with all the camera footage and strict laws that the city has.

Less than half an hour later, we fly out of the grounding zone and fly into the atmosphere. Andre shifts in his sleep and moves off of Kaedy. He stays asleep.

"Oh, I thought I was going to lose my arm there," Kaedy says as she slowly stands up. Her knees wobble slightly as she reaches her full height. "I'm going to walk around for a little bit." She stumbles her first few steps.

I end up driving alone for a while. I hear something behind me. I don't look, expecting Kaedy to say something.

"She fell asleep back there," I hear Maylene say. "She deserves it too."

I chuckle to myself.

"How's Matt doing?"

Maylene comes by and sits cross-legged next to me. "He's doing much better. Asleep as well. He needs it."

I nod, understanding their need to sleep, as I begin to feel tired. The landscape of tall grass creates a cozy, slumberous vibe that hits me, coupled with the lack of sleep and the wearing off of the adrenaline Matt shot me up with close to a day ago.

"Let me take over," Maylene says. "I've had my time to rest. Now it's yours."

I nod again. I push the button to engage autopilot and leave the driver's seat. Maylene quickly takes over, but I take her spot on the floor.

"What about getting some sleep?" she asks.

I try to stifle a yawn, but then let it all out. I smack my lips tiredly before answering. "I'll head back there soon. I just want to let the sleepiness fully overcome me so that I just pass out."

"There's alcohol in the back kitchenette," Maylene suggests. I don't respond to that, but it's good to know that she is still that same person.

After some thought, Maylene asks, "How do you think he's gonna be?"

I look up at her and see her nudge her head in Andre's direction.

"He'll be fine," I tell her. "Eventually. He'll probably want to take some time off, but I don't think he should be all alone. Knowing him as much as I do, which really isn't that well, he will probably want to rediscover himself. The thing is, there is already so much about him and so much that he has that's just...*good*. I don't think he needs to rediscover himself."

"What do you think he needs?"

I shrug. "My wisdom isn't that deep. I've never been in any position close to his, so I can't say for sure. But in my opinion, he's one of the best people I know. That means he already knows who he is."

Maylene doesn't say anything, but I can tell she agrees. I sit there for about twenty minutes. I can't really see much out the window, just the darkening sky above. Maylene concentrates on driving while getting lost in her own thoughts.

When I feel the fatigue start to kick in, I get up to head to the back, where I can get some rest. Maylene gently grabs my arm and squeezes it before letting it trail off from her grip as I walk away. Matt and Kaedy take up most of the available space, sleeping on separate couches. I climb up the ladder, jump into one of the first sleeping areas I see, and fall onto the bed, quickly falling asleep.

The dreams I have run through my head, but they make less and less sense as they go on. I can remember the night inside the Tall Building. I can remember the idyllic nature of the courtyard and the horrible choices made just moments after. I can also remember dreaming of being caught, tortured, and thrown out of windows at elevations greater than ten. That I know didn't happen. But now I can see the four of us escaping on wild horses, though they fly like my old Sonars, and Gary rides upon one with Kaedy.

I can also hear the laughter, though it belongs to my friends. Something smells warm, but I know that makes little sense.

I open my eyes.

The laughter indeed comes from below. The warmth now smells like food, and a loud growl immediately makes me sit upright, craving the food down there. I get out of the bed and jump down through the opening, skipping all the rungs of the ladder. Maylene lets out a small shriek of shock, but then bursts into laughter. She is carrying a pan with small meat-rods, which are apparently called "sausages" on Earth.

What a weird word.

The whole gang is awake. Maylene and Kaedy move around busily, heating up food from the appliances I managed to overlook. Maylene finds the alcohol and takes it out. We are no longer moving. I try to take a peek out the front windows, but I can't tell where we are, only that we are parked somewhere surrounded by trees, probably by the edge of a deep forest.

"Hey bud," Matt says in his lower voice. "How did you sleep?"

"Good," I say. "Odd dreams, though."

He laughs. "You're telling me."

I don't even want to imagine what kind of dreams Matt had, being in unbearable pain, drugged up to fight infection, and shot with too much adrenaline before then being given something to make him go to sleep. I'm surprised he hasn't had any other complications than his initial injury. I'm surprised his heart didn't stop.

I look over towards Andre. He stares forward, occasionally looking around, and putting on small smiles. We all know he's hurting badly inside. I take a cue from the others and don't mention anything to him. Andre will let us know when he's ready. And when he is, we will be there for him.

Someone taps my hip with theirs. Its Maylene.

"Have a seat," she says. "We're cooking, and you men are going to enjoy it."

I oblige and chuckle. "You don't seem the type to cook for men. Or for anyone."

Maylene laughs. "Oh, honey," she says tenderly as she sits down next to me. She looks me dead in the eye. "I'm not. If I cooked the food, it likely will taste horrible." She laughs in my face. I can smell the alcohol, but I know she isn't drunk. Not yet, at least. "Kaedy seems pretty good, though. But you're not allowed to let us know who you think made the food, so if it tastes horrible, smile and swallow it down."

A laugh comes over from Matt. "Easy for you to say."

Maylene stands up. "No, not really. I mean, yeah, easy to say. But swallowing isn't my thing. I'm more of a slurper."

"A slurper?" Matt asks, his eyes just slightly narrowing like an animation as he grins widely.

"Yeah, a slurper," Maylene asserts. "Whatever. Call it what you like."

I smile, amused, but say nothing, not knowing if they're talking about food or something else.

"Okay, food is ready!" Kaedy calls out. Her voice sounds angelic, and that's not just because she saved me from hearing more of Matt and Maylene. My stomach gives off a low growl, as if it were waiting for this.

The meat-rods are delicious. Some are way overcooked, undoubtedly done by Maylene, according to her confession. These are followed by some smoothie drinks that Kaedy promises will make us feel way better in a little while.

"This will detox all of that adrenaline and unnatural stuff you poisoned yourself with, as well as give you the nutrients you're definitely lacking. After a good night's sleep, you'll feel brand new," Kaedy says.

"Hey, those adrenaline shots probably saved my life," Matt says.

"I believe you," Kaedy replies. "When used as needed, I don't have a problem with them. I just think it's best to heal yourself after. Have you ever seen someone who took adrenaline shots even just twice a week?"

Matt snorts. "No, who is that crazy?"

"There are people out there," Kaedy goes on. "And I've seen them. Let me tell you something: they are ugly. Like some horribly wrinkled and diseased-ridden faces, and their bodies just ooze this putrid smell. Usually they don't lose hair, but their hair becomes this tangled, solid mess that becomes too heavy and petrified looking."

Matt immediately downs his smoothie.

We finish eating, even Andre, and end up leaning back in our seats, satisfied with a decent meal and time to relax.

"We believe that we've lost anyone who may have been following us," Maylene says, but I think she is mainly telling me, as I was the one who was asleep last. "But we have sensors and alarms ready in case the ship picks up anything unusual or threatening."

"Great. And where are we?" I ask.

"Somewhere ways off Gandago," Matt says. Gandago is easily a day's worth of full-time driving in an ordinary Sonars from Longfurd. Quicker, for sure, with a high-speed ship. But I don't think anyone followed us far, so I don't think we had to lose anyone trailing our tail. I don't know how. And I don't know why, but I don't think they were interested in going after us.

"Where do we go from here?"

"We'll be heading up north from here, veering slightly west," Andre answers, surprising all of us. "We have to get you going towards NEAST, but the three of us have to get back to our headquarters."

"But we won't be there for long," Maylene assures me. "I'll be taking a different route to NEAST, probably meeting you there, while Matt will follow behind you."

Guessing my concern, Matt says, "I'll be good as new then; don't you worry about me."

"And I am going to stay with you," Kaedy says. "At least for a bit. We will be picking up a new Sonars for you soon. Then I'll ride with you to Fraslia, but after that I must be on my way. But I'll be waiting for you back in Candalance!"

Fraslia is less than two days to NEAST. I've never been there before, but maybe I can make a quick trip back there once I deliver the chip.

"That sounds like a great plan," I say. None of it is selfish, none of it has to do with spending time with Kaedy. I do my best to hide my excitement, but I feel hot in my face, and my friends know me too well.

"Any new information on what happened?" I ask, cringing at the question as I remember Andre is here. "I mean, you know."

"We know what you mean," Andre says. I can't tell what emotion he is feeling. But he keeps going on. "Still no word on who Daden was working for. James won't budge, and it isn't in Mr. Canabana's nature to resort to torture."

It isn't in my nature either. I thought that James was dead, but I suppose I misunderstood what Edward said. It is probably a good thing he is alive, as James could be connected to Chlorofyx, and he would have info on who our enemies are. I don't know if I will ever get over what happened. I'm sure if I turned on the news, it would still have reports on the current state of the city and rescue efforts, though by now most are probably in vain. I wonder if, were I to stand in front of James, knowing that he knew who was behind Chlorofyx, I wouldn't resort to torture myself, purely for revenge.

18

Looking at Kaedy's face is the only thing that keeps me feeling like myself. The pain and hurt that I've felt, which I know is nothing compared to those affected by the collapsing city, makes me want to be a different person. Someone more violent. More dangerous. Someone threatening enough that they could do something about it, and that those evil enough to destroy so many lives are too scared to. The moment doesn't last long, and soon I can turn away, knowing that I am not yet becoming so vengeful.

Shortly after Andre told us that we know nothing about who was behind Chlorofyx or who Daden and James were working for, we were in the sky again. I took the first shift, and now I sit in the proper driver's seat with Matt at my passenger side. Maylene, Kaedy, and Andre clean up after us, though I know they're probably chatting amongst themselves.

I don't really know where I am going, so I have to pay more attention to the directing map on the CHAD screen than I normally do. There is also the matter of our traveling altitude, which is much higher than I am used to, so I pay careful attention to our surroundings, even if there are far fewer vehicles up here. All the Sonars of regular size fly below, though none at the speed we travel.

When we finally run low on charge, Matt directs me to a nearby city so we can get to a Platform.

"This city looks too...ancient for my liking," Matt comments as we ground. I look around for a few seconds. The buildings are tall and rusty-looking, and almost none of them go straight up. Most lean to the side, as if its weight were too much for them to bear. "Also, with this ship, you don't have to obey the grounding laws. But it is courteous to do so."

I nod, not having known that.

"If you take a right at the next signal and then move up one elevation, we'll head right into a charging station. You'll have to swing around the back, though, where the larger Platforms are, as the usual ones won't give us a proper charge."

"Okay," I tell him, slowing down for some unusually dim-witted drivers who pass by right in front of me only to stop suddenly.

The charging station is five stories tall, adorned with an antique-looking clocktower rising in the center. The hands on the clock don't appear to move, or the time just doesn't match the time on our ship, which is automatically changed to suit the current time of our location.

Around the back, there are many ships docked on Platforms, with a line waiting behind them. We sit there for nearly an hour before it is our time to charge. While we were waiting, the others joined Matt and me up front, and we spent most of that time inventing wild ideas of how to speed up the charging process.

I make to get out to go stock up on snacks, but Maylene holds me back.

"Where are you going?" she asks.

"Need to get sustenance for the road," I tell her.

She snickers. "You haven't seen our kitchen pantry, have you?"

Without waiting for my answer, she takes my hand and walks me back to the kitchen. There is a cozy nook behind a wall at the end. In here, there is a full sink, counter, and closet filled with snacks and meals. Another pantry contains water. Maylene smiles slyly and kicks open a small drawer near the floor, this one containing bottles of alcohol.

"But now isn't the time," she says, closing it gently. "Earlier was mainly for Andre's benefit, though he didn't drink any." She walks out of the nook, with me following behind her. "I don't think I'll have another drink until we're all wrapped up with this. And at this point, I need it to be. It breaks my heart seeing Andre go through this."

"Me too."

"And Matt says he's fine, and he is," Maylene goes on. "But I know he would like a small break from all of this. But he won't stop until we're done. It's actually one of his most admirable qualities."

"He's got a lot of admirable qualities."

"Oh my, are we fangirling here?" Maylene asks annoyingly.

I hear a thud behind me. Without looking, I can tell who it is, especially when he wedges in between us and wraps his arms around our shoulders.

"Nah, he ain't fangirling," Matt says. "He's just a solid guy who isn't afraid to speak the truth." He shoots an accusing look at Maylene.

"I am definitely not scared to speak the truth," Maylene laughs.

Matt shrugs. "Maybe not most of it. But some things. Hmm, yeah," Matt says, removing his arms. "One day I'll get you to see your truth."

"Oh, yeah? And what truth would that be?"

Matt walks away in front of us, though we're all heading to the front. He shrugs. "I could hazard a guess, but I wouldn't want to spoil anything for you."

Maylene scoffs but says nothing. Matt holds just the smallest of a smug grin on his face, but they both know it's back to business. At least as much business as we can accomplish while we wait for the ship to finish charging.

Andre and Kaedy walk back inside, both carrying drinks and treats. My mouth drops, and I shoot a look at Maylene.

"Why did they get to go?" I ask.

Kaedy answers for Maylene. "This ship has stuff in it, for sure, but not everything." She walks to the belly and sits on one of the couches. "But don't fret; I got you something too." She beckons me over and hands me a milkshake, though it isn't what I am accustomed to.

"This city was redesigned to imitate one of the cities on Earth," she explains. "So they've got all kinds of exotic foods here."

"Somehow I don't think Earth looks like this," Matt says. "I've seen the pictures, and they are a lot more...green."

I nod in agreement. Earth seemed naturally beautiful, with developing cities that look way more aesthetic than this rusted iron junk of a city. But so many places on Talvor try to mimic the Earth experience in hopes of attracting tourists, that there is no way all of them would do a good job at it.

"You never know if Earth just sent us misleading pictures. Or pictures only of the good stuff. But this city has food made from every recipe and description that we have gotten from Earth," Kaedy says. "So at least the food is authentic. Eat up, I got all you guys stuff too."

Andre helps her hand out snacks and drinks but keeps quiet most of the time. Before we know it, our ship is done charging. Maylene takes the next driving shift, and Andre takes the passenger seat, leaving me with Matt and Kaedy.

Our talks are enjoyable and not personal, something I was worried Matt would make so. At least, not personal for me. He mainly laughs at Kaedy's stories of men who tried to court her. When I feel uncomfortable, she reminds me that she was interested in me first and that I didn't even have to court her.

"But I'm sure anything you did would have worked for me," she says before pressing her lips to my cheek. I can smell a light scent of rose in her hair. Funny, Maylene smelled the same way, but unlike Maylene, that nice smell is usual for Kaedy. "Even if you acted like a total dork."

I chuckle. "I'm pretty sure I looked nervous and unaccustomed to talking to girls."

Kaedy shrugs. "You did. But that was okay."

"Maybe I should act more like Arch," Matt jokes.

"Funny," Kaedy says. "But laughing aside, I personally think your only problem is that you know what you want, but you're too scared to go for it."

Matt leans forward and clears his throat.

"Let's not go there," he requests in a lower tone.

Kaedy shrugs. "Okay, but you know I'm right."

All of us know she's right.

Matt doesn't say anything. Something eats at the back of his mind. Several times I think he's about to get up and walk over to the cockpit, but he never moves.

Kaedy rests her head on my chest. I can't help but stare at her, probably with some cheesy grin on my face. Matt ends up passing out where he sits.

"I'm adorable, I know," Kaedy whispers, somehow knowing that I've been staring at her. I chuckle.

"Yes, you are," I tell her before giving her a light kiss. She kisses me back, and for a moment there, we build the intensity between us. I feel myself wanting to do more, now, but she pulls away.

Good thing too.

She still rests, closing her eyes and using my chest as her pillow. I think about it, about whispering to her to head to the bunks above. But that would make for an awkward encounter with the others later. I let out a sigh through my nose, rest my head back, and close my eyes.

I don't fall asleep. Even though the time I sit there feels like forever, I find myself not wanting this forever to end. I can hear Maylene and Andre talk up front but can't make out anything they say. They sound quiet, though, like Andre might be opening up a bit.

Every now and then, I open my eyes and stare out. Kaedy is asleep on me. Matt shifts sometimes, making me wonder if he is still asleep. I can tell that it's getting dark, beyond the fact that I can see out the front windshield. There's just that feeling in the air. I expect Maylene would want to take a break from driving, but neither she nor Andre call to us.

Well into the night, I pass out myself. A solid nap, deep sleep, with drool coming out my mouth. I know this because Maylene scoops some up in her hand and smacks my face with it to wake me.

My eyes open. She's laughing.

"Classy," I tell her, slightly annoyed.

She smirks. "You too." She walks around, gently shaking Matt awake. Andre quietly climbs the ladder and disappears into one of the beds.

"We're officially in the middle of nowhere," Maylene calls out to the room of now awake people. Kaedy moves slightly, clearly comfortable, but still rests her head on me. She's going to hate it when I tell her I need to move around.

"Now I'm sure you're all just itching to get going, ready for your turn to drive for twelve hours or more," Maylene goes on. "But orders are to stay put. We will resume in the morning. Most ships our size don't travel at this time, even the cargo and freight ones, with all their laws about nighttime driving. So, to not look suspicious, we're staying here."

I nod. Kaedy gets up.

"So, I'll take the first shift in the morning," Kaedy says, stifling a yawn. "It only seems fair."

"However you want to do it," Maylene replies. "But, for now, just enjoy yourselves. Go back to sleep if you want. But if anyone wants me, I'll be outside, getting some fresh air, and looking out at the stars."

In pure Maylene fashion, she grabs a chocolatey drink mixed with booze, despite her earlier assertion to not drink more, and struts outside. The cool, crisp air blows in. A little chilly, but fresh and inviting. Kaedy stands up and walks away. I sit up and look over at Matt. He seems wide awake but still in his thoughts. What Kaedy said must have really struck him.

Speaking of who, Kaedy walks back in and tosses blankets to Matt and me.

"Let's go," she says, jerking her head towards the still-open door.

I don't need to be told twice. Though I am still tired, I get up and follow her out. Before I step outside, I turn back to Matt.

"You coming?"

He shrugs.

"You should come," I tell him. "Odds are, you'll regret it if you don't."

Silently, he gets up and follows me out.

The breeze that was pleasantly cool back in the ship feels cold outside. I can imagine snow falling down, but the bare ground is brown, littered with twigs and dry pine needles. Maylene gets a fire going out of a pile of sticks. She had already brought out four small chairs. We must have been landed for a while. We all take seats, close and cozy by the fire. Maylene passes me her drink. I'm about to decline, but with one look from her, I take it. I then pass it to Kaedy, who passes it to Matt.

The night is mostly quiet. We don't talk much at first. Even the bugs don't make much sound, though occasionally a Sonars would pass high above us. A bird of the night calls out. Still, half an hour passes, and we don't speak. There is no need to.

Maylene's drink isn't strong. By this point, I've had seven swigs of it. I feel warm, snuggled by the blanket around me. The journey thus far has brought us so close together and made our friendship so real. There is little that can compare. It's great to choose your friends. But getting this close with strangers due to circumstance beats any friendship I've had. But then again, none of those previous ones lasted long.

By this point, the warmth of the alcohol hits, along with its other qualities. Maylene lets out a laugh. It's contagious, and the rest of us do so too.

"What's so funny?" Matt asks.

"Nothing," she chortles out in response. "But also, like, every-thing."

Kaedy laughs at this.

"You're gonna have to be more specific," Kaedy tells her. "Other-wise, I'm gonna think you're kinda insane."

Matt chuckles. There is a lot of laughter going on. I let out one too, because I don't understand how we could have gone from enjoying the silence with each other's company to laughing at seemingly nothing.

"She's already insane," Matt says. "That's what we love about her."

"We're all insane," Maylene says. "Look where we are! Remember what we just did? We broke into what's supposedly going to be the next Capital of the Pacan continent and stole back something that was held under their highest security."

Something she said catches my attention.

"What do you mean the next capital?"

I'm surprised when Kaedy answers.

"There's been rumors that Longfurd has been slowly increasing its popularity and plans to overtake Praeline as the capital of Pacan."

Praeline has been the capital of Pacan since before I was born. I've learned of shifts in power over the years, but mostly those were from ancient times in lessons I studied back in school.

"Of course, a hostile or violent takeover is more noise than they want to deal with, so they've been winning over the countries so that they could do a vote to put them in power," Kaedy goes on. "When I recently learned about it, I suspected that Prodigy was going to be their biggest weapon to achieve this, but the more I've thought about it, I think the two are mostly unrelated."

I consider this.

Maylene interrupts my thoughts.

"Yeah, yeah," she says. "While this is largely unknown, I expect it to be true, but with Prodigy in our hands and still on our planet, there are worse things at stake. If Prodigy gets implanted on Talvor, it won't matter much who thinks they're in charge. Because whoever has Prodigy will be, whether the world knows it or not."

She has a point.

"But why are we talking about this?" Maylene asks. "We're already working on it. Let's get back to everything that we've accomplished thus far. Our team, this team right here, is the best I've ever known of."

"I agree," Kaedy says positively. "You guys are amazing."

"So are you," Matt says. "You handled that ship with such precision, I'm surprised you don't work for the military. They probably could use people like you. Plus, your timing was impeccable."

Kaedy blushes.

"I'm not that good," she says. "There was just so much going on, I didn't have much of a choice."

"But you pulled through," Maylene says, reaching her arm over the fire to hold Kaedy's hand briefly. "And for that, we're all grateful."

The silence between us returns. There isn't anything awkward about it. Nothing uncomfortable. Again, it is nice to have each other's company and not feel like we need to act in some way or be interesting to continue to be liked.

Maylene takes another swig and hands me the bottle again. There isn't that much left. I take less this time, saving enough for Kaedy and Matt. Kaedy takes her silently, but Matt surprises us.

"This one is for all of you," he says, holding out the bottle. "And Andre and Mr. Canabana, for not only saving the world but for bringing us together."

"And Gary," I mumble out.

"Good point," Matt says. He retracts his arm and holds it out again. "And to Gary."

We all raise our hands as if we're holding drinks. Matt finishes off the bottle and gently lays it down on the ground, where it then immediately falls over. I lean back and look up at the stars. The canopy above sways in the wind, but the night sky is clear and beautiful. I close my eyes for a moment.

And I wake up to the noise of scurrying. Something dashes across the fallen foliage. I hear the flutter of wings and leaves being ripped off their branches. I open my eyes. Sunlight filters through the trees, shining a golden light onto the ground. There is a stillness to the air and the world around me. My blanket sits on top of me, carefully snuggled around my body to keep me warm.

Across the flameless fire pit, though thin smoke still rises from it, sits Matt, with Maylene lying her head on his shoulder. Silently, I get up, not wanting to disturb them. I also don't want them thinking I caught them doing something, because they both clearly aren't ready to admit their feelings for each other.

The airship's main door is closed. I look around a bit, trying to find a switch or button. Before I do, I hear the door open. I step back, giving it room to open out. I walk up the stairs and find Kaedy.

"Good morning," she says to me. I give her a hug and a kiss on the head.

"Morning," I say. "Did you see the two out there?"

She giggles. "Yes, and I didn't want to disturb them, but I had to make sure that the airship was ready for takeoff."

"That's why you left me out there by myself."

"Sorry about that. I didn't want to wake you," she says. Kaedy walks further into the ship, towards the kitchen area. "We'll have more time to spend together. But I made sure you stayed warm."

I smile as I follow her back.

Moments later, I hear people come up the stairs.

"Hey," Maylene says.

"Good morning," Kaedy replies. She doesn't change her tone to indicate that she saw anything. For all Maylene and Matt know, Kaedy and I slept inside the ship.

"Hey, when do we get going?" Matt asks. "Because I'm kinda starving here."

"We can take flight now," Maylene says. "The sun is back up. We should be able to get to our destination before nightfall."

Matt nods and lets out a large yawn.

"Hey Kaedy, if I take the first driving shift, do you mind cooking something up?" he asks shyly. "There's just something about your cooking that I like better than mine."

"It's probably because hers is better," Maylene says. Matt looks at her and lets out a smile.

"Probably," he says, and smiles at Kaedy.

"Of course," Kaedy responds. "Maylene and I will put something together."

Matt shoots me a slightly worried look.

Maylene rolls her eyes. "Don't worry, I'm mainly going to be making morning refreshments and cleaning up after Kaedy. Her cooking is far superior to mine."

Matt smiles again, places a gentle hand on Kaedy's shoulder, and walks towards the cockpit.

Kaedy looks at me, bringing a warm smile to my lips. "You should join him," she says. "Maylene and I got this." She winks at me.

I nod, kiss her briefly, and head towards Matt.

Matt sits in the driver's seat, and I take co-pilot.

"You ready?"

I nod.

"Let's go."

Matt punches the controls and gets the airship's engines roaring, though they don't make that much noise. He flips a switch, and we rise into the air. He carefully guides us up, avoiding all the trees, until we are high above them. Then we shoot forward, on our way.

I look over to Matt. He focuses on the sky. I lean back, getting comfortable.

"Kaedy's got some good advice," he says after some time. "That's a smart girl you have there. Don't mess it up," he jokes.

I laugh. "I know. She's amazing."

Kaedy comes out front, carrying two bowls of food.

"Here you go," she says. "Hope you enjoy. Maylene and I are going to finish cleaning, but just let me know when you want a break from driving, and I'll take over."

"With a breakfast like this, I'll drive all day," Matt says with a mouthful of food.

I start eating too. It looks like it's just eggs mixed with greens and slices of meat, but it's flavored with various spices, and it just tastes so very good.

I suspect that Kaedy and Maylene are talking about some girl stuff, and that makes me happy. Kaedy fits in perfectly with my friends, and the four of us seem to get closer and closer as if we're all a second family.

Matt sets the controls to auto-cruise. I leave mine as they are, but I am ready to take over if anything happens. It is unlikely, though, with our high altitude. A few gliders pass over us. I can feel Matt tense slightly, ready in case anything happens, but the gliders seem unbothered by us and are soon out of sight.

Before the late afternoon arrives, Matt announces that we're almost there.

"We'll be stopping east of Richtka," he tells me. "There is a new Sonars waiting for you there. You and Kaedy will take it to Fraslia while the rest of us head back towards Candalance."

Maylene struts up to the cockpit. "Slight change of plan," Maylene says. "Arch and Kaedy will head to Ibarca first, because for whatever reason, Fraslia is on high watch, and we don't want to risk anything."

"Damn," Matt mutters under his breath. "It's a good thing this is all almost over."

Maylene nods in agreement. "Also, I will be taking Andre back to Candalance. Edward wants you to trail behind Arch until Prodigy is in the hands of that guy at NEAST."

Andre slowly steps forward. I didn't even see him.

"Maylene and I will be watching from afar," he tells me. "Edward has enough people around the world that we can get you backup as needed, but we're going to do our best to hinder any obstacles or threats. Be warned though, the closer you get to NEAST, the more dangerous this will likely be."

An odd silence follows.

"Edward believes that his plan is known to whoever James works for," Maylene informs me. Kaedy walks in too. I suspect she knows all about this already. "So NEAST might not be an option anymore. At least not directly. While we don't have to go into NEAST, the contact there has to remain close-by so he can quickly get rid of Prodigy."

"Who is the contact?" I ask, forgetting the name Edward mentioned so long ago.

Maylene shakes her head. "I forgot. Edward now refuses to tell anyone. Probably for the best."

"Well, alright then," Matt says. "Sounds like a cinch compared to what we've already done."

"Yup," I agree.

"We're just under an hour away," Matt says. "Let's get comfy while we can. I don't expect we'll want to stay long when we get there."

19

The city of Richtka is brilliant in the distance as we swerve away from it. With spotlights lining the city, Richtka boasts a cinematic experience. I've been there before, and it is one of the largest entertainment and cultural centers in all of Pacan. It's one of those cities that makes you feel like you can accomplish anything. The City Where Dreams Are Made and Realities Are Born.

Even Matt, guiding the vehicle, takes a long glance at the city as we pass it. We have to stay several kilometers away from the city to avoid looking like we're, well, avoiding the city.

Another couple of hours pass before the city is completely out of view. Both Kaedy and Maylene offer to take over driving, but Matt waves them away, claiming that their cooking was far more important. Taking the hint, the two of them go back to the kitchen to prepare a dinner.

"I'll help them," I tell Matt. He looks at me briefly and nods his head.

The kitchenette is packed, being such a small space and with three people already in there.

"Hey Arch," Andre says. He doesn't sound like his cheery self, and unlike before, he doesn't make much of an attempt. "How's your day been?"

"Good," I say, trying to sound neutral. "You helping with dinner?"

"Yup," he says, sounding a little livelier. "I actually know a lot about cooking. It's one of my passions."

I feel awkward because I don't know what to say.

"That's really great," I say, cringing at myself. Andre doesn't seem to mind, though.

For the most part, I stay out of everyone's way. After half an hour, I go back to the front, realizing that I'm more useful there, even if I am still doing nothing.

Matt laughs. "Did they kick you out?"

"No," I tell him. "But they know what they're doing. Evidently, I don't."

This makes Matt laugh again. "I'm sure you do, but they just know it better. Is Andre back there?"

"Yeah, he's helping them."

"That's good to hear. Soon he'll be back home, and he can finally have some alone time to grieve."

"Do you think that's what he wants to do?" I ask. "Or if that's what he needs?"

Matt shrugs. "No. But whatever it is that he needs, he'll be able to get it. Edward is expecting him, and I am sure he will know what to do."

Up ahead there are three abandoned steel barns. The building materials for these predate even my grandfather. Matt gently lowers the airship quite some Milkateet away from the largest one.

"This is our stop for the night," Matt tells us. "At least, just part of the night. But not for you, Arch."

"We won't be here long," Kaedy says, bringing both Matt and me a bowl of food. This time it's wild grains and chicken. "Just long enough for dinner."

"And for your Sonars to arrive," Andre says, peering out the front.

Matt shuts off the airship, takes his bowl, and walks out the door. We follow him, Andre trailing behind.

The wind blows into my face and through my hair. It stings at first, and I squint my eyes. Old bales of hay stand strong in the wasteland. They look eroded but are mostly intact. None of the barns have doors, and one of them is missing more than half of its roof. I look around. In the distance, I make out what appears to be an old well.

"The Sonars is in there," Matt says, pointing to the mostly uncovered barn with his fork in his hand.

"I don't see it," I say, thinking that we were waiting for it to show up.

Matt takes a seat on one of the bales. "Eat first. Then I'll show you."

Maylene smirks as she passes, telling me that she also knows where it is. She takes a seat behind Matt, their backs to each other. Kaedy takes my hand and sits me down against a stack of hay. Andre just sits on the ground, legs crossed.

We eat mostly in silence. As the sky gets darker, the wind picks up. When we're all done eating, Maylene collects our dishware and returns it to the airship. She's only gone for a couple of minutes, but in that time, I begin to shiver from the cold.

"Let's go," Maylene says, and she sweeps right past us. I quickly get up and follow her. She walks into the barn. I now know where she is headed. There's an open hatch. I should have guessed it then. Beneath us is some sort of garage. Edward must love his underground lairs.

We go down a spiral staircase. As Maylene steps onto the level ground, all the lights turn on at once, though they slowly increase their brilliance so as not to blind anyone.

I've seen them before, but they still take my breath away. Glossy and glamorous, the sleek and polished midnight black Sonars sits in the middle of the room as if waiting for my arrival. Parking bays are placed at the sides, but they are all empty. We go down the access catwalk and walk down the metal steps into the parking lot.

Even though she's done this before with me, Maylene still proudly presents the vehicle.

"Look at this fine creature," she says. She admires the Sonars for a moment before turning to me. "Hmm." She walks under one of its wings and picks up something off the ground. "Here."

She hands it out to me. I eye it for a moment and then hold out my phone to let it program the Sonars' key into my phone.

"Don't forget to keep at the normal altitude. And don't use any features that you shouldn't use unless it is *absolutely* necessary."

"Cloaking the Sonars would help a lot," I tell her.

Maylene sighs. "I know, but we can't risk it. There are some people already looking for you specifically. And Matt, actually. They want him now, too. So, the both of you need to keep a low profile."

"Okay," I say, disappointed.

"I'm going to ask Edward for one of these when we're done," Matt says.

"It's one of the things Daden really admired about Edward," Andre says. "Or so he claimed."

We stand there, saying nothing.

Andre lets out a loud breath. "I'm sorry, guys," he says, lowering his head. "I appreciate you all for just being you and not making me talk about it. For letting me have my space but welcoming me when I wanted company. And I love you guys for it." Something gets stuck in his throat. "You truly are the best friends I could have asked for."

Still, we stand there and say nothing.

Andre steps forward and places a hand on the Sonars.

"Because of you guys, I'll be fine," he says. "I'm going to take some time off. Edward has already offered me places to stay, away from everything. But I don't think I'll be there long. I want to be back with you guys as soon as possible."

Maylene steps up and gives him a long hug.

"We may have helped," she tells him. "But you are the reason you're going to be okay. You're going to be even more than okay." She looks him in the eye, her hands still on his shoulders. "I know it."

Andre moves his face a bit closer to Maylene's. I think the same thing too, and I can feel Matt tense up. Getting on his toes slightly, Andre kisses Maylene on her forehead.

"Thank you."

Maylene smiles and nods.

Andre turns to me. "Good luck, Arch. But you won't need it. You'll finish this." I nod. Andre walks up to me hesitantly. I open my arms and give him a hug.

He then turns to Kaedy.

"I'm truly, truly happy you're a part of us," he says. "I think you and Arch are amazing people."

Kaedy, knowing Andre the least out of any of us, frowns slightly but follows with a smile and hugs him tightly. I don't know if she truly means it, or if she has otherwise been lonely until we met, or if she puts on the act for his benefit. Either way, I appreciate her genuinely being nice to him.

"Time to go," Matt says after clearing his throat. I look over to him, grab my phone, and start the Sonars. The door opens.

Maylene jumps onto me, hugging me tightly.

"This time, no more near-death experiences," she tells me. "While I love the action, it's time we ended this once and for all."

Still embraced in her hug, I say, "I agree."

She releases me and takes some steps backward.

Matt comes up to me. He pulls me in, and I feel like I'm about to suffocate with my face pressed against his chest. I try to move, but his arms are too big. But I hug him back the same.

He lets go, both of us not saying anything to each other. We know. The friendship that he and I built is something that neither of us could explain, but we both understand. It's the kind that I know he would be the best man at my wedding, and I his.

Our hug lasts the longest. It's a type of vulnerability I'm not used to showing. I'm sure he isn't used to feeling it either.

He lets go and nods. I nod back. He hands me something from his pocket. It's the chip. I almost forgot about it. He carries something else his his other hand.

"The last stretch," he says.

"The last stretch." I take the chip from him. Matt then hands me what he's been holding. It's a jacket, black in color, with lines spread across it. Its collar is folded over perfectly. Made of a leather-like material and blended with a substance to enhance its bulletproof-ness, the jacket has a reflective shine. I put it on. Like all other clothes that I've been given, it fits me perfectly. Matt places his hand on my shoulder. I feel a small jolt. I know what it was. He placed a small camera on me, integrated in the jacket. The trust I have for him makes me say nothing. Maybe he is embarrassed to ask if I would be okay with it. I know that the camera is just in case I get into trouble. So, I say nothing of it. There is a moment I think he's about to speak, but he says nothing. I nod to him and Matt returns it, stepping back slightly.

Maylene and Matt both give Kaedy a hug too; Maylene's more friendly with hers, while Matt remains almost awkwardly professional.

I wave to my friends and step into the Sonars. Kaedy is right behind me. The door closes, and I raise the vehicle into the air. It is much smaller than the ship, having only two seats in the front and a bed in the back, just like my old Sonars. Underneath the bed, I can see a lot of packed storage bins. This ship has been equipped with things I need. It amazes me how much Edward can accomplish, all from one place. I want to thank whoever prepared the Sonars, but I know I'll probably never find out who.

With one last look, I drive the Sonars down the runway. There are signs facing me that tell me to go slow. Up ahead, there is a wall with painted arrows pointing up. I slow down to a stop. Above me doors slide open. Through the moonroof, I can see the heavenly sky and stars above. We rise through the opening. Once we're elevated enough, the doors beneath us close automatically. I accelerate forward, picking up speed and altitude.

It takes no time to get back into the groove of driving the Sonars, but even with Kaedy by my side, I still feel empty. She must sense something. "You'll see your friends soon enough," she says. "I'm sure it will just be a few days. A week, tops."

I sigh. "I know. It just feels like we've been doing this for so long. To be honest, I can't even remember how many days it's been since I first met Maylene. I know it hasn't been that long, but it feels like it."

"Of course it does," she says. "Traveling these great distances can make it feel like a long time has passed, even though it really hasn't. Trust me, I know."

"Oh yeah, you travel a lot too," I say.

"Yup," Kaedy says brightly. "That's actually why I can't stick with you all the way to NEAST. But when you get back, I'll be taking some time for myself."

"Me too," I say with a small chuckle. We both already know it, but it's nice to say it out loud again.

"And maybe when we're back in Candalance, Matt and Maylene will finally have stopped pretending they're not into each other."

"That would be a miracle," I say. She laughs.

Simply talking makes me feel calm and eases that aching emptiness I felt when I left the others. I feel full again. I realize that there is more to my life than just mindlessly and aimlessly traveling and delivering packages. I haven't done myself any favors in the past. But that's going to change. It has already.

Driving late into the night doesn't bother me at all. The bleak darkness that surrounds us is like an old friend, one that always leaves but never fails to return. The moon remains out of sight, as do most stars, unless I look up for them. The headlights on the Sonars are strong, easy on the eyes, and reveal nothing. Nothing but the bare distance we keep crossing.

Kaedy lets out a long yawn.

"If you're tired, you can get some sleep," I tell her. "I don't mind driving. I'm so used to it that it feels like I'm home."

"Of course I can get some sleep," she says. "And I plan to, but I'll just rest here."

I laugh. "I mean, I don't mind if you go back to that bed and get some sleep. I'll wake you in the morning or if I stop somewhere."

"Darling, it's already the morning," she says, pointing to the time. Indeed, zero-thirty. Funny how the time flies when you're flying.

It's also funny how time seems to stop sometimes.

"Yeah, well, taking into account time changes...." I trail off.

"It's still the morning, wherever we are currently," she says. "But I am a good co-pilot. I don't abandon the driver."

I smile. Until recently, I never had a co-pilot before, having done all my trips solo. I would do the same — never leave the driver's side. Unless there was some mutual agreement regarding shifts. We have about another seven hours of driving, at which point we will reach Ibarca at around five local time.

"Fair point," I tell her. I look over to her, but she appears to already be asleep. I don't know her well enough to know if she falls asleep that fast or if she's pretending. Or maybe she's just resting her eyes. Either way, I let her be, not minding one bit.

Some hours later, a call comes in. I connect it to my phone and earpiece.

"Hey Maylene," I tell her in a hushed tone.

"Why are you so quiet?" she asks. "Oh, am I disturbing something?"

"Really?" I ask, wondering if she's joking. "No, you're not. Kaedy is sleeping. We're still on our way to Ibarca."

"Oh, so sweet of you," she says. "I figured you'd still be on your way. Even in the airship, so would I. Anyways, originally I was planning to have you two stay in Ibarca for a while, but it looks like Fraslia's high alert phase is about to end. But unfortunately, Matt has detected higher than normal traffic headed towards Ibarca."

I clench my jaw slightly but don't say anything.

"They're about half a day behind you at least, so there isn't any immediate alarm," Maylene reports. "Still, we don't want you staying there for long. So, expect to take a three-hour break, maybe get some rest, and then be on your way to Fraslia."

"Sounds good," I respond. "How long will we be in Fraslia?"

"Probably just over a day," she says. "I can't speak for Kaedy, though. She'll be leaving at some point after you get there, but you'll have to ask her for the details. She already has her own Sonars waiting there, something she arranged herself."

I nod, but then remember she can't see me as I didn't allow the visual to the call. "Okay. Thanks for letting me know."

"Of course," she says. "Andre is sleeping. I'm planning to drive straight to Candalance in one go, fuel allowing."

"Stay safe," I tell her. "But I'll see you soon."

"See you soon."

Maylene hangs up.

Kaedy remains asleep. Getting hungry and a little tired, I set the Sonars to autopilot and jump to the back to see what snacks we have. I have to sift through a few containers. I find a bag with my name on it that contains clothes.

Luckily, it doesn't take me long to find the snacks. I don't like using the auto-pilot feature, no matter how safe it may be. With regards to energy drinks, I don't find any, but I there are syringes of adrenaline shots. I'm tempted, but I don't take them. I'm not that tired.

Ibarca is nestled on the side of a mountain, and on an island in the middle of a lake. Cascading water falls into the lake at the back end of the town, while the lake's water crashes down into a river at the base of the mountain in the front. Three bridges on both sides serve to provide walking access in and out of the city.

Light snow falls upon the town, gilding the structures with white. There are only two elevations in the town, and the largest building is only thirty floors tall. All the buildings are placed at the far end of the city, just before the waterfall that flows into it, though the water falls from a much higher height than the tallest structure. I heard that there are underwater caverns that were built into wide tunnels to guide water through in the case that there is a flood.

Most of the houses are placed along the water, but some of the smaller ones stand closer to the middle of the island. Though it looks small compared to most of the other cities in the world, there is still a population of over four hundred thousand. Two charging stations exist in the city, near the walkways across the lake. Airships use the lowest level out of the five.

As we approach the city, I increase our elevation and veer off to the side to properly enter. The Sonars could make it much farther on its current charge, but I pull into the second floor of the charging station anyway. The sunlight is dim, part of it blocked by the mountain in front of it. I check the time. It's almost six in the morning. We made better time than I thought.

Once parked, I gently place my hand on Kaedy's.

"Good morning," I tell her.

She smiles and yawns.

"Good morning. Did we make it?"

"Yup, we're in Ibarca."

She sits up quickly and looks out the windshield.

"Isn't it early to be getting a charge?" she asks. "We probably don't need one for a while."

"You're right, but we have to wait here for a bit until Maylene tells us it's safe to go," I explain. "So I figured I'd charge the Sonars now."

"How long do we get to stay here?" she asks excitedly.

"Just a few hours," I tell her. "Maylene will call us when it's time to go."

Kaedy leans back in the chair. "Okay, fine. Let's finish the charge and then find first-elevation parking." She looks out the window again, peering her head to see better. "Though it looks like other than the charging stations, the parking is all on the first elevation."

"Do you want to spend some time in the town?" I ask her.

"Don't you?"

"Well, yeah, but I'm tired, and I'd rather come back another day when I'm not pressured for time."

"Oh, I'm sorry. I forgot that you drove all night," she says. "Silly me."

I can feel her slight disappointment. But I also know that she understands and doesn't blame me. "I don't mind spending some time out now, though," I tell her. "Would you mind continuing the drive for a few hours when we leave? I can sleep then."

She smiles. Damn, I do love that smile.

"Of course, I'll even drive all the way to Fraslia," she tells me. "But if you're too tired now, we don't have to go out. I totally understand. You drove all night while I slept like a baby, despite claiming how I don't do that."

I jerk my head towards the window. "It looks like a very charming town," I say, knowing that I'll silently regret this later. "We should at least see part of it while we're here."

A faint bell sounds, indicating that the charging is complete.

"Let's do it," I say. I drive down to the first elevation and follow the road deeper into the town rather than across it to the other side. I park next to what appears to be a large outdoor stage. When I open the door, frigid air blows in.

Snow crunches below my feet. The walkways are laid with a stone-brick. A few people stand around, most of them tourists. They're taking pictures of themselves in front of the amphitheater. When in use, it looks like a place that gets packed. I can imagine lights in shades of blue and purple illuminating the atmosphere. As we walk further away from the stage, I notice tall pillars with lifts on each side, providing more elevated and prime space for spectators.

The water that runs through the town doesn't freeze. There is a spot, though, that was made for ice skating, and it appears that its source of water is from the rivers, but that area is frozen. There is no one using the rink.

Kaedy pulls me towards it. There isn't anyone by the booth granting access to the ice rink. Kaedy jumps over the low fence and beckons for me to follow. She does a small hop onto the ice and immediately falls backward onto her butt. I carefully step on it and help her get back up. She laughs.

"I've always sucked at skating," she says. "I also kinda wish I thought to bring gloves." As she says it, I become conscious of how cold my hands are. "How about you?"

"Yeah, my hands are freezing."

Kaedy laughs. "I'm sure. But I mean, how are you at skating?"

I shrug. "Never really tried. And never on ice."

She looks out towards the main part of the city. "Let's see if we can get across." She locks her arms with mine and pockets her hands. I do the same. Step by step, we traverse the ice rink together. It wasn't large to begin with, but it seems like it'll take forever.

Nearly falling three times, Kaedy tightens her grip on me. I keep her upright as best I can, but she manages to bring me down when we're halfway across.

The impact doesn't hurt much, but the cold feels like pain as it sends chills through my body. We fall again when we try to stand up. Kaedy unlocks our arms. I manage to make it to my feet and help her get back up.

Kaedy holds my arms as we finish our trek but doesn't lock them together. It is way easier this way.

Finally, we make it across. Kaedy lets out a breath and kisses me.

"You're going to be a pro skater one day."

I laugh and kiss her back.

A voice rings through my ear.

"Arch, get out of there," Maylene warns. "They're less than an hour away."

She doesn't say more and hangs up. Maylene's worrisome and urgent tone reflects in my eyes. Kaedy looks up at me.

"What's wrong?"

"They're less than an hour away." She knows who I'm talking about. "We have to go," I tell her. I let out a sigh. I forgot all about everything else for a moment there.

But an idea comes to my mind. I grin.

"What is it?" Kaedy asks.

"Well, we have to leave urgently, so let's take the fastest way back to the Sonars." Without further explanation, I let go of her and leap onto the ice. My jacket provides some cushion as I land on my chest, but it still hurts. My idea works for the most part. I slide more than halfway across. I turn my head back as I come to a full stop. Kaedy is laughing at me. I turn facing forward and use my arms to drag myself. It becomes exhausting very quickly. With my arms already sore, I reach the end. I look up and see Kaedy looking down at me. She smiles.

"Let's go, Mr. Shortcut," she laughs. I quickly get to my feet and follow her back to the Sonars. Apparently, I did not take the fastest way. It was still fun, though.

True to her word, Kaedy takes the seat in the driver's spot. She gives me a look, telling me not to argue.

"Good thing you got a charge for the Sonars already," she says as we takeoff.

"Yeah, good thing," I say, breathless from my intense workout.

20

L uckily, we don't see anyone coming after us, which would be a real problem if we did. But Maylene did say that they were less than an hour away, so I didn't expect to. But things haven't always turned out as I expected. We move fast, though, because that doesn't mean that they're not catching up quickly. If they're in airships, then they're most definitely going to. I call Maylene right after we leave the grounding limits of the city, but she doesn't answer. Kaedy knows nothing better to do but drive us as fast as possible from the wintery town behind us and say nothing.

Maylene calls me back.

"Go faster," she tells me.

Kaedy pushes the Sonars, urging it to speed up. It does. But we're passing the usual cruising speed for this altitude. Going up higher would look odd and invite unwelcome attention, but going this fast down here can catch the eye of Impositioners.

"Where are they?" I ask.

"They've still yet to reach Ibarca," Maylene tells me. I can see beads of sweat on her forehead. She's still traveling. I suppose that Andre is driving, but he is out of sight. "With any luck, Matt will be able to throw them off your trail. Or even better yet, stop them dead in their tracks."

I laugh. Before this job, I wouldn't have thought that statement would be literal. It is. And now I don't mind as much. I try to not let the thoughts of all those who were killed in their attempt to acquire Prodigy enter my mind. I try to push away the thought that if I had been better or quicker, then these things may have been prevented.

Too late.

With Kaedy at the wheel, I have no way to vent my frustration. The pent-up rage turns to sorrow and quickly back to rage again.

"Just keep going and stay alert," Maylene warns. "And Arch...."

I turn to look at her. I've heard every word she said, but half my mind was elsewhere. Now I listen intently to what she has to say to me.

"None of this is your fault," she says. "Matt does the same thing, where he blames himself, always. But without everything that you've both done, things would be so much worse."

She doesn't wait for an answer. She expects a comeback — something that tells her that she's wrong. A stab at her, to front the idea that I'm right and that I'm to blame. That's why she doesn't give me that chance. And now I have to sit here and think about how maybe she is right.

The drive seems to go on forever, but the world around seems so still. All I hear are the screams of the past, large chunks of concrete collapsing, dust rising into the air. I can't close my eyes, for all I see are graveyards.

The late morning turns bright, and eventually the light begins to recede. Not once did Kaedy stop. Not once did she speak. Into the sunset we fly. Maylene sent a message a few hours ago telling us to keep moving, but to not worry because Matt had handled the situation.

Before I know it, I realize I'm dreaming. But the moment I do, I can't remember what I dream about. All I can think of is my silence. Of how others view me. Of how I view myself. I wonder if my father knew what I was doing, if he would be proud of me. Or if he wouldn't care. Odds are, I won't find out. But when I'm done with this, I will see him. I'll make the best of whatever I can.

Mother would be proud, but she left this world years ago. It's sad how, when you're tired and life seems to suck, you remember all the other reasons why there is so much dread.

My thoughts turn into peculiar dreams, but again, each time I realize it, the dreams stop playing in my head.

A void. My thoughts empty out, and I am left with a void. I hear a change in the atmosphere. Shortly afterwards, I feel a drop so sudden that my stomach rises. My eyes open. The night outside looks like a void. The headlights of the Sonars are dim. I turn to look at Kaedy.

She gently lands the Sonars and flicks off a few switches. She notices me.

"Oh, hey," she says. "I hope you got some good sleep."

"Some," I say, and then immediately yawn. "Not enough, though. But I can continue the driving."

Kaedy smiles. "I'm tired, but the only reason why I stopped is because Maylene called. She said it would be better if we were to reach Fraslia during the day. So, we'll stop here for the night."

"Okay." I look around and stand up. Kaedy does too. She looks at me expectantly.

"What?" I ask, smiling.

"Lay down," she tells me. "I'm not picky where I sleep."

Oh, yeah. There's just the one bed in here. I sit back down in the seat.

"That's okay. You take the bed," I offer.

She laughs and shakes her head. "No, the bed is big enough for the both of us."

She's right. I let out a silent sigh.

"Okay."

I lay down. She rests right beside me, her back just a small space from my torso. A few moments pass.

"Why do I feel like you feel like this is awkward?" she asks me.

I shrug. "It's probably because I feel awkward."

Kaedy turns around and faces me. She makes sure to catch my eye before kissing me.

"Don't be so awkward," she says before wrapping her arms around me, as if she were giving me a hug. I hug her back, my chin just on top of her head.

Minutes pass, and I can hear her breathing get heavy, but she doesn't snore. I rest my eyes, hoping to catch some sleep tonight with this brief piece of mind.

We're already in the air. Kaedy is driving. I wake up slowly until I realize something horrific. My eyes snap open. My body reveals my unspoken desire. I don't know if she noticed. I don't know if that's why she got up earlier than I did and decided to get going for the day. I do what I can, but I fear the only thing that will handle this is depleting my bladder. I sit up, my hands in my lap.

Kaedy turns back. I flinch slightly and make sure that my hands lay as naturally across my pelvis, as if that were the most comfortable position they could be in.

"Oh, hey you," she says playfully. "Did you sleep well this time?"

"Uh, y-yeah," I stammer. My face flushes.

"Good!" She sounds so honestly happy.

I let out a quick grin but can't shake off the feeling that she knows. That she felt something.

"Are you going to join me up here? Or have I lost my co-pilot?"

I sneak a peek down. I am wearing tactical pants with lots of pockets, and while my pants are stretchable, that's more for movement, and their material is tough and hard. I can barely discern anything.

Carefully, I stand up. I do my best to keep my back to Kaedy as I make my way to the seat. All five steps. I take way longer than I should.

"I have to use the bathroom," I say shakily as I sit down.

"No problem," Kaedy replies. "We have to make a quick stop in about an hour anyways. Best to recharge now rather than in Fraslia because the city will be so packed with people. But we can't linger for long. We still have to get to the city during the day; it'll just be later than Maylene wanted."

"Sounds good," I say, breathing out and leaning forward.

"Good!"

I can't tell if she is trying to play off my acting weird or if she's trying to not act weird herself. Or if it's just all in my head. This question might burn in the back of my mind until the end of time.

The longest hour finally passes. There aren't many rest stations in the world, as most Sonars and vehicles can pass through at least three cities on one charge. They're all more of a novelty than convenient, but in my case now, it is definitely more convenient.

Of course, by the time we land on a Platform, the perilously embarrassing moment has passed. Still, I am grateful for the quick break to relieve myself. I ask Kaedy if she wants anything to eat, but she says she'll be grabbing something herself.

Twenty minutes later, we're back on our way. Kaedy insists on driving, and I give up trying to convince her otherwise. Her breakfast smells so much better than mine: greens, eggs, and meat wrapped together, while I have a bag of chips and a stick of meat.

"Is that what you usually eat?" she asks me.

"No," I lie. "But it is easy."

"So, it is what you eat usually," she says. "At least when you're on the road."

I nod in defeat. "I usually enjoy healthier meals in restaurants. So yeah, I'll go three days sometimes eating like this, and then I'll make up for it later."

Kaedy nods in disappointment. "I'm gonna talk to Matt about that. Maybe he can convince you to do better."

"What? It's not like I'll be eating like this for much longer. I do not plan to continue making deliveries once this is over with."

The words feel like a confession to my ears. I've known this for a while, but I haven't so bluntly stated it out loud. I didn't know that it was something I had to hear myself say until now.

Kaedy ponders for a moment.

"Is that what you want? Or are you just saying that?" she asks.

"It's what I want. I want somewhere I can call home," I tell her. "I want people I can call home."

The words sound so lame, so pathetic, to my ears.

"You have people you can call home."

"I know," I sigh. "I do now. I didn't before. Back then, I was always on my own, doing my own thing. And I thought about my future, but never really faced trying to even make one. It was just one day after the next. Just some faint notion that would probably never come to be. Honestly, if I hadn't taken this job, if I hadn't met you, Matt, Maylene, and Andre, I would probably have kept on at it. And then realize one day, when I am sixty, that I never even tried to build something for myself. Never gave myself the chance."

Kaedy doesn't say anything, but she gives me a slight nod and looks at me with those beautiful eyes, telling me that she's listening. But I don't have any more to say.

When she's sure I'm done, she speaks.

"As long as you're sure and that you're doing it for you, I'm sure you'll be happy," she says. "Because the only time we aren't happy is when we lie to ourselves."

I nod.

"I'm sure."

"Good," she says, though this time she sounds tender and supportive.

"What about you?" I ask her.

Kaedy lets out a sigh. "I want to keep doing what I'm doing," she says. "I love collecting art. But I don't have the funds to do it all myself, so I'll help others find those things that they find beautiful, the things that give them light, and then one day I'll become a collector myself." There is a glint of a dream in her eye. "And then maybe when that day comes, I'll hire some aspiring young woman who was just like me, and I'll help her along her path."

I smile.

"And when I've stuffed my home full of art, I can open a museum. Preserve the works of artists for time immemorial."

Again, I smile. I turn my head away from her and look out the windshield. But she doesn't say any more.

"Were you scared to tell me that?" I ask her, having felt like she was.

"Just a bit," she answers. "I thought that because you were done traveling, you'd hope I was too. Because I'll be away a lot."

"And each time you go, I'll be waiting for you to come back."

Kaedy smiles.

We don't say anything the rest of the way to Fraslia. We make it well before the sun begins to set, but still after the high afternoon.

Maylene calls in. "So, you've made it," she says. "And during the daytime."

Maylene looks better than she did the last time I saw her. But it doesn't look like she's made it all the way back to Candalance. I thought she would have by now. She sits inside a large room, but there are couches and even a bed in the back.

"Mr. Canabana asked us to meet him here," she says. "It's one of his hotels known for their more charming spaces rather than large penthouse suites."

"It looks nice," Kaedy says, stealing glances whenever she can.

"It is," Maylene replies. "It's not far from the ocean. Andre is still around. He seems happy here. I think he's finding himself again, whatever that means for him." Maylene genuinely sounds happy for him.

"That's good," I say. "Tell him I said hi."

"I will. Anyways, getting back to business. There is a Canabana Hotel in Fraslia, but Edward also has a home there, and that's where you will be staying. I've set your navigation to it. You'll like it. It's very nice."

"Sounds great," I say.

"And Arch, just make sure you leave tomorrow during the day. You should make it out fine and do your best to make as few stops as you can until you reach NEAST. Be alert for any changes, though. We still aren't sure where exactly you're meeting Edward's guy."

"Got it." I smile, still wishing I could remember his name.

"Talk to you soon," Maylene says. I swear I see her shoot me a quick smirk before closing off the video call.

Fraslia is like most large cities: tall buildings, most of them just large blocks. The higher elevations have floating houses, just like those in that city where I met Gary. The navigation system on CHAD directs us to take a turn to go up to the eleventh elevation. For a moment, I sit stiffly, fearing that we will be staying in one of the floating-house-death-traps.

We don't. Kaedy turns away from the houses, and we head towards a large structure. We pull into parking. A message from Maylene comes through CHAD that tells us that access has been given to our phones.

The parking structure is huge, but not many Sonars are here. We walk through the automatic doors and enter a large and empty foyer.

"Suite ten," Kaedy says.

"Yup."

We walk down the hall. I don't see any doors. But we keep going. We reach the end of the hall, passing by only two emergency exits.

"Maybe we missed it," Kaedy says, walking back.

When we return to the foyer, the doors are painfully obvious in sight. Shaking our heads, we walk up to them and enter the suite.

Half of the building is used for parking, while the other half is used as living spaces. Each suite appears to be four stories tall, with a small fifth one at the top. There are stairs that lead one floor down to what would be a basement, though none of them are underground. Right above this penthouse is parking, while right below is also parking. Each suite has its own parking that is also five levels tall, and they are arranged in a zigzag so that you are never directly over or under your neighbor's homes.

The home is massive. There are too many bedrooms to decide where I want to sleep. Kaedy hears my stomach growl and takes my hand. She quickly finds a restaurant, and we enjoy a healthy dinner, according to her. But the food is good.

"This is better than that wrap you ate this morning, right?" I ask her.

"Yeah, but that's not fair," she says. "It was a charging station wrap, nothing special at all. But still better than what you ate."

I laugh.

"Okay, fine. You win."

"Of course I do."

After dinner, we go back to the suite. We watch a movie in the theater room. There are large red cushioned seats and sectional sofas. We opt for the sofa, and she rests her head on my chest. When the movie is over, Kaedy asks if I want to watch another. With nothing better to do, I agree.

Halfway through the movie, I feel Kaedy's eyes on me.

"What is it?" I ask her, looking down.

Kaedy turns the volume down.

"Tell me a story," she says.

"What kind of story?"

"You pick. You owe me a story."

I nod. "Okay, uh...."

"Tell me about when you first met Maylene and how you got into all of this."

I smile and begin to tell her. I tell her of that night in the hotel, my disbelief in Edward, but that he offered a lot of money and seemed convinced in what he was saying, so I went along. I make it clear that I didn't just do it for the money. I'm not that type of person. I tell her the night I met Matt and how he saved me when I was attacked in that hotel. How I was so shocked and overwhelmed that I couldn't help but notice how attractive the guy was.

Kaedy laughs.

"What?"

"I understand the appeal, but I am more into you."

I look down into her eyes. Kaedy leans up and keeps her mouth close to mine. She's waiting for me to make the move. I kiss her deeply. She kisses me back. It doesn't take long until I feel what I felt this morning. Kaedy places her hand there, and now I know that she had noticed it. I roll her off me slightly and move on top of her. I undo the three buttons on her loose-fitting shirt. I take off my jacket. Kaedy breathes heavily. I move further down until Kaedy lets out a few gasps. I keep at it, but she tilts my chin up and locks eyes with me.

"I'm ready," she tells me.

I sit up, unzipping my pants. She sits up too and pushes me down on my back. She slips my pants off, my briefs. She takes a short, long taste before moving closer. She sits down and tilts her head up.

We go like that for some time. She eventually takes me to the nearest bedroom, and this time I go on top of her. I kiss her. A lot. This is something she and I have been waiting for, but there was never really a moment that offered this chance.

21

"So." Kaedy speaks just barely louder than a whisper, pausing for a moment. I lay on top of her for half a minute, trying to slow my breathing. We lock eyes. She, too, is breathing heavily. "Tell me a story."

I lay on my back next to her, smiling. I look up at the ceiling. My right hand finds hers.

"I was traveling once and had to stay the night at this hotel on the water," I say slowly, still catching my breath. "It was late, but I was hungry, so I went down to find some food."

Kaedy smiles. Her bright teeth shine, reflecting the moonlight that comes through an opening in the curtains. Her eyes reflect the lights outside, but then soon I see the reflection of my eyes in hers.

"Go on," she whispers.

"I was sitting there, minding my own business, when this loud girl came up and started talking to me."

I smile as she snorts out a laugh.

"I'm not loud!" she cries out. I laugh, raising my eyebrow at her. She stares at me, a remnant of a laugh still on her lips.

"Well, you felt loud that night," I tell her.

She scoffs. "Yeah, it's probably because you were just so nervous."

I nod and grin wide. "I was nervous because I wasn't used to talking to anyone as beautiful as you."

A moment of silence passes between us. She scooches closer and kisses me. Before I know it, we get back into it. I pay attention to the details, the way she breathes in suddenly, the way she stares into my eyes, how she arches her back and gasps when I place my hand on the small of it.

She asks me to tell her another story when we're done. Not wanting to use the same move twice in a row, I carefully start to tell her about my younger life, back home, those years I remember with my mom, and those first years without her. She listens intently. The way her eyes hold their gaze, I can tell she's genuinely interested.

She listens well, as if she really wanted to hear a story. I tell her about my father, someone that she knows about, just like most of the world. And I also tell her how I felt about him leaving.

While I tell her my story, I realize that I probably took on this job, the job of making deliveries, as a way to hide from the fact that I feel like I don't have a home. But I smile as I think of it, because after all those years of feeling so lonely, I feel like I have a place in this world. I have people that I care about, and they return that same love I have for them.

I know my father loves me. But he made a choice and jumped onto the opportunity he had. And I respect him for it. I am grateful for it. It gave me the means to live an easy life and find out who I am. Most people don't ever get that luxury.

"Everyone is just looking for their home. Everyone wants to feel at home, no matter where they are. Home is where they feel safe. And home can be anywhere. That was all I wanted," I say, thinking of my father. "He was there for me after mom died," I whisper as an afterthought. At this point, Kaedy is smiling while drifting off to sleep. "He never really abandoned me, despite his grief. But things never felt the same. Sometimes it takes a while to get used to that kind of loss." The more I face the truth of it, the more I realize that it was his work that made us grow apart. He did the best he could. And when an opportunity came, he went for it. I can't ever blame him for it. It made our lives so much easier, if not also so much lonelier.

Kaedy's eyes are closed, and her breathing is much louder. I know she's asleep. She still wears that smile though. I can't help but smile back. She's snuggled up to me, her face on my shoulder.

"But in the end," I say, knowing she can't hear me but still wanting to say it. "If all those years of being alone were the road to finding you, then I'd walk them another four years if I had to." I stop, holding back my next thought. But I decide to say it anyway. "I love you."

Gently, I move her off me and slide out of the bed. I have been holding in my bladder for too long.

I plan to tell her what I just told her when she is awake, awake on a different day. Maybe tomorrow. Maybe when this is all over with. Sometime. Sometime soon.

After getting back into bed, I pass out very quickly.

I wake up peacefully. My body feels like it got the long rest it was so desperate for. There is a hot, fresh scent wafting in. It smells like syrup, bacon, and a bunch of other things that make my stomach growl with hunger.

My eyes open after realizing that Kaedy is no longer beside me. Damn, she's an early riser. I sit up slightly and see her walk into the room. She is carrying a tray with two plates of food.

"Good morning, handsome," she says, walking closer to me. "I got you breakfast."

"Breakfast in bed," I say with a smile. I sit up fully, the white blanket still covering the lower half of my body. "Isn't that something I am supposed to do for you?"

She sits down next to me and gives me the tray. "Maybe one day you will. But just because I'm a girl doesn't mean I can't do it for you.

C'mon. You know better than that," she says. "After all, I can probably drive just as good as you. If not better."

"Oh, so she wants to compete!" I say, before taking a bite out of some pancake toast. It's got chocolate chips and melted caramelized sugar inside it. Potent. But delicious.

"Well, it might not be much of a competition." She laughs and whips out a fork I didn't notice that she was holding. She stabs a piece of bacon-wrapped sausage and eats it.

She catches the look I give her.

"What? I need to eat too; this isn't all for you. That's why there's two plates," she says. "And before you ask, no, unfortunately, I did not make this. But Edward suggested we order it, so I got it delivered. Apparently it's the best breakfast place in the entire city."

"I believe it," I say as I inhale more of the food. I try to go slowly so that Kaedy has a chance to eat what she wants, but she doesn't seem particularly hungry. I get the feeling that she ate some before bringing it in to me.

Kaedy turns off the privacy of the electrochromic windows that line either side of the room after she finishes eating, while I finish up the last of it. When it's all gone, I toss the tray towards the foot of the bed. Kaedy comes by to sit next to me. For a while, we just watch the morning make its way towards noon. The rising sun, the rush of the Sonars driving by, and the warm colors of early morning turning into a blazing blue.

"I need to get going," she tells me, breaking this brief breath of serenity. The real world outside still awaits, and I still have a job to finish.

"Yeah," I say, slowly making my way to get up. "I do too. I probably should have left a while ago."

Kaedy gets out of bed. Her back faces me, and the light from the sun glows over her. She turns around to face me. "I think you'll be on time. It's less than two days from here to NEAST. And we still don't know who we're meeting, or who you're meeting, I should say."

"Odds are I'll probably find out an hour before I get to NEAST," I say. "Just to make things more interesting."

Kaedy shrugs. "It might be safer that way."

I nod, agreeing. I get out of bed too and follow her into the living room. She starts walking toward the door. I don't want her to leave yet.

She looks back at me expectantly.

"You coming?" she asks.

"Now? Oh, I, uh." I don't know what to say. I feel like I'm going to jumble my words. "I wanted to shower now while I have the chance."

She shakes her head. "Of course, I forgot that you might not have that choice for a couple days." She walks up to me and gives me a lingering kiss.

When our lips unlock, we hold each other's gaze.

"I'll see you soon," she whispers. I know it's gut-wrenching for her to leave like this. But I understand. She has a job to finish, just like I do.

"See you soon," I whisper back as she leaves. The front door behind her closes and locks automatically.

I head back to the room we shared and take a shower in its bathroom. I don't linger, but I let the hot water run down my body for a moment. Elated with last night, the somber loneliness now begins to creep up, and for me, that means getting back on the road. But like Matt said, it's the last stretch.

It is entirely possible I end up in a hotel tonight, but things change so constantly. The only thing I'm sure of now about this job is that I am right at the end of it. Even if that means my last two days end up being four. It doesn't matter. Because it'll be over. And everything that Edward stood for, that all of us have stood for, will have been accomplished.

It's funny how the condo feels so empty without her here. We spent only one night here, so the whole place should feel foreign to me, but it had felt like home.

And now it feels like the embodiment of emptiness.

I grab the bag I took from the Sonars and walk out. It's a little heavier than I remember. In the empty foyer, I place the bag down and take a look. I can't help but smile. Kaedy packed some of that breakfast for me.

Getting into the Sonars brings back so many memories. For the longest time, being on the road was home for me. And in a way, I still feel the lingering spirit of the sense of home it gave me. With a sad smile, I get it started up and make my way out.

I won't give up driving. Kaedy loves adventure, so I'm sure we'll take many trips. There is so much of the world to see and experience. But with her by my side and with my friends, everything will feel like home. Because it will be.

It takes almost an hour to get out of the city. I managed to hit the lunch rush in addition to the traffic of the time of day, where some people start midday shifts at work while others are getting off from their night shift.

Kaedy sends me a message, telling me that she hated leaving that way. I smile and tell her that I understand but that we'll see each other soon. I hate just leaving in general. It would have been so perfect if everything else was finished; that way I could spend all the time in the world with her. At the same time, I wouldn't have it happen any other way.

Maylene sends me a direction shortly after. No destination, but simply just *drive that way*. I do so. I hold back calling her or Matt, as

I am sure they're hard at work making sure that I make it to where I'm going.

On this side of the city, far beyond its limits, the land is ragged, brown with shades of red and purple, and mostly with the same elevation, though small mounds and craters fill the Talvor as far as I can see.

Fraslia is mostly known for selling rare minerals. That's because of the caves that I'll be passing over. Contrary to most other open places I drive over, Sonars here are more prevalent. No later than every twenty minutes do I pass another one. It would be nice to visit the caves and mines one day, but they are likely inflated in cost as a tourist destination.

Most cities have easy access to almost anything because of how abundant everything is. Farms grow out in the countryside, close enough to the cities so that they don't have to rely on another part of the world. Most cities even have indoor farms. Materials are everywhere, and the governments trade what they don't have readily.

But what if the world being united this way is really nothing more than just one long, well-thought-out plan? What if that makes it easier to use something like Prodigy? Or is even thinking this making me some conspiracy theorist?

A world united and at peace is without a doubt a good thing. But there must be safeguards. If Prodigy were in the wrong hands, Talvor could be a world united but fully enslaved. A world where all humans must bow down to those who control Prodigy or risk being terminated in whatever way.

I drive just a bit faster. The world has done so great so far with peace between the nations. But what I carry could change everything.

While the rough land is quite something to look at, it gets mundane very quickly, and I end up just gliding over with little thought to it, and before I know it, I've passed the caves and mines and soar over fields of short grass.

A call comes into the Sonars. It's Edward.

"Hi, uh, Mr. Canabana." I feel awkward and uneasy. I feel like I've never spoken to him before. Maybe it's just because he hasn't called me directly before now.

"Yes, Arch. How are you?"

He's so polite.

"I'm good, yeah," I say. "Just making my way towards NEAST."

"So, I've heard," he says, a near-sarcastic undertone accompanying his voice. "I'm very proud of what you have accomplished so far and, indeed, how far you've come. This has been my longest, unresolved ambition, but I can taste the end now."

I remain silent, not knowing what to say.

"I appreciate everything that you've done," he says, probably sensing an inability to take a compliment on my part. "When you're closer to NEAST, I will give you a call and let you know who my contact is."

"Okay," I reply. "But didn't you already tell me?"

He pauses for a moment. There is no visual, just an audio call. He doesn't answer my question.

"Arch, you don't have to act nervous around me," he says. "Really, there is no need to."

I let out a laugh. "I know; I don't know why I feel so self-conscious."

"Neither do I, but it isn't you. And you are a very different person than the night we first met, and that night you were very much yourself; not at all shy about what you believed in," he tells me, hitting me just in the right spot. Of course he's right.

"How many people do you think are after this?" I ask him after a moment of contemplating. "How many people want Prodigy?"

Edward sighs. "I can only guess. But if I found out about it, and if the others who have already tried to take it know about it, I would have to say that probably every large government and every large corporation in the world, knows about it."

"Every large corporation," I say quietly.

"I wouldn't worry about it, though," Edward says, sensing exactly what I'm thinking. What if my father is behind any of this? Is that something that he is capable of? Or someone else close to him? He had been a hero years ago, exposing a criminal mastermind hiding as a CEO. That's how he became what he is. He fought the evil; he wasn't part of it. But people change. People hold grudges, and many probably hate my father. The thought puts a feeling of unease inside me that I didn't know I could feel.

"But it's still possible?"

Edward sighs again. He knows exactly what I'm talking about. "Yes, but not likely. PlatTech hasn't made enemies of the people at large; some other corporations have, and while they ignore the accusations or shift blame back to their accusers, there is likely some truth behind every rumor. Those are the guys we should worry about."

"Still, it's probably a pretty long list," I say.

"Yes, it is, which is why you just need to keep your head down. Don't worry about anything else. Matt and Maylene are working very hard to help you reach your destination. So don't worry about who the bad guys are, or who the good guys are, because what we're doing now will save our world."

I nod. "Yeah." A small pause. "Yeah."

Another moment of quiet. Edward knows he's made his point. Now there really isn't anything else to do but complete this delivery. This mission.

"Okay, talk to you soon," he says before clicking off.

I spend the next hour red in the face because I feel embarrassed about feeling embarrassed when he first called. Face-to-face, I wouldn't have felt that way at all. But my determination to get to NEAST increases tenfold.

I pass over a large lake. Glistening water sparkles as it rides the wind, moving in small waves and ripples. I lower my Sonars, kicking up more water. It is these small moments that can be made to seem so magical with a single photograph; that one perfect shot. Reality doesn't quite look the same. Still, if you look around, there really is beauty in everything.

The lake is massive and is dotted with islets, though some of its islands are big enough to hold a moderate house and a Sonars or two. I know there are cities just an hour away, but I'm not headed toward those.

As the day goes on, the land I pass over becomes drier. There is less vegetation and more plain, solitary-colored ground.

I munch through my snacks throughout the day, and when it gets dark, I stop somewhere briefly to eat some of that breakfast Kaedy packed for me, even though I know I'll regret not having this kind of food in the morning.

Looking out my window, I sigh at the black night ahead. I'm not sure how long Maylene wants me to go for, but to get this over with, I clench my teeth and get moving once more.

For whatever reason, the stars out here don't shine as bright, even though there isn't much light pollution. But I do know at NEAST, which is located in the middle of the desert, has so much going on that it's hard to see the stars there unless you're using their equipment designed to look out into the far reaches of outer space.

After another couple hours, I stop by a charging station location in a small town. There are several of these towns around, dotting the outskirts of the high desert. I charge up just because I'm already here and go inside to grab some more food. I'm not hungry at the moment, and I grimace at the meal choices I have, knowing that it will be all I have to eat for tomorrow.

When I get back into my Sonars, I change into a plain white shirt and put on the jacket Matt gave me. I realize that the jacket is designed to keep me warm or cooler, depending on the outside temperature. Being that it is nighttime, it is very chilly outside, but during the day it might get a little warm. Then again, the Aclojade Desert is quite unpredictable. I put on some tactical pants with the same temperature effect and place the chip inside a small pouch and into one of my pockets before snapping its button into place.

"Where are you?"

I turn around quickly. Maylene is staring at me through the screen.

"Hey!" I shout at her. "I was just naked!"

Maylene laughs. It looks like she's made it back to Candalance. "You weren't naked; I saw the whole thing."

I raise an eyebrow. "Yeah, but still." I trail off, not caring to discuss any further on the subject.

"Well, you shouldn't feel embarrassed around me," she says. "You know that."

I force out a chuckle.

"So how far out am I going tonight?" I ask. "Whatever it is, I'm okay with it. I bought some booster drinks to keep me going if need be."

"At this rate, you'll probably only be traveling for another hour before stopping until the morning," she responds. "So far, no one has been tracking you, or chasing you, so you're in the clear. Unfortunately, we must still be cautious, so you will be sleeping in the Sonars tonight."

I sigh and sit down. "That's okay. It's kind of what I expected. But couldn't I just stay here?"

"Hm, no," she says. Maylene peers into her camera, making her face look quite big on my screen. "There's too many people out there." She must be looking out of my front camera. "I think it would be better if you stopped in Meladrosa."

"I've never heard of it."

"Most people haven't. That's the point. There are much fewer people there, and a random Sonars parked off the road for the night isn't unusual. Most people who do that never even learn the name of that town," she explains. "It's a very private place, where most people like to be left unbothered."

"For some, that sounds like heaven."

"For some, that is!" Maylene laughs. "That's why they moved there! But it really wouldn't be my style. It's a bit too much peace and quiet. Too much of that, and everything seems suspicious."

I start the engines and buckle in. The Sonars rises off the ground a bit, ready to get going.

"The peace and quiet will be nice for just the one night," I say. "But I agree with you. I could probably never live there."

Maylene laughs and then snorts.

"Sorry, I just thought of something. Maybe when you're as old as Gary, it would be an appealing place to live."

I give her a confused look. "Is that what was so funny?"

Maylene squints her eyes, holding back a laugh. "Yes," she says in a slightly higher pitch than normal. "The picture in my head was what was so funny, imagining you as a grumpy old man."

I roll my eyes.

"If you could have imagined what I did, you would have laughed too," she says. "Anyways, head to Meladrosa, but don't stop at the charging station for the night, because that would look suspicious to the locals. Instead, just find somewhere near the edge of the town that isn't in front of anything. If you leave by nine tomorrow morning, you should make it to NEAST well before dinner. Edward will call you and let you know where exactly to go."

"Copy that," I tell her. She smiles.

"Good night, Arch. See you soon."

Maylene clicks off, and I get going. This town has two main streets and no elevations. I'm sure all the settlements around here have no elevations. As such, there are no grounding laws, but it is courteous to stay low to the ground and follow the marked roads rather than fly above.

I keep at a slower speed until I'm well out of the city. Once through, I push my Sonars forward, rising high into the sky. Looking below, I see nothing. It doesn't matter much, as nearly everything beneath me is a bare wasteland.

I'm still hours away from the high desert, and it is unlikely I'll get much closer tonight. Maylene sends me my destination, steering me slightly off course. I can tell from the navigation system that there are two towns closer to NEAST than where she sends me, but I head there without questioning.

A message comes into CHAD. I read it from the screen while silencing his narration. Kaedy asks me to call her when I stop for the night. I send her a message back, telling her that I will, and that it looks like I've got another hour left.

She responds with *perfect*.

The closer I get, the fewer stars I can see. Still, those few that do appear in the night sky are blurry, but their light continues to cast that perfect utopian atmosphere over the naked and dry land.

Sooner than I thought, I lower my Sonars down to the ground and pass through a quaint town. Everything is closed, even the single charging station. There is just one road that forks into two on the other side. Most of the structures look like they are made of a hybrid wood-and-steel. Some of the larger structures, while tiny compared to the cities, are made from stone and lack a front door.

There are three other Sonars parked off to the side at the edge of the town. I pass by them and set down my vehicle near them, but a bit further apart than the others are.

I spend a few minutes outside, walking for a bit. The dry, cold air makes my lips feel chapped immediately, but I happily breathe it in. There is a distinct freshness to the desert air at night, making it stand out from most other places in the world.

There is a single-room structure in the middle of the fork, between the roads. There is a small garden in front of it and a gated backyard. The gates are purely ornamental, short, and have several openings. I have to walk closer to see what lies inside.

Headstones are randomly placed throughout, some with small boutiques, others with piles of dead leaves. There are two with burning candles. I don't go inside, but I walk by it. The building almost looks like an old church. It is possible that the townspeople come every once in a while to pray and pay their respects.

The garden in front is bountiful with all sorts of colors, almost like an oasis in the desert. It gives a striking contrast to the rest of the otherwise monotone town. There is a heavy scent like perfume from the garden, making my head slightly dizzy. I walk away from the garden and then head back towards my Sonars.

As I walk back, I can feel eyes on me. I subtly look around, trying to see if there is someone following me, but I catch no one.

When I get inside, I immediately call Kaedy.

"How was your day?" she asks.

I smile. "Good, just lots of driving. What about yours?"

"Oh, same here." Kaedy looks like she's staying at a comfortable hotel, though the room looks smaller than the places Maylene has been setting me up. "I'm actually going to be trying to sell an art piece tomorrow. It's not something I usually do, so I'm a bit nervous about that."

"Don't be," I tell her. "You'll do great. You always do."

She smiles and looks down. Is she blushing? Kaedy stays quiet for a minute.

"So, uh," I say, and then clear my throat. "I had a great time last night."

Silence. Awkward. More silence.

The quiet only lasts about three seconds.

"Me too," she says. "Honestly, I can't wait to see you again."

I laugh nervously. I don't even know why. "I feel the same way."

Her face brightens up, and inside my heart melts. Nothing compares to her beauty. I start to feel oddly warm and take off my jacket. That's not supposed to happen. The reason I feel hot must be unrelated to the temperature. Another look at Kaedy through my screen confirms this theory.

"We definitely should meet in Fraslia when you're done," she says. "That should be just about three days from now, depending on how long it takes to drop off that thing you're carrying."

"Yeah, or even one of these quaint towns," I say, looking around as if I can see them all. "But they are a little creepy. I went for a short walk, and I felt like someone was watching me."

Keady giggles. "You're disturbing their peace," she says. "Of course they're watching you."

"Yeah, that makes sense," I say absentmindedly. I'm just thinking about meeting her back in Fraslia. "I like your idea better."

"Then we can spend a couple days in Ibarca," she says. "You know, really experience that city. I think it will be wonderful."

"Oh, absolutely," I tell her, snapping my attention back. "I'm all for that."

Kaedy gives me her perfect smile.

"Then it's a date," she tells me. "Just be sure to let me know once you're all done. Because once I make this sale, I'm taking time off. Even if I wait for a couple of days doing nothing. It'll be worth it."

We talk for about an hour into the night until I realize that the next day already started. I tell her that I should head off to sleep. She wishes me goodnight. Those words I said to her last night while she slept linger on the tip of my tongue, but they don't come out. Kaedy looks like she's either expecting me to say something or like she's gonna say something herself, but when no words are exchanged, I tell her good night. She smiles genuinely and closes out.

22

It took me a while to fall asleep last night. I was entirely enamored with the memory of the time I spent with Kaedy the previous night while also mentally slapping myself for being such a sissy when we last spoke. I want to tell her so bad. I want to tell her that I love her. I feel like she feels the same way. We took things slow, not by choice but by circumstance. But even so, especially with those circumstances, I truly believe we've become that close.

I wake up to a blinking message on the CHAD screen. There's no words, just a destination. I get up and move over to the front seats, opening up the map. They're sending me to the middle of the desert. The location must be just under an hour away from NEAST, and that's to the property line. I've never been there before, but from the pictures and footage I've seen, it's a long road to the gates and then another road to the actual base of operations.

While I picked up snacks last night, I neglected to get water. And this is one of those mornings when I wouldn't mind having a cup of coffee. Knowing I need to get going soon, I quickly put on my jacket and head into the town. It's still chilly out, but not nearly as cold as it was last night. Even though it is nearly midmorning, most places are still closed. I manage to find a shack just opening and I use the best puppy-eyes I can muster to encourage the disgruntled man into selling me a quick cup and a bottle of water. I highly doubt it worked; it's likely he just wanted to be rid of me.

I jog back to my Sonars. The three others that were parked here are gone. I quickly jump into the main driver's seat and get going. For the first half-hour, I sip down the coffee, not paying much attention to anything else.

As I go on, I can sense the temperature rising outside, even if it doesn't change at all for me inside the Sonars. The sun begins to glare down on the barren land. Dried plants struggle to survive, no longer gasping for moisture but leaning over in dread. The farther I go, the less solemn the vegetation looks, and soon the sad plants are replaced with those that thrive in the intense sunlight. Plants covered with glochids branch out, some of their stems bigger than the roots of trees you'd normally see in the city.

When the glare gets too bad, the Sonars automatically dims the windshield, making it easier to see but reducing the usual far-reaching visibility. Above me, several airships zoom past. None of them give me a second look. Most bear the NEAST insignia, a small "v" inside a larger one, with the words National Exploration Agency of Space Technologies arched over, but the last word the largest beneath everything else.

It probably could be pretty sweet working for them. It is also entirely possible that it's overhyped, and that most positions there are just what I consider to be boring desk jobs. But if we ever have missions into space, traveling to other planets, that's probably where I would want to be.

Matt calls me. Anxiety creeps up. I've both been looking forward to catching up with him and not. Using proper manners, Matt waits for me to answer rather than force himself into my communications system.

"How's it going, bud?" he asks me. He gives me that wide grin. Due to his surroundings, I can tell he is traveling. His Sonars looks similar to mine, though the inside of his is darker.

"You know, same old," I tell him. "But we're nearly there."

He laughs. "You know it," he says with a yawn. "Anyways, I'm probably about two hours behind you. We'll keep it that way, and after you've delivered the package, I'll be taking you back. I've got your location marked on my screen and your traveling speed, so I'll make sure to not be more than a couple hours behind. Maybe I'll catch up a bit too."

I don't respond. He also has that camera on me. While I trust him not to use it, I can't help but wonder if he saw everything the other night. I try to hide my thoughts, but my facial expression gives me away.

"What's wrong?" Matt asks, slightly frowning at my face.

"I, uh," I look down for a moment as I speak. "I was planning to meet up with Kaedy before heading back to Candalance."

Matt stares at me, his mouth open slightly. He then laughs. "Okay, so either you guys finally did it, or you didn't, and that's something you need to rectify immediately."

I don't say anything. But at least that mostly confirms that he didn't see anything private.

"I can only imagine," he says. "With someone like that, I'd be beating myself up, unable to think of anything else." He stops for a moment. "Yeah, I'd be losing my freakin' mind." Matt peers closer at his screen. I can see a couple thousand thoughts run through his head. Still, I say nothing. He can figure it out.

He stares at me, having reached his conclusion. But I know he wants to be right, so I remain silent.

"You look okay," he says finally. "Maybe a bit sleep deprived, but okay. Which means you two did it."

"Did what?" I ask after a few seconds.

Matt's eyes go wide. "Hey, I'm here to congratulate you! Not for anything else, but—just for finding someone who is so great, because you deserve it man. You really do."

I can't stop my smile. "Thank you," I tell him. "And yeah, it was great."

Matt nods. He looks away for a moment. I look at the navigation. I'm less than two hours away from my destination. Still, it seems to be in the middle of nowhere. I wonder if Edward will call me soon.

"Well, it's nice checking in on you," he says. "This will all be over soon."

"What about you?" I ask coyly.

Matt looks back as if there was someone else there. He knows what I'm talking about. "Not yet," he says. "But when I get back to Candalance, be sure I'll be making my move."

I grin and nod. "Glad to hear it. Because you too deserve someone great."

A silence passes between us. It's almost unreal how close we are to finishing the mission that brought us together. The future, my future, is mostly unmapped. Is it really possible to go back to such a normal life after living this life for the past several weeks? I'll be finding out soon. We all will.

"After I pick you up, I can take you to Kaedy," Matt says. "I'll call her to make sure she has a vehicle for the both of you to come back to Candalance when you're done." He pauses for a moment. "You said you are coming back, right?"

I laugh. "Yeah, I'm definitely coming back."

'Good, good."

Another moment of silence.

"I'll see you soon, bud," says Matt. He waits for me to respond before clicking off.

The grandness of the desert evolves into something bold and extravagant, yet extravagant in wholly nothing, as not even cacti or birds of prey are around. Badlands at their finest. The land below me appears to be entirely unhabitable. It's probably why this was the chosen area for NEAST. It's so far out of the way, and any experiments that go wrong are unlikely to affect anything living. That is, anything else but those who are stationed there.

After an hour, the driving becomes rote. The airships that flew above me are gone, and I encounter no more. The land remains mostly the same, with the only difference being the shape, size, and direction of the large cracks in the ground.

I set the Sonars to autopilot for a moment. I know I'm still some hours away, but I head back and lie down for a bit. I don't fall asleep. The anticipation of delivering Prodigy and of spending a couple of days with Matt while we head to Fraslia keeps me awake. And the thoughts of the week I'll spend with Kaedy comes to mind. Everything. Everything I'm going to do and everything I'm going to accomplish. The thoughts don't stop. Good thoughts. Great thoughts.

When I feel like I've been out of control of the Sonars too long, I get back up and head to the front seat. Even though it feels weird, I put on the jacket, knowing it will help keep me cool when I meet Edward's contact from NEAST.

As I sit down and disable the autopilot function, Edward calls me. His blue eyes are piercing, even from the screen. Like Matt, Edward appears to be traveling.

"Good morning, Arch," he says politely. "I hope everything has been well since we last spoke?"

"Yes, thank you," I tell him. "Matt checked in with me a couple hours ago and told me the plan. Everything is all set."

He nods and looks away quickly. I see him adjust some things on his dash. He then picks up the camera and walks to the back of his

Sonars. It's white inside and has noticeably more space than mine. It doesn't look like an airship, though.

"Not everything," he says as he sits down on the bed in the back. "You still have to meet my contact." He swipes up in the air, causing a hologram to appear, facing him. I can't really tell what it is.

"Yes, of course," I say. I want to ask him who I am meeting, but I'm sure he's about to tell me. Or he won't. Either way, I know I'm in good hands.

Mr. Canabana continues to move his fingers around, changing a few things on the screen that only he can see.

"I've locked out your navigation system," he tells me. "I've also disabled CHAD." He contemplates for a moment. "Isn't it funny, calling it CHAD? I always thought that was an odd name."

I laugh. "I just thought it was a name." I know it's more than that.

"Oh, yeah, it is, but it stands for something. Most people forget that," he tells me. He's right. But I'm not one of those people.

"Communicative, Handy, And Detailed."

Edward raises his eyebrows, apparently impressed.

"I misjudged you," Edward says. "But clearly I made the right choice in picking you for this mission."

I just have one question. Maybe more, but just the one important one. "Why did you disable CHAD? And how are we still talking, then?" So, two questions.

"My apologies; I should have been more clear. I disabled CHAD from all use except for with me. I control your CHAD at the moment. There is no geographical location enabled, no navigation, and no communication with anyone." I take a deep breath. "It must be this way. We cannot risk someone hacking into the system and knowing where you are and what you're about to do."

I let out a small sigh. "Okay. I get it. Makes sense."

"I know it will feel lonely and monotonous these last few hours, but I assure you that you are not alone," he says. "I am here. Even Maylene is here."

I hear her chime in briefly.

"Hi Arch."

I say hi back, but there is no response.

"Forgive her," he says. "She's quite busy at the moment. But when you're with Matt, feel free to give her a call. We'll all have time to breathe and relax then."

"Okay. So how do I know where I'm going?"

Edward nods. "Right. Let me fix that." He plays with his holographic screen. The lights are a pale blue, hardly discernible from where I sit, but vivid if you're in front of the proper side of them.

The image of Edward Canabana projects out of the screen, and his head and surroundings float above the CHAD screen. Replaced by the footage are two green lines. Testing it out, I turn the steering slightly on the Sonars. Two red lines appear, accompanied with a beeping.

"Just stay in that path and you will reach Jasmine," he informs me.

"Jasmine? Is that your contact at NEAST?"

"Surprised?"

I shrug. "Just a little. For whatever reason, I always thought he was a he."

Edward smiles. He swipes up on his screen. Another projection shoots out of my CHAD's screen. Next to the footage of Edward, there is a lady, probably in her late forties, standing there, slowly spinning around. It's just a picture of her. She has long, dark hair, fair skin, and weary eyes.

"This is insane," I say. "How are you doing this?"

"I own several companies, some of which create new technology. I would be remiss if I didn't test them out before selling them to the public," Edward answers simply.

"This is unreal, but absolutely amazing."

"Well, thank you, Arch," he says. "I'm glad you're enjoying it. Perhaps when you're back, I can show you some of the other projects I've been working on."

"You sure seem to do a lot," I say.

Edward nods and claps his hands once. "Prodigy is just my most urgent enterprise, something you've been a great help with."

"I'm glad."

We let the moment sit for a few seconds, but Edward then gets straight back to business.

"Jasmine will be meeting you in her small rover. Those are quick in the desert, and she'll be able to quickly get Prodigy safely onto the next shuttle to Earth. She is quite talented, if I do say so. She began working at NEAST at just fifteen years old, so she is quite respected there. Of course, she isn't without those who mean to do her harm. NEAST is full of people who want to advance our world into the next great thing, and there are those who just love the stars and space, and then there's the ones that aim to develop and implement technology that will suit them, and damn everyone else. It's almost a shame that Prodigy has to go, as I am sure I could have found a good use for it."

"Keeping it is just too risky?" I ask.

"Oh, I tried for years. But people still manage to track it down before I have time to get anything accomplished with it," he tells me. Edward almost looks regretful, but he doesn't say more.

"Does she know what I look like?" I couldn't help but ask. "Jasmine, I mean."

"Oh, yes," Edward says, fluttering his eyes like he had been in deep thought just seconds before. "She's been expecting you for some time now. But she understands the delays we've had."

"Great."

Edward taps some things on his screen. The projection of Jasmine disappears.

"Any questions?" he asks me, closing his computer-hologram.

I do have one. Just the one.

"Where are you?" I ask him.

Edward chuckles. "I'm around." He blinks. "Bye now," he says, and immediately hangs up. The projection of him disappears, and all I see are those two green lines, telling me that I am still on track.

I should have asked him more about Jasmine because I could have sworn the name he gave me before was a different one, and that's why I thought I was meeting a man. Maybe it was a fake name he gave me back then.

The road now seems even more unpleasantly boring now that there is nothing to look forward to. I understand his precautions, but that understanding hasn't stopped me from wondering if I was missing something. Is Edward not who he says he is? The thought lingers only for a bit. If he wanted Prodigy, well, he had always had it. I still trust him in that he wants to rid our world of it. Clenching my fist, I push the Sonars harder, moving along quicker than before.

It doesn't take me long to realize that because there is so little out here, flying faster than normal is unlikely to get me into trouble, so I speed up, pushing the Sonars past reasonable speed for my current traveling elevation.

I don't ascend higher into the atmosphere, as that would look out of place, and I don't want to get caught by an Impositioner, even if it's unlikely, when I'm so close to Jasmine.

I realize that Mr. Canabana never told me how I would know when I made it to Jasmine's location, but I figured there would be some marker on the screen. At the very least, I can look out for a parked rover.

When another hour passes, I slow down a bit and start looking out for anything on the ground, just in case that's all that would tell me that I've reached my destination. The thought of staying in the Sonars for two hours while I wait for Matt isn't inviting, but maybe I could just nap during that time. I'm sure my CHAD will still be disconnected; it is likely the Sonars itself is being abandoned entirely.

It stays cool inside the Sonars, but the harsh sunlight makes it feel like it is hot. Sweltering weather outside makes the skies look both hazy and beautifully blended with shades of blue. Some parts of the ground below look distorted, and I am unable to see if it's because of a trick of the light or if the ground is just that messed up with fissures.

I munch on some snacks, leaving the Sonars on autopilot for five minutes. I wipe my hands on my pants when I'm done and sit back down in the driver's seat. I am about to flick the button off when I notice a large ship pass overhead. It's been a while since I've seen anything.

Then I hear the quick beeps. I check the thin screen above, which shows me the view from behind. A Sonars rises into view. It's black with a thick, gray stipe on both sides. It looks like an Impositioner. Instinctively, I slow down. It doesn't.

When I look ahead, I slam on the brakes. My heart jumps out of my chest, replaced by my stomach. The airship that passed above lowers rapidly. I maneuver out of its way. Then I see three additional Sonars. Still, even after I decrease my speed, they seem to come right at me, faster and faster.

I punch it. These aren't Impositioners. These guys aren't NEAST. Someone's found me. They must know this is their last chance. There's something different this time. They're coordinated and perfectly positioned. Edward's plan to keep my location hidden didn't work.

I quickly set all my controls to modes that aren't considered legal. I cloak the Sonars, though it won't do much good as they've already spotted me. I disable the safety driving precautions, making my Sonars as fast as the airship, maybe faster. I shoot down to the ground, hoping they follow. They do.

My plan doesn't pan out. When I'm near the ground, the airship launches a rocket, forcing me to quickly swerve out of the way. Chunks of the land are blasted into the sky while shards of rock violently fly through the air. The Sonars following me trail behind until the debris clears.

The four Sonars continue their pursuit. Paying close attention to what's behind me, I attempt to put as much distance as quickly as possible between myself and the airship. The ship slowly turns to face my direction. Impossibly, the airship then darts forward, closing the distance between us.

Horrified, I do all I can to drive faster, but it seems I've pushed the limits of the Sonars. I can feel it vibrating, unsure of how it's moving as fast as it is. I'm lucky that there is so much open space, because I am not giving the sky in front of me the amount of attention I should to safely travel.

When the airship inevitably closes in, it launches another missile at me. I shut down the main control for the Sonars, something that is usually locked in position while traveling, but I had disengaged the safety protocols. Without its electro-magnetic systems, the Sonars plummets to the ground. The airship passes over me. I flip back on the switches. I shoot forward, catching up to the airship, but then quickly turn around and head in the opposite direction.

For a second, I think I had lost the other Sonars chasing me. They quickly come into view, but now there are five.

Another blast comes my way, but this misses me easily, almost like a desperate attempt or hope for a lucky shot.

It's a good thing that my Sonars is faster than the other Sonars. Using the time I have, I continue flying far from the airship. But one look into my rearview shows me that the airship is back on my tail. It is unlikely that they will let me use the same tactic. Whatever I do, I can't let that airship get near. Too close, one decently aimed shot from its launcher will annihilate me.

I fly in a straight line, moving only when I need to avoid any more projectile launches.

"Can you hear me?"

My head turns towards CHAD's screen. There is nothing there.

"Arch, can you hear me?" Edward's voice crackles through.

Feeling silly, I answer, "Yeah." I don't know if he can hear me. I don't know how he's reaching me. All my communications systems seem off. I try to activate CHAD, but the program remains silent.

"ARCH!"

"I hear you!" I shout back, frustrated that nothing seems to be working. I dive down again and swerve to the right to avoid another fire. A second missile comes right behind, and I move out of the way just in time. My Sonars shakes violently and feels ripped from its directional force. I have to adjust my steering firmly to stay in control.

"Arch, are you there?" The screen flickers on. In that second, I see Edward, but then the screen turns blue.

"I'm here!" I cry out. "I'm here."

"There you are," Edward says. "Sorry about that. They seem to have jammed all communications, but I knew I'd get through. Maylene is nearby, working on getting firepower out here, but she might be too long. Listen close. You're going to see me soon; I will be flying towards you. No matter what happens, continue straight. If you don't, what I'm about to do might kill you."

He says all this very fast. There is no time for me to think about anything he says, so I just agree.

Instantly, the cloaking of a Sonars goes down, and way in the distance, a white Sonars hurtles towards me. It's Edward. He must have been near me the entire time. I keep going straight, as he said. I hear firing behind. Another missile is launched at me.

I want to move. Every cell in my body is telling me to move. I have to. If I don't, the entire Sonars and myself will be blown up. But Edward's words are like frantic shouting in my head. Whatever happens. I close my eyes for a second, but that doesn't help me. I take a deep breath, clench my fingers around the steering, and continue straight.

The missile comes close. Something shoots out of Edward's Sonars, but I can barely see it. Right behind me, a forcefield glows as the missile makes contact. The missile doesn't make it and breaks up into several pieces. The force field flickers but holds. Two of the dogging Sonars crash into it and are obliterated. Again, the field flickers, but I can still make it out.

The airship fires another missile, nearly breaking apart the shield, but not quite. Even so, it did enough damage to it. When the airship hits it, it breaks it apart and passes through with little incident.

"Good job, Arch," Edward says. He steers his Sonars around, heading forward like me.

"You too," I breathe out. "And thank you."

"Don't thank me yet; we're still in the heat."

I raise my altitude, going higher than the airship. The airship doesn't move. It appears to be going after Mr. Canabana now. The three other Sonars still chase me.

"Don't worry about me," Edward says, noticing the same shift as I do. "I'm here to make sure you make it to where you're going. Remember that."

I nod, even though I'm sure he can't see me.

A missile is fired at Edward. He dodges it easily. The Sonars he drives is slightly different in shape than mine; it's sharper and more angled. He cloaks it again. It disappears fully.

The airship keeps at it, moving towards where Edward was. They probably have sensors to read heat or motion and can likely still track Mr. Canabana. They fire again, but the missile gets lost in the distance.

"They were way off," Edward says with a chuckle. "That means that my new design is working." He waits a second. "Are you ready to do it again?"

"Yes," I tell him, eyeing the Sonars behind me.

"Good. Slow down."

I do as I'm told. The Sonars begin to gain on me. I force myself to ignore my instincts. I shift slightly but pay careful attention to where Edward might appear. Then I see it. The hazy and indistinct distortion flying through the air. I make sure I'm out of its path. Again, just behind me, a field appears, and another two of the Sonars are vaporized. The shield holds strong this time.

The last Sonars must have seen that there was a trap coming, as it slows to a stop before hitting it. Unfortunately, the shield can't last forever, and while I increase the distance between us, he is soon after me once more.

A missile heads in my direction. The airship must have given up on chasing Edward. I dodge it.

"I should have seen that coming," Edward says. He uncloaks his Sonars. He isn't far from me, heading in the same direction, almost parallel. "The cloaking mechanism is also equipped with a heat diffuser, making it very hard to track even with other sensory equipment."

Sand begins to settle on the windshield, something I think is odd until I realize that the wind is blowing it all around. A light storm is passing through. I look around as best I can. So far, there is no sign that the storm will worsen.

"That airship is only faster than you right now because it isn't as hit by the wind like you are," Edward says. "I am sorry for not having the better model ready by the time you picked that up. But let's see what we can do to use the wind to our advantage."

Edward drops to the ground. I follow him. I know he decreases his speed so that I can stay close. The airship lowers too. Another missile comes after us. Edward goes to the left, while I go to the right. We still decrease the altitude, and the missile hits the ground, kicking up more debris, but this time I mostly just see more sand.

In the strong winds, the sand creates a thick cover. It's hard to see much while inside, but it is likely that the airship can't see too.

With all the recent motion, I forget that there is another Sonars after me until now. I look around, trying to spot it. When I move out into view, I see the Sonars underneath the airship, which is now moving at a slower pace.

Ahead, two Sonars fade into sight, deactivating their cloaks. They may not have been as good as Edward's, but with the reduced visibility, there was little chance that I would have seen them.

Edward and I dart out of the way. Luckily for him, Edward wasn't their target. The two Sonars catch up and flank me. I try to raise the Sonars, but I can't move it. Then my Sonars vibrates, and I've lost control. I am unable to steer. I look out to the side. Radiating energy spills out of the two Sonars, locking me into whatever position they desire.

Behind me, the airship begins to pick up speed. The Sonars that rode beneath it is nowhere to be seen.

"I can't shoot out that forcefield," Edward says. Before I can respond, he then says, "Oh, perhaps I can."

Panic floods my body. "No, wait."

It's too late. Edward shoots out another beam, though this is off target. However he does it, I don't know. I don't even know how it works. The Sonars to my left crashes into the activated shield and is torn up. I'm so surprised that it worked that I don't take the moment to free myself.

That moment is soon gone. Another Sonars from below rises to take the last one's place. Once again, I'm pinned between the two tractor beams, tethered and at their mercy. I struggle with the controls of the Sonars, but to no avail.

"Shit," Edward says. The tone in his voice isn't good. This situation isn't good. Edward shifts the direction of his Sonars and flies towards me. He moves off to the side, making sure to avoid getting too close to the Sonars that have me pinned. I shout out in frustration, unable to do anything else.

I can feel it. I can feel the airship behind me about to fire. They're going to sacrifice two of their own to shoot me down.

Then it happens. The airship launches its next missile. It flies in a perfect line towards me. Again, I try to move my vehicle out of the way, but still I remain suspended between the two Sonars.

I look into the rearview. The missile is fast approaching, and I have just seconds. But then I see Edward make his way towards it. His maneuvers should be physically impossible. Edward falls in line with the missile and shoots something out towards me and the Sonars to my sides.

Mr. Canabana is then hit with deadly accuracy. The impact and explosion aren't nuclear by any means, but shards of projectile and Edward's Sonars cut through the air. There is no surviving that.

The beam Edward shot disables all the Sonars, including mine. Five more below are forced out of their invisibility cloak. We all plummet towards the ground. It's just like what happened back in Chlorofyx. I turn off my systems and quickly engage them again. I make air again and zoom forward. None of the other Sonars were quick enough, and they splatter on the ground.

Unphased, the airship continues its pursuit. I do my best to not think of what just happened, but knowing that Edward is gone doesn't make any of this easier, especially when he was my only support. All I can do is hope that Matt and Maylene know what's happening and that they're sending whatever help they can.

No matter how much I push, that airship is gaining on me. It doesn't shoot any more missiles. It probably knows it has already won. I keep at it. I have to keep at it.

There is a small moment where it looks like I'm getting away. I don't look back again to properly judge it. I just keep going.

I move as quickly as possible. I see a wave of energy rush towards me. It penetrates my Sonars and deactivates it. Again, I drop to the floor like a bird killed mid-flight. I struggle to get the controls back on. I finally do, way too close to the ground for my liking.

Something hits the side of my Sonars and I am blasted off course. The impact shuts my systems back down. The belt holding me to the seat is disengaged, and I slam into the side, my face pressed against the window. I slump to the floor, my head pounding. I scramble to my feet. The crash cushions should have activated by now.

Surely, I am seconds from smashing into the ground with no chance of pulling through. A million thoughts race through my mind. I check that Prodigy is still on me. It is. I tear apart CHAD's screen and plunge my hand into the inner parts of the Sonars. I punch down anything I can find. Finally, I find something that activates the cushions. Their force almost breaks my arm. I retract my hand from the guts of the Sonars and try to position myself comfortably. The thick padding is larger and softer than the last Sonars I was in that crashed to the ground.

Still, when I hit the ground, I am tossed over multiple times. I hit my head on three occasions and start to lose consciousness, but don't quite black out. And now all I can think of and all I can feel is the pain of smacking into the ground, flipping over in the air, and banging back on the ground again. Just like the last time this happened.

23

I know I'm not there. I don't even think I'm here. My head hurts so bad. I can feel myself tossing over and over, each impact on the ground seemingly more painful than the last. It is cold. I can feel the metal floor. But heat radiates out of my body, and I feel like I'm burning up. There is little solace in my numb mind. I don't know what is. But I remember everything that was. I remember everything that happened.

I can't wake up. But I am not sleeping. Everything feels wrong. I open my eyes, yet they stay shut. So I close them again, not that anything has changed. There is nothing here. There is nothing there.

I can't control my thoughts. I try to feel the pain of losing Edward. I try to feel sad. I try to discover where I am. Nothing. There is nothing. I feel like I'm experiencing the worst of a hangover. A loud burp escapes my throat. I gag, I retch, but nothing comes out.

And then I start to shiver. The heat still feels like it's pouring out of my body, and my body is an infinite source of energy radiating warmth. Wait, is it the ground that is shaking? Or is it me? It is impossible to tell.

The pain is constant, but occasionally a new wave of stronger feeling overcomes me. I shout out, but I can't hear my own voice. But now there are voices. What are they saying? Are they talking to me?

My eyes open. I spit out involuntarily. I can't see anything. All around me is black. Darkness. My face is pressed against the floor. It indeed is metal, that much I can tell. I lay there for a while, unable to move my body. My breathing intensifies, anxiety rippling through my skin as I ponder what the fuck is happening to me. I can feel all my senses slowly come back. I stop shivering, even though the ground still feels cold. I can feel the cold air blowing on me, but there is heat coming straight down. Things still make little sense.

My finger. My right index finger. It twitches. I try to make it twitch again. I struggle with putting all my will into it. Nothing happens. When I give up, it twitches once more. And then again. It becomes more frequent.

My other hand starts to get feeling. I then realize that most of my body had no tactile sense of anything. But my face always did, at least the side that has been pressed down against the floor. I don't think there is anything on me, but it sure feels like there is. As the sense of touch pervades me, I begin to ache. The bruises I sustained feel fresh. Something is injected into my body. I squeal at being startled at the sudden jab of the needle. It was something warm. I can feel it fill my blood vessels.

The pain slowly starts to fade. Perhaps Matt has saved me? But I don't think so. Why would it be so dark in here unless my eyes are still closed? I try to open them again. Instead, I blink.

It must be hours that I lie here. At an unbelievably slow pace, I am able to control more and more parts of my body. It sure is aggravating. I can move my head around; I can even make it so the other side of my face is pressed against the floor. But I still can't get up.

Then the feeling fully comes back to my hands and my chest. Then my arms are free. I try to drag myself across the floor but come across a wall. I follow it along, turning along each new wall I come across. Four times I turn. I'm in a box.

Defeated, I lay there, slumped. Not like I have much other choice. Hours later, even with functioning legs, there is still nowhere for me to go. I still can't see anything. Frustrated, I bang my fists against the ground. It hurts, but the pain quickly fades. I do it again, harder. It hurts more, but again, the pain disappears. With difficulty, I get to my feet. I manage to stand for a grand three seconds before collapsing on the floor. My forehead takes the brunt of the impact. Searing pain tears through my skull, into my eyes, my ears, my nose. It stays there only for a few seconds. And then I feel fine. Numb, but fine.

Maybe it's Matt and Maylene? And I'm stuck here until I've fully recovered? Maybe I'm not really stuck. Perhaps it's a puzzle that Mr. Canabana created, and I have to solve it, and at the end he'll congratulate me.

I shake my head. I know what happened. Edward Canabana is dead. But these delirious thoughts still creep into my mind.

I close my eyes. I can see a younger version of myself. Mom is there. But her back is turned to me. I call out. She doesn't look back. And then she disappears. I see myself standing next to my younger self. I smack my younger self across the back of his head. I pick him up and start walking. Instead of all white, we're now at the beach. This version of my younger self can't swim. So I toss him into the churning waters, hoping he'll drown. I can be that person no more.

Fear snaps my eyes wide open. I feel like I'm crying, but no tears fall. I remember the love I had for my mother, but that was a lifetime ago. It's been so long since she left us. And while the kid I was then essentially died, I am not the same person, but I still remember being that kid.

What am I talking about? These delusions are changing the way I think. The idea of forgetting who I am crosses my mind. These thoughts are forcefully being driven into my brain. Someone is trying to program my mind. But that isn't possible, is it?

No, it's not. But with Prodigy, maybe it could be.

With Prodigy in my hands, I could change the world.

I slap myself across the face. Those aren't my thoughts. I know they aren't.

I stand up again; this time, sheer will keeps me upright on my two feet. I check my pockets. Prodigy is still there. I kick and punch the first wall I find. I still can't see anything. I shout, and then shout louder. I use more force as I pound away at the wall.

Then I feel it move. I punch it again, then slam my fists into it. I hear a creaking, like an old and rusted metal hinge being used for the first time in a very long time. A loud bang follows as the wall hits the floor. I take tentative steps forward, still unable to see anything.

I go straight for a while, arms outstretched to catch any walls or objects in my path.

"Can you hear me?"

The words echo around like a faint whisper. I can't tell who it is.

"Arch, can you hear me?"

Again, those words trickle through. I can't tell where they are coming from.

"I can hear you," I say, getting sudden déjà vu. "I'm here." Tears form in my eyes as I say it quietly, knowing that I had been speaking to Edward and that now I am not. "I'm here," I say again.

There is nothing. No response.

I keep walking. I keep the straight line I walk in, but I can feel open space all around me. The thought that I'm dead comes to mind. Maybe this is the afterlife, and I'm supposed to find my way to the good part. Maybe this is the bad part — punishment for failing to save the world.

"Can you hear me?" the voice echoes, this time stronger.

"I'm here," I say again.

"I didn't ask if you were here. I asked if you can hear me."

"I'm here."

Silence.

I keep walking. I keep the straight line I walk in, but I can feel open space all around me. Am I dead? Is this the afterlife? Was I good, or was I bad?

Maybe this is the bad part — punishment for failing to save the world.

The thoughts repeat in my head. I can't stop them. Over and over and over.

I keep walking. I keep the straight line I walk in, but I can feel open space all around me.

Maybe this is the afterlife. Was I good, or was I bad?

I can't stop the questions from repeating in my head. I don't feel like I am even thinking these thoughts, more like the thoughts are thinking for me. It's constant. Over and over and over. I hear my own voice ask these questions. And still, I walk forward to an unknown destination. Straight path. Nowhere else to go. But always the same straight line. Always the same open space.

Is there even anybody that I should be?

I cry out. My mind is overloaded, and I don't know why I am thinking this way. I don't know what's happened to me.

"It's time," the voice bellows out. The echoes last for a while. Only when it is completely silent again do I respond.

"Time for what?" I barely speak louder than a whisper, knowing that there is no one I'm talking to. The voices I hear are in my head, and my head doesn't count as anyone. It's not even the real me. It is a fake, an imposter of a personality.

My outstretched hands make contact with a wall. For whatever reason, I knock. Just the once.

The wall falls over, and blinding light sweeps in. I have to squint and cover my eyes with my arm. The light is overbearing.

It takes almost a minute for my eyes to adjust. I'm back in the desert. But the sky is more beautiful than anything I've ever seen. Dusk is approaching. The sky is a deep blue, shaded by purple and pink clouds. I can see shooting stars. The moon sits in the sky, full, unlike when I was last in the desert.

In the distance, a figure approaches. My heart sinks as I quickly realize that there is no way it's Edward. But still, I hang onto that thread of hope.

The thread snaps.

And then my heart shatters. There is something else wrong here. Something else is at play. I know him. It's been too long. This should be a happy moment. I know it's not.

As my father approaches, I notice an army of Sonars land to my sides. Men jump out of them, all holding weapons pointed at me. There must be over two hundred of them. I turn back. There is nothing there. Nothing but the desert. No semblance of a cubed prison that I felt like I lost my mind in. But, perhaps now I can escape. Though if I tried to run that way, I would be gunned down instantly.

When he speaks, his voice lacks affection. "Hello, son."

I start to shake. Rage drowns out all emotions. I can't believe it. All along, my father has been a part of this. No. He hasn't been a part of it; he's been the one behind it. Edward was wrong. But how would he have known? I never would have guessed it myself. But still, it doesn't add up.

Aldon Caldor takes purposeful steps toward me. I wait, unmoving. I turn my head back, realizing again that there is just open land, no box or building or whatever it was that I had just been in. This could all be a simulation. It's either this or the dark building I was trapped in for hours. Or both. But if it is a simulation, is it created by my father or someone else? And why am I so sure that my father is real?

Maybe deep down, I always knew.

The radiating sun blazes down, and even though it is much later in the day, I feel the back of my neck start to sunburn. It shouldn't be this hot right now. Sand is kicked up by random gusts of wind, slowly falling back down. It's hard to see anything beyond the Sonars that surround me. Even my jacket doesn't help much with the heat.

My father doesn't get as close as I would have hoped. If he were within my reach, I'd strangle him right here and now. He probably knows that. He is dressed in a jacket like the one I have. His pants look clean, almost like they belong to a suit, but its pockets are plentiful.

"I've been tracking you for some time," he says after a while. I say nothing. He takes one step closer. Still, too far from me for me to do anything.

Even if it kills me, if I get the chance, I will kill him. There is no sadness inside me. Just understanding. A horrible understanding of who this man really is.

"You don't have to talk. I'm sure there is nothing for you to say. So I'll do the talking for the both of us. But let's save us the trouble and get that burning question in the back of your mind answered," he says, talking slowly, his voice deep and his words clear. "Yes, I am the bad guy." He pauses for a second. "But think about it. Am I really? I am now the richest person on the planet. I own nearly three-quarters of the largest corporations in this world. The amount of charities I've supported, no one else can even compare. But still, I was never doing enough. So, when I heard about Prodigy and what it could do, I knew I had to have it. And no one else."

I stare at him. I don't snarl; I don't let any features of my face change except for my eyes, which narrow each time he speaks.

Aldon looks at his feet and sighs. "I knew I should have killed you when I killed your mother."

I flinch but do my best to remain expressionless. He killed mom? There's no way. He wouldn't have. He loved her so much.

"That's right. She disagreed with me on many things. I let it go for a while. But when I knew that the world had to be fixed, that's when she lost it. She threatened to expose me and take you away from me. Taking you away never would have mattered. If anything, she would have been doing me a favor." He takes another step. Still, not close enough. "But exposing me, no, no," he says as he waves a finger. He chuckles. "No. That could not happen. There was still so much to do to save this world. And I was the only one doing anything about it."

"Edward Canabana was saving the world," I blurt out, unable to help myself. "He's done so much more than you."

"Edward Canabana cared about saving the *people* of this world," my dad retorts. "I want to save the world from the people."

"What do you mean?" I ask, curious as to how deranged he is.

"Humans have progressed so much that they forget to take care of their planet."

I shake my head. "We live in obnoxiously large cities, none right next to each other, so that there would be plenty of nature and land to remain untouched. The humans of this world, our ancestors, found a way of life to support the growing population without de-stroying the ecosystem."

"Well, they still are."

I stare at him. He holds the gaze.

"Ah, who am I kidding," he says. "I actually don't give a shit about that. Trash the world, for all I care. But do as I say. Under my leadership and management, I can take our people to the stars and beyond."

"That's what NEAST is doing," I say.

"NEAST has found a way to communicate to another planet that sustains life, with people that speak our language, and have refused to let anyone go there. For *decades,* we've been in contact with Earth! We have the technology to make it to Earth! They could have sent people. They never did."

I can almost see Aldon shake with rage.

"I won't be like that," he says. "We can keep building our cities, but we can also go to new worlds. These large governments don't rule over their land for any reason other than the plain fact that they *conquered* them. We live in a time of peace. That peace will be disrupted. But I can prevent that. I can prevent war. Prodigy will let me rule the entire world without anyone knowing it. So there is no one to be jealous of. Warmongers who rise up to create trouble for whatever reason, I can get rid of instantly. And when we find other planets that can sustain life, we will also conquer them, and then we can save them."

"And what about those who are like mother, who disagree with you?"

"With Prodigy, they won't be a problem."

"You can't just kill people because they disagree with you."

"Oh, and what makes you think that?" he asks, a grin on his face that I can only describe as ugly and evil. "Because I already do. And with Prodigy, it'll be even easier. Less bloody, even."

"Is Prodigy all you care about?" I seethe. His logic is...illogical and corrupt. He truly is a psychopath. "Is it all you ever cared about?"

"No, I care about my family."

"*I'm* your family."

He laughs. "No, you're not. I have two sons, and a daughter. And they are far better children than you ever were. You were always too much like your mother. But, there is something inside you that they don't have. And that is potential. The potential to take my place when my time is done. That is the only reason why you're still alive."

I gulp down the saliva that spilled from my glands.

"I also care about my power," he tells me in a quick afterthought. "And I am selfish about it. I won't let anyone take it from me. But my family now supports me, something your mother never did. Something you clearly don't."

I look up, not knowing what to say. Everything looks the same. The time of day hasn't changed at all. That's when I see it. A flicker. This isn't real. This is just like the dark room.

"You're in the desert," Aldor says, observing that I noticed something off. "But you are seeing what I want you to see. While you were in that ship, I put into your brain a programming link that lets me alter what you can see and what you can hear. Even what you can feel. So, yes, the desert here is very real. I am very real. Those men with their air rifles pointed at you are real. But the sky, no. It is not there. Not the way you see it, at least."

I don't know how long it's been. But Matt may not be far behind. He likely knows I'm in trouble. I know he will come. I just have to stall long enough. I must give him enough time so he can save me. But how long was I trapped for? It could have easily been an entire day. It could have been more.

My father begins to laugh, bellowing out deep noises as he looks around. I don't see what he finds so entertaining.

"Do you not see, Arch, that I've been planning this for years. I knew the wrinkly Edward Canabana had Prodigy, and I knew that he was working on sending it out of this planet. But after you guys broke into the Tall Building, oh damn, I never would have thought you were a part of his plan. Before that, I thought you were useless, a nobody who would end up alone. That's why I gave you my money. I knew you would never use all of it. You never cared to give yourself the importance you deserved. But that's the thing. If you don't think you deserve it, then you don't. You have to take what's yours. If you don't, then it doesn't belong to you."

I look away for a second, but then turn my eyes back to him. He takes another step. At this rate, it will be hours before he's in my grasp.

"So, what's your plan then?" I ask. "Kill me, take Prodigy, and then starve the world?"

He chuckles. "The first step was confirming that you indeed do have Prodigy on you. Second, yes, I take it. Do I kill you? Not necessarily. Because even with all that you've accomplished, you are no threat to me. So as long as you keep your head down, I'll let you live. I'll even continue giving you access to my money."

"I don't think I can do that."

"Do what? Give me Prodigy, or stay out of my way?"

"Both."

Aldon scowls. "Don't play that game with me. You cannot stop me."

I look up. Still no sign of Matt. I begin to tremble. I curse at myself, willing my body to be still. I think of Matt and Maylene. I think of Andre. I think of Kaedy. Looking up at the sun makes me remember how her eyes are so much more beautiful when the sun is in them. How the whole world lights up when she smiles. This can't be the end. I won't let it be.

"Fine. But what will you do once you have Prodigy? I deserve to know that," I say. "I deserve at least that."

"Good, you're listening to me. You're taking what you want. Fine," he says as he takes another step forward. "I'll tell you. Starting with my competitors, I will drain their bank accounts and make it look like they are stealing from each other. They will go to war, but they won't want to make it public. It will look bad. Eventually, they will drown each other. While that's happening, I will gain access to all footage in this world. Think, government cams, phones, recordings inside buildings, anything and everything. All of it. Depending on what I get, I'll make my next moves. It won't take longer than five years to rid this world of the muck that poisons it. Of the muck that keeps us mired down in the stone ages."

He is delirious. He is the muck of the world. And he doesn't see it. He knows he's the bad guy, but he can't see how evil he is. Or maybe he's just afraid of someone else doing this to him. He isn't the only one dying to get their hands on this program.

Something still isn't right about me. I hear his words, but they take time to set in. The fact that he replaced me with a new family hurts. It shouldn't. It really shouldn't. But for some reason, it does. But while I should feel more emotion, more anger, I don't. My father isn't my family. My friends are. In it's own way, it is sad as to how little I feel. And the Tall Building? If he was watching that, then that means he was behind Chlorofyx. He's the guy that Daden was working for.

"How does that sound?" he asks.

I can't speak. Sweat drips down from my forehead. My hands are clammy. I close my eyes.

Something changes in the wind. I look up. There is a Sonars flying overhead. It looks like the one I was driving.

Just as my spirits rise, the Sonars is shot down. I can't see where it crashes. Everything happens so fast.

"I'm going to do you a favor and let you know that Matt was not in there," my father says. It takes me a moment to hear him. My eyes go blank. I don't know what to think. I don't know if I should believe him. "But I know you're waiting for him."

"What?" I say, letting just that one word escape.

"That Sonars wasn't real. Just in your mind. None of them saw it." He points to the people around me. They stand there, still as stone. I almost forgot they were even there. "But I need you to pay attention to me. Because I assure you, whatever happens here, I will kill them. I will kill them all. Matt, Maylene, Andre. Even Gary, despite the fact that he's senile. And yes, I will then come for Kaedy, because everyone that was connected to Edward Canabana must be dealt with."

"And me? Why not kill me?"

Those brave words are unlikely to do me any good.

"Why not kill you." It wasn't a question. "How much easier things would be if I did. I don't know; maybe some part of me still thinks you're my son."

We stare at each other, my eyes glaring at him, as if somehow the look in them will be able to kill him.

Then a spasm of pain shoots through my body. I fall to my knees, too hurt to even let out a sound other than a sharp intake of breath. Then my head feels like it's about to explode. When I open my eyes, I don't see the desert, or my father, or any of the guards that surely are still aiming their weapons at me. I see Kaedy dead on the ground, blood coming out of her eyes. Maylene is stuck to a torn Sonars, impaled by a long piece of metal. Matt is still alive, though blood leaks out of his mouth. He opens it, trying to say something to me.

I can't hear what he says. He gurgles on his own blood, unable to speak.

"Don't kill them," I say, shutting my eyes, knowing that none of it is real. "Don't." The pain leaves my body.

"Ah, that is not a choice I have," he tells me. "All the meddling and plans they had to keep Prodigy from me for so long. No. And the technology they have access to. I'm pretty good, but Edward thought out of the box. He thought of the simple things, and those things were perfected by him. His technology is too valuable. So, I won't destroy it. I will take it. I will take everything he thought of and created. But I'll dispose of your friends quickly and painlessly. I don't need them to get into Canabana Industries. I already have people on the inside. They don't work for anyone but me. How do you think Daden got there? Daden was obsessed with me; I knew it, so I toyed with the pathetic faggot. He knew I would never take him, but he devoted his life to me."

It's hard to take all of this in at the same time. Andre deserved better. Everyone did. I can't even imagine why anyone would work for my father if they knew what he was really doing. It could be that they share the same delusions and the same falsities that make them believe that they are gods. But if Aldon has had people on the inside for so long, why did it take him so long to realize I was a part of this? Was Edward really that secretive about this mission? Maybe it was just the handful of us who knew about it.

"Creating armor that can make you invisible," he goes on. He must still have been talking, but I didn't catch what he was saying until now. "That has been attempted by so many. Edward Canabana finally had a prototype, and it worked. But that was put on the back burner. Getting rid of Prodigy was too important to him. And he was smart. He was slick. But, alas, I finally got him in the end." He speaks as if he were telling a long and sad tale. He speaks as if he is the hero of the story, the hero who had to struggle and suffer to reach that happy ending.

I now get the feeling that he is stalling. But what would he be stalling for?

"I can't let you have it," I tell him firmly. A million thoughts race through my mind, all with undesirable outcomes. If only there were some sort of final gambit I could play. But it looks impossible. My only hope is Matt. But I don't think he's going to make it. Even if he knows what's happening, there is little he could do on his own to save me. Maybe Maylene will pull through. Odds are, we'd all end up dead. Odds are, Matt is beating himself up, not knowing how to save me. That's okay. I'll figure this out. He's done so much for me already.

"Fine," he says, surprising me. "But let me see it."

There's something in his voice that sounds sincere. I pull the chip out of my pocket and hold it up. It's obsidian glint reflects the sunlight. He takes three steps toward me. Still, he's too far away. If I move, even if I move quickly and suddenly, he is surely able to step back and let his men finish me off. There has to be some other way I can coax him to come closer. Because if I can take him out, at least that's one less person who poses a threat to Prodigy.

I let out a slow breath. There is also a chance that he's been lying about the men. Maybe they aren't real. But then that would mean that the Sonars that I see aren't real, and they are my only way of escaping.

I put Prodigy back in my pocket.

"Stunning, isn't it," he says. "With the current technology I have, I was able to make you hear things, see things, feel pain, and take it away. I could have altered your whole rationale, and made you a completely different person if I tried long enough. Those who knew you wouldn't recognize the person you'd become. They would see Arch, but you would have no sense of identity. I could have done all that to you. But I didn't. I just wanted you to have a taste of what I could do. Prodigy will let me do it without even trying. I don't want to destroy the world. I don't want to rid it of all the people. I want people to be happy. I want them to live their own lives."

He's now sounding like a decent human being. I don't think he's being honest.

"But I can't let people think their own way," he explains, revealing the truth behind his words. "That poses a threat that this world has seen for centuries. But if I can control how they all think, then I don't need to kill people. We can grow and thrive as one mind. And no one will know the difference. They'll think they have individuality, and they will, so long as I accept it."

I shake my head. The talking is too much. I need to get out of here. Few options are presented to me, but I must make my move. I know Matt can see everything. I still wear the camera he placed on me the last time we saw each other. I know it, even if I don't understand how it works. I take a step forward. Aldon tenses. The men at my sides shift uniformly, readying their weapons. It shouldn't be like this. It doesn't matter that he's my father. There are other men just like him.

Weeks ago I thought it was all a lie. But something inside me told me to go for it anyway. I listened. I'm glad I did. Because otherwise I wouldn't have seen just how messed up our world is.

Prodigy would be able to save billions. But too many people seek to use it as a weapon. Edward was right. If we can't destroy it, Prodigy must leave this planet. Even though the world won't be safe from rising tyrants, it will be safe from Prodigy. And maybe then we'd all have a chance at saving humanity.

Full scale war isn't the answer here. Removing their trump-card is.

"No."

My word is simple. Clear. I know my mission. There is no need for explanation. I ready myself. I have to be quick with what I do next.

"It's a shame how even now I was right," Aldon says. "I won't second-guess myself ever again. You should have died with your mother."

I turn my foot to my right and make to charge at the men. Something hits me in the back. Or at least it feels like it does. I barely move anywhere. I can't. My body is frozen. I am still facing my father. It's another one of those tractor beams, like what they used to suspend my ship.

Aldon pulls out a simple, ancient gun and points it at me. The faint click, the blaring crack as the air shatters — all senses come back. And for less than a fraction of an instant, I feel a burning pain.

24

He closes his eyes. The pain inside his body is unbearable at times. There isn't a proper cure, just something to delay the inevitable. And even then, it does little to ease the pain. The nanoparticles that swim in his body act like a cancer, but they are engineered and robotic. True cancer can be healed. There is no stopping this.

The echoes of his failures haunt his every waking moment. Those failures are worse than the physical pain he feels. They let him have little sleep. Not that it matters. Sleep isn't something he cares about anymore. There is nothing left for him to care about.

Except for one thing.

It's been five years. His face is pressed against the small window. The rain outside splatters across it, giving the window a cool feel to it. The old cabin had been abandoned. Once part of a museum exhibit, it now stands derelict and alone. Even so, it is one of the still-standing structures in the ruined city. Traveling has become increasingly difficult. They are after him. But he is smarter than he ever was. Better. He has to be. Otherwise, he would already be dead.

With Prodigy in no one's hands but his, the world has been ripped apart in search of it. All efforts to maintain secrecy were abandoned. They couldn't bear the fact that they had Prodigy once, and it was taken from them. Again. So, more cities fell. The governments of the world had to band together, but little did they know they were secretly fighting each other. But when they found out, things started going bad.

But there was a silver lining to it all. The governments had exposed themselves as a system corrupted by those who only sought power. It was clear they never cared for anything else, or anyone else, for that matter. The people of the world started fighting back. And they were winning. They still are. The future of Talvor looks bright. A world more united than ever. Though there is still the matter of Prodigy. Prodigy, in the wrong hands, would undo everything great that came from a planetary civil war. That's what started it all, and now most of the world knows of its existence. Politicians and businessmen alike either want to use it, safeguard it, or rid the world of it. But it is hard to trust each other after the bloody massacres. Who was truly responsible for it all?

He knows. He knows very well who is behind it. And he wishes he could do something about it. But he has little time. It's either rid the world of Aldon Caldor, or rid the world of Prodigy. The mission has to be finished. Prodigy must go. And then he would be able to die peacefully, knowing that he had completed the mission that his friend died for.

The mission that all his friends died for.

Matt looks at his watch, noting the time. It belonged to Edward Canabana. A simple, black leather strap, three hands inside a large enough dial to hold twenty-five numbers written in letters, with a gold trim and black backing. There are a few cracks in the glass.

After the incident, Matt made his way back to Candalance. He only answered Maylene, but he didn't tell her much then. At least, he didn't use very many words.

"They're dead," he said. "They're dead. Arch's father has Prodigy."

He turned off all communications after that. He even shut down the Sonar's radar systems and navigation, making it nearly impossible for

Maylene to force her way in. It wasn't that he didn't want to talk to her. He did. He wanted to say so many things to her. But Maylene wouldn't understand. No matter what, she never would see what he saw. He watched the live footage from the camera he put on the jacket he gave Arch after Edward's tracking sensor blinked off. He watched it all, from the crash until the end. And he played it over and over while he traveled back.

As he knew she would, Maylene was waiting for him back in Candalance, but she gave him space. The only thing she did to acknowledge his arrival was catch his eye for a brief second. She didn't nod; she didn't smile. Matt knew that she was also torn apart inside. She probably wanted his presence and assurance, but Matt wasn't ready to be there for her. He wasn't sure if he could be there for himself.

Matt proceeded to let out his rage in Edward's office, destroying most of everything inside. Desks were tossed over, chairs were thrown at walls and even windows, though the windows never broke. Screens, small computers, and other technological supplies were kicked in or to the ground. That which was destroyed included the watch that he wears now. A relic Mr. Canabana kept, reminding himself of earlier days and simpler times. That was also why there were so many computer screens. Matt threw it against the floor-to ceiling-window, imagining that it would smash right through, but all it did was crack and fall to the floor, leaving the window unharmed.

Then Matt broke down. Memories flooded his mind. That night he met Arch for the first time in person. At the time, it was just another mission. But imagining the watch break through the glass on the window, even if it never did, reminded him of their stunt of crashing through that window in the hotel building. Matt couldn't quite tell back then that he knew that would turn into a friendship that would last for a lifetime, but thinking about it now, he realized that somehow he always knew, ever since he first spoke to him in Maylene's office.

Matt never thought that the lifetime would be cut so short.

He stood up. He stopped the tears in his eyes. He was stronger than that. Matt resisted the urge to destroy everything else in sight. He bent over to pick up the watch. Gently, he placed it around his wrist. A hand placed itself on his shoulder. He hadn't heard anyone come in. Still, despite the surprise, he didn't flinch. All Matt did was become completely still. He knew that hand; he knew that touch.

"You shouldn't be in here," he told her.

She didn't move. She didn't remove her hand.

"Why not? It's my office."

"What do you mean?" Matt said, brushing her hand off and turning around to face her.

Maylene frowned slightly. She held her palm upward and swiped at it with her other hand. A screen popped up. There was a document, hand-written. Matt recognized the handwriting immediately.

Final Request, Testament, and Legal Transfer

I, Edward Martin Canabana, hereby appoint Matthew Versaillex Schwae as the legal and rightful owner of all my belongings and properties, including but not limited to, my residences, vehicles, assets, and most importantly, Canabana Industries. In the event that Matthew cannot, for whatever reason, accept this, I appoint the above-mentioned to Maylene Markell Mayfield.

In regard to Canabana Industries, I appoint Maylene Markell Mayfield as Chief Executive Officer. As the Ownership of Canabana Industries will reside with Matthew, he has the right to revoke this decision.

~ E. Canabana

"Upon his passing, this document was sent to both of us, as well as his attorney and the governmental law authorities."

Matt blinked and looked away. Maylene swiped the screen away.

"That reminds me," Maylene said before injecting a syringe into Matthew's forearm. He almost caught her in time but only managed to shove her hand away, leaving the needle in his arm. But it was done. Whatever was in it was already in him.

"What was that for?" he asked, his mind racing.

"That was a computer Nanolink to connect to your body. It lets you access and control any of your devices from the palm of your hand, without those devices being on you. It was developed by Edward, but he never released this to the public, fearing that someone would use it for devious means," Maylene explained.

"Then how do you know about it?" Matt was still suspicious.

"After I learned that Arch didn't make it," Maylene shuddered and took a deep breath, forcing herself not to choke on her grief. "I came back here as fast as possible. I wasn't far. Not with the way I drove. I dove into all of Edward's stuff. He left many instructions for us on how to handle everything, including his developments, what he wanted the world to have, and what he didn't. I guess that he always knew deep down that his future would end abruptly."

Matt pondered that for a moment.

"Show me."

Matt and Maylene spent the rest of the day going through everything that Edward had left for them.

"Isn't it dangerous to have you appointed as CEO?" Matt asked after reading another dissertation of Edward's, one noting a cover-up from NEAST regarding something they discovered about Earth. They were both kneeling on the floor. "That puts a large target on your back."

Maylene laughed. "Aldon Caldor already knows about us. He will come. It doesn't matter. It might be safer this way. Because I am already a very well-known target."

Indeed, she was. It was already on the news: Edward's passing, Matt's inheritance, and Maylene's appointment. There was nothing about Arch, though. To the whole world, Arch was a nobody.

"Are you really that worried about me?" she asked.

Matt looked into her eyes. "I always worry about you."

Maylene chuckled a breath. "Why? I'm pretty capable. I can take care of myself."

Matt knew that she could. Maylene knew that Matt knew. He sighed and looked down at the floor. He clenched his jaw, and after mustering up the bravery, he looked back up at her.

"Because I care about you."

They both knew what he meant. Maylene didn't drop her gaze. Matt leaned in slowly, and when Maylene didn't pull away, he kissed her. She kissed back.

But she quickly broke it off.

"Sorry, not now," she said. "I can't do the cliché of us getting together after such a tragedy."

Matt let out a small chuckle. "And here I thought you were going to tell me that I wasn't your type."

Maylene smiled lovingly, her eyes unmoving, looking at Matt with such a tenderness that he wasn't quite sure how to feel. "I think deep down I've always known you were my type."

Matt smiled.

"I should get going," Maylene said. "I have a company to run, and if I don't make an appearance, I'm sure there will be a lot of noise. We don't want that."

Matt smiles at the memories. Maylene kept him feeling like himself. She gave him hope that not all would end horribly. Of course, nothing would last.

He and Maylene had gone straight to work, keeping Canabana Industries running while locating Aldon Caldor and Prodigy. They never shared another moment like that. Just four weeks later, Maylene had gone missing. Matt didn't sleep the whole time. He searched everywhere for her, increasing his radius further and further out. Two days after that, her body was found discarded in an alley on the first elevation in Candalance. She never left the city. Her throat had a hardened, metallic substance inside it. Aldon Caldor had gotten inventive and brutal in his methods. Remembering what he had told his own son, Matt quickly sold all of Edward's properties, except the hotels, and used the money to lay off everyone who worked at Canabana Industries, leaving them with enough to take time to find new work. He wouldn't risk their lives for something they didn't even know about.

The memories are bitter and cold, gray and faded, and of a different life. He had tried to contact Kaedy and break the news to her, even though he was sure she knew. But as promised, Aldon got to her first. When Matt finally hacked into her camera, he found that it was underwater, along with her body, trapped inside a Sonars. The chances of an accident like that occurring were less than one in ten billion.

He remembers how Gary supposedly passed away in his sleep. Matt wonders about Andre. Andre had never been found. At least, not that he knew of. Matt hadn't heard from him after that first week when he got back to Candalance. Andre was still taking some time, and the news of Edward and Arch didn't help his cause. That was when Andre disappeared, never to be heard from again.

Matt stands up and walks towards his Sonars. This one is small, like any normal Sonars, not usually used for long trips, but that didn't stop him. A dull silver in color, there is nothing evidently special about it. There is no bed in the back, and there is only one seat. He gets in and powers it up. The cloaking system initiates upon starting the engine. The best thing about it is how quick it is.

He sets off into the wind. The ruined city is close enough to the town where Arch stayed the night before he was killed. But Matt isn't heading there. He is heading to NEAST. Before she was killed, Jasmine hid a shuttle programmed to head to Earth. She left him with instructions on how to activate it. Finally, the mission will be completed. Jasmine knew that she wouldn't have enough time left in the world to do it herself.

Twenty hours. That's how far he is from the shuttle's location. Of course, it isn't directly inside NEAST. After Aldon was able to activate Prodigy, NEAST itself was compromised.

Retrieving Prodigy from Aldon Caldor's grasp was difficult. Without support or help from anyone, as everyone else had been killed, Matt spent the better part of a whole year devising a plan to get it. In that time, Aldon had destroyed one of the Canabana hotels. But no one was inside. Matt may not have sold those properties, but he closed down all operations related to Canabana Industries. There were no casualties. He also deleted every record of anyone who ever worked for Edward, leaving Aldon with no way to go after them, except maybe with the power of Prodigy, but it was too much work for Aldon to go through. At least, Matt hoped it was.

And that was his opening to reclaim Prodigy. It turns out that Aldon did care about the personnel files. In a furious and desperate attempt to gain access to Canabana Industries, Aldon entered the deserted corporate headquarters in Candalance. Matt knew that place inside out and left a trail for Aldon to follow. Aldon used Prodigy in the main network system located in Edward's old office. And Prodigy itself landed right into Matt's hands. There had been no breaking in — not on Matt's part, at least. There were no deaths. Matt used no weapons. He just set the trap. A once impossible task had become so easy.

Realizing what had happened, Aldon proceeded to demolish the entire structure. He went building after building, any previously owned by Edward. Of course, people noticed, but there was no news coverage. Even without Prodigy, Aldon still controlled most of the world. Matt had to lay low for another year. But he wasn't careful enough. Someone, a man who presumably worked for Aldon, injected Matt with the most painful substance he had ever felt. Matt grabbed the man's head, smashing it against the ground until the man breathed no more. It was too late. The damage was done. Matt knew that a slow death was on its way. That was when Jasmine contacted him. Of course, doing so cost her her life. But she didn't die in vain. None of them did. When he can get the shuttle out of orbit, Aldon will realize that his reign over Talvor has ended. And the people of the world will finish the rest. That was what Aldon deserved — not a quick death, but the horror that everything he ever did resulted in failure and that he would never win. What the people did to him after, he didn't care.

Matt smiles. He looks out at the desert wasteland. There is a peace inside him. A glorious peace and sadness. Arch loved the world, the lands, the cities. He always found something to appreciate.

A spasm of pain shoots through his chest. He tastes blood in his mouth. He spits it out, the blood falling onto his pants. Time is running out. Matt ignores the echoes of pain that follow. He's used to it by now.

Night comes quickly and begins to fade back to a faint light. He made better time than he thought he would. Just another couple of hours. And then just one hour left to go. Arch had made it this far. Matt tightens his jaw, locking his eyes forward. He's going to complete this for the both of them.

Daybreak sits just below the horizon. Finally, Matt sees his destination. He lowers the Sonars to the ground before parking it next to a large and decayed crate. Matt steps out of the Sonars, checks his pocket for Prodigy, and then collapses to the floor. He spasms in a short seizure. His eyesight fades. For a moment, he is blind in one eye.

The pain goes away. Blood leaks out of his mouth and nose. Matt extends an arm out and tries to pull himself forward. He is too weak. Matt sighs and lays his face in the dirt. He closes his eyes and wills for the strength to stand. Slowly, he rises to his feet. A short step, and another. Many more, and he makes it to the crate. The shuttle sits within it. With feeble effort, Matt bangs against the crate, trying to break it. It doesn't budge.

Matt coughs up more blood. It splatters onto the sand. He looks up at the sky, the twinkling stars beginning to fade with the rising dawn. He lets out a yell and throws the full weight of his body against the wood. Nothing. He does it again and again. Finally, the wood splinters but isn't quite yet broken.

Out of breath, Matt forces himself to do it again. His head gets dizzy. The pain is everywhere. He can feel blood leak from his eyes in place of tears of pain. The crate breaks enough for Matt to reach the shuttle. It is much smaller than he thought it would be.

Remembering her instructions, Matt places Prodigy on top of the oval shuttle. It is not bigger than a chunky cat. The machine absorbs Prodigy inside it when it recognizes its presence. A small touchscreen is revealed where he had placed the program chip. There is just a green and red button, so simple in nature. So outdated in regard to technology. How is this thing supposed to make it light-years away to Earth?

Ignoring his doubts, Matt presses the green button. He falls to the sand. Like before, he extends his arm, but he doesn't try to move his body. He just barely touches the shuttle, brushing against it ever so slightly. It rises into the air. Matt tries to follow it with his eyes, but the blood makes it hard to see.

The shuttle moves forward, higher and higher. Matt catches one last glimpse of it as it ascends out of the atmosphere, gleaming briefly as the rising sun shines its light over it. He knows Arch would be proud. "I did this for you, buddy."

Knowing that he's done it and that he made all their efforts and lives worth everything that it had cost, Matt curves his lips into one final smile.

Several nights ago, Matt had recorded a message into Prodigy to alert those on Earth.

"This...this is a warning...."

About the Author

Self-published, constantly writing, and recently realized there are so many words I need to put down, so this is all the effort I'm putting into a bio at the moment.